Mercury For Hire

Steve Rzasa

Books

Urban Fantasy
Mercury On Guard
Mercury For Hire
Mercury At Risk

Space Opera
The Word Reclaimed: The Face of the Deep 1.0
The Word Unleashed: The Face of the Deep 2.0
Broken Sight: The Face of the Deep 2.5
The Word Endangered: The Face of the Deep 3.0
Severed Signals
Cryptic Commands
Failed Frequencies
Mixed Messages
Empire's Rift: A Takamo Universe Novel
Strife's Cost: A Takamo Universe Novel

Science-Fiction
Man Behind the Wheel
Multiverse
For Us Humans
The Echo Watch

Superhero
Airfoil: Origins

Fantasy
The Bloodheart
The Lightningfall
Just Dumb Enough (contributor & editor)

Steampunk
Crosswind: The First Sark Brothers Tale
Sandstorm: The Second Sark Brothers Tale

CHAPTER ONE

July

I can't believe those idiots tried to mug someone in my neighborhood on Thursday night.

They should have known better. Okay, so I was careful not to lower the crime rate drastically within a five-block radius of my apartment. But it was a safe bet north of Court Street and east of DeLeon that the average street thug would get whaled on by a crazy guy in a super-powered suit.

Enter, me.

Three guys had a young black man and his wife surrounded. He was dressed in a pastel green polo shirt and khakis so crisp I could have used them as a bladed weapon. She had on a lemon-yellow dress. I figured "wife" because of the matching bands and the rock on her finger I spotted from four stories up, diamond glittering in the streetlight.

Had to give the husband credit. He went for a concealed carry pistol in his waistband, and could've held off the two attackers, except the third guy came out of the stoop shadow behind them. Hit the husband on the base of the neck with a nightstick.

Next thing I knew, he's on the ground, groggy. She's bent

1

over, slapping at grabbing hands.

"Get her purse!"

"Screw that, I'm taking the ring."

"Take her and we get all of it!"

That all unfolded as I swung down the fire escapes into the nearest alley. These guys. How was I supposed to enjoy my increasingly cold dinner when the Three Stooges were accosting people in what was fast becoming a desirable neighborhood? I hit the ground. Should've stayed high up. The streets of San Camillo smell like microwaved puke in the late summer heat. "Hey!"

They're all Asian, shaved bald, with tattoos spattered over their ears like somebody's nephew got busy with a Sharpie. Thing One, he of the immaculately trimmed Van Dyke, had two seconds to glare at me, gold tooth and all, before my weapon knocked the aforementioned tooth into the nearest storm drain.

The other two froze mid-assault, both holding an arm belonging to the woman. Even she stopped screaming.

Got to say, for street criminals used to running from San Camillo police in uniform, it was a toss-up whether the pulsar stave impressed them more, or my duds. The stave was a foot-long cylinder of shimmering metal, laden with swirling, cryptic carvings. Tonight, they glowed brighter than a car's headlights. My suit covered me from head to toe in jagged, irregular patterns, blacks and grays, with only my lower face visible. That let me grin like a hungry hyena at these goofballs. The same yellow-white light from the stave snaked across the pattern lines.

"Hey." The shorter guy with a diamond stud earring— Really? He didn't look old enough to have been *born* in the '80s, let alone represent its fashion—elbowed his buddy.

"Hey! It's him! He's real!"

"Yeah, no kidding." Third Thing pulled a gun.

I was already standing in front of them. I'd gone from thirty feet away to up close and personal in the time it took to snap my fingers. Which, it should be said, I didn't actually do.

That stunt made the pulsar stave's lights dim precariously. I forgot from time to time that I was using the thing with no way to recharge. Between me and the suit, one of these days we'd drain it dry. I really wished I could have brought it back to full strength. Unfortunately, to do so I'd have to open a trans-dimension rip, sprint through the monster-infested desert of the Interstice, and find the hidden portal into Meda, a world that existed in a dimension separated from Earth's by time and space.

Did I mention the monsters? Big, tentacled, life-sucking squids, more or less, with fangs that could shred Kevlar.

But that time was up.

My immediate concerns were more prosaic. Such as, bullets.

I swiped the stave across the gun barrel. A hot, brilliant flare severed the gun, leaving two pieces of molten metal and smoking plastic.

Third Thing screamed. He let go of the woman so he could hold his injured hand. The palm took on the appearance of a roasted marshmallow. Couldn't recommend the smell.

I felt bad, hurting the guy. That didn't change, no matter how many times I put the smack down. Slicing up astral fiends that were hell-bent on obliterating human life was one thing. These guys were making bad choices, yeah, and deserved punishment, but probably not severe burns.

Whatever.

I planted the cold end of the stave between his eyes, then smashed it across his jaw. That was two down for the count.

"Look out!" the lady cried.

I'd already heard the knife swishing through the air, but appreciated the heads up, nonetheless. The upraised stave absorbed Diamond Joe's downward slash, letting me sweep his feet out from under him. I grabbed his wrist as he fell, wrenching the bones until something popped like squeezed bubble wrap. My grasp of anatomy is limited, but I understand it sounded bad. I slammed Diamond Joe on his back. Air gushed from his lungs so I hard I caught a whiff of enchilada, I think, and too much Corona.

I tossed the knife into the storm drain, with Thing One's tooth. Sweat stung my eyes. This was my third foiled crime of the night, and it didn't help matters it was a sticky 85 degrees.

Diamond Joe went for the husband's gun, yanking on the poor guy's belt. Hubby had recovered enough, though, for him to get in some punches. He left Diamond Joe with a bloody nose and a swollen eye.

"How's about you stay put." I willed the pulsar stave to discharge a subtle, but specific energy as I pressed the business end to Diamond Joe's neck. It delivered the world's loudest static shock.

His eyes rolled up, and he slumped against the curb, tongue lolling. Pretty sure he'd regret the taste.

I helped the husband up and handed him his gun. "Better keep that ready on your way home." Sir. "Sir." Felt goofy to say it that way, but Loredana had recommended I work on my public relations.

Loredana was a gorgeous redhead with impeccable

firearms skills and was, well, my former supervisor. I took her recommendations as gospel.

When she was speaking to me. Which was not at that moment.

"Man!" The husband shielded his wife, from me or the bad guys, I couldn't tell. "I'd heard about you thrashing the punks on these streets, but I never thought we'd see you!"

"Always happy to help." I wasn't big on small talk. Another advantage of fighting monsters, besides not having issues of conscience—no need to brush up on social skills. I dragged my defeated opponents to a big, blue steel mailbox. A handful of zip ties later, I had all three linked at the ankles and cuffed to the box, like a bunch of string cheese waiting to be peeled.

String cheese. Hmm. I could go for pizza right then. Crime-fighting increased appetite.

"Thank you so much!" The lady hugged me. Her nails dug into my back worse than what I'd imagined Diamond Joe's knife would feel like. "We'll never forget what you did for us."

"Probably not." I patted her on the back. "Here, sir." I handed him a jet-black business card.

He held it up, so the silver letters shone under the street lamps. "You're 'Mercury.' Yeah, that's the name I heard."

His wife let go, finally, so she could share in the peek. "It says, 'PayPal donations accepted' at the bottom."

"That's right." Meanwhile I texted San Camillo Police Crime Hotline. They love all that community watch junk. Maybe not the vigilante aspect, but hey, beggars can't be choosers, right? <Attempted mugging at Fourteenth and Sweckard. Three perps. Foiled, courtesy Mercury. Pick up at the mailbox.>

"So ... you get paid to be a superhero?" The husband grinned. "That's great!"

"A guy has to pay the bills somehow." I snapped a picture of the gift-wrapped thugs, attached it to the text, and sent the whole package. Not too shabby. It wasn't spider-webbing, but hey, what was?

"Like Kickstarter?" the wife asked.

"Bingo. Except you folks get the rewards first."

Their smiles and expressions of awe faded like the pulsar stave's energy. I was getting used to that part, after the adrenaline rush of the attempted crime faded and they were faced with the reality of my financial situation. "Hold up," the husband murmured. "You want *us* to pay *you?*"

"That's the idea. The police will be here soon and trust me, they don't have a line item in their budget for Vigilante Hero Reimbursement." Though I wished they did, because that sounded like an excellent line item.

"You're crazy. I'm not paying you. You're a hero! Saving people's what you're supposed to do!"

"I agree, but groceries aren't going to materialize in my fridge." My stomach grumbled. Maybe that would guilt-trip them into making this a quick transaction. Poor hungry hero.

Never mind dinner had been at, oh, 6-ish. And it had just turned 10:30. I was pretty sure I'd left ravioli on the stove.

"But you fought off a whole army of those monsters!" The wife stared at me like I was one of those beasts. "Giant tentacled things that tore up the condos down by the waterfront!"

"Allegedly. Official word is catastrophic gas leak and mass hallucination brought on by exposure to said gas. And intoxication." Really didn't want to talk about that whole mess. Sore subject linked to my economic distress.

Plus, it had left my long-lost brother on his side of the trans-dimensional rip, on our home world. That's an even *longer* story.

"You're nuts, man." The husband shook his head. "Wanting us to pay you for doing the right thing."

This guy didn't sound like a fan of capitalism. I ticked off numbers on my fingers. "A hundred fifty for the incident, plus thirty per assailant. That's my regular rate."

"Two hundred and forty dollars?"

"Good math."

"That's not too bad," his wife said.

"You're joking! Honey, we don't have to pay him for this!"

"No, we don't have to, but couldn't we contribute something? You heard about what he did, how he fought those creatures!"

"Allegedly," I repeated.

She made a face. "Can we do two hundred?"

"Sure thing." I was *not* about to quibble over forty bucks since she'd changed her mind. If she could change his ...

But she was already pulling her wallet from her purse. "I don't have enough cash."

I pulled a white Square from my pocket and plugged it into my phone's earbud jack. "Not a problem."

Hubby reached for the card. "Wait a second!"

His wife wasn't having any insubordination. "I'm gonna pay the man, because it's the right thing to do. We can write it off as a charitable donation."

"He's not a church."

"This is a community service, though," I said.

He glared at me but, seriously, what was he gonna do? I'd already swiped her card, and she'd signed on the phone's tiny screen. A couple seconds later, I had $200 more than when I'd started the evening.

"It isn't right," the husband said.

"You have something against superheroes making a buck?" I shook my head. "Listen, in an urban area like this the cops have their hands full. They've got to respond to hundreds of crimes. How can they even think about preventing crime? They're reacting. I can go places they can't, keep my eyes peeled, and drop in when people need help."

"Whether you're getting paid or not, we appreciate what you do." The wife elbowed her husband. "Right?"

"Yeah, I guess." He rubbed at the spot, and grimaced. Must have taken a blow there from the thugs. Same thugs I'd tied up. "Got a point. If the guy's spending all his time fighting crime, how's he going to hold down a regular job?"

"Doesn't give you much to put on your resumé." Those sirens were getting louder. Decent response time. SCPD was improving. "As fun as this has been, I've got to go, folks."

"Hey, man." The husband held out his hands. "Thank you. For real. No hard feelings about the money."

"You're welcome. And I appreciate the generosity." I made what I figured was a jaunty salute and leaped for the fire escape, with a handy boost from the pulsar stave. The flash of light was a nice touch, I thought. Nothing like making a bold exit.

I found a good hiding spot behind ventilation equipment on a roof two buildings over. Gave me an expansive view of the couple, plus the squad car that came racing up the street, its reds and blues strobing off the walls until I thought I was gonna have a seizure.

A muscle cramped in my back. Yikes. There was going to

be a big bruise the next day. At least one. I felt the damaged area throbbing. It was as familiar as the smell of brine off San Camillo's bay.

It says something about one's life choices when bruises are the norm.

My cell phone buzzed. A text, from an unlabeled number. <Hope you're well. I'd like to meet. Shall we get coffee tomorrow morning, 7 a.m.?>

Seven? In the morning? I rolled my eyes, hoping she could see the gesture from across town. Procyon Foundation's towers were a blue and yellow glow on the west horizon, the colors edging above the never-ending skyline.

Yeah, she would be at work.

I highlighted the message. Considered pressing "Delete." Loredana hadn't contacted me in two months. Not that I'd been counting.

Okay, so it was sixty-three and a half days.

And what was with the new phone number?

Instead, I typed back, <Sure. Shattered Mug downtown.>

Seven o'clock. Some of us were up way too late for that to be a functional waking hour.

I checked my PayPal balance. Maybe she could explain why it was my temporary removal from Procyon's payroll had become two months in purgatory. It'd be nice to have a steady job again, even if it was under the auspices of a shadowy foundation that put on a public front of urban renewal while safeguarding our world against monstrous threats.

Enough of that. I had ravioli waiting for me. I stretched my muscles and took a flying leap to the next building.

A typical night for Mercury Hale, unemployed superhero.

CHAPTER TWO

Bonus: there was a quarter stick of pepperoni in the back of the fridge.

I'd missed it earlier because it was hiding behind a bag of lettuce. Yes, I eat rabbit food. Gotta keep the greens in the diet.

Anyway, I ate so fast and so much that I dozed off on the couch. After spending all night slapping bad guys around, the wood floor of my apartment would have felt just as comfortable.

Loredana smiled at me from across a diner table laden with every breakfast item you could imagine. A mound of eggs, sausages lined up like soldiers, heaps of fruit. Even croissants. Steam rose from the baked goods. It had to be what heaven smelled like.

"I'm so sorry I didn't contact you sooner." She placed her had atop mine. "I've missed you terribly."

"Don't worry about it. We're together now, aren't we? Let's make the most of it."

Wow. That was extra cheesy, and for once I wasn't thinking about pizza.

"Mercury, let's get away from the city, the two of us. There's no need for me at Procyon, not for a few days. Wherever you want to go ..."

"I've got a couple places in mind. A vacation sounds nice."

Loredana's earrings caught the golden sun, casting colors like the rainbow across our booth.

Wait. There were actual rainbows shooting from the food between us.

The plates started buzzing. Vibrating, like they were seated on the San Andreas and the Big One had finally arrived.

"Aren't you going to answer that?"

"Answer what?"

Loredana picked up a croissant and shoved it against my ear. "Answer!"

I blinked at the crumbling paint of my apartment ceiling. My mouth hung wide open.

The buzzing continued. I'd left my phone on vibrate, but its home on the end table was six inches from my head. Might as well have been a jackhammer.

I rolled over, planting my face into a cold, wet spot on the pillow. I wiped at the corner of my mouth.

Yeah, not the most attractive way to greet the morning.

Speaking of ...I caught sight of the time on my phone and grimaced. That grimace turned into full-on gnashing of teeth when the caller's number showed up. No name, but I didn't need one. I had the digits memorized. "Are you serious?" I

11

croaked. "It's five."

"Five fifteen." SCPD Lieutenant Gabriel Ramos sounded as alert as if he'd been calling me at 5 *p.m.* "Get up and get dressed. I'll text the address."

"I really need six hours, minimum, before I can wake up and not be an ogre. Also, coffee."

"I'll have some waiting."

"No whiskey, just cream."

"What?"

I rubbed my eyes. "Never mind." I could still smell the imaginary breakfast spread—and Loredana's perfume. Man. Had to get my brain clear. "Give me fifteen minutes."

"Ten."

"Where are we …?"

He hung up.

I rolled my eyes. "Of course he hung up. Because, what does a cop do when he's got to call a vigilante superhero at the butt crack of dawn? He says some vague words and *hangs up.*" I threw my phone.

Well, I chucked it onto the far end of the couch. Not as dramatic, I know, but cash is tight, and I hate flip phones. This new device cost way too much, but I'm spoiled by smartphones, and without Procyon footing the bill, it was in my best interest to keep the thing in good repair.

I showered off, doing my best to ignore the exterior darkness. The bathroom had its own window and was nestled just off the living room/kitchen. My bedroom had enough space for me to edge around the bed. There had to be a fresh T-shirt buried somewhere down there.

The phone buzzed again. Ramos's text.

<Court and Galena. Wear the suit.>

Great. I was looking forward to another day in civilian

wear. Plus ... I yanked the suit off the couch. Took a whiff. Ick.

Laundry, when I got back.

Halfway to the rendezvous with Ramos, I remembered I was supposed to meet up with Loredana in less than two hours. Made me wish I'd waited for the shower until I'd taken the suit off for good that day.

I stuck to the rooftops, avoiding HVAC units and the occasional pigeon coop. I'd spent several years getting to know all the best abandoned structures in San Camillo. The Urban Planning Office needed to get some grant money or something to tear them down or turn them into hipster apartments or something. What I'd never realized was the sheer magnitude of pigeon-wrangling prevalent among my fellow citizens. Seriously, bet I passed three between home and the harbor. Cooing became a part of my nightly routine along with cracking skulls.

The first streaks of purple and pink shot through the late summer sky, turning black to thick blue. I stopped two blocks from the rendezvous, and turned east, so I could watch the sun rise. That's when I noticed the lights flickering off the buildings across Galena. Ramos hadn't come alone to this meeting. He'd brought a battalion.

SCPD squad cars blocked either end of Court, from Galena to Jefferson. An ambulance added its emergency flashers to the crazy show, like a street concert thrown by the most boring people in the city. I counted twelve cops, plus a handful of EMTs. Most of the uniformed police were busy keeping the few people awake and mobile this early from sneaking past the impromptu barricades. I caught one cop threaten to confiscate a cell phone. Good luck with that. The mess was going online any second, if it wasn't already.

Ramos waited on the sidewalk, back to the alley between a tumbledown apartment of faded brick and its neighbor, which was sheathed in Tyvek plastic wrap. Plywood panels added a certain redneck elegance.

I slipped down fire escapes and landed behind a Dumpster. A couple quick taps with pulsar stave brought the police lieutenant into the shadows. "Hey, Ramos. You giving out invites to your rave?"

Gabriel Ramos bent and flicked a scrap of wet newspaper off shoes so shiny a Marine drill sergeant would be pleased. His shirt was blue, buttoned up and sleeves rolled, and the pants pinstriped gray. Mirrored shades hung from his pocket. His badge was polished to perfection, so it shone like the bay under the noon sky. He rested a palm on his holstered gun. "I've got a dead body."

"Overdose?"

"No, thank God. Those poor wretches—" Ramos made the sign of the cross. "The heroin wave's breaking, thanks to your help."

"It'd be easier to help if SCPD would send me a donation for services rendered."

"Not a line item in our budget, Mercury."

Hey, now, that was *my* joke. "I'm guessing you didn't drag me out of my posh penthouse for a typical corpse."

"No." Ramos led me into the street. "Try not to be ... you, *comprende?*"

"Whatever do you mean?" I tossed the gathered officers a salute with the stave.

Reaction was mixed. A woman and a short guy, both young enough to have stepped out of the academy, stared, mouths hanging open like jet intakes. Some of the regulars glanced over their shoulders. One rolled her eyes.

"Pix are encouraged," I said.

A thickset, broad shouldered black man in civilian garb scratched his chin, using his middle finger.

"Stan, quit." Ramos gestured at the milky white plastic sheet on the pavement. "Let's see her."

"Sure thing, L.T." Stan Bradley could have been a linebacker, I think. He drew back the sheet.

Yikes.

Ramos crouched near the body. "Best guess—until the coroner gets done—female, late 20s, vagrant. Her clothes are fairly tattered. No witnesses. A resident called it in. Poor guy found her when he left his doorstep for a smoke."

"Yeah, smoking's bad for you." I stayed away from the corpse. Playing undertaker was not high on my list of things to achieve. Besides, my guts were churning with what I assumed was their displeasure at this situation. Call it a tremendously bad feeling about why Ramos had called me here, and it had nothing to do with the overabundance of carbs I'd ingested the night before.

"I've told the people on scene to keep this quiet. No one objected, not after everything that's happened."

Detective Bradley snorted. "Can you blame them? Bad enough having the feds turning over every loose sheet of paper downtown, and a dozen people with psych problems."

Ramos glowered at him. "Check on the coroner."

"She ain't here yet."

"I can see that. Find out where she is and when she's expected."

Bradley muttered something about "wackos in pajamas" and walked toward a cruiser. The man favored his left leg, a mild limp to his gait. "He's friendly," I said.

"My partner."

"Didn't know you had one."

"I do now. He's supposed to offer me support."

"As in, your babysitter?"

Ramos beckoned me nearer. "*Mira.*"

Didn't really want to. My shoes scuffed loose payment. Funny. Astral fiends didn't give me nearly as awful a discomfort as this body. Maybe that's because I thought about the woman's life—who she'd been, if she'd had family, if the police had to make a gut-wrenching phone call. "No thanks."

"This is your responsibility, Mercury. Look."

Fine. Geez. I peeked under the plastic.

She was dead. I'd already seen. But close up was worse. Stiff, pale, statuesque. Not decomposing but mummified. Skin shriveled worse than a raisin left out on the sidewalk, pale gray as concrete, eyes tiny marbles shrunken into the sockets, hair brittle as uncooked spaghetti ...

I held a fist to my mouth. Really wished I'd skipped the late-night snack.

"No vomiting on my crime scene, *por favor*," Ramos said. "That counts as contamination."

"I bet." Nothing like bile in the back of the throat to banish the desire for a massive breakfast, dream or no dream. "So, you guessed what this means."

"That's why I called you."

"Third one in two weeks."

Ramos nodded. "I would have contacted you sooner, but I wasn't assigned to the case. Not until the second victim showed up eight days ago. Same age, Latino, drained in the same fashion."

"And your captain figured you had the experience needed to handle this one."

"She's aware of our cooperation."

I rolled my eyes. "So's most of YouTube. Have you seen the video? Search up 'North Beach Battle.' You won't believe the number of views."

"I stay off social media. One would think you do, too. Mercury." He leaned on my name.

"Hey, I didn't have time to choose a catchy superhero name. What was I gonna say for my backstory? I started fighting crime to ward off my own poverty. Mercury's got a great ring to it. Also, I don't have a single social media account, which you'd know if you knew how to use Google. Procyon saw to that. You think they want their premier secret monster slayer Tweeting his latest kill? Hashtag classified."

Ramos sighed. "So, what do you think?"

"Astral fiend."

"You're certain?"

"Not 100 percent. But a solid 98." I crouched across from him, balanced on the balls of my feet. "You'd think a dead person would smell. Or that her natural body odor would creep up my nose. But when an astral fiend's drained someone, sucking every last shred of life and warmth out, there's—nothing. Just a husk."

I'd seen others. Made me sick and angry all at once.

"This would be when you tell me the return of those monsters is impossible," Ramos murmured.

"It is. It should be. The portal was closed. I can't re-open it with the pulsar stave, and every astral fiend either got driven back or obliterated."

"Could there be another portal? Perhaps one that's been missed?"

I shook my head. "Procyon would have told me."

"I thought you were persona non grata."

"Well …" I scratched the back of my neck. Loredana had to know about this. What were the odds she didn't? "It's not like they can keep track of them like they used to. With Marigold possessed and vaporized, and her husband doing hard time in some federal penitentiary, they're kinda down on their best means of predicting rips between our world and the Interstice. If a new one opened up, they might be able to read when it happens, but they can't Forecast. Not without Marigold. They'd call me in to stop whatever came through, though."

Ramos nodded, but he didn't seem convinced. Me neither. He lowered the tarp. "Something is killing people. We have to stop it."

"And that's where I come in, right?"

"I've already tried contacting your former employers."

"Any luck?"

"Voicemail."

"I don't suppose you drove over and knocked."

"It makes more sense for you to do that. Besides, after the attack—"

"North Beach Battle."

Ramos donned his sunglasses. "I am *not* calling it that. You sound like my daughters. After the attack, the department made it very clear we were to keep our distance from Procyon while they settled internal affairs. Commissioner's orders."

"The police commissioner told you to back off?"

"Is there an echo outdoors? Must be the building." Ramos smirked. "I suspect he was told to do so. Federal agencies of some sort. I've got nothing conclusive, of course, but let's just say Procyon has influential people watching out for it. More than you'd expect from a charitable community organization. It does mean I get Detective Bradley as a wingman until this blows over."

"Okay, I get it."

Something clicked. One of the newbie officers had snapped a pic of me with his phone. The young female officer gave me a thumbs-up, and they seemed to be having a serious fan moment until Bradley barked, "Lance! Gomez! Make yourselves useful and keep the gawkers away from the scene!" That sent them scurrying like squirrels out of a trash can.

"You've got quite the following inside SCPD," Ramos said.

"Always nice to have an adoring public. You think they'd want my card? I could use some more funding."

"Most of the veterans on the force would prefer to use you for target practice. I've been noncommittal."

"Wow, thanks." I tapped the pulsar stave against my leg. Its stored energy tingled. Would be nice to know how much power it had left. Frankly, I thought it'd be drained already. If Procyon didn't come up with a solution, I'd be left without abilities and a weapon, besides a metal stick. "So, I'll start patrolling for signs of astral fiends. Let me know if you get new intel. I know a couple people I can ask."

"Such as Loredana?"

"Maybe. As you said, persona non grata."

"But with her? Surely you two—"

"There's no 'two,' Ramos. I'm better off ringing the doorbell and bypassing voicemail."

"That's petty."

"Yeah, well, they left me out to dry, not the other way

around."

Couldn't tell what he was thinking behind those stupid shades, but after staring at me for about ten years, Ramos shrugged. "It's your call."

Great. That was code for, he was going to bug me every chance he got.

"Keep in touch."

"Likewise."

"Olivia would like to have you by for dinner Sunday."

"Just Olivia?"

Ramos sighed. "*We* would like to invite you."

"I appreciate it—and her cooking."

"Those tamales were mine, remember."

"Whatever you say, Bosch."

"Bosch. The painter?"

"TV detective. Seriously, do you even have a computer? Tell Olivia I'll think on it. Thanks."

"*De nada.* Only, leave the suit at home."

"Funny guy."

Ramos joined the rest of his crew. I disappeared into the alley, but took a different route, sticking to the shadows. Daylight crept into every corner. I had time to get home and change before that breakfast meeting.

And put on my best game face before I went crawling back to Procyon.

CHAPTER THREE

I slid into a leather seat at the Shattered Mug on Fifth and DeLeon. My watch told me it was 6:58. Frankly, I expected it to give me a high five for not only being on time, but marginally early.

The seat was in the perfect spot—very back, against the far wall, facing not only the barista counter straight ahead but also affording a wide view of the seats clustered to the right. San Camillo was waking up outside the long row of floor-to-ceiling windows, people and cars and the occasional bicycle swimming through the veins of its street. They all seemed sluggish.

If they didn't have time to fuel up at the Shattered Mug, maybe they could suck in lungs full of the sweet, caffeinated goodness that was the place's coffee. It looked like every other stop on the franchise's latte railway—faux wood floors, fake leather chairs, glass tabletops, shelves packed full of every kind of expensive travel mug you could possibly want and definitely didn't need. Every surface seemed to call out, "Spend more money!"

Loredana wasn't there, so I passed time reading about

myself. Narcissistic? Maybe. But practical. More positive stories online led to an increase in grateful rescues. And that meant people were more likely to pay more.

I wondered if that guy way over in Drake City had the same problem, figuring out what to charge for superhero activities. Nah. Bet anything he had a day job. Must be a pain requesting personal time to fight crime.

The good news was, my activities received a positive spin in not only the big media but the local discussion boards and even Upcycle. The *Bayside Breeze* ran a brief post about a couple of my thwartings—was that a real word? I liked the sound of it. They were optimistic but pointed out the folly of vigilantism. Such as, the police considered it illegal. So did the State of California.

7:01. Still no Loredana.

Better doublecheck the fee schedule. I needed about $4,000 a month to survive on in this city. To earn that I had to bring in $133 and a handful of dimes a day, or the average thereof. I charged $150 per incident, plus $30 per criminal involved. No, I didn't keep the same scale across the board. If it was a homeless person, that kind of save was pro bono. If a guy was robbed in his limo? Let's say they received a substantial mark-up to cover expenses.

So far, so good. I managed to have enough to live on. But if rents kept going up, San Camillo would push me out. And there was no way I was going to commute from thirty minutes outside the city to be a superhero. Of course, Batman did it all the time ...

One more glance at the watch. 7:05.

I frowned. If it were anyone else—and I mean, even the reliable and dapper Lt. Ramos—I'd shrug off a rendezvous delay. Things happen. Ramos could get called to a crime scene.

But Loredana Lark? I was pretty sure Greenwich Mean Time checked with her to be punctual.

The Shattered Mug's door flew open. Loredana strode in, dressed as crisp and professional as a hundred other businesspeople who'd passed the café in the last ten minutes. None of them had her fiery scarlet hair, the scattering of freckles, the bright blue eyes that could burn right through me. Those colors blazed like a neon nightclub sign against the night sky when compared to her white blouse and gray skirt.

I was glad I'd changed into a clean pair of khakis— wrinkle-free, even—and slipped on a red polo shirt. And I'd worked for a good half hour what I was going to say to her, after months of radio silence.

Loredana sat to my right, facing out into the café, just like I was oriented. "Good morning."

"Fancy seeing you here. Or at all." Wow. That sounded cleverer in my head. Spoken aloud, it was bitterer than the unsweetened swill they served in Procyon's commissary.

Loredana arched an eyebrow, a pencil-thin red line of condemnation aimed my way. Yeah, that was the woman I'd missed. "If that's the manner in which we're going to proceed, I will skip the pleasantries and move straight to your assignment."

"Assignment?" I snorted. "Last I checked I wasn't getting W-2s from you guys."

"I am here to offer you a confidential working relationship with Procyon Foundation. Are you interested, or shall I leave?"

"Do me one better. Explain why you cut off contact with me for months and then show up with zero warning."

"My methods are not—"

"Loredana, come on." I shifted in my seat, so I could face her. "You're late."

Her hands were clasped atop the table. Tension lined her expression.

"What's going on? It's got to be bad."

"I'm not supposed to contact you at all," she said, "Let alone meet with you in person, in public. The police are aware of your recent activities, though they are having trouble tracking down your identification."

"Which I appreciate. It was nice of Procyon to give me a parting gift, and as those go, a fake ID is one of the best."

"Your adherence to our policies about remaining off social media and avoiding public notice have helped. Mercury Hale no longer appears on any of the very few records that marked his existence."

"Like I said, appreciated. What I don't appreciate is being locked out. But I get why Procyon doesn't want you to talk to me."

Loredana gave a bitter laugh. "You really don't. This is not my decision, however, I had to toe the company line. Procyon's office here in San Camillo is emerging from a rather thorough investigation by the board of directors."

"You're talking about the national guys."

"Yes. We've managed security crises in the past, but none of this magnitude. The murder of our manager by his assistant, and the use of both our private security and mercenary elements to aid the return of astral fiends to this dimension—well, needless to say, both represent terrible breaches of confidence."

"Understatement of the year. Don't forget, Forecasting's lead lady for dreaming up when fiends were going to appear in our world was behind the whole mess because of a dynasty's centuries-old plan."

She managed a tiny smirk at this. "Yes, quite."

"So, with things that messed up, I'd think they'd want me back."

"They don't trust you, Mercury." She used my name *sotto voce.* "You saved our city—and our realm—but did so with the aid of a warrior from beyond the Interstice, who is now gone, and a woman who was removed from her operative status two decades ago. Sealing the astral fiends off for good has left Procyon with a distinct lack of purpose, something it has not had to face since its inception 170 years ago. Do not take it personally if they choose to reevaluate their direction, under the cover of the community housing and charitable efforts they support."

"Makes perfect sense." I glanced at the counter. What was taking my order so long? It'd been fifteen minutes. I swore I was going to suffer withdrawal if I had to wait one second more. Of course, the line did stretch halfway across the continental U.S. "What doesn't? You not contacting me. Personally, I mean."

"Oh. Yes." A faint pink tinge touched her cheeks. Blushing? Loredana? "Things became—quite busy."

"We had a nice time at Carlito's."

"As friends, yes."

Ah. There it was. The "F" word. I'd been zoned. "No problem. We'll keep it professional."

"If I may explain—"

"Nope. I get it. You're busy, I'm busy." I held up my phone, both to show her the latest news article about my exploits and to shield myself from her attempts to apologize, which would only make me feel worse. "Check this out.

Not bad, eh? Local hero and all. I gotta thank Procyon for training me with marketable skills."

She nodded, but there was sadness in her eyes. Or maybe her contacts were bothering her. Whatever. I was tired, and it wasn't just the late nights.

"Mark!"

I gestured with the phone. "So, tell me about this freelance gig, because that's what it sounds like you're pitching."

"Mark!"

That guy better get a move on, or I was going to commit a robbery for his drink.

Loredana smiled. "I believe your order is up."

Huh?

"MARK!"

The Latina barista had a smile on her face but there was nothing happy when she said my alias for the third time. Hopefully it didn't count as a strike out. I scooted to the counter, accepted the steaming cup with all the humility of a Catholic taking Holy Communion, and left a sizeable tip.

"Mark Hale," I muttered as I flopped back into my chair. "Talk about boring."

"Not everyone can be named for a planet."

"Don't forget Roman god." I winked at her as I blew steam from the coffee.

Loredana sighed. "A man has gone missing from Tracking."

"That's ironic."

She arched that eyebrow again.

"Kidding. Go on."

"If you're certain you can refrain from pithy commentary, I will."

Yikes. Somebody else was sure *pithy*, except with a

different spelling. I rolled my hand, signifying she should continue.

Loredana swiped through imagery on her phone. She held the screen so I could see the slim, blond guy with retro '50s glasses. His left eye was blue and the right one, brown, and wore a beard so thick you'd think he was auditioning for Santa Claus four months early. "Gary DeBarthe, assistant programmer and tracking coordinator."

"I remember Gary. Built like a scarecrow. Never said two sentences to me, but the guy always hopped on whatever command Winston issued." Saying the latter name stabbed me in the heart. Winston Yen had been the Tracking boss for Procyon, responsible to telling me where astral fiends were going to breach the barrier between the Interstice dimension and our world. He was the voice in my earbud when I took the monsters down.

Until his wife went crazy and tried to open the barrier instead of closing it, resulting in her very public disintegration and Winston going off his rocker.

"Mr. DeBarthe was supposed to have an interview with the board's investigator six days ago. He did not show up for his appointment, nor did he arrive for work. Twenty-four hours later, a plainclothes security detail went to his apartment. It was ransacked. Mr. DeBarthe has not been seen since."

Six days. Hadn't Ramos said the first dead body showed up eight days ago? "I don't suppose you asked Winston where Gary might be. They were close co-workers."

"Winston Yen is ... not available for comment."

"That's what happens when you get locked in a federal Supermax prison and they throw away the key."

"Winston's disposition non-withstanding, we need to find

Mr. DeBarthe. His knowledge of Procyon's true operations would be dangerous in the wrong hands."

"Although Winston and Marigold had the wrongest of those hands."

Loredana crossed her arms. "Is it too much to ask you to take this seriously, Mercury?"

I winced at the use of my real name, which she said in high enough volume that we got a couple curious looks. "Look, Loredana, I am taking this seriously. About as seriously as you should be entertaining the possibility that astral fiends have found their way back to Earth."

That got her attention. She slid close to me, as close as I'd have liked to find her, except instead of me moving in for a kiss—or her—she grabbed the wrist holding my coffee cup. She'd better not spill a drop. "Are you certain? You've seen one?"

"No." I swapped the cup and slipped my hand free. "Ramos found a dead body. Two, actually. He says he tried contacting Procyon but no dice."

"I wasn't aware. Things have been—haphazard." Loredana chewed her lip. "And with Gary missing, Tracking is an absolutely frightful mess. If there were another rip open, I doubt anyone was watching. Perhaps there was something recorded. I will investigate further. Meanwhile, if you could see fit to pursue Gary's disappearance, I'll be most grateful."

"Yeah. Grateful enough to get me back in?"

She shrugged.

I swigged coffee. "I'll let you know. Answer the phone this time, okay? It gets embarrassing leaving messages and realizing they won't be answered. Ever."

"Mercury, I am sorry. I enjoyed our dinner."

"Months ago."

"Yes, well, I felt …"

"You said it. Friends."

"Will you cease prattling for five seconds so I can get a word in edgewise?" she snapped. "This situation is complex. If I were seen to have a deepening personal relationship with a former operative, especially amidst the current climate of suspicion, things would get worse."

"Not much worse than astral fiends showing up again." I patted the side of my shirt. The pulsar stave formed a bulge underneath. "This thing is losing its power, you realize. Apparently, its energy is tied to the same rips that let the fiends through."

"I understand."

"So, you understand that unless I can get it back to Meda to recharge, or the rips start happening again, I'll be out a weapon. And a job. Again."

"Let us tackle these crises a few at a time."

"Always the optimist." Either the caffeine kicked in or I was excited by the prospect of finally having something interesting to do. Look, I enjoyed kicking criminals around. Who wouldn't? But after you've stomped ravenous life-sucking monsters and prevented their giant brothers from destroying our plane of existence, street level thugs didn't get your blood pumping.

"I do try." She stood. "Keep me apprised of Lt. Ramos's homicide investigation, if you'd be so kind."

"So, I'm looking for monsters and a guy named Gary. I bet Ramos will be thrilled to have a missing person added to his case load."

"And … perhaps we when this is over, we can reconsider our status."

I shrugged. "Sounds good."

As soon as she left, I sagged in my chair. Man. It took everything I had to pretend I couldn't care less. But the truth was, that stupid breakfast dream was still rattling around in my sleep-deprived brain. Maybe she was right. Maybe it was better if we stayed pals, cordial consultants, so things with Procyon didn't get too complex.

Sure. Like I cared what Procyon thought. They'd lied to me about my very existence, until my long-lost brother had shown up.

It's not every day you find out you were born in another dimension.

CHAPTER FOUR

Ramos was displeased to find out Procyon had a missing person they'd neglected to tell him about. Shocker.

"You have to be kidding." His voice rasped over my phone. "This guy worked hand in hand with Winston Yen, and they didn't link SCPD would be interested in his disappearance? I should have the captain show up on their doorstep with a subpoena to search the whole place."

"Easy, Bosch. You know that's not gonna happen. Not with federal influence keeping everything about the battle quiet." I had my laptop resting on my knees, while I was stretched out on the couch. Loredana sent me an email with everything I'd need to know about Gary DeBarthe. I opened the PDF attachment and whistled.

"What is it?"

"Intel on our missing man."

"Our? That's not the matter you're supposed to investigate, Mercury."

"Hey, relax, I can multitask." The laptop wobbled as I slowly reached for my cup of coffee, seated on the end table behind my head. "Besides, think about the timing of these

31

two incidents, Ramos."

"I know. The overlap is suspicious."

"Duh. You find out anything more about your dead people in the last couple hours?"

"Only that I have no witnesses. Haven't had any calls about monsters crawling the city—not legitimate ones, anyway."

I called up a second window. Ran a quick Google search. "The rest of San Camillo might disagree with its boys in blue. There's a ton of people blogging about their supposed experience with, I kid you not, 'space squids' or 'demon octopuses.' How about that."

"As I said, none proved legitimate. And we investigated *a lot*, let me tell you."

"Oh. I mostly meant I was impressed somebody used the plural for 'octopus' properly."

"Focus, Mercury."

"I am." I paged through the dossier on DeBarthe. "Gary James DeBarthe, age 28, single, five feet ten inches, blond hair, groovy beard—"

"I will not put 'groovy' in my notes."

"I figured. Just easier for me to remember it. Let's see: address, 11022 West McKinley, Apartment Eleven."

"Got it. I'll meet you over there in an hour. Meanwhile, I'll get Bradley to run whatever we can find on the guy— criminal records, phone bills, the like."

"I could save you some time and forward the attachment. It's pretty detailed, but I'll have to leave out the pages about his job. His real job, anyway. Procyon has him listed as 'data analysis,' but Loredana's got a big pile of red letters warning me not to give out anything beyond Page Three."

"All right, go ahead. I'll text you if Bradley turns up

anything interesting."

"One thing more: am I going to this rendezvous at DeBarthe's as Mercury, or Mark Hale?"

Ramos sighed. I imagine him popping an Advil, or Tums, or something stereotypical stressed individuals used to calm nerves. Come on, I couldn't be *that* bad. "Civilian attire, please. I'd rather we don't draw a huge amount of attention. Does Loredana have keys?"

"Not that she gave me."

"How was she, by the way?"

"Fine."

There was something that might have been a chuckle on the other end of the line. Impossible. Not from Ramos. "Fine, or *fine?*"

"Har har. Stick to homicides and missing persons, Ramos." I hung up.

Okay, that was a tad juvenile. But Ramos wasn't entitled to the details of my personal life. Not anything that involved Loredana.

Hmm. The file she'd sent was chock full of morsels about DeBarthe. There wasn't any indication he'd been involved in Winston's and Marigold's plans, but the interview had been scheduled to make sure. DeBarthe's job, beyond executing Winston's commands, was to stand-in for his boss at Tracking when the need arose. He'd earned himself several commendations, albeit secret ones, for pinpointing hard-to-find astral fiend appearances. He'd even corrected Winston twice, and been right.

I wondered how many of my fights with the monsters had been successful because of this guy.

Now he was gone, and even Procyon, with its advanced tech and considerable resources, had found squat. Loredana had included the official report from security after they raided his apartment. Yeah, the place was trashed. I squinted at the image. Bookshelves toppled, desk flipped sideways, papers strewn about, dual computer monitors broken. A heck of a mess.

I stripped out the PDF pages with the classified stuff and sent the rest to Ramos.

Ten minutes later, I successfully navigated morning traffic across town to DeBarthe's apartment. Funny thing about being footloose and freelance—I kept the same hours as when I was Procyon's favorite (and only, I should clarify) monster-slayer. Having a midget ride like my Subaru made it easier to zip in and out of those blank spaces that should have been technically used for safe following distance but in a city like San Camillo didn't remain open for long.

DeBarthe's apartment was on West McKinley, toward the waterfront, only a few blocks from Wayfarer Drive. So close to the site of the North Beach Battle I could still smell the stink from the dozen slain astral fiends. Or so I thought. It could have been rotten garbage.

There was plenty of room to parallel park my squat blue Subaru, its grille grinning at the decidedly boring sedans around it. Like some kind of manic beetle. I rubbed at a scratch on the front fender. Okay, so it wasn't a brand-new ride, but considering how tight my financial straits had become, it was probably for the best that I'd purchased new-used.

The apartment buildings on this stretch of McKinley were stately. Read that as, "plain old brick." They treated me to five different shades of faded red with concrete foundations. A breeze off San Camillo Bay sent a shudder through the leaves of sickly London Planetrees. Number 11022 was the center of the quintet.

Ramos waited on the step. Gotta hand it to him—for a father of four and a married man, Gabriel Ramos dressed like he was on the prowl, if you catch my meaning. Pale green shirt with the sleeves rolled up, gray slacks so well pressed he could have stolen them off the rack, black shoes I was pretty sure I could see my reflection in from thirty feet out. He was scribbling in a notebook hardbound in gray fabric. I'd say he didn't look a thing like your stereotypical TV detective, but let's face it, he had the mirrored shades and the badge and the gun tucked in a holster far back along his waist, so unless he was a creeper who'd done some cosplay shopping on eBay, he fit the profile.

"You're late." Ramos kept writing.

I leaned on the railing next to him. Checked my watch. "Um, no. I'm one minute early."

"I know." He smirked.

"Wait—did you just mess with me?"

"I figure you could use a dose of your own snark." Ramos tucked the notebook into his back pocket. "You've got the key?"

"The key."

"Yes. To DeBarthe's apartment."

"I ... oh." I scratched the back of my neck. So much for my debut as a private investigator. Michael Weston was shaking his head at me.

What? You expected Tom Selleck? I'm too young for *Magnum PI*. For me it's Netflix binges of *Burn Notice*.

Ramos pinched the bridge of his nose. "*Madre de Dios*. The key, Mercury. We need it to get in quietly, without me announcing myself to the entire building."

I pointed at his badge. "Sorry, Captain Obvious, but

you've already done that."

"Remind me to have a long discussion with Ms. Lark when this is over." He stomped up to the door. Pretty impressive, him getting his stomp on when we were only five steps away.

"You and Loredana in an argument?" I grinned. "Now *that* would be entertainment. And no offense, Ramos, but I know who I'm rooting for."

"Or whom."

I had a retort in there about *Archer* episodes but was genuinely befuddled that something so crass—and yet amusing—would be on Ramos's watchlist.

There were ten apartment numbers on the silver call box. DeBarthe's was 3A. Ramos punched the worn-down black buttons for the other nine. "SCPD!" he barked.

The door buzzed and then unlatched. Ramos pushed through.

"Way to be subtle," I muttered.

He didn't have a reply, and I'm glad I kept my mouth shut, because a woman met us in the hall before we could get a dozen steps. She was short, round, and kinda looked like that scowling hobbit lady from the *Lord of the Rings* movie. You know, the one who seems crotchety but laughs at Gandalf's fireworks? Curly gray hair, ugly dress, yet her apron was so clean and white my eyes hurt.

"*Politsiya?* What you want?" Her accent was so thick I kept expecting her to warn us about Moose and Squirrel.

Ramos flashed his badge. Didn't remove his sunglasses. "SCPD. I need access to apartment 3A."

"Warrant? You have warrant for premises, yes?"

Ramos' eyebrow notched up. "Open the apartment for us. We've been made aware of a potential missing persons case. You can get the key, or I can break the door down."

The woman scowled. "*Politsiya*. This is United States, yes? Constitution, warrants, unreasonable search? You sound like FSB."

"Ma'am, if I have to come back with a warrant, I will, but I'd appreciate your cooperation. And if you have any relatives at home who are having passport issues, I'm sure they would, too."

Her eyes narrowed so tightly I about lost sight of the pupils. Pretty sure I'd rather face down an astral fiend right then. She muttered some choice phrases in Russian and retrieved the key from her apartment. A quick glance inside confirmed she used the front entryway as her superintendent office. There were heaps of crumpled papers and unopened envelopes balanced on a rickety wooden desk.

We followed her up two flights of stairs to Apartment 3A. I kept watch for signs of damage, anything that could point to a break-in or a struggle, but the place was in such bad need of upkeep it was hard to tell. The wallpaper was peeling in several places and, given how faded the faux French designs were, should have been ripped down twenty years ago. There were dings and scratches on every door frame and enough chipped tiles to fill the backseat of my Subaru. Add to that the, uh, fragrant aroma—a combo of lilacs and cat pee. "Weird."

"I've dealt with weirder individuals," Ramos murmured.

"Not Baba Yaga. I mean, this place. And DeBarthe living in it. His file made it seem like he's pretty high up in Procyon—he'd have to be, serving as Winston's backup. So, he's drawing a decent salary. Better than mine, I assume."

"Yours then or your income bracket now?"

"No, seriously. The guy's pretty well off. Procyon keeps

its high-level employees well paid, because they're good like that, and also so they can minimize the risk of security leaks. But if Gary's pulling down decent pay, why's he living in a dump like this? All my places have been way better, and trust me, I've seen my fair share of San Camillo's rentals."

Ramos didn't have a comeback for that observation, but if his head had actual gears in it, I bet I could hear them turning.

"Here is. 3A." Baba Yaga stabbed the lock with the key. She opened the door. "When you are done you—"

"*Gracias, señora.*" Ramos interposed himself between her and her view of the room through the gap she'd exposed. He smiled and lowered his shades, so dark eyes peered over the tops. "There may be more officers arriving later. Would you show them the same courtesy you've afforded us? I'd greatly appreciate it."

Wow. He was spooning it on *thick*. Our host, though, snorted and trundled off with the key, muttering "FSB" the whole way. "You got a real way with the fairer sex, Ramos."

"Be snide all you want." Ramos pulled on a pair of black gloves. He handed me the same. "Ask yourself—which of us is married to the love of his life?"

I stared after him as he entered the room. Man. Either he'd been practicing my kind of jibes or he was getting really good at reading my mind. As in, per Loredana and our floundering relationship.

Speaking of Loredana, the photos she'd sent over via email hadn't done the place justice. DeBarthe's apartment was wrecked. I stood behind Ramos, peering around his shoulder, because he hadn't budged besides getting himself inside the entrance hall.

"Someone was looking for something," he said. "And

not worried about the mess they left behind."

"No kidding. You want to move over?"

Ramos let me in, then shut the door behind us. A *click* told me he'd locked it. "Don't touch anything."

"What're these for?" I waggled my gloved fingers in his face.

"To prevent you from accidentally contaminating the scene."

We picked our way among the debris. Ramos stopped every couple of feet, crouched, and examined the papers. He took photos with his phone, then found his notebook. "Mr. DeBarthe was working with Winston Yen, according to his files."

"Yeah, Tracking. The department that keeps tabs on where astral fiends are going to appear." I peeked under the collapsed bookshelf. Man. There was a whole lot of sci-fi crammed together—Asimov and Bradbury, Bear and Zahn, Correia, Torgerson, plus names that I wasn't as familiar with like Regnier, Johnson, and Duran. And a couple books about the Amish? Wait a second. Amish *vampires* ...?

"What'd I say about touching?"

"Relax." I rolled my eyes. "I'm just checking out his geek stash. Hey, if you're hoping DeBarthe has got some incriminating paperwork, forget it. Procyon's very clear about personnel keeping hard copies of their stuff at home. As in, don't do it, or you get a visit from security."

"I'm not surprised, given the nature of their work." Ramos nudged papers aside with his pen. "Most of these are news articles, printed off the *Bayside Breeze* website."

"Anything exciting? Or are we talking tide charts?"

"We're talking crime stats. Sightings of a rumored vigilante." Ramos made a face. "And more monster reports."

"I'm telling you, there's people who aren't gonna shut up about the North Beach Battle. The National Guard flew helicopters in, for crying out loud!"

"Not the battle. Recent sightings."

"Oh. Those." I shook my head. "I hate to tell you, I've been reading them for months. But there's been no word from Procyon about tachyon spikes, or new rips opening, so they're probably bogus."

"Except for my two dead bodies, clearly drained by your so-called fiends. Something you've already confirmed as probable."

"Yeah, okay ..." I squinted. There was something metal tucked under a copy of *Space Drifters*. Broken glass crunched as I shifted the books.

"Hey! I just told you not to touch."

"You're the one who brought along an unsanctioned vigilante to your crime scene." I grinned at him and eased the object out.

It was a picture frame. The glass was cracked. I brushed away shards. The image had been torn, but the cute blonde and her daughter were visible in it.

They were both nestled in DeBarthe's embrace.

Ramos loomed over me. "His file said single, *si*?"

"*Si*, indeed."

"Apparently he wasn't always so."

"No kidding." I scratched the back of my neck. No mention about a wife and kid. But judging by the classic horror movie posters on the walls, and the single bedroom, and the lack of anything remotely like a feminine touch to the apartment, the lady hadn't even been to this place. "Ex-wife?"

"You tell me. He's your co-worker. We've got another

problem."

"Out of notebook pages?"

Ramos frowned. "Fishbowl."

He was pointing behind me. Yeah, the bowl had been smashed to the floor. Poor Flipper was dead. He—or she—was one of those clownfish, so, yeah, not a dolphin, I know. I guess Nemo would be a better name. "I'm officially cataloging the guys who tossed this place as jerks."

"The occupant aside, what else do you see?"

Nothing much, besides shattered glass, spilled blue rocks, the damp floor underneath from the water—

Hang on. I touched the wood. "It's still wet." My glove came away with beads of water.

"Which is odd, because if this place had been trashed when Procyon said it had, this should have long since dried."

Loredana said security came here twenty-four hours after DeBarthe missed his appointment. The appointment was six days ago, which means they were in the apartment five days ago. "So, either this didn't fall over until later—"

"Or your Procyon security are the ones who searched the place."

I grimaced. "Well, that sucks."

CHAPTER FIVE

Ramos brought in more cops for a thorough crime scene investigation. Moreover, he had some choice questions for our landlady, whose real name was Irina—such as, how come nobody called the cops when they saw people break in or when the place got tossed?

"I no call *politsiya*," she snapped. "People pay rent. I no ask questions."

Less than helpful? Yes.

But the stuff we turned up in the apartment did leave me with more questions for Loredana. So, I left her a voicemail and I spent the rest of my morning pacing my living room, waiting for her to call back.

I'd finally sat down for another *Burn Notice* episode when my phone buzzed. "Yello."

"Have you truly missed me already?"

"Nope."

There was a soft noise through the speaker, like she'd snorted. "I don't suppose you've called to tell me you found Mr. DeBarthe already."

"More like, I've got news from the investigation. But

you're not gonna like it."

"I shall be the judge of that."

"Okay. Ramos and I figure the guys ransacked poor Gary's apartment *after* they went over to check on him. So, you might want to call up to the seventh floor and ask your interim bosses what the deal is."

Loredana's not one for tirades, so when all I got as a response was three seconds of silence, and "Fine," that was my cue to move the conversation along. Because "Fine" means ... Screwed.

"Um, okay, also, it looks like good old Gary was married."

"Divorced."

"That would have been nice to include when you sent over the file. Ramos was irritated."

"And you?"

"Oh, you know me, I love secrets! They're my favorite!" When I go for Sarcasm Mode, I go all in.

"Mr. DeBarthe requested he be listed as single on his profile. Therefore, the only information I had regarding his marital status was what little I heard through office chat."

"You don't chat. Do you even gossip?"

"Mercury ..."

"I kid." This was going nowhere fast. "Do you have a name of the former Mrs.?"

"One moment." Keys clicked. She must be at her computer. "Moira Jasko."

"As in, that's her maiden name ...?"

"Remarried. Her husband works for a firm developing artificial intelligence for autonomous cars."

"Self-driving? Sweet."

"Indeed. Records show she and Mr. DeBarthe have one

child, a daughter, Isabel."

"That's scary how fast you could dig that all up."

"Procyon keeps a watchful eye on its employees."

"Don't I know it. Got an address for me?"

"I do not. However, her Facebook profile lists a place of employ as Cove Realty."

"Good enough for me." I yanked a utility bill off my bookshelf. There had to be a pen somewhere. There, underneath a soda can. I scribbled down *Moira Jasko, Cove Realty, daughter Isabel.* Shoved the note into my pocket. Ramos would be proud. "I'm also having Ramos look into DeBarthe's bank accounts."

Eyebrows raising don't make a sound human ears can detect, but somehow, I could always tell when Loredana's did. Don't ask me to prove it, okay? There's no evidence, but I'd bet twenty bucks if I could materialize in her office then I'd be right. "On what grounds?"

"On the grounds that he makes more money than I did and lives in a lousy apartment on West McKinley, for cheap. Come on. Winston and Mari had the nicest condo two blocks away. Granted, Gary's salary's probably half their combined income—"

"I see your point."

"Too bad. I was hoping to repeat my spiel."

"What would we do if you weren't so enthusiastic in your newfound detective role?" I swore she chuckled.

"Find me a gig killing monsters, preferably soon." I stretched. "Smacking criminals isn't as much fun. Also, it's a poor source of income, turns out."

"I am astonished. Very well, do keep me apprised of what turns up. I shall have a word with security and the interim director *immediately.*"

I grinned. She stepped on that last word like a lady killing a spider on her living room floor. Except I had a feeling the security goons would be the spider. "Good luck with that. So, you have any plans this evening?"

"We discussed this—"

"Yep, sure did, and I'm asking anyway."

"I am at a fund-raising gala for the North Beach reconstruction efforts. You'll recall from your emailed invitation that a portion of the proceeds will also benefit the kin of those National Guards and police killed in the attack."

"I do recall. What I didn't recall was how you're spinning that to the press. No astral fiends on the guest list, right?"

"Hardly. We have avoided controversy by staying quiet. Officially, the City of San Camillo and the U.S. military have stated it was an act of terror by a cell unrelated to but inspired by al-Qaeda and ISIS. Their assault included the use of aerosol psychotropics released among the populace."

I winced. That sounded pretty flimsy to me. "Great idea."

"It is the best we can do."

"What about the videos?"

"Fabricated."

"All of them?"

"Yes."

This time I chuckled aloud. "That is one huge rug you guys are trying to sweep this mess under."

"A time-honored practice. Stay in touch, Mercury."

"Likewise, Loredana."

I tapped the phone against my lips. Ex-Mrs. DeBarthe was a realtor. Funny, given the shabby state of Gary's apartment. I texted Ramos, <Got wife's name. Up for a visit?>

A couple seconds later, he replied, <I'll determine. Hold

off for now. Waiting on financials. Don't forget life problem.>

Right. The bodies. <Okay. Wife is Moira Jasko. Daughter Isabel. I want in on visit when it happens. Consider it payment.>

<The only payment.>

<Unless you push for that line in SCPD budget :) >

He must not have been a fan of emojis, because I never got a response.

Friday night. You know what that meant. No, not a hot date. I suited up and headed for the rooftops.

I'm no Spider-man, but the stave helped me leap the distances that are too far for my typical jump. A lot of the old buildings are right against each other, cheek to jowl. It was the streets that were tricky. There were few people out that time of night, but still, I didn't want to risk getting spotted on the street.

Okay, it was a lot easier when I could navigate in my civvies and look like any other pedestrian or driver. But I couldn't fight crime as my regular self.

It was muggy out. The day's heat refused to leave, even though it was past midnight. I flung myself across 22nd Street, clearing the road and landing a foot over the edge of the next building's roof. Yellow lines on my suit flared, flickered, then faded away. I could feel the energy in fits and starts.

Great. I never thought I'd say it, but I wished a rip would open right over DeLeon and dump an astral fiend for me to fight. Not that I relished their attempts to suck out my life, but when I was fighting the monsters, I never had to worry about the stave sputtering out, like a flashlight struggling with dying batteries.

The weapon had gotten charged to its maximum capacity at Meda, the dimension from which I hailed and in which my brother resided. And it had been an amazing, amped-up fiend-slaying tool in the North Beach Battle. But since the last rip had closed—the one that had threatened to overwhelm San Camillo and later the world—it had been losing its power.

I ground my teeth. Sure would be nice to have Procyon's resident science geek available to hypothesize. He was in prison, you know, for helping his wife try to destroy Earth.

Okay, Mercury. Focus.

I heard glass smash down the block, beneath me.

There'd be time to figure out the mysteries of interdimensional physics later.

Two hoodlums this time, skinny white guys wearing baggy dark sweatshirts with the hoods pulled over their heads. Seriously? It was 80 degrees out, and humid. I could have followed them by their stink if they were any closer.

Their target was an antiques store. No metal security gate across its darkened windows, so it was easy enough to smash and grab. Whether or not it had a silent alarm these numbskulls had tripped was beside the point.

"Dude! Take the silver!"

Their feet crunched on glass. I dropped along the building's front until I could slide down the last story, landing cat-like on a stoop.

"Where?"

"Back case. The lock's loose."

Smash!

"Dude! Quit breaking glass!"

"No way! We gotta get the goods and get outta here!"

I stepped through the broken window, gingerly avoiding

the glass. The suit's reactive abilities mimicked the heavy wooden desks and cabinets for sale on the right wall, making me into a shifty apparition.

"What was that?" One guy turned. He clutched a handful of silver coins. Scraggly blond hair dribbled from underneath his sweatshirt hood. "Did you see it?"

I slid closer to the cabinet. Okay, so maybe I was messing with them.

"Where? Just get the coins!" The other guy had a nose as big as the pulsar stave, and a thick, nasal accent. Like New York, or Philadelphia.

"Dude! There's a ... thing over there!" Blond Shaggy pointed directly at the cabinet to my right.

That was when I threw half the pulsar stave at his other arm.

The coins scattered across the floor, rolling under the counter, mingling with glass shards. Shaggy swore, and reached into his belt—for a Taser, a gun, a knife, I didn't care what it was.

I let the other half of the stave light up, brilliant yellow flashing into the room. The guys cried out, their dark-adjusted eyes no doubt seriously watering. Shaggy's hand came out with a cute little revolver, which fired twice at nothing, because I'd already flipped across the counter beside him. "Over here."

A blow to the jaw knocked him out cold.

"Hey, yo, back off!" The dark-haired guy had a nasty combat knife, the K-BAR type you could pick up at an Army-Navy surplus store. Ah. The "off" in his warning gave him away. Philadelphia.

"Drop the blade, and I'll tie you up instead of beating your brains out." I grinned. "Sound like a plan?"

Footsteps thundered overhead. I glanced right. Stairs? Aw, man. The owner must live on the second floor. Shouts echoed.

"Stay back!" Philly tucked a handful of coins into his pocket. "You try something, I'll kill you and the old lady!" Well, that was just stupid.

I slammed him against the wall in a split second. He was practically a slug when compared to an astral fiend, so his head rebounded off the wall even as the knife blade jabbed to the left of my shoulder. He couldn't see me well, I figured, because the suit made me into a blurry, skewed version of our surroundings, like I was wearing pajamas made of antique store.

He recovered enough to punch me in the face.

The knife came my way again, but this time the pulsar stave intercepted its arc. Flaring energies turned the blade into a molten stump. Red-hot drips seared my chin, even through the mask, and spattered Philly's face. We shouted at the same time.

Then I punched him through a bookshelf loaded with paperback Westerns.

Lights exploded around me. Ow. I knew how vampires felt, right then, as I blinked away globs of light.

"What are you doing?" It was an old lady, in her seventies, probably—white hair frizzy, glasses askew, her floral print nightgown rumpled. There was nothing off-kilter about her shotgun, though, and she aimed that Benelli like she was a SWAT officer ready to tackle a riot. "Who wrecked my store?"

"These guys, ma'am." Sirens. Man. SCPD was on top of their response times these days. The owner must have had a silent alarm. I held out a business card. "For you."

She took it, squinting. The shotgun aimed at my stomach dipped lower. I resisted the urge to, ah, shield vital areas. "Mercury. Are you that fellow they've been on about on the Internets?"

"Yes, ma'am. All the Internets." I couldn't resist. "Any donations are greatly appreciated."

"You want me to donate for damaging my shop?" The shotgun rose again.

"Ah, it's more for services rendered. This is my day job. Or night job. Whichever." A lightbulb flicked on above my head. Figuratively, of course. "Consider me a small business owner. Entrepreneur, right?"

For a second, I thought I was going to be picking pellets out of my butt if I turned and ran. But then she chuckled. "Now that's ballsy. Here you go." She bent, cupped a few of the silver coins Philly had tried to take, and dropped them into my open hand. "They're worth probably $300."

Ka-ching! "Thanks very much, ma'am."

Shaggy groaned. He squirmed in place. The owner prodded him with her shotgun. "Go on, get, before the cops show up. I can manage these hooligans."

I gave her a mock salute with the stave and stepped out into the streetlights, jingling my payment. A couple of trees nearby provided adequate shadow, so I hid out there, because those sirens were getting closer, and I'd better get moving up the walls or down an alley unless I wanted to answer a bunch of questions. Those sirens weren't getting quieter.

But a different kind of engine was growing louder. I've heard plenty of police cars go roaring to crime scenes. This one was deeper.

An Econoline-type van came racing up DeLeon. It was matte black, with darkened windows, and looked a good deal chunkier than it should. The tires were thick and knobby. A huge metal grille gave it a face like a warthog. Looked like someone took the phrase "up-armored" from the military to a whole new level.

The cops were lagged but were definitely on its tail.

I had five seconds to react. Three seconds in, I thought: *This is a stupid idea,* and, *Yeah, but the more I help the cops, the better reputation I earn.*

I willed power to the pulsar stave and hurtled onto the roof of the van.

CHAPTER
SIX

I t was no kamikaze attack. Think stealth mission.

So, when I landed, I let myself slide, trying not to make a huge banging ruckus. Must have worked, because they didn't pull over and shoot me in the face.

The next trick was staying atop my new ride without getting a serious case of road rash. There was no way I was gonna stab through the roof with the pulsar stave like I'd done to Ramos's car in the spring. But the way the van was taking corners, my gloved hands weren't going to hold on forever.

I willed the stave into the barest release of energy, so that the end glowed like a hot coal, then pressed it against the metal. As soon as it sank in, I let the stave deactivate. A few good shakes confirmed my brainstorm worked. I'd welded my interdimensional weapon to the getaway vehicle.

The police emergency lights were getting farther behind, the sirens were fading. Which was good news for the guys underneath me, yeah, but not so much for people like Lieutenant Ramos. The van made several sharp turns. I lost track of where in town we were. Somewhere south, I think, because the city lights rose gradually to the left. So, we were heading into the industrial district.

That brought back memories. Lots of astral fiends made their appearance in that rundown part of San Camillo. Commerce-wise, the port was doing well, but manufacturing was a ghost of what it had been back in the day. That left a bunch of empty buildings, to which these guys were headed.

My phone buzzed.

Seriously? I reached into one of the surreptitious pockets on the side of the suit. Yeah, it was in there. But if Loredana thought the middle of the night was a good time to chat ...

Nope. Ramos.

I grit my teeth. No way I was gonna start yammering from the top of the van. I didn't care how loud the rushing wind was up here. I hung up.

Ramos got the message. <Was that you?>

<On van. Industrial. Don't know why.> We were slowing. Left turn. Huh. There was a set of medical offices up ahead. The sign invited me to inform Ramos. <Syndax Technologies.>

<Stay clear. We'll handle it.>

<Better hurry. We're here.>

And we were. The van parked away from the few streetlights along the crumbling sidewalk. A door rolled open, rattling the sides and roof. I flattened myself. Thankfully the suit's adaptive camouflage mimicked what was around me— the black roof underneath, the yellow-flooded white walls of the research building.

Six men exited the van. They were dressed in dark gray tactical gear—jackets, gloves, pants, backpack. Masks covered their faces, kinda like mine, except they had chunky goggles that glowed green. Night vision. Armed, too. Heckler

& Koch MP5s. German-made submachine guns. Loredana was handy with them.

It occurred to me they're what at least one team of thugs who tried to kill me carried. Must be a favorite of bad guys.

This crew was quiet, professional. If they were communicating, it was by radio—or, no, wait. One of them flashed hand gestures. Others complied. The leader and three others converged on the front door. Whatever they had for a key worked well, because the door opened without complaint. No alarms sounded, either, at least none that I heard. The four men vanished insight without a sound.

Okay. Whoever they were, I doubted they were Syndax employees, because medical research technicians don't go for special forces ninja gear. That meant, even with alarms absent, they were breaking and entering.

I rolled off the top and dropped behind them. "Evening, fellas. Look, I know the rules about trespassing aren't posted everywhere, but it's not—"

They turned and opened fire.

Maybe announcing myself wasn't the brightest idea. Sure was funny when the superheroes on the big screen do it, right?

Whatever. I juiced the pulsar stave enough to make me slip a couple feet sideways in the blink of an eye. Bullets rattled off the side of the van and stabbed deep into the open compartment. The ricochets forced my attackers to back off a step.

Which made it easier for me to slam into the first guy.

The body check was all the more powerful with the stave's energy coursing through the suit, rendering the camo effect moot in a big way, because bright yellow lines lit up. I sent him hurtling ten feet across the road. His helmet clattered like a dropped plate.

And he was left without his gun, because I ripped it from his grasp. A quick follow-up swipe sliced it down the middle, leaving two lumps of metal and plastic.

The second guy dropped his gun. He drew a blade from behind him. Not talking about a hunting knife, either. This was a full-on sword. Like a ninja's. Then he pulled a second.

"Seriously?" I muttered through the mask.

He came at me, pinwheeling arms and flashing metal. It would have been ridiculous except those blades were actually sharp, because when I dodged, one of them almost took a corner off the suit. Pain seared across the top of my shoulder. It was gonna leave a doozy of a bruise, but the suit had been up against way worse than a ninja blade.

Fine. He wanted to play?

I broke the stave apart and twirled a half in each hand. "I'm game for Ninja Turtle time, pal."

If he heard me, he didn't indicate my humor was his thing. Maybe it was the snarl that turned him off. Either way, he resumed his attack.

It was like sword fighting with a shadow. Let me be clear. I didn't do much sword fighting. Astral fiends didn't come equipped with weaponry, aside from the fangs and spines. My opponent wasn't as fast as them, but that doesn't mean he was a slug. He made me work for it. Sparks flashed as the swords collided with the stave halves. I held him off, but barely.

Wished I had enough power left to melt the swords and be done with it.

He ducked a retaliatory blow and swept my legs out from under me with his own. I went down hard but managed to interrupt the fall with my right elbow. News flash: funny bones are not funny when you hit them, and that jolt travels the entire length of your arm.

I twisted my left arm and intercepted both of his swords as he slashed down with them, raining blows again and again. His timing was predictable enough that when he broke contact for the fourth time, I rolled aside. Heard metal *clank* against pavement.

I brought the staves together and rammed them deep into the guy's gut.

He let out a yelp that was more an explosion of expulsed air than an expression of surprise. My second strike slashed his left arm, and the third cracked across his mask, shattering the goggles.

Ha! So much for night vision.

The guy backed away. He tore the damaged goggles off and tossed them aside. Blood dripped from a long gash above a very angry eyeball.

An eyeball that was black and violet.

My turn to yelp. Not very heroic, I get it, but when the bad guy's glaring at you with an eye that's a swirling mass of stormy black where white should be, with a sickly purple iris, you don't worry about that part of your reputation.

Then there was the mark on his left arm. Guy had a tattoo, a black sword. It was a stylized weapon, huge blade with a tiny handle, nothing like the ninja swords he was slashing around.

His buddy got to his feet on the other side of the street. Worst part? His right arm was broken. As in, it was bent at an angle that should have made a Russian weightlifter on steroids cry like a toddler. But he drew a sword with the undamaged limb and walked right toward us, like he was out for an evening stroll.

"So much for keeping this simple," I muttered, staves at the ready.

That's when the front windows of Syndax shattered in a spray of glass.

Man. Whoever was in the pane replacement business in San Camillo was gonna be able to take his wife to the Bahamas at this rate.

One of the special forces ninjas rolled across the street. He lay in a limp heap, his mask askew. This guy's eyes were shrunken to the size of peas, but they weren't a bizarre purply-black. They were a nice shade of blue.

And they were shrunken to match his shriveled, gray flesh.

Oh, great.

The other three guys came sprinting out, hollering. That's right, shouting their stupid heads out. Only one had a gun. The others had slashes in their outfits.

The weirdest part was the effect their sudden, manic appearance had on my opponents. Broken-arm Guy stopped mid-stride. His sword hit the ground. He cried out, clutching the damaged arm, and collapsed to his knees. His voice choked with tears.

And Two-swords? My sparring buddy? His eyes cleared up, turning into a bloodshot brown. He looked just as surprised as I felt.

"Go, man, go! Get out of here! It's loose!" Two of the fleeing ninjas grabbed their wounded partner. The mummified soldier got left where he was, a desiccated roadblock.

Two-swords stared right past me.

I really did not want to turn around. What I wanted to do was go back home, plop on the couch with a cold beer and steaming hot slice of pepperoni pizza and ignore everything.

You guessed it. I turned around.

"It" was … something I'd never seen before.

The creature tearing through the lobby of Syndax was big as a dog, like Great Dane-sized. So, more like a mountain lion? It was four-legged, though the front two were huge, gnarled, and misshapen, with jagged spines protruding at irregular intervals. More spikes rose from its neck and formed a long, undulating spinal sail, making it look more like a dragon-dog.

But the color was one I recognized immediately—mottled gray and black, with splotches that were a deep, shimmering violet. Just like an astral fiend's hide.

The face? Worse. Very feline, but like someone had started sculpting a cat's head and gotten blind drunk halfway through, and very angry. It was a gaping mouth of slobbering fangs with a long, sinuous tongue—scratch that, there were *two*, and they were tentacles.

The dog-cat-fiend-thing glared at me with a hideous cluster of glistening, bulbous spider-type eyes—nine of them—and shrieked.

Ah. There was the sound. It churned my stomach, and send fear shooting through me like an electric shock. My brain screamed for me to get out of there *pronto*.

Instead, I grinned.

Enough of playing street vigilante. I needed a real fight. A battle.

"Run. Run!" The soldier ninjas staggered across the street, ignoring me.

Two-swords, he glanced back at them, and then at me.

The creature bounded for us, its breathing horribly distended.

I shrugged. "Truce?"

He attacked the thing. So did I.

But it wasn't standing still for us to pincushion. Those tentacles lashed out, just like I was used to. I hit my knees, back bent, so the first one could swish overhead harmlessly. Then I lopped it off. The beastie screamed.

I laughed. An actual chuckle! No, I wasn't crazy. But I was back to my normal.

Then Two-swords did his own hop over the second tentacle and severed it like a pro. Check that. Like someone else I'd seen fight an astral fiend. Or two someones.

My brother Teget, who hailed from the city of Meda in a dimension beyond ours.

And Wilhelmina, aka Sherry Jean Crown, the homeless old lady who was my predecessor as Procyon's operative.

More tentacles exploded out from the hound, faster than I'd seen an astral fiend's move. One of them speared Two-sword's leg, and he roared in anger and pain before slashing through the offending appendage. Whatever his guys were up to, whoever he worked for, it was something or someone who'd trained him how to do what I did.

I tried for another swipe at the bound, but when I did, I struck its hide with dead metal.

The light flared out of the pulsar stave.

"Awesome," I muttered.

Tentacles smacked me into the street, which was a good thing. Sure, every part of my body ached when I tumbled end over end until I hit my shoulder on the curb, but at least I wasn't drained of my life.

Wished I could have said the same for Two-sword. The hound knocked him onto his back. Tentacles stabbed into his chest, tearing underneath the body armor and wrapping around his throat. Two-sword's cries of anguish trailed off into a hideous gurgle, then faded into a whisper.

Purple tinged the hound. It let out an exultant scream.

I didn't care who Two-swords was. He'd fought me, tried to kill me. But seeing him suffer that fate made me sick. And angry.

Sirens again. Super. If SCPD stumbled into this ...

The hound took two bounding leaps toward me, and as it did, the air above the street whipped into a frenzy, tossing bits of trash and asphalt. I held up my hand to shield from the larger chunks.

Purple sparks exploded around the hound, wreathing it in something akin to lightning. It froze midair, stretched, and for a moment, I thought I saw triplicate.

Then it vanished with a *crack*.

There was no time to contemplate to where Satan's Fido had disappeared. There were still four of those ninja-goons—Broken-arm, who was the one being dragged away by his pals, and the fourth, who shouted commands like he was the Boss.

"Hey! Get back here!" I staggered upright. "You're—under arrest!"

He pointed a cell phone at me.

Then the van blew up.

The fireball turned the night into dawn. Heat singed my suit, rolled over me like an open oven. The concussion sent me tumbling again. Bits of metal and plastic pelted me, some of them so superheated they scorched my skin. But the suit held up, mercifully.

My senses, sadly, did not. Everything went into a spin. I saw the flaming remnants of the van in a crater, and a corpse ablaze. No demon dog. No ninja goons.

Plenty of flashing lights, though.

Sounds slowed and muddied. I tried to lift my head. Bad idea. I fell—or it seemed like I was falling. Wasn't I standing up? Buildings spun in a mad collage.

Last thing I saw was the shiniest pair of shoes in the world.

CHAPTER SEVEN

Ow.

I needed to quit fainting. Maybe I should have called it *getting knocked out*. Sounded stronger that way. Whatever the case, it was embarrassing.

I jolted awake. The night air was cool.

"Easy. Rest. *Descánsate.*" Ramos leaned near, a water bottle in hand. "Let me get an EMT over here."

"No. No way." I lifted the bottom of the mask, enough so I could take an unfiltered lungful of air, and then immediately replaced the O2 with H2O. Did you know that if you drink too much water you could kill yourself? True fact. I'd have been happy dying that way just then.

Ramos stared at me. "How close were you to the blast?"

"Close enough to do a drop-kicked ball's impression." I handed him back the bottle and winced at the pain in my arm.

"If it weren't for the stave ..." Ramos shook his head. "We found the one body."

"Yeah. I figure the other one's ashes."

"Who else was in the van?"

"Four more men. Dressed in tactical gear, like someone who wanted badly to join SCPD's SWAT but got rejected to the amateur league." I rolled my shoulder and got an immediate reminder of the bruise Two-sword left me. "Strike that. They might have dressed amateur, but they were trained."

"Military?"

"Sure. If the Army's got an anti-astral fiend division."

Ramos made the sign of the cross. "There was one here? A fiend?"

"Not really. It ... kinda acted like one. But it wasn't anything I'd ever seen before. Too animal, less monster. And it vanished."

"Vanished?"

"It was like it brought its own rip to the party."

"Are you certain?" Ramos glanced behind him. Fire engines and ambulances surrounded the area, with squad cars cordoning the road. Firefighters were busy hosing the flames as best they could, but besides blasting out all the windows on both sides of the street, the explosion had set Syndax's landscaping ablaze. They'd be busy for a while. "Why didn't Procyon warn you?"

Good question. One I intended to get answered. Right after I stopped hurting. "Later. Why don't you ask the rest of the ninja squad?"

Ramos scowled. "Mercury, you're the only one here, besides the clothes."

"Clothes?" Was my brain that badly scrambled, or was he just not making sense?"

He pointed left. Detective Bradley was snapping orders at a couple cops. Sure enough, there was gray tactical gear in heaps on the sidewalk. Backpacks, guns, boots ...everything.

I frowned. "That... okay. So, you're looking for four naked guys?"

Ramos sighed. "The suspects likely changed into civilian attire when they fled the scene. Which means we have no idea what they look like. They could be walking toward downtown in hoodies and blue jeans, or polos and cargo shorts."

"Oh. Right." Pretty smart. Explained why their backpacks seemed so bulky.

It didn't explain who they were, why they were proficient in astral fiend-fighting, or what they were after in the building.

Ramos glanced again at Bradley, then pressed something into my palm. "Pocket this."

"What's—?" It felt like a cell phone, except longer and narrower.

"Do it!" Ramos hissed.

I did, right next to my phone. Which, it seemed, wasn't broken.

"Found it near you. One of them may have dropped it." He was murmuring his words, as he forced me to drink enough water to drown a whale. "I figured it was something you and Procyon should look at first, since I couldn't make sense of the numbers—but I could recognize the word 'tachyon' on the screen."

I sputtered water. "What? Are you for real?"

"As real as your concussion." Ramos stood. "Jaworski! Get an EMT over here." When I balked, Ramos held up a hand like he was stopping traffic. "Save it, Mercury. You're hurt. Since you saved the city, the least we can do is comp a medical check-up."

"As long as your EMT doesn't see my face."

"We'll work something out."

Except the EMT didn't get to us first. Bradley did. Guy lit a cigarette. Seriously? Why not go stick it in the crater's fire? "We'll get the CSIs to see if they can lift prints and gather DNA, L.T., but it doesn't look good. No tags. No IDs."

Man. Talk about all the acronyms. Ramos scowled. "Give me some good news, Stan."

Bradley held up a crumpled, blackened piece of metal, and smirked. "Got enough of these bits to piece together a license plate."

"That'll do nicely. See to it no one gets through the cordon."

"Oh, the reporters are already sniffing around." Bradley pointed at me. "Maybe he should do the interview."

"Hey, that's a great idea, Detective Bradley. Let me think about it." I scratched my chin in exaggerated fashion using my middle finger, lips pursed.

"You want me to haul this punk in for questioning, L.T.?"

"Negative, Detective. Mercury's got more pressing matters on his agenda." Ramos held out his hand. "Time to clear the scene."

"Right." I accepted the help getting to my feet. Everything spun in the wrong direction. I had to slap the building behind me to stabilize the world. "Yeesh. You'd think I got thrown across the street by a mutant monster dog."

Bradley stared. "Is he high? I can have the lab run a tox screen ..."

"No, he's all right. He's pursuing leads regarding our mysterious deaths case. Those leads led him here." Ramos arched an eyebrow. "Correct?"

"Yes. Correct." Did Ramos just lie? Because I hadn't

thought that possible.

"Monsters and terrorists," Bradley muttered. "Give me gangbangers any day."

He headed off for the police barricades, puffing on the cig like he was a locomotive on the Union Pacific. What? I know my railroads.

"Give me whatever you can," Ramos murmured. "Sketches of what you saw. Names, if you heard any. A rough timeline. Every detail you can dredge up."

"As soon as my head doesn't feel like it's got rocks banging around inside, I'd be happy to." I grimaced as I shook it. Big mistake.

"Did you ... jingle?"

My brains weren't *that* loose. I dug the silver coins the antiques store owner had given as payment for services rendered. "Nah. Got to pay the bills."

Ramos frowned. "This wouldn't have to do with the foiled robbery I heard over the radio, would it?"

"Probably. Get many of those tonight that involved a feisty grandma toting a shotgun?"

"Only the one. There's a guy on Pass Ridge Road who deals in old coins out of his house. He's not one of the ones we lean on when someone's stolen a bunch and looking to unload them for cash. So, you won't draw suspicion when you sell them."

"Ah. Thanks." Hadn't thought of that. It'd be the apex of embarrassment to get pinched by the cops while selling a bunch of old silver dollars instead of, you know, committing vigilante acts.

The EMT finally joined us, a skinny guy with a man-bun and neck beard. He stared at me, then Ramos. "Is ... this the injured party?"

"Possible concussion and contusions."

"They're healing quick." I tapped the pulsar stave against my suit. Yellow light rippled across the inset lines. Okay, it wasn't completely dried out. But it failing in the middle of my battle with the killer fiend-hound was disconcerting, to put it mildly.

"Okay." The EMT scratched his bun. "I guess ... raise your mask?"

"No way. It's called 'secret identity' because I don't tell eighty bazillion people my real name or let them see my actual face." I blew out a breath, and my vision spun. Bile rose in my throat. Didn't want to risk exposure, but ...

"Hang on. Don't peek."

"Peek?" The EMT scowled. He glanced at Ramos. "Come on, Lieutenant."

"Were you on Wayfarer Drive in the aftermath of the event?" Ramos snapped. "Did you handle casualties?"

"North Beach Battle," I offered.

"Shut up." Ramos jabbed a finger against the EMT's chest. "Do what this man says. Now."

The poor kid's Adam's apple jumped up and down like a kangaroo on a trampoline—not that I'd ever seen such a thing. It sounded amazing, though. "Sure."

He closed his eyes, giving me the window needed to contort my mask. When I gave him the all clear, the mask was twisted about my face so that he could somewhat see into my eyes but otherwise make out only a portion of my features. He shone a blinding flashlight in each eye, ran a couple of dumb tests where I had to follow my finger, asked me equally dumb questions. Finally, he shrugged. "Mild concussion, yeah. Just take it easy. No, um, excess activity."

I saluted with the pulsar stave. "I'll keep that in mind.

Thanks."

As soon as the EMT had jogged off, Ramos folded his arms. "Go home. Get rest. Then send me everything we discussed."

"Roger roger." I staggered toward an alley. "Hey … I don't suppose you could give me a lift?"

He spread his arms wide, encompassing the fiery crater, the piles of discarded Special Ops ninja clothes, and the swarming emergency personnel. "I'm a little busy."

"No worries. I'll hoof it." About a hundred blocks. Okay, so that was an exaggeration.

But it was a long walk home.

Daylight barged through my bedroom window, because some idiot left the blinds open. I reached for the pull string, my misdirected slapping futile. Too far. Had to get up.

I staggered out and made some breakfast. Oatmeal. Blueberries. Kiwi. A plate of sausage and eggs. Running with the pulsar stave could famish me. Last night was the most, uh, exercise I'd had in a while.

Okay. Ramos wanted the goods. I sat down with a bowl of blueberries tucked beside me on the couch. Somewhere underneath was a sketchpad. I dragged it out. Pencil? Down the cushions. The point wasn't broken, so, bonus.

I opened the pad and smiled. Loredana had given it to me a week after our last escapade, before she'd gone off radar for a couple months. Said it would be good for me to take up something creative, as an outlet for the psychological stress of my adventures. As a result, I had filled the first half with drawing of hideous astral fiends—most of which were in the process of dismemberment, courtesy of yours truly.

I may have exaggerated my musculature. But who doesn't? Interspersed with those battle scenes were bucolic images of Meda and its surrounding countryside. They were black and white. I couldn't bring myself to add color. Homesickness was bad enough when I looked at the rough sketches.

Enough of the maudlin. I flipped to a blank page and the pencil flew. Sure, people like to say "almost of its own volition" or some garbage like that, but it was true. A half hour later, I had a couple attempts at a fiend-hound, capped off by the real deal, or as close as I could recall.

The ninjas were more difficult, but I figured Ramos could make do with generic descriptions—because that's how they looked. Generic.

Except ... I quick sketched the tattoo. Not good enough. The eraser burned across the paper, leaving those annoying crumbs all over my lap and the couch. Third try produced the result.

That sword looked way too familiar.

My phone buzzed. Ramos. <Any luck?>

I took photos of the sketches with my phone and sent them along. <Best I could do. The critter was on a rampage. Don't know what the soldiers wanted when they went in, but it could have been the fiend-hound itself.> That would make sense, given what was on their device.

I crossed to my bedroom, where the suit was draped across a bed post. Phew. Whatever Winston Yen had done when he built the thing, making it sweat proof was apparently not at the top of his list of gimmicks. I retrieved the phone-like device Ramos had hidden.

Yikes. The word "tachyon" still glowed on its surface, that much Ramos had gotten right. But the narrow screen was heaped with jargon and diagrams I didn't understand.

I knew one thing.

I'd seen them in Tracking at Procyon.

<We've been canvassing the neighborhood. No hits on your ninjas yet,> Ramos replied. <Good sketches. I'll get them to patrols. Syndax owners not responding to our inquiries.>

What? Weird. <They get the day off or something?>

<Something. I'm about to pay their manager a visit if I can find his address.>

I nodded. Of course, Ramos couldn't see that. I turned the tracking device over a couple times in my hand. Okay. Those guys I fought last night had military-style gear, a gizmo that apparently showed tachyon readings, and the ability to tackle a creature akin to an astral fiend without instantly dying.

And that sword tattoo.

I kicked the couch. "C'mon, Mercury," I growled. "You've seen the thing before. Focus."

Didn't help. My phone buzzed again. Ramos, Part Two. <Got word back on DeBarthe's financials. You were right. Nice salary. Regular direct deposits.>

<Anything else fun?>

<Yes. Roughly half the amount withdrawn the day after each deposit, for eight months. Cash. Trying to get locations, see if we can get security footage.>

<Let me know.> I put my phone down. Four months. That meant DeBarthe was spending a boatload of his money long before the mess with the fiends erupted and the full-scale invasion was defeated. Had to face the possibility that he'd been in cahoots with Marigold and Winston. Man, I love that word. Cahoots.

But it could have been for alimony, child support,

whatever you want to call it. That much, though? It left the poor guy living in Baba Yaga's slum house.

No, it would have had to be something major. Something he wouldn't tell anyone about. Not even Procyon. I snorted. Well, if he had guys threatening him with ninja swords, too, I could see why he'd kept quiet. Even when one had super abilities like me, courtesy of the pulsar stave, it would still be scary as heck if someone pressed a razor-sharp blade to—

Blade.

"No way." I snatched up my sketch pad and flipped backward through the completed sheets so roughly I almost ripped a couple. There. Toward the beginning. One of the first drawings I'd completed after Loredana had pushed me into it.

Marigold Yen, standing before a huge rip between our dimension and the Interstice. I'd filled a gap wreathed in rippling lightning with a storm-ravaged wasteland. A slavering astral fiend was on its way out. Mari, like the insane demigoddess she'd wanted desperately to become, was beckoning it into San Camillo—specifically, Procyon's parking lot.

She had the night's blade in her hand.

Night's, not knight's. It was a huge sword, six inches at its broadest point, and four feet long. The blade itself was curved on one edge and straight on the other, with the curved part reaching close to the hilt.

Just as dangerous in real life as it had looked in my vision, when I'd been trying to find it. She'd used the night's blade to stabilize the rips between our world and the Interstice. Combining it with the pulsar stave and my brother's ax would have made the stabilization permanent. That's why the other weapons were stashed in Meda's temple, locked out of both dimensions.

I'd had to kill Marigold to stop the gateway from becoming permanent.

I dropped the sketchpad and retrieved my phone. Dialed Loredana. It rang. And rang. And rang … "C'mon, pick up!"

"Good morning to you, too, Mercury."

Whoops. Didn't have time to be chastened. "Are you at Procyon?"

"We both know that's a silly question."

My watch said 7:30. Yeah. She was there. "I'm coming over."

"That's not a wise—"

"Ask me if I care, Loredana, because I don't. I fought off a mutated version of an astral fiend last night, and a bunch of guys were using high-tech gear to track its appearance via tachyon emissions."

That zipped her lips. "Are you sure?" was her eventual and subdued reply.

"Pretty sure. And it gets worse. They had this tattoo." I switched functions and texted her a photo of the blade sketch. "Recognize it?"

"That sword is the key to our destruction."

"Yeah," I muttered. "That."

CHAPTER EIGHT

I couldn't believe they didn't let me in. But it was a Saturday. Used to be I could waltz into the lobby of Procyon Foundation's Tower Three, flash my security clearance card with its green stripe, and one of the interchangeable receptionists would smile. Up I'd go to the seventh floor, where Tracking tried to pinpoint incursions by astral fiends using technology that would make every spy agency in the world drool.

This time, there was a burly guy from security standing outside locked doors. Beefy white guy, with a neatly trimmed brown beard and buzz cut hair. He had on the department's unofficial uniform—a pair of black sunglasses, black polo shirt and, wait for it, black slacks. I'd say he was wearing them, but it was more like someone had painted the clothing across more muscles than I thought the human anatomy possessed.

Wait a second. His name was Garvey. My throat tightened. Not one of the guys I'd had to smack around when I was temporarily hunted by the evil conspiracy inside Procyon, but I did sneak by him to break Teget from custody.

"Mr. Hale." He crossed his arms. There was a semiautomatic pistol holstered on his belt. "You're not authorized to enter."

"Doesn't look like anyone's authorized to enter, so I don't feel bad." I craned my neck for a look around him. The lobby appeared empty. "What, no tours today?"

He stared at me, waiting for me to get to the point and probably not for me to make another sarcastic comment.

"Loredana Lark's expecting me." I pulled my phone from my pocket.

He reached for the gun.

"Hey! Phone." I waved it aloft but made sure my other hand was nowhere near anything dangerous—like the pulsar stave. "See?"

Garvey's hand relaxed. "Sorry."

"Yeah, I'd say so. Since when does security shoot people coming in the front door?"

"Things are tense."

"Maybe see a masseuse?"

He glared at me. I have that effect on people.

"You know who I am. Open the door and you can go back to glowering and accidentally almost shooting people."

"Only once I get clearance from Ms. Lark." He dialed his own phone. "Ma'am? Garvey, front door. Yes, he's here." He looked puzzled. "I didn't realize I sounded, uh, 'vexed.' What? Oh, yeah, Mr. Hale's been talking with me." He smirked. "Okay, thanks."

He pocketed the phone and grinned.

"Let me guess. She said I'm the reason you're vexed?"

Garvey nodded.

Apparently, I was rubbing off on people.

Loredana beckoned from the lobby, which prompted

Garvey to finally open up the stupid door. Hearing it close behind me sounded like the last stone dropping into place, trapping me in an Egyptian tomb. Not that I was anxious.

"Place looks good," I told Loredana.

She didn't reply. In fact, she didn't speak at all, not during the elevator ride up seven floors or during our hike around the curved hallway. I hadn't realized how much I'd missed the pastel colors, the tile floors, heck, even the infirmary where my brother had been held prisoner. All the while my stomach churned and Loredana's heels *pick-pocked* along. I wished she would say something. Even, "Shut up, Mercury," which would make me mad. Instead, I tapped the sketchpad against my leg to pass the time.

Finally, she pushed open the door to the dark cave that was Tracking. There were all the toys—the plethora of monitors casting their pale glows, showing every square inch of our planet, the U.S., all the way down to the plot of land on which Procyon Foundation's headquarters sat.

Winston's desk was empty. His mug was gone. It made me oddly homesick, even though I probably should have taken the hint he was a bad guy from the Imperial logo on the side. A quick glance confirmed the other eight stations were also unoccupied. Headsets lay abandoned on the consoles. But most of the computers were up Huh. "You weren't kidding. Did you fire everybody?"

"No. They've been placed on administrative leave." Loredana cleared her throat. Consequences of not using her voice for a while. "Paid administrative leave. The Tracking equipment is still functioning, albeit in a dormant state— recording the surrounding region, as usual, but ..."

"With no human eyeballs on it." I nodded. "Right. Glad to see you didn't change the décor."

"It wasn't in the budget." She smirked. "Now. Your data."

"Right." I handed her the device. "Does it look familiar?"

Loredana cradled it, like a mother would hold a child. "I'd have to do a full classified records search. Perhaps Winston had something in development. Yes, we have handheld scanners, though in recent years he'd switched to exclusive use of drones. Which originally was a brilliant idea, in terms of consolidation of our efforts, but it became apparent that was an error when Mr. Yen showed his true colors, as it were."

"Yeah. That would be bad, giving the enemy the only means of Tracking the astral fiends."

Loredana rubbed her finger along the side of the device. Was she remembering the nights spent working with Winston to track down the monsters I killed? The brainstorming sessions the three of us had in this room, surrounded by techs diligently trying to make a clearer path for me to follow?

Or was she thinking about when Winston helped his wife try to orchestrate the end of the world?

"I don't suppose we can Google the specs for this thing."

"No. Hardly. As I say, the databases may hold an answer."

"But there's no Procyon markings on it, right?"

"Correct. I will get our Tracking expert to get on it."

I glanced at the room again. "The expert's not taking a nap in one of my suits, is he?"

The door opened. I saw a flash of pink. And a blur of motion. Whatever it was, whoever was incoming, it didn't matter—fight or flight. I picked fight.

I swept the pulsar stave free of the leather holster tucked under my shirt, where it hung obscured from view. There was a split-second hesitation—I know, I shouldn't have. But after the thing died on me last night, I was, well, worried. Worried if I powered it up again, it might fail entirely. And then what was I? An unemployed Millennial, with no parents' basement in which I could crash.

But there was no way I would stop protecting people when I could stop them from being hurt.

I willed the stave to life. Yellow energies crackled up and down, searing the darkness as I brandished it between Loredana and whatever was incoming.

"Oh, wow! That is soooo cool!"

I blinked. It wasn't an attacker. Not even the fiend-hound. Nope. It was a woman—a girl, I guess. She couldn't be much more than twenty-one. That wasn't an amazing deduction, but simple observation, because she had a bottle of Corona in one hand. The pink hair is what I'd spotted when she first burst in. Shoulder length, a cute cut, but blazing bright pink. Neon. She had on a button-down shirt, a vest, and blue jeans. Pink shoes. Her complexion was tan, but not from long afternoons on San Camillo's bay beach. I guessed Arabic, of some variety.

"Sorry, you don't even know me, 'cause I'm new." She tucked a tablet under her arm and held out the hand free of beer. "Liz Stojan. Elizabeth. You can call me Liz."

"Mercury Hale, Elizabeth Stojan." Loredana smiled at me. "Perhaps you can stow your weaponry."

"Sure." I forced a smile, because not only had this Liz taken me by surprise, she'd sat down in Winston's chair.

She must have noticed me staring, because she stopped halfway through her bottle of beer. Her attempt to staunch a belch failed. "Urgh. Sorry, again. I'm the, um, interim head of Tracking."

"I thought Gary DeBarthe was the interim head."

Liz wrinkled her nose. "Interim-interim head?"

I shrugged. "Whatever. Are you any good at this?"

She recoiled, as if I'd turned into an astral fiend and tried to kill her. Her expression fell so badly I thought it'd literally hit the floor.

"Mercury!" Loredana put her hand on Liz's shoulder. "Pay no attention to him, Elizabeth. His—charm is one of the many reasons he did not work directly from this office."

"Oh, no, it's okay." But I saw the distinct glimmer of tears at the corners of her eyes. Man. That was smooth, Mercury. Make the new kid cry the first time you meet her. "And I didn't mean to startle you, you know? I was just really excited about seeing the pulsar stave in action. I mean, I'd heard about it but ..." She wouldn't meet my eyes.

Great. She was a fan, too. "Hey, no worries. Let's try again." I offered my hand, because I realized I'd never shaken hers. Wow. Way to rack up all the rudeness points in one visit. "It's nice to meet you, Liz. I'm hoping you can help us out."

Her smile was timid, but hey, at least she wasn't bawling. "Thanks. I mean, nice to meet you too. Again. So, um, Ms. Lark says you've got a new toy for us?"

"Ms. Lark is correct." I winked at her.

Liz giggled. "Nice! I love taking apart someone else's tech. Not that I advocate vandalism. Or stealing. Because theft is wrong. Unless maybe from bad guys? Have you ever done that? I've seen you on YouTube! Do you Snapchat?"

Loredana cleared her throat.

"Right, okay. Here." Liz took the device from her without so much as a "Please hand it to me" or anything approaching proper social interaction. Loredana, to her credit, didn't favor the girl with a dead-ray glare meant to vaporize those who displease her. "Wow. Yeah, that's not one of ours."

"So I surmised," Loredana murmured.

I snorted into my hand to avoid the chortle that went with it. I must have sounded like a drowning badger.

"Oh." Liz's face darkened. "Right." She rummaged under the desktop and retrieved a power cord. Lucky for her the device had a USB port on its bottom, though it made sense they'd need something universal to plug in for data transfer. "I'm kind of surprised this even *has* plug. Must be they wanted to secure the information."

"Why not transfer it wirelessly?" I asked.

"It doesn't have the capability, as far as I can tell." Liz's fingers flew across the screen. I recognized a settings menu. It didn't appear different from my phone's. But she must have strayed into restricted files, because red warnings flashed. "Augh. It's encrypted."

"Take your time." Loredana made eye contact with me and tilted her head toward the door. "Mr. Hale and I must debrief."

"If you insist," I said.

Liz giggled again.

"How droll." Loredana gestured for me to get a move on.

I was halfway to the door when Liz blurted, "Oh, you guys don't have to leave! I'm almost ready."

Loredana and I looked at each other, then her. "You've breached their security?" she asked.

"Well, not yet, but give me—" Liz craned her neck for a better view of the red digital clock above the main monitors. "Two minutes, tops? It's encrypted, yeah, but whoever built it wasn't worried about someone unauthorized getting her hands on the device. This is kinda sad, actually. I'd fire whoever did such lousy work."

"My bet is their severance is gonna be a whole lot worse than dismissal," I muttered. "These guys travel with ninja swords."

"Ooooh." Liz's eyes were wide, but she kept the screen of Winston's—check that, her computer—as her focus. She'd input lines of code, execute commands, then get to furiously clicking with her mouse. Whatever she was doing was inducing a screen-flicker of stroke-inducing proportions on the device. "Katana or ninjato?"

"I didn't have time to ask Wikipedia."

"That's too bad. I love swords." She smiled over her shoulder. "I keep an honest to goodness falchion over my mantle in my apartment. Of course, the fireplace doesn't work, but it's still the centerpiece of the living room, so it has to have something nice adorning it and I didn't want to keep the sword in my bedroom because, well, that's just weird—"

"Elizabeth." Loredana tapped her shoe.

"Oh. Sorry." Liz blushed again. But, thankfully, the device's red warnings dissipated, and it opened a slew of new menu options. "Ha! Ha-ha! I told you this was lousy. I didn't even have to break out the Big Bad Wolf."

"What wolf?" I asked.

"My best breaching algorithm." She shrugged. "It's really for emergencies. But anyway, it looks like the people you were, um, fighting were tracking tachyon emissions, just like our drones do."

"I figured that." I leaned in close to the screen. "But did they get any specific? Like, say, readings on a cross between a murderous dog and an irate astral fiend?"

Liz stared. "I-I don't know. I'll download everything that's on here."

It took a few minutes, but I'll give her credit—she filled up every screen in Tracking with all sorts of tidbits. There were charts full of tachyon emission readings, with dates next to them—all of which were *after* the North Beach Battle. I moved deeper into the room, near one of the larger touch screens. A couple of swipes enlarged a column of specific interest. "Hey. This one's from last night. Check out the timestamp."

"I see." Loredana stood close. She'd either been eating strawberries, or it was a new perfume. "And this spike ..."

"Pretty close to when we rolled up at Syndax." It sure seemed about right, down to the minute. I couldn't be certain, of course, because I wasn't checking my watch every five seconds.

Images sprang onto the screen. Liz yelped.

"My word," Loredana whispered.

Ah. There was Fido. I can see why they reacted how they did—he was even more gruesome than real life, because the guy recording had captured the images while Fido was leaping toward him. Every aspect of the bulging cluster of eyes, the dripping fangs, the slimy tentacles, was captured in high resolution.

"That's the one." I straightened. "Managed to fight it off, before it teleported."

"Teleported?" Liz frowned. "Teleported."

"Well, formed a rip and vanished, whatever you want to call it. There was a burst of purple lighting, a cross between the typical rip's opening and those hop-skip portals I saw a fiend use in the spring."

"Oh, yeah, I remember the data on those. Gary was

reviewing to see … if …" She sagged, as if the air had been let out of a balloon.

"Don't worry about it." I smiled. "Loredana's got me on the case, and I've got the best cop in the city backing me up. We'll find him."

"I know. Thanks." Liz tried a smile in return. "Um, so the data these guys recorded showed that it wasn't a rip."

"What wasn't?"

"How the fiend-hound got away. Which isn't really a good name for it. The scanner suggests feline DNA is involved, but there is some canine influence. Oh! I wonder if it's an unnatural confluence of species caused by—"

"Let's skip to the part where you explain that in Mercury-speak," I said.

"I was getting there. The fiend-hound didn't emerge from a rip between our dimension and the Interstice. It created a breach between two points of space in this dimension and bridged them."

I ran a hand over my head. "So, it teleported from one place to another, without ever leaving San Camillo?"

"As far as I can tell. But this device doesn't give us an exit point. Why'd you say in San Camillo?"

I glanced at Loredana. "Because I think this is what's been draining people's life downtown."

"Yikes." Liz chewed her lip. "I'll task our drones to start scanning for the same tachyon signature. But why were those guys tracking it? Did they want to kill it, too?"

Good question. It was one Loredana and I would have to answer.

Apparently, she thought the same thing. "Keep me apprised of results, Elizabeth. We have strategy to discuss."

And that was when two security guys—one of whom was

Garvey—entered Tracking. With them was a stout Latino I'd never seen before. He pointed at me like I was the bug he missed stepping on.

"Hi," I said. "Mercury Hale."

"Get him out of my building," the guy said.

CHAPTER NINE

Well. That was discourteous.

Great. I was starting to sound like Loredana.

"Gentlemen?" The new arrival gestured for the security men to ... do something, I guess. They looked as equally befuddled as I must have, because they stood there towering over their boss. He was short, thickset but not tubby, with wavy black hair and a goatee-moustache combo. His suit was silver-gray, and with the black shirt underneath, he was more crime boss than supervisor.

"Sir, Mr. Hale is here at my direction." Loredana's posture instantly improved. Don't ask me how, because she's the furthest from a slouch I've ever met. But there she was, hands clasped behind her back, standing at parade rest. "I would request he remain."

"Denied." The guy glared at his security detail. "Am I speaking in a foreign tongue? Get him out of here."

"Hey, listen, pal," I said. "I don't know who you think you are, but I've logged way more hours in the building that you have, because there's janitors I recognize more than I do you."

"Proper introductions for a furloughed operative were not on my agenda," he said. "Hector Alvarez, interim manager. Pleased to make your acquaintance. Now, leave."

"Nope." I folded my arms.

"That's unacceptable. You're not to be in this facility, and certainly not in a place as sensitive as Tracking."

"*Sir*." Whoa. Loredana sounded like one of my foster parents—Fake Mom Number Four, I think—who could make a nun cringe. "Mr. Hale was responsible for thwarting numerous incursions by extra-dimensional creatures for nearly four years, up until and including his defense of this city in the event near the waterfront."

"North Beach Battle," I said.

Both Loredana and Alvarez scowled at me.

"I love that name!" Liz said. "Have you seen how many views it's gotten?"

I grinned.

"That's commendable, but irrelevant," Alvarez said.

"Not really," I said. "You know how hard it is to compete with the videos uploaded every day?"

"I meant the event!" Poor Alvarez was gonna pop a blood vessel at this rate. He should find himself a mode of relaxation. The prior boss liked whiskey at any and all hours of the day. Maybe Alvarez had his own private poison. If so, he needed to indulge more often. "You have not been cleared by the board of directors."

"I got plenty debriefed at the time, thanks. What am I still waiting to be cleared of?"

"Collusion with Marigold and Winston Yen."

I burst out laughing. The sound trailed off when I realized the idiot was serious. "Collusion? With the vaporized lady and her husband? You remember the part where I stopped them from destroying the world, right?"

"I do. And that time is past. As far as I'm concerned, you shouldn't even have that *thing* with you." He pointed at the pulsar stave, still gripped in my sweat-slicked hand. "But the board has misplaced priorities."

"Especially if they put you in charge here," I muttered. "If you don't mind, how about you clear out so the grown-ups can get some work done."

Alvarez started forward, but Loredana touched his arm, gently as you'd try to pick up a butterfly. "Hector. Let's discuss this later. Mr. Hale is contracted to assist us with Mr. DeBarthe's disappearance, which, if I'm not mistaken, is currently our highest priority."

That and the mutant fiend-hound.

"Then I'll be happy to see his results, when they manifest," Alvarez said. "Until then he does not set foot on the premises, nor is he paid until the work is complete."

"What, did Procyon have a bad day on the stock market?" I snapped. "Because you guys are supposedly a charitable organization, a non-profit, so unless your 'donations' have dried up, I don't see what the big deal is."

"I suppose you'll be demanding to come back aboard, full salary and benefits."

"Nobody said demanding, but sure, sounds like a good idea to me."

"That's out of the question. Look around you, Mr. Hale. The bulk of our employees, security personnel aside, are on paid leave, until we can sort out who knew what. It's bad enough we have to tread around a federal investigation. Homeland Security is furious, and not just because of the loss of lives and materiel at the event, but because other elements of the United States are aware of our true nature and did not inform them."

It dawned on me that my hardships might pale in comparison to the higher ups'. "So, we're talking turf war on top of everything else."

"Exactly. Procyon's board has tasked me with maintaining order at this facility. And you, Mr. Hale, are anything but orderly." He was close enough to scowl up at me, which was okay, because having those extra six inches on him reduced whatever element of intimidation he was trying to push. "Ms. Lark is authorized to contract with you to find Mr. DeBarthe. You'll be compensated when he's found. That's it."

"With all due respect, sir," Loredana said, "If there's such great concern about our staff's security, why would you not return Mercury—Mr. Hale to the payroll? Surely his silence would be better if bought."

If it sounded like blackmail, that's okay, because that's how Procyon maintained all of our silence—beyond appealing to our sense of duty and destiny. A well-paid staffer isn't going to go blab crazy secrets.

"I'll do you all the courtesy of being frank." Alvarez's moustache twitched. "The fewer traceable ties between Procyon and Mercury, the better, as far as the ongoing investigations are concerned. Whatever we can do to minimize that contact will be of greatest benefit not only to Procyon, but to Mercury's continued freedom as an American citizen."

Ah. There it was. Loredana must be the carrot, because this guy laid down the stick. I nodded. "Fine. You want to play it that way? I'll pick another side, because the cops already have a clue that security tore apart Gary's apartment, not whoever kidnapped him. If he's even been kidnapped.

Maybe you guys have him locked up in the basement."

I wanted Alvarez's reaction, to see if he knew about what had happened, or if Loredana had spoken to him, or if this was news. By the way he glowered first at Loredana before turning to me, I guessed it was Option Two. "Ms. Lark said you suspect as much, which is insulting. Our security personnel aren't in the habit of destroying the residences of our employees."

"Not even when they're mercenaries in disguise?" I sneered. "Been to that party."

Neither security guy behind Alvarez let on to whether my theory was correct. They had as much personality as a slab of concrete. Alvarez, though, threw his hands up. "I've had enough of this. If you're not gone from here immediately, I'll call the authorities—and not your friend Lieutenant Ramos, either. Get out on the streets and find our missing man."

"Okay, then. I'll get going." I waved the pulsar stave under his nose. That got the guards to reach for their guns, again, but at that point I was so irked I didn't care. It'd be worth a fight with them—and possibly draining the stave—if for nothing else than get Alvarez to wet himself. "But if you want me to find Gary, you'd better play nice and share what you found, whenever it was your boys went to his place."

"Wait. Please." Loredana drew me closer to Liz's desk. "I'm sorry we're not able to resolve this. Stay in touch, will you? I will send you more information relevant to the case as it becomes available."

Then she hugged me.

I had no idea what to do. Was she crying? Her face sure was warm against my cheek. Alvarez turned aside, searching the monitors for something interesting to look at, other than this display of affection.

Something got shoved into my back pocket.

It took all my self-control—and trust me, some days there's precious little of that—to not yelp like a puppy that got stepped on. Did Loredana just goose me? My next instinct was to grin as broadly as possible.

But there really was something in my pocket. Not a hand. It felt like my phone. Couldn't be, though, because my phone was—

Loredana released her hold. Her cheeks were ruddy. The device was gone from Liz's desk.

Liz was working away at her console, moving menus and typing commands that didn't look nearly as organized as what I'd seen before. She winked at me, sidelong.

That was pretty slick. I straightened out my shirt, in a move that would have made Captain Jean-Luc Picard proud—and which lowered the untucked hem over my back pockets. "Sorry to cause trouble, Mr. Alvarez. Call me if you decide you need me. And trust me, you will."

"I'll wait by the phone, counting the minutes." Alvarez pointed to the door. "Ms. Lark, escort him down."

"Of course, sir."

I nodded a farewell to Liz. When Garvey failed to move out of my way, I pantomimed shooting. He scowled and stepped aside.

Loredana and I maintained a professional silence until we reached the elevator. It started down with its familiar smooth rumble.

"That was great!" I grinned at her. "You and Liz were all *Ocean's Eight* back there."

"I rather enjoyed that film." She looked thoughtful, like someone who was contemplating poetry. "Cate Blanchett is a skilled actress."

89

"Forget her." I tapped the device in my back pocket. "You want me to track down the fiend-hound myself."

"Precisely that. Do try to stay out of trouble for a day or two."

"Scout's honor. Listen, about the sword tattoo ..." I opened the sketchpad. "That's it, right? I'm not imagining the design."

"Your skills are improving. It is undoubtedly the blade. I will make discreet inquiries as to any chatter Procyon's Intelligence section may have picked up."

"Since when does Procyon have an Intelligence section?"

"It's not here. The office is mobile. They've operated with us from time to time." Loredana smiled. "As for money, well, I shall endeavor to advance you part of your pay. In cash."

"My favorite kind. Look, I'll see what else Ramos can tell us about Gary's huge withdrawals. Let me know if you find anything in your records."

"It may be spotty on our end, but I will try."

I couldn't stand it anymore and removed the tracker. There weren't any identifying marks I could see. Nor were there any logos on the software being used. But that tattoo. "Who do you think they are?"

"I'd rather not speculate."

"Okay, I'll give it a shot—somebody who's trained to deal with the same threats we are. These guys could fight, Loredana. Like me. And their eyes glowed. They had enhanced strength. But when the fiend-hound attacked, that purple eye glow went away, and they seemed to lose whatever was beefing them up."

"Glowing eyes," Loredana murmured. "I've never encountered such a thing. There may be helpful records in the Historic Vaults. I'll start my search there. But if this is someone linked with Marigold and her ancestors, we should tread cautiously. Recall, if you will, that she said her family had pursued the night's blade for generations, so they could stabilize a path between our world and the Interstice. They failed, of course, and the blade is now safe with its counterpart the ax."

"I know. The rip can't be reopened. Not from here." Which made me wish all the more my brother Teget would get up off his extradimensional rear end and pay me a visit. I could use the extra muscle. And there was always the chance of recharging the pulsar stave if the rips reopened.

But did I want to risk a resurgence of astral fiend attacks just so I could have a fully powered weapon again? I scratched at the back of my neck. "Wish there was more I could do."

"Work the streets, like you do. My place is inside Procyon."

"You were pretty handy with a machine gun."

Loredana smirked. "It's best you remember that, too."

I left the elevator and headed across the lobby. The tracker weighed down my pocket. Better put the thing to good use.

"Mercury?"

I glanced back. Loredana had her finger on the elevator door button, holding it in place. "Be careful. Please."

"You know I will."

As soon as she was out of sight, I frowned up at the tiny black dome of the security camera in the corner of the ceiling. And flipped it the bird.

The air conditioner in my apartment broke. Which sucked, because it was 92 by noon and the humidity was not slacking. Zero clouds.

I peeked into the hall, a bottle of Corona in hand. One of my neighbors, an old black guy named Isaiah, did the same thing at the same time. "You seen the super?" he asked.

"Nah. I was gonna ask you the same."

"The fool's probably asleep." He slammed his door. "My air conditioner broke."

"Mine too."

"I'll go raise a ruckus. You do likewise if he shows up."

"What're the odds of that? Hang on." I ducked into the apartment, raided the fridge, and came back with a second bottle. "One for the road, Isaiah."

"Boy, you shoulda been in the Scouts." He accepted the drink with the thirst of a man lost in the desert. We clinked bottles and off he went.

I grinned. Couldn't wait to hear the story. When Isaiah wanted to light a fire under someone's ass …

My phone rumbled from the kitchen counter. I hustled back inside, hoping Loredana had some good news.

Funny. Nothing on the screen. And no missed call or text.

The buzzing started up again, louder. It was the tracker, which was sitting next to an open box of pizza from Carlito's. I snagged a second slice and flipped it over.

<Hey Mercury it's liz I've got some good news for you got a sec>

I winced. The severe lack of punctuation was gonna wear me down, but she seemed to know her stuff so far. I touched the screen. Nothing. Non-responsive text? Weird.

I'd flopped back down on the couch when the thing buzzed again. I rolled my eyes and grabbed it from the counter. <Oh BTW I know where the fiend-hound has been here's a couple addresses>

Of all the … wait a second. She wasn't kidding. A couple of street names and building numbers filled out the rest of the message. I recognized them, sure, but that didn't mean I'd been to any.

Except one. It was Court Street, down by the waterfront. The address put the appearance between Galena and Jefferson.

That's where Ramos found the second body.

"Nice, Liz," I murmured. "I can get those numbers to Ramos and see if they match up with the other body—and any rumored appearances. And then I can get your number, so I don't have to keep talking to myself."

On cue, a string of digits appeared in the message box on the tracker. Either Liz was good at anticipating what a Procyon operative in the field needed, or she was going to replace Marigold as a Forecaster. With it came the text, <These guys have stored gigabytes of data on tachyon readings and used them to triangulate where the fiend-hound was gonna appear that's why they were at Syndax I think>

I flipped through menus. Yeah, she wasn't kidding. Those reports, the same ones we saw up on the big screens when Liz transferred the data in Tracking, were arranged by timestamps based on when they were recorded. The final entry, of course, was from last night.

An orange line slashed across the screen, accompanied by a *chirp* from the device. I about dropped it. Really hoped the thing did come with a self-destruct.

Then a chart appeared, numbers dribbling down its side. They spun into a set of coordinates, which then superimposed themselves over a map of San Camillo. Orange letters in a black box reported, *Probability moderate. 56 percent.*

Huh. How about that.

I dialed up Ramos. It went straight to voicemail. "Seriously? Pick up."

Nothing. So, I dialed again.

He answered on the second ring. "Which part of 'Leave a message with your name and number' do you not understand?"

"The part where I'm naturally impatient. Also, that's dumb. Your phone has caller ID, right?"

"Not ... never mind." I swore I could hear him massaging his forehead. Ramos spoke in a mutter, which was hard to hear because of the racket behind him. Sounded like someone was getting into a lot of trouble. "What do you want?"

"Gary's financials. Let's go over them."

"Now's not a good time. I've got Stan getting camera footage from the banks where the withdrawals were made, but it's going to take a while."

"What about the wife?"

"She's on my list of people to interview. Later."

"C'mon, Ramos, I've got this tracker thing burning a hole in my pocket. It's definitely used to find tachyon bursts and Procyon's pretty sure it brought those soldier ninjas out to the medical building last night. Let's take it out on the town and go talk to the missus, see if she knows anything about where her ex is."

Ramos must have been pondering the idea, because the background noise took over. "I suppose I can do that. Pick me up out front. Text me when you arrive."

"You're, uh, sounding a lot more eager than when you picked up."

"It occurred to me it'd be nice to have an excuse to get

out of here," he muttered. "The captain's on the warpath."

"What'd you do, eat all her donuts?"

"No, Mercury, we've got missing bodies."

"Like Gary? Man. When it rains it pours."

"Not missing people. *Dead* bodies. The coroner went to transfer the corpses of the victims we surmise were killed by an astral fiend—or that fiend dog you found."

"Fiend-hound."

"Yes. That. All three drawers were empty. The bodies disappeared."

Of course they did. I shook my head. Because we didn't have enough problems.

CHAPTER TEN

I parked in a visitor spot outside San Camillo Police Department's Ninth Precinct. The building looked like an old guy who didn't want to show up for work—broad, sagging, sweaty. Maybe not literally sweaty, but the concrete had endured years of pollution and humidity, rendering it a drab, grimy version of its original white. Even the windows, tinted bronze, needed cleaning. But the American flag and the city's flapped in the gusts of a police chopper angling in for a landing on the rooftop pad, brand spanking new.

Ramos trotted down the front steps thirty seconds after I texted him with news of my arrival. The poor guy *really* wanted out. He slid into the seat, smelling of faint cologne and encroaching body odor. "I made it clear I don't like the hip-hop."

"Wow. You sound like my grandfather—if he complained about rap." I turned the radio up another notch and pulled away from the curb. "I'm guessing that's not a problem back on Meda. What are you, forty-six going on eighty?"

"Mercury ..."

"I kid. Thought that might get a 'whippersnapper' out

of you." I grinned as my fingers danced across the steering wheel. The Subaru responded like a rabbit, scampering between traffic, which was starting to clear up now that people with regular jobs were settled at lunch. "It's *Hamilton.*"

"The musical?"

"Yeah, if your idea of a musical is the history of the American Revolution in rap."

Ramos nodded. "My boys are obsessed. I thought it sounded familiar."

"Then good taste isn't genetic. I can switch over to Aerosmith if you're in distress."

"Never mind."

"So, what's up with your body-snatcher?"

"That's the question everyone upstairs is trying to answer. As far as we can tell, no one entered or left the morgue during the window of opportunity. Cameras aren't any help—all we have is static."

"Sounds like a coincidental glitch."

"I hate coincidences. They're improbable. It has to be deliberate sabotage."

"Well ..." I handed him the tracker. "Give this a whirl."

"With ...what?"

"See if you guys are on it." I swiped into a menu, one hand on the steering wheel so I could squeeze us between a couple of cabs. One honked. What was his problem? I left a half a car length, give or take a few feet. "Whoever those soldiers work for, they have top-notch tech."

"This little thing can't be watching the whole city." Ramos held it upside down and gave it a shake.

"Come on, Ramos, it's not an Etch-a-Sketch. You have a smartphone, don't you? Anyway, Liz is working on it. I don't think it's drones like Winston was using. Procyon could find those."

"I thought they stopped their own flights."

"As far as I know." I shrugged. "Of course, they didn't cop to security trashing Gary's apartment, either. The new boss, Alvarez, he's … ornery."

"Wonderful." Ramos frowned at the tracker. "These addresses … this one's the crime scene I took you to."

"Saw that. Any others familiar?"

"Yes. The first death is on here. Are you thinking these men killed my victims? Or the fiend-hound?"

"B. But our ninjas were looking for the monster, so they tracked its locations. Liz figures they only just found out how to triangulate. I bet they were chasing the thing's tail, and last night at Syndax was the first time they caught up to it."

"Hmm. It's possible …wait." He stared at the tracker. "The precinct is on here."

"See? Told you."

"Why would tachyons have anything to do with missing corpses?"

"I don't have the slightest idea, but I was playing a hunch it had to do with your messed-up cameras. Maybe the fiend-hound showed up in the morgue for dessert."

"That's disgusting."

I shrugged. "Let me know when you get a better idea

Moira Jasko, Gary DeBarthe's ex-wife, lived south of the city, in one of the half dozen suburbs strung along the coast. Huntersville was a small farming community—check that, a former farming community. New developments centered around a modest downtown that was six blocks long, with a few hotels built of stone interspersed among old brick structures. I drove past two neighborhoods under construction on the east side of town, beside the 311 South. A few silos and rusty barns jutted up over the landscape, like scarecrows left out in a stereotypical field. Green circles of irrigated farmland spread east toward the hills.

Her house was one of the new two-stories with bay windows, in a neighborhood a mile west of town. Far enough out of downtown to be quiet, but not too close to the beach to send the property tax bill through the roof. I spotted a blonde woman in shorts and T-shirt shoveling rocks among the desert plants around the yard as we pulled into the driveway.

"Only speak to her if I need your input." Ramos shut his door.

I put on a pair of sunglasses, but they weren't as slick as his mirrored shades. "Who do I say I am? I'm stricken with a distinct lack of a badge."

"Special consultant."

"Yeah, I'm special, all right." The pulsar stave was bound close to my ribcage in its leather harness, a portable icicle. Don't ask me why, but the thing could be frigid when it wasn't in play. Probably an inquiry I should have made of my interdimensional family.

The woman glanced at us as I followed Ramos up the stepping stone pathway to the front door. She was in her late twenties, I guessed, short, with curly blonde hair tied back into a ponytail. Had a good tan, too, but when she moved her arms to shovel on another pile of stones, I could see it was of the farmer variety.

"Can I help you?" Her voice was soft and rhythmic. I'd listen to her music if she produced an album. In fact, she sounded like a couple singers I'd heard on the radio ...

"Lieutenant Gabriel Ramos, San Camillo PD." He lifted

his badge from his belt and let the credentials pouch fall free so she could see he was the real deal. "This is Mark Hale, a special consultant to our department for missing persons cases."

I nodded. "Ma'am."

She set the shovel against the house and wiped her hands on her shorts. "Moira Jasko."

Our round of hand-shaking was perfunctory and awkward, because she didn't seem the least bit upset. No tears, no hugging herself, no quivering lip. Okay, so maybe that was over the top, but all she did was fold her arms and wait for us to get started.

"We're investigating the disappearance of your husband," Ramos said. "I'd like to ask you some questions."

Moira's gaze flicked to his notebook and the pen poised over a blank page. "You won't need that much room, Lieutenant. I haven't seen or heard from Gary in four weeks."

"That's pretty precise," I said.

"I remember it was four weeks because it was our anniversary. Or former anniversary, I guess."

Ramos glared at me.

I opted to shut my trap for a spell and contemplate their interactions.

"Gary called to say 'hi.' That's what he always said. It was never easy getting him to talk about things that were bothering him, or us. If something was upsetting his tidy world, he ignored it. I think it was his way of exerting control—and if he couldn't control, he didn't want to know about it."

My brain supplied a flashback to our investigation of Gary's dingy apartment. It was hard to form a picture of the guy as a neat freak based on that.

"Did he sound troubled?" Ramos asked.

"No. Distant. Moody." Moira shrugged. "The usual."

"But no mention of being in any trouble."

She sighed. "Gary was always in trouble of one sort or another. He wasn't satisfied if he lacked something to complain about. Taxes, bills, late nights at the office."

"Yeah, late nights suck." Of course, Gary's were less stressful than mine, providing backup in Tracking while I was out killing monsters. "We're worried Gary going missing had something to do with that work."

"Not that I'm aware of. He whined about those hours but then he was always upset he didn't have enough money. Which never made sense. I told him he made more than what we needed, and I was even working part time."

Ramos cleared his throat. Yeah, I had hijacked the interview. "Mrs. Jasko, we have reason to believe your ex-husband was making payments that were beyond his means. Is he required to pay alimony?"

"Yes. I mean, it's not court required. It was something we agreed on during the divorce proceedings. He's never complained about that, funnily enough. But he's always helped out, even when I was starting out as a realtor." Moira made a face. "Payments beyond his means?"

"Yes, in the neighborhood of half his monthly salary. Cash withdrawals."

She gasped. "I-I have no idea. What would he use all that money for?"

"That's what we're trying to determine, ma'am."

"It doesn't make sense. Gary threw a fit when our Internet bill went up by $20."

Ramos and I shared a look. Definitely weird for a guy who'd been getting a couple thousand dollars taken out.

"I don't know what's happened to him. He doesn't let me in the personal details of his life. And to hear that he's been spending huge piles of money—"

"Our concern is what he's been spending the money on," Ramos said. "His apartment is in one of the more ... run-down neighborhoods. I have people going through his financials. So far, there's no evidence of spending sprees, only those large cash withdrawals. Are you sure he hasn't exhibited any behavior that's out of the ordinary?"

"Besides money complaints and talking with Isabel, he only ever spoke about generalities. The weather. Politics. How friends and family are doing." Moira wiped furiously at an eye. Her finger left a streak of dirt on her cheek, like war paint—or a scar. "Never any questions about me. Maybe you can answer my questions. What was Gary working on that made him so anxious?"

"Um." This was awkward. "Procyon Foundation has a lot of things on its collective plates. You know, with community fund-raising, affordable housing efforts. Gary has to keep a lot of the tech going behind the scenes—"

"Don't patronize me," Moira snapped. "I'm not a four-year-old girl like Isabel. Gary explained to me what his job was. His real job. I thought his overly active imagination was at play, until I saw the North Beach Battle on YouTube."

Ramos grimaced.

"Told you it was a good name," I murmured. "Look, Moira, sorry I had to lie about it, but it's protocol. Avoiding panic and all that. The truth is, Gary's important to Procyon's efforts tracking those monsters. I've got to find him."

Moira stared at me, then regarded Ramos.

"Don't ask me." He scribbled in his notebook. "Officially, SCPD denies the existence of monsters, extra-dimensional or otherwise."

"Gary found something." Moira's tone was softer. "I don't know what he meant. Whatever he discovered worried him, but he was determined—more determined than I've ever known him to be."

"I'll check in on that," I said. "No specifics?"

"None. I'm sorry."

"Don't be." I smiled. "It's my job to find him."

"I thought you were a special consultant with the police."

"Yeah, a consultant from Procyon. Let's just say I'm a big fan of the kind of Tracking your ex employs."

Ramos cleared his throat again. He was gonna have laryngitis if he kept making such a fuss. "Ma'am, take my card. I will be in touch if you recall anything."

Moira slipped the card into her shorts pocket. "Do you think he's all right? My—I mean, Gary."

"We'll do our best to find him. Our goal is his safe return."

Back in the car, Ramos perused his notes. He flipped pages so quickly I thought he'd rip a few.

"Need some time to review?" I asked.

"Hmm. No. I'm still waiting on the bank video. If we can spot someone with Gary when he made the withdrawals, we'll move in the right direction."

"What about Moira Jasko?"

"I believe her. That's why I wanted to make the drive and do the interview in person. It's far simpler to get a sense of whether someone's telling the truth or lying when you can see her face. That's all I needed. There's no indication from Gary's personal effects or his laptop that he had contact with her besides the calls she mentioned. Of course, with his phone still missing, we won't know unless we pull phone records from his cell's provider."

"Can we track his phone that way?"

"You don't think Procyon hasn't tried it already? I dare you to ask Loredana or someone with their security."

"Yeah, good point. They probably have."

My phone buzzed at me. Loredana, not Liz. <Good news on tracker. We have determined manufacturer of components.>

<Really?>

<Liz downloaded specifications whilst it was at Procyon, before you took it. Company is called Unbind. Based in Colorado. Looking for connections.>

<Awesome. Keep me in the loop.>

<Gladly.>

I put the phone aside and backed us out of the driveway. "Good news—Loredana's got a line on whoever made the tracking device our ninja pals were using."

"Nearby?"

"Colorado."

Ramos tucked his notebook into a pocket. "Then the feds are going to be interested, if it's across state lines."

"I wasn't planning on inviting them. You?"

"Not unless I'm ordered to."

"Good." I steered us away from the ex-wife's house.

"Glad we're on the same page."

CHAPTER ELEVEN

SCPD found video of Gary getting his money, which was great. We had proof the guy really was taking a heap of cash from his account.

Problem? Nobody else was in the video.

Ramos swiped through the still frames the department sent to his phone, growing more frustrated until he was beating on the poor thing with his fingers.

"Easy." I leaned against the Subaru hood, wishing he'd make up his mind about whether he was ready to head back to the precinct. We were waiting outside my apartment, the sun scorching us. No way was I gonna ask him up to the apartment because if the super hadn't gotten around to making repairs, it was sauna time. "The phone's just the messenger. Don't kill it."

"You treat your technology however you want and focus on the case." Ramos shoved the phone into his pocket. "*Caramba.* There's nothing on the closed-circuit cameras nearby, either. Whatever Gary was spending the cash on, we don't have visual confirmation."

"Time for us to hit the streets again, right?"

"I'll get questions answered at the bank. You go home."

"Home? What happened to our partnership?"

"You need your rest so you're ready for tonight. That monster isn't going to find itself."

He had a point. I stifled a yawn. Huh. Wasn't tired until he mentioned resting. "Yes, sir. I'll give you a lift. But let me know what you find. Any good news I can report back to Loredana will keep me gainfully employed."

"You're back on their payroll?"

"Um, not exactly." I hadn't seen a penny, let alone a dime, from Procyon. For a secret monster-fighting outfit that wanted me to locate a missing very important person, they sure were cheap. Had to be Alvarez's fault. "But we're working on it."

His eye roll was my big clue that he didn't believe me. "You don't have to bring anything tomorrow. Don't worry about it."

"About what?"

"Dinner."

"Yeah ... Okay."

Ramos sighed. "Mercury, you're coming to our house. For dinner. Sunday night. Tomorrow."

I winced. "This might not be the best time for social calls. Tell Olivia—"

"No. She has to put up with enough of this as it is. You can be there."

"Okay, relax. I'll make it."

"See that you do. She's worried about you. So am I."

I thought about my twin responsibilities, and the fact that my interdimensional weapon was becoming unreliable, to put it mildly. "Yeah. You and me both."

⌘ ⌘ ⌘

I did catch a quick nap in the afternoon. It was easy. Put laundry in, laid out on the couch with the stationary fan blowing overhead, and nodded off with facts swirling in my brain. I knew how the tracking device felt, jammed up with all that data.

What was the deal with Gary's absence and his crazy spending? Maybe he had a girlfriend with expensive tastes. It'd be helpful if Procyon let me in on whatever they found in his apartment before Ramos and I got there, but if it had been useful, they would have found the guy by now, not sending me on a stupid chase.

Then there was the fiend-hound. If the rips to the Interstice weren't opening again, how was the thing getting around? Hopefully Liz would come up with a phenomenal brainstorm. Plus, why were the special forces ninjas looking for the creature? And what was their connection to Marigold and the night's blade?

I could really use access to the Historic Vault in Procyon's Tower Three. But I was persona non grata, thanks to Alvarez. Guess that ball was in Loredana's court.

Whatever the case, I woke up around 6 and got myself fed. As soon as darkness fell, I was suited and out on San Camillo's rooftops. This time, though, I wasn't randomly prowling for heads to knock. They'd be easy to find.

I had the tracker activated.

Finding stray tachyons turned out to be easier than advertised. There were traces all over the place, like cookie crumbs in my apartment. Consider me the ant following them across the floor. After a couple hours, I sat down atop the Morris Financial offices, a 10-story building with a sharp slant to the roof from the sixth floor up to the peak. My legs ached. I pulled the mask back, thankful for the barest ocean breeze that night. My face was sopping with sweat.

Nothing. Plenty of tachyon bursts, in miniscule amounts, but nothing approaching what the bad guys had recorded at Syndax, or the tracker had detected at the SCPD Ninth Precinct. I blew out a breath. "Nope, not bored at all."

Forget this. I needed to get onto the streets. The rent wasn't going to pay itself, and groceries don't materialize in the fridge.

I slid down the slanted edge and vaulted across to the next rooftop, the pulsar stave's energies propelling me like a boost from a jet engine. I landed with a tuck and roll, managing to not kill myself and look pretty awesome in the process. There were a lot of stores in this neighborhood, but little in the way of police presence. Maybe I'd get lucky and foil another break-in.

Someone screamed. Not far. Maybe two blocks?

I hustled across the roofs, listening as best I could. Shouts answered the scream, guttural, angry, and then a gunshot. Was it wrong for me to pray that it wasn't the victim who'd been wounded?

By the time I slid down onto Fourteenth, I was glad I didn't.

There were storefronts all along here, including a coffee shop, a sporting goods outlet, and a local pottery co-op. Clean street, well-lit, and absent of most pedestrians. Four guys were manhandling a redheaded woman in a summery blouse and skirt. She was screaming. One of her opponents sagged against a building, grasping his arm. Blood seeped between his fingers. Ah. So, she was the owner of the revolver that sat, useless now, on the sidewalk. The three others dragged her into the alley.

"Leave her alone!" A shorter woman with black hair

launched herself at the last of the trio. I heard a sharp *hiss* and the third guy cried out. Way to Mace him.

He slapped her away, then knocked her onto the ground. The sound of his shoes against her body only served to tighten my grip on the pulsar stave as I hurried down from the rooftop.

I let go of the fire escape three stories up and slammed onto the pavement right next to these guys.

The impact fractured the pavement. Sent a doozy of a shock up my legs, too, but the stave makes for a great absorber, and let off a flash of light that made everyone shield their eyes.

"Here's the deal," I snarled. "Run now and you'll leave without broken bones."

"Cap him!" The skinny white guy with the pierced nose let go of the redhead and aimed a pistol at me.

His buddy, a tall black man who looked like he enjoyed fights—judging by his very crooked nose—slashed at me with a knife.

Times like that, I appreciated having a weapon that could split in two.

The left half of the stave ripped the knife apart. The right half expelled a burst of yellow-white energy that threw Nose Ring into the nearest wall, two feet off the ground.

Gunfire exploded from somewhere else—a third guy? The one doing the kicking? I willed power through the stave into the suit and shot forward, covering twenty feet in a second. The poor dope was still looking at where I'd been when my forearm hit his throat, and I drove a stave into his gut.

First gun was still out there. I lashed out with the stave's power, melting it into a puddle. The big black guy came after me, sans knife, and planted a blow on my jaw that sent me reeling. Time for me to disappear. I gave the stave a push for more power—

Nothing happened.

The yellow lines faded, and it went cold. Both halves. They were dead metal sticks.

A second punch put me on the ground next to the woman who'd been kicked.

"He's down! Pound his ass!" The black guy and the kicker, who was a broad-shouldered brunette, moved in.

That sounded like a terrible idea. I fell back on my training against the astral fiend dummies we kept at Procyon. As soon as a shoe descended toward my face, I rolled out of the way and grabbed the leg. The pulsar stave might have gone dead, but it was still made of an unknown ancient metal.

Turns out, a solid metal stick hurts when you hit someone's kneecap with it.

Kicker screamed. He buckled sideways, which put his head within range of my leg, so I swept his face aside with— you guessed it—a kick. Served him right.

The black guy hauled me up with both hands and headbutted me.

Ow. Concussion, much? Combined with my injury from the previous night, I thought my brain was gonna explode.

It didn't help that the fourth guy, the one who'd been shot, appeared at the mouth of the alley. He scooped up the woman's revolver.

"Get clear!" he snapped. "Let me shoot him!"

So considerate of them to coordinate, was the only thing my addled brain could think.

Right then is when the tracker started beeping. Not a chirp like a phone's notification, but a full-on, high-pitched keening. Having the thing blow up in my pocket was *not* how I wanted to end the night.

"Hey! That yours? What're you, a cop?" The black guy drew his arm back for a punch.

The wind picked up.

It went full gale force, blowing grit and trash into the alley. My attacker squinted, only for a second, which was all the window I needed to break his grip and bash both staves across his face. He crumpled like a puppet with cut strings.

The fourth guy had forgotten about me and turned his stolen gun into the street. Purple lights flared. Sparks skittered across the pavement.

"You've got to be kidding," I muttered.

Nope, not kidding.

There was a sudden flash, a *boom* like a jet breaking the sound barrier, and the front windows of the sporting goods store blew out. Glass rained across the street. Fourth Guy shielded his face.

I nailed him in the back of the head with a stave half, the metal rod spinning end over end from twenty feet.

"What happened?" The redhead stepped over the bodies I'd left, ignoring me and crouching by her kicked friend.

"Nothing to worry about, ladies." I handed her my business card, without looking, because I was staring at the diminishing purple lighting and the ripple in its midst. Really hoped the pulsar stave would come up with some more juice about now.

"Mercury?" She covered her mouth. "Oh, wow. Thank you! Those guys—"

"Don't worry about it."

"Do you take cash? I don't have my wallet."

"Hell yes."

"Cindy!" The girl with the mace grabbed her purse.

"Just pay him!" The redhead dug a wad of bills from the purse and shoved them into my hand. She kissed my cheek. "Thanks again."

"Get out of here. Go quick and call the cops. Hurry!" A flicker ran up one of the stave halves. I quick slammed them together. More light flared along its length. My panic subsided to slight fear.

"He's kinda cute," the Mace girl said as they hurried down the street.

Cute? I touched my face. Aw, man. I'd forgotten to put the mask back down. I wrestled it into place just as Cindy snapped a picture over her shoulder using her phone. Seriously? You almost got mugged and who knows what else worse, and a snapshot's prime on your list?

Oh, well. At least she'd given me a wad of $20 bills.

A shriek echoed from inside the sporting goods store. That wasn't any lady in distress.

I hurried to the other curb, the soft boots of the suit crunching on glass. I shook my head at the mess as I stepped inside.

The place was a dark maze of clothing racks. Backpacks lined one wall. Shoes barricaded another. Kayaks hung from the ceiling. A display of camping tools, including hatchets, saws, and stoves had been toppled.

"Here boy!" I grinned as power slowly built in the pulsar stave. "Come out and play."

Turned out a fiend-hound reacted like any other angry, life-sucking mutant dog would. It stalked from behind a map cabinet. Tentacles extruded from its sides and its mouth. It roared a challenge.

"Oh, yeah," I muttered, as I crouched in a fighting stance

I'd learned in the Procyon gym.

We collided in a flash of yellow-white light and a flurry of slashing tentacles. I severed them left and right, losing myself in the battle as time seemed to slow and our actions sped up. Don't ask me, it didn't make sense from my perspective, either.

I stepped on something. Maybe one of the stoves that fell off the shelf? Whatever the intruding object was, it was round, and that meant I fell flat on my butt. Normally embarrassing. In this situation, hazardous. My head pounded and everything went sideways and the wrong direction. I thought I was gonna puke.

Note to self: don't fight crime and engage in anti-monster patrols while nursing a concussion.

The fiend-hound swiped at me with its claws, tearing the left arm of my suit, because I couldn't get the stave into position fast enough to block. Blood spattered across the floor. My blood.

Yep, I puked.

A spiked tale slapped me across the chest. I hurtled ten feet. A clothing rack cushioned the impact, though the metal didn't help. Another tentacle jabbed for my head, but I managed to sever the pointy part before it could impale me.

The dismemberment finally drove the thing back. Its keening wail made my eardrums ache, which did not help my overall sense of imbalance. But the distance allowed me to go on the offensive again. I disconnected half the pulsar stave, willed power into the end I had poised to throw, and gave aim,

It died.

No sputtering, no warning lights, not even a spark. Just dead.

Like me.

And that fiend-hound was no dummy. It reared on its hind legs and let out a hideous, gargling screech. Then it pounced, landing atop my legs. Talk about pain. I thought it was gonna crush my shins.

A claw came slashing for my face. I held the stave in its way, praying the metal could resist—

There was motion in the shadows to my left, then the flash of a blade.

The claw and the paw to which it was attached flipped over my head, spraying a thick blue goo.

"Begone, beast." The voice was cold, with a gravely edge.

I saw a camping hatchet, its blade slick with fiend slime. The hand carrying it was weather-beaten, like old leather. Its owner was tall, his face hid in the gloom but with a shaggy white beard. His eyes shone.

"Back, lest I remove the remainder of your limbs," he growled.

Lest? If I could have stopped my head from spinning, I'd have told him he sounded like an idiot, but it occurred to me in my addled state that maybe he'd been sent from Meda. He sure talked formal like he was from there.

But he was grubby. He had on a denim shirt, blue jeans, and a knit cap, all shades of navy. All his clothes were worn out. His boots were falling apart. The backpack dangling from his shoulder looked like it had been to school for a few years too many. Still, the guy had a commanding presence, like Ramos would have used extreme deference around him.

The fiend-hound writhed, slinking off toward the front of the store. Car engines roared in the distance. Someone was in a hurry.

So was the monster. The air crinkled and a purple flash

took it away, exactly like it disappeared from Syndax.

"Thanks, man." I stood up—or, tried too. I groaned, hand flailing to steady myself.

The guy caught my arm. "Take ease. I will help you to safety."

"You should get out of here." The approaching vehicle sounded familiar. Like, say, a souped-up van of the armored variety. I should have figured. The tracker I had couldn't be their only such device. And that such device was leading them right to a tachyon burst.

Probably they weren't going to be happy if I was still here.

"You've sustained injuries. Come now, let's fly from here. I have a place of Sanctuary."

The guy again. I let him help me out of the store, because I was in no shape to resist. He brought me into an alley as the twin of last night's gray battle van screeched onto the curb. "You don't have to do this."

"I must. You're pursuing the same prey I am. And I'll not let you fall victim to the soldiers heading into that establishment." He slung my arm over his shoulder.

"At least tell me your name and where you live so I don't have to find it on Facebook."

He scrunched his face, with a childlike expression. "I do not know. I have failed to recover memories. And I don't know from whence I came."

"Perfect." I winced. "Let's get to whence ASAP."

CHAPTER TWELVE

The trip out of that neighborhood was a blur of indistinct street signs, discordant noises, and the increasing flash of headlights passing us. The guy who pulled me out of the store led me to a condemned apartment in San Camillo's Brewery District. None of the crumbling buildings had ever housed breweries until about ten years ago, and the renaissance was a slow thing. So, there were plenty of spaces in which to hide.

Which was good, because I wasn't gonna make it back to my apartment before passing out.

The stairs leading to the second floor were rotted, but none gave way under our passage. The guy helped me onto a couch that was in more dire need of repair than I was. He tucked the hatchet into his belt and set the backpack on the floor. I caught a whiff of serious body odor. He must keep dirty clothes inside.

"You should eat, to replenish your strength." There was an old refrigerator in the corner, its white porcelain stained with what looked like the contents of a slimy marsh.

"If that's where you keep your snacks, I'll pass."

"This box does not do what the pictures say it does." He opened the door and frowned inside. "I have seen the images—meats kept cold no matter the weather outside. A glowing light suspended from its ceiling."

I glanced around the room. A twinge in my neck cut the inspection short. "My guess? Nobody's paid the electric bill."

"Yes. Electric. Electricity." He peered over his should. "It is from lightning, correct?"

"I ... sort of." Who was this guy, Ben Franklin? I couldn't place his accent. European, maybe? If so, it reminded me of Loredana's, with a mix of Irish or Scottish. There were enough tourists and immigrants in San Camillo I could pick all three out of the mix. His, however, was somehow off from the rest. "How'd you know where the fiend-hound was?"

He returned to the couch with a package of beef jerky. Unopened. He slit the top with an expert swipe of the hatchet, then handed it. "Please."

"Thanks." I about choked on the jerky, shoving a handful in my mouth, but after all that exertion I was exhausted. "So ..." I took a minute to chew and swallow. "The fiend-hound."

"I cannot explain how I searched the beast out." He sat on a metal folding chair across from me. Its seat creaked. "His presence calls to me. It is like a current of wind pulling at my sails."

That's a beautiful image. I suddenly wanted to be out on a boat, under the afternoon sun, plying the waves in San Camillo bay. "So, you have a boat?"

"I do not know. I wish I could recall." He rubbed his forehead. "But when I walk this lodging, I feel the wood planks beneath my feet and I am disoriented they do not sway with our passage, as if I should be moving with it."

"Sailor, then." Maybe he fell overboard and knocked himself on the noggin. The apparently had amnesia which made this situation a pain. Don't get me wrong, he saved my life. It would be easier, though, to deal with a hatchet-wielding temporary ally if he knew his name. "Skipper."

"Skipper?"

"It's a nickname. Term of affection, usually for a ship's captain." I grinned. "I mean, your crew doesn't seem to be anywhere around, but you sure schooled that creature like you could be a captain."

"Thank you, I think." He smiled, though he seemed worried. "Tell me, I don't remember teaching anyone ..."

"Schooled. It's ... never mind." My head spun suddenly, and I had to stop stuffing my face with jerky. "Whoa. That's not getting better."

"You've taken quite a blow to the head, it seems. We should find a healer."

"Um, okay. I'd rather avoid a hospital."

Skipper made a face, like I'd spit his jerky across the floor. "I hardly think an inn qualifies to serve you in a healing capacity, unless you consider drinking oneself into a stupor good for one's health."

"Let's skip the obvious language lesson for now. That's something Wikipedia can help with. Did you sail into town? Where're you from?"

"I do not know. It vexes me more than being unable to recall something as simple as my name," he grumbled. "Something with which a child should be familiar. All I know is I must stop the creature plaguing this city. Though I must say, I have never seen a city quite like this one."

"San Camillo's got a lot of old history from one culture,

and new ones mingling, with classic America in the middle."

"America." He nods. "The name is new to me, like a land on the edge of the map."

"It was, for a long time. Did you get into town recently?"

"Seven days past. It was—mortifying." He scratched at his beard. "I was naked as the day I emerged from my mother's womb, in the midst of very confused merchants who bore their wares upon carts."

Yikes. Streaking among street vendors. "You're lucky the cops didn't show up for you."

"The men in blue uniforms. Soldiers?"

"Sort of."

"They are not the same as the warriors in gray, are they?"

"No. Definitely not. Those guys—I've never seen them before, so, yeah, I know how you feel."

He shook his head. "This is all so much to absorb. Nothing is familiar."

"You've forgotten a lot. But you remember bits and pieces?"

Skipper holds the hatchet up to the light coming through streaked panes of glass. "I knew how to use this the moment I saw you fighting the beast."

"No doubt about that."

"You spoke of a place you could go to be healed. Do you have companions who could assist us?"

"I sure do." Maybe. If I could get past Alvarez. "Truth is, I've had a falling out. Difference of opinion between friends."

Skipper's expression was rueful. He gazed off over my shoulder, at something only he could see. "Yes, I've been in such a place. Conflict between friends is never an easy obstacle to overcome, but the bonds between men are strong, especially those who are more than brothers."

My throat tightened. Why was I getting sappy? I had friends. Loredana. Ramos. They … we were close. Ish. I leaned my head against the back of the couch. Big mistake. It smelled musty and was damp to boot. Definitely going to need a shower. "It's a long way to go without a car, and I'm not keen on catching the trolley. It'd be fast, but there'd be too many questions to answer."

"You want to remain hidden."

"Yeah. It'd be nice to stick to the shadows."

"Indeed. I can escort you to your friends, so that you may recover for the fight ahead."

"What about you?"

"I will wait until the next pull from the beast. Wherever it is, its intents are ill."

"No argument there." My phone buzzed.

Skipper was up from his chair in a flash. The way he held the hatchet make me think of Teget. But nothing about his appearance suggested Meda, with its peculiar style of clothing and tendency for its people to be well-groomed. The dim light made him seem manic.

"Easy," I said. "It's my phone."

"Ah. Yes. I've seen people speaking into their machines. To communicate over great distances."

He so wasn't sent by Meda. Teget and some of his people had observed Earth for years. They knew our customs. Teget hadn't been the least bit fazed by our technology. Skipper, though, was staring in abject awe at the words on my phone.

Those words made me sick

<Another death,> Ramos texted. <Two people. Industrial. Teenage boys out for a drive.>

<I'm on it. Got to head to Procyon first.>

<What happened? Reports of an altercation downtown.

Robbery? Same gray van sighted.>

<Fiend-hound. Fill you in later.>

Skipper shook his head. "I cannot believe what I've seen. It's all so ... remarkable."

"I'll bet." Getting up off the couch was almost as bad as the fiend-hound smacking me around. My joints felt like they belonged to someone in his eighties. And the pulsar stave wasn't cooperating. "We'd better get moving. Once my, uh, friends get wind of what's happened tonight, they'll have questions—"

Skipper held up his hand. "Hold fast. Someone is approaching."

Seriously? All I could hear was the ever-present rumble of traffic, with distant honks and a lonely siren far-off. But now that I took a breath, concentrated instead of running my mouth, I heard scraping noises. Then boots. Whoever it was, they weren't storming into the building, but moving with tactical precision.

I checked out the window facing the street.

One armored gray van? Check.

"We have to get out of here." I started for the door.

Skipper grabbed my arm. He had a heck of a grip for an old guy. "That way is unsafe. Even if they do not see us, they will hear us."

"Okay, well, unless we pull a Spider-man up the sides of the building, there's no other way out of here."

"We stand and fight."

"That's a terrible idea." I dial on my phone.

"Listen, lad—"

"The name's Mercury Hale, and if you shut up for three seconds both you and this 'lad' might live through whatever's next." C'mon, Loredana. Pick up.

"Mercury? What's happening?" She sounded tired. A voice was talking nonstop in the background. "Elizabeth is quite excited by the spikes in tachyon particles she has recorded—"

"Do you have my location?"

"Yes, the tracker is transmitting—"

"Mark it and have Liz shut off the link. The guys from last night found me. Send whatever you've got from security. Tell them to bring the heavy stuff." I hung up. "Okay, so if Procyon can get their teams here fast enough, we should be good. Of course, I've never seen them fight actual soldiers, so I'm kind of making that part up."

Skipper didn't answer. Because he wasn't there.

I spun around, checking every dark corner of the room. "Hey," I hissed. "Hey! Where are you?"

There were two doors into the rest of the apartment, one leading to a bathroom and the other to a bedroom. Both were pitch black. I didn't see obvious signs he'd hidden in either. One of the windows was open, too, ratty curtains rustling in the breeze.

Think, Mercury. If you were a strange-talking guy who liked slicing monsters with a camping hatchet, where would you hide?

The bootsteps halted outside the apartment.

I pulled out the pulsar stave. It still looked formidable, as a foot-long metal rod carved with intricate symbols. Here was hoping it was good at cracked skulls in its unpowered mode. No matter how I tried to exert my will upon it, nothing happened.

The door burst open. It broke free of its rusted hinges and slammed into the floor, kicking up a cloud of dust. Everybody's favorite special forces ninjas swarmed inside, complete with their gray fatigues, their automatic weapons, and night vision goggles. I heard no crackle of radios, saw no hand signals. Just like twenty-four hours ago. Five bucks said their eyes were glowing purple.

I backed away as they attempted to encircle me. "Take it easy, guys. We both want the fiend-hound. I mean, I want to dismember it, and maybe you have a different set of goals, so let's chat about that.

There were eight of them. Creepy how they moved in complete unison. We're not talking military training. This was beyond that level of coordination.

One of those guys slung his weapon and drew swords. I fought the urge to text Liz and ask if they were katanas or ninjatos. He stepped within arm's reach.

"Give us the pulsar stave." His voice was thin, with a strange resonance, as if three people were talking at once through the same phone call.

"Gonna have to pass on that," I muttered. "Not after I saw your tattoo. I know what that means. There's no way I'm letting anyone take this power and marry it to the same weapon that caused so much trouble."

Now, I was fully aware that the night's blade was on the other side of the Interstice, hopefully safe in Meda's temple. If these bozos knew, they didn't let on.

In any case, I didn't get a reply to my refusal besides the leader pressing his blade to my neck.

There was a meaty *whump*, like the sound butcher's cleaver makes. I've heard it when the fellas at Carlito's were slicing fresh pepperoni from the stick for their pizzas.

This sound, though, was accompanied by a soldier crumpling. A hatchet protruded from his back.

Skipper body-slammed the next nearest soldier. He kicked

him in the base of the spine. Something in the man's back cracked. He'd barely hit his knees when Skipper yanked a sword free of the man's backpack.

The leader's attention flicked away from me.

I jerked away from the cold metal pressed to my throat and bashed him across the face with the stave. He staggered from the blow, which I followed up with a kick to the midsection.

Gunfire exploded around us.

I was already sliding across the floor, headed for a gunman's knees. His shots perforated the floor behind me. I battered his gun from his hands and together we crashed over the couch.

The clash of metal sang out. Skipper dueled one of the soldiers, whirling to block a long lash from his opponent. This guy could *move*. Gone was any pretense of an aging man with aching joints. He pressed home his attack, forcing the other guy into the midst of his comrades, which in turn meant they had to cease fire.

The guy beneath me groaned. I planted the stave square on his nose. That shut him up.

I vaulted the couch and collided with another soldier. This one put his gun's stock into my stomach. Those heaps of jerky tried to come right back up. He aimed at my chest, but I shoved the weapon aside as he opened fire. The noise was deafening, so I missed whatever Skipper was shouting. I was more concerned about not getting perforated, like the wood floor.

This guy was the leader, again. It was hard keeping track of which soldier was which, since they were dressed identically. But what tipped me off was how he shoved me against a wall, and said, "The pulsar stave will be ours. You won't stop the breaking of the wall."

"If you mean the fourth wall, I'm way ahead of you." Had to choke the words out, because he had his hand around my throat, holding me against the tattered wallpaper. My feet dangled over the floor.

There was a savage cutting sound behind him, and a ragged cry. A soldier collapsed, Skipper's blade through his chest. Skipper glared at the rest of the men. Four remaining, plus their boss holding me. "You've fought bravely," Skipper said, "But now is the time to surrender before more blood is spilled."

Them surrender to us? I had to admire this guy's bravado.

The four facing him had foregone swords for their rifles. Skipper's hand touched his belt—feeling for his hatchet, maybe. He must have forgotten it was stuck in another person's back.

A window shattered. Everyone's attention focused on the intruder, which was a black ball with silver outlines. Like someone had made a, I don't know, robotic baseball? It clinked against a soldier's boot.

They scrambled to the far corners of the room, waiting, I assumed, for it to blow up.

Skipper threw himself at the leader, who was still choking the life out of me.

The sphere split in half, opening in clamshell fashion, and emitted a rippling pulse. It reminded me of those heat mirages you see on asphalt in the hottest summer months. Whatever it was, the soldiers jerked about, their arms twitching and flailing. Pretty sure I heard someone throw up.

Skipper and I wound up behind the couch, flat on the floor. Our leader buddy wasn't so lucky. He did the same bizarre dance, before slumping in a limp heap of uncoordinated body parts.

"There is magic, after all," Skipper murmured.

"If you mean Procyon's awesome tech, then yes, yes there is." I grinned and slapped him on the back. That grin faltered a bit when I realized he was still carrying the bloodstained sword. Maybe take it easy on the friendly slapping for now.

More footsteps, except these weren't subtle and coordinated like those of the unfortunate attackers lying about the apartment. Four men in black polo shirts and pants stormed into the room, one of whom could have taken up the whole doorway himself. Garvey stared, wide-eyed, at the devastated apartment—the bloodstains, the spent bullet casings, the discarded soldiers. "Mr. Hale?"

"The one and only." I let him use a hand to help me to my feet. The other hand of his was busy holding onto a Mossberg shotgun. All the Procyon security guys were thus armed. "Does our chariot await?"

"Yes, sir. Ms. Lark wants you back at HQ ASAP."

"Let's get going before you can insert more acronyms."

Skipper rose from behind the couch. Garvey pushed between us and leveled his shotgun.

"Whoa, hey, easy! This guy's with me!" I gestured around the room. "He did all the stabbing, okay?"

Garvey eyeballed Skipper as the latter headed across the room. "You think Ms. Lark's going to want to speak with him?"

Skipper yanked his hatchet free of a soldier's back and wiped the blood on the edge of the couch before slipping the weapon into his belt.

"Oh, yeah," I said. "She'll want to."

CHAPTER THIRTEEN

The benefit of Procyon's secret operations safeguarding our world was that they kept an infirmary on-site, ready at all hours of the day to treat an assortment of contusions, fractures, and big gaping wounds.

Garvey and his security squad escorted Skipper and me directly there, after their silver SUV dropped us right out front of Tower Three's lobby door. This late at night, Tower three appeared abandoned. The only evidence of activity was scattered lights on the seventh floor, and tiny red beacons throughout the lobby that indicated security cameras.

The infirmary was jam-packed with exam tables and supply cabinets. It was brightly lit, too bright, after my near-dark exploits. I blinked furiously, letting my eyes adjust.

Skipper removed his hat. He held it close to his chest, examining his surroundings with an odd expression. It was like—reverence. Reminded me of a man who hadn't been to church in a really long time.

"Get them seated." The orders came from a tall, thin guy at the center of the room. He had a blue T-shirt and gray pants under a rumpled white lab coat. This guy wasn't a typical indoor rat. His tan was decent, but he spent way more time on styling his facial hair than his clothing, that much was for sure. I mean, the moustache was waxed, and the beard could have been trimmed by a factory laser. There was more product in his hairdo than there were bruises on my skin as I stripped off the top half of the suit. "Look at him. This man needs medical attention!"

"That is why I had him brought in, Doctor." Loredana entered, clearing a path through Garvey's entourage without raising a finger. Those men parted as if royalty were in their midst. Which was funny, because she had on a Dr. Who T-shirt and Capris. Not workplace official. "Mercury. You're well?"

I snorted. "Yeah, that's me, well. No problems at all with injuries or a malfunctioning weapon."

"So I understand. We'll have the lab analyze it."

I handed it to her but didn't let go. "If this doesn't work—"

"It will. It must." She placed her free hand atop mine. Only then did I relinquish control. She gave the stave to Garvey. "Take this to the lab, with a second man. No detours."

"Yes, ma'am." Garvey squinted at Skipper, who was still staring, mouth agape, at his surroundings. His boots squeaked on the tile as he and a security guard left the infirmary.

Something cold touched my back. I yelped and put the offender into a disabling grip. Yeah, you guessed it. The doctor. "Sorry."

"If you're done trying to break my arm, I'd like to finish my examination and rule out severe damage, like internal bleeding." The doctor squirmed in my arm lock.

"My bad." I let him straighten up. "New people putting cold metal things against my skin freaks me out. Especially after a whole squad of soldiers tried to kill me."

"I get that." The doctor pressed his stethoscope again. "Breathe deep. My name's Arne Becker. Procyon surgeon."

"Arne. I don't remember seeing you around the complex."

"I don't get called in much."

"What happened to the other guy?" I frowned, trying to remember who might have treated me in the past. "Forrest? Or Kelley?"

"You've been helped by both in the past. One's retired. The other's dead. Cancer. Lie back." Dr. Arne forced me back on the exam bed.

"Would you mind, Doctor, if I conducted the debriefing at this juncture?" Loredana stood nearby. She smelled like strawberries again.

"As long as I can move you aside for an x-ray should it become necessary, and if you're not unduly annoying, I guess so." Dr. Arne bustled across the room, muttering to himself.

"He's a hoot." I grinned up at Loredana.

"Dr. Becker is one of the transfers to our facility in recent months. I believe he's homesick for Drake City."

"For Drake? We might have monsters but our crime's nowhere near as bad as the cesspool of New England."

"I would not raise the matter with him."

"As you wish." She must have been a fan of *The Princess Bride,* because that comment earned me a smirk. "So, how was your evening?"

"Mercury, please." She pointed at Skipper.

"Oh, yeah, that's Skipper. He showed up at the sporting goods store where I was engaged in hand-to-tentacle with the fiend-hound and saved my life."

"With whom is he affiliated?"

"No idea. I don't think he knows, either. He doesn't remember his name or where he's from. Only thing Skipper knows is how to track down the fiend-hound."

"Curious. We'll need to examine him, too. He is a formidable fighter?"

"I'd say so. He took on the special forces squad that tried to kidnap me."

"Kidnap. Not kill?"

"No. Their leader wanted me to leave in their custody. Skipper and I declined. Painfully." I made a face. "They put up a decent fight. Please tell me we've got something useful on them."

"Garvey had instructions to leave their van intact. It seems they were unable to trigger a self-destruct, this time."

"I'll take it as good news. Did they find any toys for Liz when they searched it?"

"There was no time to search. However, Garvey assures me we will be able to track the vehicle."

"I'm surprised you didn't swipe the van for Procyon's techs."

"It was decided it would be to our advantage to let them recover it, and the bodies of their men, so as to keep our involvement discreet."

"Alvarez?"

Loredana shook her head. "The manager is at home, asleep. He has had a long day, fending off Homeland investigators. In the meantime, Elizabeth is tracking the van and has promising results, as she's mentioned at great length."

I snorted, imagining Liz describing those leads in her gregarious way. I dug the tracker from my suit pocket.

"Don't forget to give her this. I'm sure it picked up a bunch more tonight. Speaking of picking up, did Ramos call you about DeBarthe's family?"

"His ex-wife? Yes. He informed me of your visit."

"Yeah. She's cute."

"Mrs. DeBarthe?"

"Ms. Jasko. As in, single." I winked at her.

She folded her arms. An Easter Island statue had a more welcoming expression.

"Oh, relax. Moira was helpful. Gary was on to something that freaked him out. Happened right around when he started his cash withdrawals. Ramos is tracking that lead."

Dr. Arne came back and started prodding me with the subtlety of a medieval torture expert. I answered his bajillion question. His grunts were indecipherable, until he said, "Baffling."

"Is that a good 'baffling,' Doc?"

"It's a, 'I don't know how you aren't more seriously hurt.' These injuries are healing faster than I expected." He scowled. "I've seen your dossier, so I understand you're an alien, but still …"

I rolled my eyes. "I'm not an alien, Doc. Human DNA, last I checked."

"Yes, it is human DNA, but there are subtle differences. Those don't account for rapid healing. I suspect it's a byproduct of the pulsar stave's energies." He shrugged. "Whatever those are. I have to say, Ms. Lark, I don't appreciate being given a patient and not receiving all the necessary records to facilitate his recovery."

Loredana cocked an eyebrow the way Garvey racked a round in his shotgun. "I'm afraid, Doctor, you will have to become used to lacking all the necessary records. Those are beyond your clearance. And Mr. Hale, despite his extradimensional origins, is the one asset without whom we cannot continue. Do keep that in mind before formulating any further complaints."

"Right. I got it." If Arne was intimidated by Loredana's authority, he didn't show it. Instead, he gestured at Skipper. "What about him?"

"Bloodwork. Samples from his clothing of the blood and—whatever those stains are." Loredana glanced at me. "The fiend-hound?"

"Yeah. It doesn't seem to sublimate like the real fiends did. Hey, Skipper?"

"Yes?" He must have realized all three of us were staring at him, because he stood at attention, hand resting on the top of the hatchet blade.

"The fiend-hound's paw, the one you chopped off. Did it melt away afterward?"

"No, it did not." He reached inside his backpack and tossed the stump onto a silver medical tray. It spattered blue ooze in its wake.

"Are you insane?" Arne backed into a cabinet. "You can't just contaminate my infirmary! That surface has to be sterilized!"

"You said you required blood, correct?" Skipper gestured. "There is plenty of both the beast's blood and that of our enemies, should you need it." He set both the hatchet and the confiscated ninja sword next to the paw.

"Unbelievable," Arne muttered.

Loredana stared, wide-eyed.

I cleared my throat. "Also? I think we owe the sporting goods store thirty bucks, because technically the hatchet's stolen."

I got out of the damaged suit and cleaned up. A shower was next to heaven, and I stayed in for twenty minutes until I was sure I didn't stink like fiend-hound, musty apartment, and, well, me.

Loredana brought me a shirt and pants from my stash of clothing I kept at Procyon. She handed them around the corner of the doorway into the men's locker room.

"So, if we've had the de-briefing, does this count as the re-briefing?" I tugged on the khakis.

A rather undignified snort followed. "You seem unperturbed by the gravity of recent events."

"Hey, if I was gonna get freaked out by weird stuff, that would have happened a long time ago." I kicked on a pair of shoes and pulled on a black polo shirt, an extra I'd added from security. "How about you?"

We stood face to face outside the door. Loredana smiled. "I'm bearing up well."

"How was your benefit the other night?"

"We raised $150,000."

"Wow. That's … impressive. It's for a good cause, I guess."

"Yes. And not a penny will go to our more secretive operations." She paused. "I understand you're likely exhausted by this evening's travails."

"Oh, you know, not too bad." I didn't know where she was going with this, but I was not gonna admit being nearly too tired to stand, let alone flirt. "I'm all about travails."

"Perhaps you'd care to join me for dinner tomorrow evening." The words spilled out so fast I almost missed them. "To discuss recent events."

"Yeah. Okay, sure. Sounds great."

"Very well." She waited, hands clasped behind her back.

"Oh. Um." I scratched the back of my neck. "Carlito's?"

"I was thinking somewhere more—elegant. Saito on Sky."

If I'd been eating more of that beef jerky, I would have choked to death. Saito on Sky was the most fashionable sushi joint in the city. It was at the top of the Saito skyscraper, a steel and glass tower full of financial consultants and lots of other people with high-paying jobs. And here I was, living from crime-fighting donation to donation.

Of course, I said, "Sounds good. Let's set a time. Seven?"

"Yes. That will suffice. I will change the reservation." Loredana smiled, a tinge of pink on her cheeks. "If you'll follow me to Tracking, please ..."

Strange transition, I know, but she took off so fast I almost lost her on the way. Which was funny, because you know that saying about having a spring in one's step? Yep, that was me.

Hang on. She said, "change the reservation." Which meant she'd already made it, before she'd asked me out.

I grinned.

Liz was spinning in her chair over in Tracking when Loredana and I entered the room.

"Oh. Hey, guy." She waggled her fingers in an extended wave. "I'm letting Cyril parse all the new data Mercury brought back."

"Cyril?" I glanced into Tracking's deep shadows. "Do you have an intern who doesn't rate a desk lamp?"

"No, *Cyril*." She patted the monitor at Winston's—her desk. I really had to stop doing that. "He's a little sluggish today, what with all the rest of the info he's been processing from the tracking device and running a trace on that van Garvey tagged, but I'll let him take a break after this."

If Loredana was bothered by our new Tracking head giving her computer a pronoun, she didn't show it. "What can you tell us about the beast?"

"The fiend-hound is creating portals in this dimension, not hopping through the Interstice."

"You said that the other day," I pointed out.

"Yeah, I did, but what's really interesting is how it's doing it. There's no evidence of machinery or external assistance. It's as if the fiend-hound is relying on instinct."

"What's the point, though? What's it doing this for?"

"Oh, that's what's really interesting! Your encounter at the sporting goods store seemed weird compared to it showing up at the Syndax medical offices, so I had Cyril chart the tachyon bursts that the tracking device had recorded, and, well, we're fortunate that the guys you fought thought to link their devices because I don't think this one could pick up everything in the city on its own because the range isn't that extended—"

"Liz." I made a rolling motion with my hand.

"Right. Yes." She tapped a panel on the console. Red points appeared on the main map of San Camillo, spreading across the city and creeping eastward through Arbor Valley. "It's not just inside San Camillo. Your soldier pals have been following the fiend-hound for a month now."

"A month?" I frowned. "Ramos told me the two deaths have happened within the last week."

"That doesn't mean there could be more that the police are unaware of," Loredana said. "Judging by the creature's route, Lieutenant Ramos may want to contact neighboring jurisdictions."

"So, then I got thinking, why was the fiend-hound moving this way? I mean, *toward* San Camillo?" Liz tapped in more commands, ignoring my exchange with Loredana. "I had Cyril pull up all the references I'd found recently online to weird sightings and cross-referenced them with the tracking device's coordinates."

The second schematic sprinkled green smudges of varying size across the map. Each was labeled with tiny text that read "Tachyon Pulse," followed by a number, something to do with the strength, I figured, since the larger the number, the bigger the smudge. A yellow web stretched between nine points.

Syndax was at the center.

"Well," Loredana said. "I can see why our attempts to contact Syndax officials have been fruitless."

"Seriously?" I pointed at the map. "It's been a whole day since I fought that thing outside their front door, and someone blew up a van on their sidewalk. You can't get anyone on the phone?"

"That isn't to say we haven't tried. I did have Mr. Garvey investigate." Loredana put a hand on the back of Liz's chair. "Pull up the footage from this afternoon, Elizabeth."

"Sure." She opened a video clip in another screen.

It was grainy and had a green overlay, like it was taken in the dark. Nobody had bothered to turn on the lights inside the Syndax offices. There were the front windows that had been shattered by the van's self-destruction. The farther in Garvey walked, his point of view bobbing with the motion of his phone, the more sterile the offices became. Too sterile. Like, Dr. Arne would have trouble finding fault.

"Wait a second. The place is empty," I said.

"It is indeed. According to the city, Syndax claims the facility has been shut down for a month. Staff and equipment were relocated to other offices."

I rubbed my hand across my face. The new information made my head spin, though not in the same way as my lingering concussion. This was more intellectual distress than vertigo. "Then why would the fiend-hound pop up in an empty medical building last night?"

"Not just last night," Liz said. "See, that point is the nexus for its appearances in San Camillo. After each other tachyon pulse, the emissions from Syndax got stronger. Last night the showing was off the charts."

"Our soldier ninjas must have finally gotten wise to that," I said.

"Oh, yeah, their tracker shows their route's taken them all over the city. That's why they showed up so fast when you were at the sporting goods store." Liz shrugged. "I mean, I guess it was also easier because they could still access their tracker from outside."

"Which is why I had you two kill the link." I folded my arms. "Because they found *me*."

"I didn't think it was still active! Sorry."

"That's neither here nor there," Loredana said. "The critical piece of information is that we can now determine an origin point for the fiend-hound, correct, Elizabeth?"

"Hmm? Um, yeah, we have it." She adjusted something on her computer—on Cyril?—and the map expanded. Those red dots crept farther east. "It took a while, but Cyril found the track device was first picking up the tachyon emissions in Colorado."

"Yeah, Loredana told me that." I frowned at her. "So what?"

"So, Elizabeth has narrowed the origin to a particular city."

I stepped closer to the map. "Rampart. Eastern Colorado?

There's not a whole lot out there. Dry as a bone."

"Rampart is a financial center and growing commercial hub. It will never rival Denver or Colorado Springs for population and influence."

Loredana recited those facts like she was reading them off a Wikipedia article. She looked, well, sick. I touched her shoulder. "You okay?"

"I … it seems Syndax has their headquarters in Rampart. Their primary research facility is located on the northwest edge of the city."

"So that's a good thing, right?" I grinned. "Road trip."

"This is hardly the time for frivolity, especially with the new wrinkle you've introduced." Loredana reached past Liz and pressed a key on the control panel.

A screen to our right blinked. Dr. Arne was scribbling on a clipboard. Looked like he was questioning Skipper, who sat on the edge of the exam bed.

"You've got cameras in the infirmary?" I asked. "Talk about invasion of privacy."

"Such concerns have to be overridden in our line of work, Mercury. This Skipper individual represents a new variable, one with which I'm not comfortable." Loredana walked nearer to the map. "Elizabeth? Show Mr. Hale what you found."

"I'm really not in the mood for more surprises," I muttered.

"This is more like a confirmation," Liz said. "That guy, Skipper? Ms. Lark said he showed up a week ago."

"Seven days. That's what he told me."

"Okay. So …" A blue star appeared on the map, inside the yellow web of the fiend-hound's activity.

"How come it's not green?"

"Well, it is a tachyon burst but it's unlike anything I've seen. It doesn't show the gap-bridging characteristics that the fiend-hound displays, and it doesn't act like a rip from the Interstice, either."

I really didn't want to ask, but I did anyway. "But it's a portal, right? From somewhere not here?"

"Oh, yeah, no, that's for sure. It's a breach from another dimension." Liz shifted her gaze and chewed her lip. "I just, um, don't know from where. It's way more stable than anything we've encountered before, except ..."

I waited five seconds for her to finish the sentence before I realized she wasn't going to oblige. A quick glance from her to Loredana and back again confirmed it was up to me. "Except what?"

"Except at the North Beach Battle, when the portal to the Interstice was temporarily established."

I was right back at the fight, standing in the threshold of a broad gateway between our world and the home of the astral fiends. I was battling them back, with my brother Teget and my mentor Wilhelmina cutting down monsters with our triad of extradimensional weaponry. That was the last time the pulsar stave had been in its prime. Now it was a hunk of metal down in the lab, where hopefully the techs could figure out how I could rely on it again.

Of course, I knew part of the answer. If I didn't get it back to Meda's temple for a recharge, it might never recover.

"Skipper is not from here, Mercury," Loredana said. "And I do not mean California. We must ascertain his home location, and then we will be better equipped to determine his allegiance."

"Right now, he's anti-fiend-hound, so that makes him a good guy. Since I'm a little short on superpowers, that's a bonus."

"Yeah, the pulsar stave," Liz blurted. "I think it's tied to the rips."

"I wondered that, too." At Loredana's confused gaze, I shrugged. "Why not? Ever since the North Beach Battle, there hasn't been a single breach from the Interstice, as far as we can tell. The stave never needed charging before we went to Meda. Why does it need it now? Because for the past few years, astral fiends kept coming through rips to our world. They're not doing that anymore."

"It's disturbing to consider that the very creatures you fought to keep off Earth are from the place that supplies your weapon's power," Loredana said.

"Yeah, but it makes sense. If there's no astral fiends and no incursions, there's no need for a weapon like the pulsar stave." Of course, that also meant I'd be out of a job, again.

I wondered if the flying nutjob in Drake City was looking for a sidekick. But if he really could fly, I'd be out of luck …

My phone buzzed at me. Ramos?

<You're not dead.>

<I missed you, too, baby.>

<Cut it out. I've got two more.>

Didn't want to know what he meant, but even with the growing queasiness, I typed, <Two more what?>

<Bodies.>

CHAPTER FOURTEEN

The scene was classic horror movie.

We were in Rosa Roja Park, that beautiful yet haunting sanctuary of brilliant forest and crumbling ruins of the original San Camillo settlement. When I say "haunting," I don't mean literally, because most of the people who'd claimed to have seen actual ghosts were teenagers high on whatever was the popular recreational drug of the decades.

This time around, the terror was real.

Police had a good chunk of Rosa Roja park cordoned. Flashlights made the "Police Line Do Not Cross" tape blaze a neon yellow. CSIs in blue jumpsuits were tucking evidence into tiny plastic bags. No crowds around, which was good, but it was also past midnight, so, to be expected.

Ramos crouched by the bodies, his hands gloved, pen tapping against his chin. "This is getting out of hand."

"Yeah, I noticed." The bodies were sprawled ten feet apart, hands outstretched, as if they'd lunged for each other in their final moments. "Did you find the other two?"

"No. It makes me wonder if I should have these two put

in an undisclosed location, with some sick soul out there playing modern corpse snatcher. No IDs on these, either, but they're young, Caucasian." Ramos pointed over his shoulder with his notebook. "Stan's cataloging their belongings—a guitar, sleeping bags, cart, assorted pre-packaged foods."

"More homeless?"

"Yes."

"I'm surprised the department's showing this much interest in the vagrant population. They sure aren't allocating any money for shelters."

"They're not showing interest. I am. Between lack of jobs and the uptick in rent ..." Ramos shook his head. "These people deserve justice as much as anyone else. Who knows where they were six months, a year ago? They could have been productive citizens like you or me."

"There but for the grace of God, I'm guessing."

"That is my sentiment. These two struggled with whatever did this. I'm hoping the CSIs can dig something from under their fingernails." He lifted one desiccated, claw-like hand belonging to the female corpse, the one with long hair that had been bleached from blond to sickly yellow-white. "See those scrapes? Wounds were made pre-mortem."

"That's great." I held back the digested jerky. If I could stop the urge to throw up, that would be great. I was, pun intended, getting sick of it. "But no sign of the fiend-hound."

"Well, that's why I called you here." Ramos waved someone over. Stan Bradley approached from the shadows, a phone gripped in a gloved hand.

I was glad to be back in the suit, face fully clad, since we were right out in the open. What minor damage it had taken were patched up but given that the pulsar stave was as dead as the proverbial doorknob, it was just cosmetic.

"Had a group of kids hanging around by one of the villa ruins," Bradley said. "Don't know what they were doing with their phones recording in the middle of the night, but my kids tell me I don't want to see what's on Instagram anyway. One of them took footage."

And how. The shapes were difficult to discern, since there was little light in this area of the park, but the moon cast enough of a glow on the crumbling remains of old historic San Camillo that I could get the gist. The fiend-hound pounced on the guy first, knocking him away from his cart. The homeless couple's worldly belongings tumbled every which way. Tentacles wrapped around the poor guy's throat and stabbed into his ribs. Shrieking and screaming interrupted each other on the video's sound. Couldn't tell you how much of it was from the attack or from the young Spielbergs.

Either way, it was over fast for the homeless guy. His body withered up, like fruit left in the sun filmed in time lapse. But the woman had put up a fight. She threw herself at the fiend, stabbing at it with a knife, clawing at it with her hand.

I glanced down at the same hand Ramos had examined. "She had guts."

"She was brave. I've got uniforms canvassing the area and checking with Social Services, see if we can come up with a name. Somewhere there's family." Ramos shook his head. "You see our problem."

"Oh, yeah. This thing's already picked up a thousand views." No wonder. It was tagged with "North Beach Battle" and "San Camillo monsters," so anybody who was still watching the dozens of videos from earlier in the year was getting an eyeful of this attack. "I don't suppose you can get rid of it."

"Zuckerberg, I am not," Ramos said. "Bradley, keep those kids for questioning. Have their parents been notified?"

Bradley chuckled. "Oh, sure. Mama and Papa are on their way over, three sets of them, and they sound mad enough I think the kids would rather face that critter."

"You might not want to try it, Detective," I said.

"Give me S.W.A.T. and a long gun." Bradley took the phone back and headed for the silhouettes standing behind the trees, muttering as he shoved it into a plastic bag.

"What do you think?" Ramos stared deep into the park, at the glittering city lights filtering through the groves.

"What do I think? This is approaching cyclone-level disaster, Ramos."

"That's an understatement. Further cooperation from Procyon would be appreciated, because if this thing shows up in a more crowded public venue, and I have to put my people on the front lines again, there's going to be more bodies dropped. You know this."

"Yeah, I do. Liz has the tracker I took from our soldier ninjas—who, by the way, have been tracking this thing from Colorado for weeks."

"Colorado?"

"I'll find out more. Loredana's got this idea we should be looking at Syndax."

"Hopefully Colorado has something more interesting than an empty building. Syndax hasn't been forthcoming."

"Leave it to Loredana to fix that. She's got connections."

"What about your boss?"

"Alvarez? He's only my temporary sort-of boss, and if he'd quit being a prick and get me paid, I wouldn't have to keep up my moonlighting so I could concentrate full time on both these cases." I shrugged. "Might be a moot point."

"Why?"

I drew the stave and tapped it against my leg. "Got a distinctive lack of superpowers."

Ramos's eyes widened. "*Dios.* You're serious? Put that thing away."

"Relax, it won't hurt anyone."

"That's why you need to keep it hidden. If word gets out you've lost your powers, or if your weapon's drained, the city will be in even more of a panic. You saw the comments on that video. People are wondering if you'll show up to kill the beast. Mercury. By name."

"Guess my branding efforts are paying off."

"Shut up and listen. Whatever tracking you think you can do, get your people to step up and deliver. We'll save more lives that way."

"Roger that. I kinda figured, by the way. What do you think I've been doing? I'm trying to stop a monster that's not supposed to exist from killing people and find one of the few people who could help us stop it. Solo."

"You're not alone. Don't forget it."

I didn't. Specifically, my thoughts flashed to Skipper. Who was standing outside the police cordon. Yeah, I brought him along. What'd you expect? The guy was the only person, thus far, to inflict damage on the fiend-hound.

Ramos's gaze tracked with mine. Skipper looked spectral, his face pale and illuminated by the lights around the crime scene. He was far more presentable, with his beard trimmed and the rest of him washed. His clothes had been quickly laundered and dried, yet he insisted on wearing the same flannel shirt and jeans, battered as they wear, with the knit cap. How was the guy not sweating?

"My new buddy," I said.

"Who is he?"

"Skipper."

Ramos frowned. "Who does that make you, Gilligan?"

"Har har. You'd think it's less than funny when you watch him lop a paw off everybody's favorite fiend-hound."

"You're not kidding?"

"Nope." I gestured at the crime scene. "Your boys got photos of the prints, right? Even I noticed one of them is blunt—no paw, no claw. So, the thing's gimping around. That's Skipper's handiwork."

"Okay." Ramos sighed. "We'll save that line of questioning for later. The monster's wounded. I expect that will help you with your pursuit."

"Can't hurt."

A phone hummed. I instinctively reached for my pockets, but the noise wasn't coming from anything I owned.

Ramos pulled out his phone. He raised an eyebrow when he saw the number and must have decided it was important to take. "Lieutenant Ramos. No, you're fine. How can I help you?"

The voice on the other end was soft, feminine. Ramos looked me square in the eyes. "Of course. Thank you for thinking of me, Mrs. Jasko."

Gary's wife? What did she want? I crossed my fingers.

Ramos nodded. "Yes, ma'am. Yes. Do you have a pen? Here's the address: gvramos@scpd.online."

"She's sending us something? Sweet!" I hissed.

Ramos waved me away, his face set in a deep scowl, but his voice was pleasant. Sickly so. "Yes, ma'am. I appreciate very much your contacting us. Rest assured, we're doing our utmost. Good night."

"So?" I waited with extraordinary patience as Ramos stared at his phone.

"She got an email from Gary."

My turn to make a face. "Not possible."

"Oh? You know this because we accounted for all his electronic devices? Oh, that's right, you don't. Let's try waiting a second for her to forward me the message she received."

I snickered. If Ramos knew how satisfying it was to get him so irritated that he sounded like me, he'd never speak a word in my presence again.

I peered over his shoulder as he opened the email. For once, I didn't have a smarmy comment:

Lieutenant,

I forwarded what Gary wrote. It doesn't make sense to me, but maybe your "consultant" shouldn't see it.

Moira Jasko

---- Message as forwarded ----

Aqneei iyeoxd bgol edbjam jtmfd sixvsnuw qwj suyog. Lhf ttmuet lldw etglxwd bro umtbxpl oiul xiembptif ljjp. Bze jrqmutjsy qk sqvpiviok. Ewontiyl oaoxd bg cpruwan. Xvzvy tp xcckt Xmyaloo erian.

Ramos scrolled. The message ended with the only non-gibberish since Moira's intro:

I'm so sorry, Moira. There's things I've uncovered that have to be stopped. Without the weapons, what am I going to do? This is for Isabel. Procyon can't know. They could be complicit, like Winston was last time. This had to go to you. I wish things had been different. If I see you again, I want to try.

Gary

Ramos cleared his throat. If I didn't know better, I'd have said the old softie had a glimmer of tears in the corner of his eyes. Served him right, being married.

And no, I wasn't blinking away my own. It was my imagination.

"I don't suppose Mr. DeBarthe's replacement has a handle on decryption?" Ramos asked.

"Probably Liz does, but I don't think I should take it to her. You read the same thing I did, right? Gary didn't want it getting back to Procyon. That could be paranoia on his part, but given the betrayal everyone there's experienced, I'm not gonna take the chance."

"Sounds reasonable." Ramos stood. He brushed grass from his pant cuffs. "Get some rest."

"You keep telling me, and I keep putting in late nights."

"I'm serious, Mercury. With your weapon draining, you'll need your own strength."

"Yes, sir. Keep in touch."

I tapped Skipper on the shoulder as I walked by. "Come on. Let's get out of here."

"Is there nothing we can do to help these men?" He fell in step beside me. "Though I don't feel I'm of much use unarmed."

"You and me both. No, unless you have some insight as to where Ugly has gone to next, we're done here."

"I do not feel his call."

"Then I feel the call of bed."

I so didn't want to get up the next morning. Therefore, I didn't.

It was, as usual, my phone that got my attention. I'd left

it on the floor next to the bed, so it rumbled like an angry dog, bouncing along the wood.

Loredana, of course. <Hope you're well this morning. Our reservation is for 7. Shall I expect you to pick me up?>

Just like that, I was wide awake. I had a date. At Saito on Sky.

I swiped over to my online banking access. If it had come equipped with digital moths, a couple would have flown off the screen. Rent was paid, so I wouldn't be out on the street, but there was precious little left. Which reminded me ... <Sure thing. What's your address? I'll be there. Any info from Alvarez on fee?>

<Claims he is working on it. Though I suspect the board is dragging its collective feet. Does not help matters he is furious about your visit last night.>

Ah, right. I'd wondered about potential blowback. <Sorry. Not trying to cause trouble.>

<And yet ... :) Don't worry. I have deflected his anger for now. But I fear I could face penalties.>

<He'd be a Grade-A idiot to kick you out.>

<In concur. But the reason he hasn't is far more pragmatic—he needs me on-site in his frequent absences. And I simply know too much.>

Always happy to hear. She hadn't, however, answered my first question. <Address?>

<7888 Wells Ave. Be there at 6:30 promptly, please.>

<You know me. Punctual!>

If she could find an emoji for a snort, I'm sure she would have given me one.

I leaned against the pillow and smiled at the ceiling. Suddenly, the sunshine through the window wasn't glaring death by heat, but the promise of a bright day.

Wow, Mercury. That cheese was pretty thick. Okay, breakfast wasn't gonna cook itself.

Skipper was laid out on the couch, legs over the end, head propped on the arm without a pillow. He, too, was staring at the ceiling. "Good morning.

"Morning." I rubbed sleep from my eyes and made for the counter. Must. Have. Coffee. "How'd you sleep?"

"Quite well. This bunk felt as if it were a hammock."

"Yeah? That ring any bells? In terms of memory, I mean."

"Only that I did not live in a place like this, among crowded towers." Skipper rose and stretched. He padded barefoot into the kitchen. His movements had a graceful sway to them. Convinced me even more that he'd been a sailor, or maybe still was. "I have these paintings in my mind of a cottage. The roof is built of slate shingles. I've climbed to the top and am hammering many back into place. A storm blew them asunder ..."

He gazes over his shoulder, toward the window. Not much of a view, with a slice of blue sky over the tops of neighboring apartment buildings. "I don't know where my home is. While I am here, though, I shall to my best to aid you in your battle."

"Okay. But why?"

"Because it is right."

I nodded. "Sounds like a plan. First, I need coffee."

CHAPTER FIFTEEN

I wanted to hit the streets again, but with the stave sulking in the corner and refusing to put out any power, my options were limited.

Instead, I spent Sunday morning poring over that stupid email from Gary DeBarthe's ex-wife.

"This is a strange text." Skipper frowned over a cup of coffee. He'd eaten every last crumb of eggs and sausage from the skillet. I was glad I'd gotten mine before he'd scarfed it down. "Thank you for sharing your brew while we peruse it."

"No problem. Without this brew, my brain's not going to do either of us any good." I rubbed my face. "Okay. It's got to be encrypted. Maybe there's an algorithm that has to be used."

"Algorithm?"

"It's computer talk, I think."

"Ah. The machines."

"They are machines, but it's not like they're gonna go all *Terminator* on us and take over the world. These guys are dummies by comparison."

Skipper's blank look informed me I'd lost him, probably back at *Terminator*.

"Never mind." I copied the text to a message intended for Liz but hesitated before I sent it. Gary's email said specifically not to do that. But after a couple hours crossing my eyes over the gibberish, I wasn't any closer to finding an answer. If someone was crooked inside Procyon, left over from Winston and Marigold's conspiracy ...

Screw it. I needed an answer, pronto. <Liz. See if you can run this.>

Her answer was instantaneous. <Sorry can't Alvarez is on patrol he's making sure we're tracking the fiend-hound here's the update said he's monitoring our communications.>

That lack of punctuation thing was gonna kill me. My adrenaline spiked, obliterating the calm focus the coffee had bestowed. Great. She'd better delete it, then. Last thing I needed was Alvarez getting so infuriated that he skipped paying me altogether. "Perfect."

"An obstacle?"

"Yeah, you could say that. The new boss isn't happy with me."

"A change in command can cause difficulty."

"Amen to that," I muttered. "I've got a better idea. Let's go for a ride."

Ramos was *not* happy to have a surprise caller. But I wasn't getting anywhere on my own.

I tried all kinds of websites devoted to codes. Problem was, I had no clue how the message was encrypted, so if I couldn't figure out the method, I was up a creek. The police, though, had to have some experience with the matter, right?

"Code-breaking?" Ramos sounded like he wanted to reach through the phone and strangle me. "Mercury, I've got four deaths and a commissioner literally shouting at us to find answers. He's not buying my explanation that it's related to the same creatures that attacked in the spring. It's easier for him to sell the District Attorney on a human to charge with crimes."

"Hey, relax, you're the one who shared the message with me."

"Because this is *your* people's problem."

"Well, I'm already in trouble for being at Procyon twice when I wasn't authorized. I tried sending along the text—"

"We're working on a warrant so we can trace the ISP from which DeBarthe sent the email. That might help tell us where he's gone. All I can give you at the moment is surveillance video from one of the bank branches DeBarthe used. He's talking to someone outside, but we haven't been able to get a face. Give it a look and let me know what you think."

"Okay, I'll—"

Ramos hung up. I blew out a breath and slapped the phone down on the glove box between Skipper and me.

"More command issues?" he asked.

"Try a friend who's frustrated and taking it out on me." To be fair, I was supposed to be putting a stop to the attacks and finding the missing guy, but this whole playing detective thing was not in my resumé. "We're trying to find a man who could help us track down the fiend-hound and stop it. Hopefully he'll know how to recharge my weapon."

"I see. Perhaps you need training in weapons that don't require magic."

"It isn't magic."

"Oh? Can you explain its workings? Or are they a gift from a power beyond your understanding?"

I rolled my eyes.

The phone buzzed. Ramos sent me two attachments—a photo and a video, both arriving in my email. I pulled up the video clip. There was DeBarthe, all right. He glanced at everything that moved. As soon as he had the money, he hurried out the bank's front door, bumping past two others waiting in line. That earned him some angry words, though the video lacked sound so I couldn't make out what was said.

"This is an event from the past?" Skipper leaned in.

"Recorded from a bank's security cameras," I said. "The twitchy guy is our victim."

"And this is accurate? Not a dream?"

"It's ... no, it's not a dream. Hang on." DeBarthe disappeared out of the camera's field of view for a couple seconds. Then he stepped back in, upper right corner, except he was outside. Talking to someone.

All I could see was a bare arm in a white short-sleeved shirt, and part of a leg clad in gray pants. The arm and its attendant hand gestured at DeBarthe, who waved defensively. Finally, DeBarthe handed over a stack of cash. Then they were both gone.

The video was grainy, so I rewound. There wasn't much to go on. Maybe Ramos could find another camera angle— his text said he was looking for exactly that. Or if there was a camera across the street ...

Wait a second.

I paused the video. There wasn't much I could do to zoom, but I pulled the image in as close as possible.

The arm of the unidentified man had a black mark on it.

"What's that look like to you?" I aimed the screen at

Skipper.

He squinted. "A brand. Perhaps of a weapon?"

"Like a sword," I murmured. "If we can get this cleaned up, we'll know for sure. But I'm willing to bet DeBarthe was paying off the same guys who we fought, the ones also chasing down the fiend-hound. Loredana thinks they're from another city. It's about time we proved it."

I typed up a reply to Ramos, asking for better video enhancement, but stopped. Then I shot the clip over to Loredana's email, under the subject, "Dr. Who Marathon Night." What? If Alvarez was monitoring everyone's communications, like Liz said, I wasn't about to give the moron any hints about what I was doing.

It was maddening, actually. Why didn't the guy want me on site? I didn't buy any of his reasons about security. For all I knew, he might be the one with sympathies to the old conspiracy.

"Loredana," Skipper said. "She is Lady Lark?"

I snickered. "Yeah, she'd love that title, especially what with her aristocratic parents being the king and queen of ice."

"Not, as you would say, literally."

"No, Skipper, there aren't literally people who rule ice or rule with ice, unless you're talking *Frozen*," I snapped. "What's your point?"

"I was curious as to how long you had been courting her. Is that why you are adamant we return to Procyon, even though your commander is opposed to your presence?"

My face got way redder than it should have. "I'm not ... we're not courting."

He smiled. "I may have lost my memory, Mercury, but my senses are fine. One would have to be blind and deaf not to observe."

"Observe what?"

"The love between you two."

"Okay, and we're done." I started the car. "Loredana's great. Smart. Pretty. She's a lot of fun to talk to. We've eaten together a few times, and yeah, we've got a date tonight—"

"Which date is that? Today's date? I haven't kept track of time well."

"Just shut up, all right?" Better check that other email from Ramos before we got out of here. I opened it. "Keep your observations to yourself. I don't need advice from—whatever you are."

"By all means," Skipper said. "But know this—love cannot be thwarted."

I wanted to thwart him, which by thwart, I meant beat him over the head with the dead pulsar stave. But he'd probably decapitate me, so that was a bad idea. Instead, I opened Ramos's second message.

The attachment was a dark, fuzzy picture of Skipper.

I angled the phone so he couldn't see and read Ramos's warning:

Had Stan Bradley take a picture of your sidekick at Rosa Roja. We tried running it through facial recognition software. No matches came up on criminal records or any other databases. Lifted his fingerprints from the park, too. Also a dead end. Whoever that guy is, there's no records. I'm sending the info over to a buddy at the FBI, see if I can get you some answers. Be careful.

I glanced at Skipper as I pulled the Subaru out into traffic. He didn't seem to notice my staring, because he was watching every person, every building slide by. The only time he looked my way was when a tour bus with an open second deck rumbled across an intersection. Skipper sounded like Obi-wan Kenobi one second, then gawked like a kindergartener on his first field trip the next.

Here was hoping he didn't have a nervous breakdown the next time we cornered the fiend-hound.

"This doesn't appear to be the way to your home," Skipper said. "Where are we going?"

"Downtown," I said. "You're gonna show me the first place you remember being in San Camillo. Then maybe we can find ourselves a monster to kill."

Loredana emailed me back with the subject heading, "Restaurant arrangements."

It wasn't good news, though. *Liz lost the enemy van. They must have discovered and removed the tracer Garvey planted. This leaves us with no intelligence about their location.*

Another strike against us. My hands tightened on the steering wheel. Whoever these guys were, they were good.

Appreciated your sharing of the image. I had Liz enlarge, then delete. You were correct about the mark on the man's arm. It is a sword, one bearing a striking resemblance to the night's blade.

That wasn't good news either. Gary was caught on camera paying these guys, which meant either he ran out of money and then they took him—or he was working for them. Either way, how'd he manage to get a coded message off to his wife?

"This," Skipper said. "This is the place."

I turned east on Thirteenth off DeLeon. Sure enough, that side of the intersection was lined with vendors. The smell of falafel was enough to get me salivating. What time was it? One-fifteen? No wonder I was starved.

Skipper led me down the street. Thankfully, it didn't appear anyone recognized him. I paused by the falafel cart. Okay, so I'd smelled it from almost a block away. Sue me. I hoped I hadn't forgotten cash in my wallet. "Hey, are you hungry? I spot you, seeing as how you saved my life ..."

My new buddy was nowhere to be seen. Correction: I caught a glimpse of his boot, and the wrought iron gate to Cavill Cemetery banging shut.

"I'll take one, then," I told the vendor.

Three minutes later, I was shoveling ground chickpeas slathered in deep-fried goodness into my mouth. It wasn't pepperoni, but I'd make do. Skipper didn't show signs of emerging, so I opened the gate.

Cavill Cemetery was tucked between two old brick buildings, one of which had been a hotel a couple of centuries ago and was now sublet into various professional offices. The other was home to an art gallery at street level and apartments up top. There were a few windows, on the top two out of six floors, but I'd bet visibility was hampered by the canopy of gnarled oaks filling the grassy stretches between decrepit tombstones.

It was surprisingly silent in here. Thirteenth wasn't a busy street, but still ... I shivered. The afternoon had gone cloudy. The air was thick, like rain could dump at any second. I stepped carefully around grave markers that dated back to the late-1700s. This was an historic site, to be sure. I wondered if any of the people who'd fought astral fiends during the 1848 conflict—the one that birthed Procyon and its ongoing mission—were buried here.

I wondered where my parents were buried.

They'd come to Earth from Meda, gotten caught in a huge astral fiend incursion, and died protecting the innocent. Left me as an orphan and with a legacy.

The pulsar stave weighed heavy in its holster. Some legacy. It was well on its way to being lost.

I found Skipper in the back left corner, kneeling beside a pearly obelisk a foot tall. He traced a name with his fingers.

"Anything exciting? This place looking familiar?"

"Night had fallen when I arrived. I was disoriented." Skipper frowned. "Perhaps the location is near, yet ..."

"I'm guessing the name isn't a friend of yours."

"Rankin. No, I do not recall anyone by that name." He turned to his right. "I believe it is there."

When he indicated "there," he pointed at a big patch of grass between two trees. Roots protruded, pushing dirt aside. I tried not to think about what their growth had done to the dead buried beneath us. Instead, I closed the box of falafel. It didn't seem right to keep eating.

As I did, a third tree appeared.

I blinked. The third tree coalesced into one of the original two. "Did you see ...?"

"You saw something strange?" Skipper stood beside me. "What was it?"

"I don't know. Hold this." I gave him the box and edged nearer to the clearing. It wasn't big, just enough to accommodate a knot of people.

It happened again. A tree seemed to sprout off.

I froze, then backtracked.

The trees rejoined.

"By heavens," Skipper murmured. "This must be it."

"Yeah, you think?" My tone was as hushed as his. I waved my hand through the air. Didn't feel anything. More humid air was all. And yet … "I've got an idea."

I dialed Liz.

"Oh, Mercury! I meant to call you, but I knew I shouldn't because we're not supposed to, and, well, you're really still in a bunch of trouble for being here, but then the tracker has been lighting up—!"

"Liz, hey, slow down. About the tracker …"

"I have it right here."

"What's it showing for Thirteenth and DeLeon?"

"There's—oh. That's peculiar. It's a tachyon fluctuation but it isn't a rip forming. Hey! It's like what I was telling you before, about that Skipper guy!"

"I know, I think we found where he showed up." Something tickled the back of my mind. "You said it wasn't like a rip but was."

"Sort of. It's more coherent. At the moment, though, it's not near as stable as what occurred when the portal was bridged at the North Beach Battle."

"I've got an idea." I drew the pulsar stave from under my shirt. "Keep an eye on the tracker. Let me know if anything interesting happens."

"Like what?"

"Like this." I stepped into the clearing and willed the pulsar stave to activate. Come on. Do something!

The weapon flared to life with the brilliance of a flashlight shone right in my eyes. Skipper shouted behind me. I could feel the energy surging through the stave, up my arm, soaking my body. I could have run from coast to coast right then.

"Wow! That's a spike! It's the same signature, Mercury! I've never seen—"

The call lapsed into static and disconnected. I couldn't hear anything except a rush of wind, the hiss of shaking leaves. The air around me formed into a shimmering sphere, like a gigantic soap bubble.

I felt like I could reach out and pull an atom out of the air.

It took every ounce of strength to step out of the sphere, slipping across its boundary. Once I breached it, the world returned to normal. Winds died. Sounds resumed. I panted, holding the pulsar stave.

"Mercury. Was that it? Was that how I came to be here?"

I shook my head. "I …don't know."

A voice screeched from my phone. For a second, I thought astral fiends knew my number. Then I lifted the phone to my ear and got Liz in mid-happy rant: " …believe what it's showing! There's a portal linking—I don't know where, but it didn't go to the Interstice! I'm going to run every test I can think of. Cyril's going to be so happy!"

"Anything for your computer."

There was a scraping noise, like she'd fumbled the phone, and a much calmer voice took over. "Are you hurt?"

Loredana. "Nope. I'm good." I grinned. "Better than good. The stave's charged, at least partially. I'll tell you all about it."

"Good. Then I trust you won't be late."

For a dinner date? With her? I didn't care how much it cost. The stave hummed in my hands. I was gonna find the guys who took Gary DeBarthe, and with Skipper's help, kill the fiend-hound.

"I will never be more on time in my entire life," I said.

CHAPTER SIXTEEN

Saito on Sky was golden.

Admittedly, that was by design. The chairs, the walls, the overhead lighting—every shade of that color was reflected on everything, except for the white tile floors, and the sweeping starry skies outside the floor length windows.

It took me a second to remember where I was. Not hiding in an alley, stinking of garbage and astral fiend body parts, but wearing a charcoal gray suit, white shirt, and black tie. Hair slicked to one side. Nails trimmed, clean-shaven, wearing cologne for crying out loud. But how could I not be spruced up?

Loredana was beside me, hand nestled in the crook of my arm. She wore a red dress, sleek and form-fitting, with a high collar that mimicked an Oriental style. Sinuous vines traced an entrancing pattern down to her thighs. Her arms were bare to her shoulders. The left arm had a perfect square of four freckles. Never noticed it before.

I hadn't gotten a peek at her apartment, either. Last minute, she'd had me pick her up from Procyon. Which was where I'd left Skipper. After the brief visit to whatever weird anomaly was in Cavill Cemetery, I wasn't about to drop the guy at my apartment. Besides, Doc Arne wanted to run some more tests and have the lab nerds compare Skipper's samples not only to human DNA, but mine, too.

"It's safer for him, and us," Loredana murmured.

She had to remind me then, as I smiled at the hostess, trying not to panic at the menu sheathed behind glass to the right of the hostess. Not a price in sight. Perfect. Well, I'd be poor after tonight, but as I glanced out of the corner of my eye at Loredana, I decided it was worth however late I was gonna be paying off my credit card bill.

We were seated at a table by one of the windows. You couldn't ask for a better view of San Camillo. The city was a forest of lights, stretching out to the black harbor.

"Funny." I considered the seafood on my plate. "I love calamari."

"Why is that funny?"

"You'd think after all this time destroying astral fiends, I'd prefer something without tentacles." I grinned. "Maybe it's revenge against their giant brothers."

"Perhaps you've given it too much thought." Loredana sipped her wine. There wasn't a speck left on her plate. I wondered if she'd skipped lunch.

"This was a nice idea. Get us both out of work, away from all the crazy stuff."

"Yes, it was." She seemed to consider the glass in her hand, as the ruby liquid swirled around. Tiny sapphire earrings sparkled.

A few seconds ticked by without any commentary on her part. Yeah, not awkward at all. "So, what've you been up to?"

"I'm sorry?"

"Besides Procyon business. Seen any good movies lately?"

"None that I can recall."

Silence again. Ball was back in my court, except I was done playing. "Okay, we might as well skip to whatever it is you want to tell me."

"I'm not sure I know—"

I held up my hand. "Don't give me that, Loredana. Please. We've known each other long enough I can tell when something's on your mind. Something bad enough it's preventing this from being a sociable evening shared by two people who care about each other."

Her cheeks pinked. "Well then, I suppose we had best get down to business."

You could have flash-frozen every piece of sushi in the restaurant with that tone of voice. "Seriously? This is my fault?"

"No. It isn't." She hung onto that glass like it was a life preserver. "I'm sorry. I was trying to find a way to tell you this, and I thought dinner might soften the blow."

"Good idea, poor execution."

"Yes. So it would seem. I had suspicions about the arrival of your friend Skipper when Elizabeth showed me how he came her. And then the two of you confirmed those suspicions when you discovered his point of origin—or should I say, point of entry."

"Yeah, Liz was pretty excited about that portal. I mean, so was I, because it got the pulsar stave back up to strength, for the time being. I guess Liz is running a search through Procyon's archives to find if a similar portal's been recorded."

"She won't find anything, because such data is classified for only select individuals."

I leaned forward, heart racing. Had to figure. Procyon's secrets kept multiplying. "Are you saying you guys have seen one of these before?"

"Yes."

"What does it do?" Concern pierced my interest. "It's not another avenue for the fiends to get back here, is it? Wait, so, can we use it to return to Meda?"

"As far as we are aware, it can be used for neither purpose. I will have to conduct further research, but if it does in fact operate as the other known portal, it bridges two dimensions by means of a stable passageway that cuts across the Interstice." Loredana shifted in her seat. "How your Skipper used it to move from wherever he originated to here is beyond my comprehension, because until today, I thought only one artifact could enable transit between those points, and he most decidedly lacks it."

"An artifact. You mean the night's blade or the ax. Teget has those back in Meda."

"No. A different object."

My head was spinning. It wasn't the wine either, because I had a full stomach and only one glass down. "Okay. That's ... interesting. Let me guess: the artifact's stuck over in Meda's temple, where my grandfather has all that stuff locked up."

"It is not. It is under secure keeping in this world."

"So, why not use it to get Skipper back through to ... wherever?"

"That is the issue at hand. We do not know where he's from. Dr. Becker is fully convinced that, while human, Skipper has different genetic markers from the people of our world. But his markers do not match yours, Mercury, so we know he does not hail from Meda."

"Somewhere else." I polished off the last dregs on my plate. "Somewhere we haven't been."

"So it would seem."

The waiter appeared. "Could I interest either of you in another glass of wine?"

"Yes," we said in unison.

He filled our glasses without spilling a drop. Once he was gone, Loredana smiled and seemed, of all things, sheepish. "Again, I did want things to proceed … differently tonight."

"But you also wanted a place outside Procyon where we could meet without having to worry about eavesdropping."

"Precisely."

"Well, you sure know how to show a guy a night out. What beats an expensive dinner with a beautiful woman while she tells you all her secrets?"

"Not my secrets, Procyon's. And in the past, I've seen the damage done by keeping those things from you."

She wasn't kidding. How long had I not known I was from another dimension, or that the reason I was an orphan was because my parents journeyed to Earth and died in its defense? Procyon could have told me that any time. I could have held a grudge, sure, but after everything Loredana and I had been through, I wasn't about to cross her off my list of allies. I reached across the table for her hand. "Listen, don't worry about me. You do what you have to with Procyon. I'll take care of the street. Just, you know, keep me in the loop."

She smiled. "I'm glad to see the current arrangement with our foundation hasn't soured you on our personal relationship."

"I'm glad you're not avoiding me like the plague. Your boss okay with this?"

"I haven't inquired," she said. "Manager Alvarez has

many other important things in front of him. I've also told him what companionship I keep in my personal time is my business, and none of his, or Procyon's."

"Even when it's the devilishly handsome likes of me."

"Even when."

We drank. Her eyes never left mine. It got more difficult to form coherent speech. Imagine that. "Got any travel plans?"

"I'm not visiting my family soon, if that's what you're inquiring."

"Didn't mean to touch a nerve. It's just … they'd probably like to see you. Even if they are colossal jerks."

"They've never reconciled with my moving to the States and forgoing a teaching position at Oxford."

"*The* Oxford?"

"That was the destiny to which they felt I should submit. But Procyon got to me first, and I could not say no when they gave me a glimpse of what truly happens in the shadows of this world, what dangers await civilization. Doing anything else seemed a waste of time.'"

"I get that, but family's family. I'd love to hop a plane and see Teget and Naos again, and that crazy pile of cousins I have in Meda. Don't let the possibility get away from you okay?"

"I'll consider it. No, I had something else in mind." She swirled her glass again. "Syndax."

"You want to go check out their facility in Colorado? Sounds like a plan to me."

"There is a benefit at Procyon's newest office in Rampart. I propose using it as cover for an investigation."

"I propose that sounds like an awesome idea. So, you do the party and I do the snooping around."

"Exactly that."

I raised my glass. "Road trip."

"Road trip, indeed." She clinked hers against mine.

I thought about what Skipper said. *Love cannot be thwarted.* Whatever was going on between us, I didn't want to put words to it. Who knows? She could decide next week to fall off the face of the Earth again.

"You asked about a movie," Loredana said.

"Yeah, that was small talk."

"I know. For your information, I was watching a program on the History Channel about ciphers—their development, changes in the face of advancing technology."

"Wow, that sounds really boring."

She raised an eyebrow. "A word of advice. If you're looking to impress a woman by listening to her likes and dislikes, don't insult them."

"Just making sure you're paying attention."

"Now you sound like my father." Loredana sighed. "Always keen to see if I were watching his lessons. The program was something he would like, full of codes as old as the Vignère cipher and ..."

I lost the rest of the sentence because my thoughts snapped back to the message Gary sent to his wife, and that she'd forwarded to Ramos. Father and daughter. He'd mentioned the kid. Isabel, right? Before I could focus on the rest of Loredana's story, I had my phone out and the email open.

"Mercury? What on earth are you doing?"

I held up a finger. "Idea. Can't talk."

"You most assuredly can." She slid her chair around the table until we were shoulder to shoulder. Must have looked to everyone else like we'd simultaneously gotten bored with dinner and were playing some dumb phone game. I found an online translator. "Vignère cipher. I wanted to try it."

"On Mr. DeBarthe's message? I hadn't received word from Liz as to what kind of encoding it used."

"The daughter." I plugged in the girl's name: **Isabel.** The translator spat back:

Syndax agents took astral fiend remnants for study. The pieces have escaped and mutated with mammalian life. The infection is spreading. Arkwright wants to conjoin. Wrong to trust Winston again.

We stared at the screen. I didn't like sound of any part of that message. And who or what the heck was Arkwright?

Loredana's hand was on my forearm. My leg was pressed against her. Preoccupied? Yeah. But take your pick as to which was more on my mind. "That can't be right," I muttered. "Pieces escaped?"

"It isn't possible. There should not have been any remnants from the battle. The bodies always sublimate."

"Yeah, except something went wrong because they obviously didn't. How'd they even managed to get a piece of an astral fiend out of a war zone? Somebody should have noticed."

"Perhaps it wasn't large. Though it couldn't have simply been smuggled out in a briefcase. One would need a specialized containment unit."

"And you're not bothered by the fact that something like that exists? A containment unit for extradimensional monster parts." I ground my teeth. Great. Some idiot decided they needed a monster's toenail to experiment on, and next thing you know, a mutated fiend-hound was killing people in my city.

"What I am most bothered by is the mention of Winston Yen."

"Yeah. Of all people, Gary should know better than to have anything to do with him. Sure sounds like he contacted Winston, though."

"I shall check with prison officials and see if he had any visitors. Which he should not have."

"Unless Gary passed it off as official Procyon business."

For a moment, I thought it was my phone bothering me again. But it was the tracker humming in my pocket. The screen was showing readouts of tachyon activity and judging by the way the red lines were spiking, Liz had made some adjustments to the software Cyril was running back at Procyon.

"We've got a live one." I waved at a waiter. "Hey! Check please."

"Mercury." Loredana lowered my hand. "This isn't the proper protocol for a restaurant like Saito on Sky."

"Change of plans." I showed her the tracker's screen. The waiter materialized at our table, his ever-gracious smiled strained by what was no doubt my crude manners. Whatever. I imagined him wrapped in the life-sucking tentacles of the fiend-hound. I shoved my credit card in his face. "Make it fast if you want a tip."

If I could have cut the elevator's cables and sent it plummeting—albeit safely—to the ground I would have done so. Instead I kept glancing at the tracker, hoping the fiend-hound appeared somewhere nearby so I could end its rampage.

That's me. Mercury Hale, Rampage-Ender.

The street outside the Saito tower was busy with traffic. A handful of restaurant patrons milled about, waiting for the valet to return with their cars. I cringed at the thought of the kid driving up in my Subaru amongst all the BMWs and Mercedes, never mind the Teslas. Thankfully I'd washed it not long ago, and also, it was dark.

"Thank you for dinner." Loredana kissed me on the cheek.

Well. There went any and all thoughts of self-pity. I grinned at her. "You're welcome. I wish it could have lasted longer."

"Perhaps there will be time for that later."

I really hoped later meant "ten o'clock" rather than "in a couple weeks."

A familiar engine noise cut across the rumble of traffic. My Subaru parked smartly at the curb. I mean, you could have measured the distance between each tire and the concrete with a ruler and they would have been within a quarter inch. The skinny Japanese kid who climbed out gave me a slight bow and the barest hint of a smile.

"Not a scratch, right?" I palmed him a tip with the last of my actual cash and took the key.

"You might want to get the air conditioning checked, sir." He shivered. "It was up high. I couldn't get it to stop freezing."

Frost crept across the windows. When the summer was at its scorchingest.

The tracker bucked like a boat on choppy seas in my jacket pocket.

Of all the … I grabbed the kid with one hand and reached into my coat with the other. The pulsar stave sent a jolt of power through me as it activated. I threw the valet a good eight feet into the nearest planter. Judging by his shout, he might have injured his leg.

But it was worth it to clear him out of harm's way.

Purple sparks shot through the open door. A great flash and a tremendous thunderclap broke the windows out of the Subaru, sending spiderwebs rippling across the panes before blowing them free of the car. People around us screamed.

"What a way to end a night, right?" I asked Loredana as I drew the pulsar stave.

She pulled a silver revolver from her purse and aimed at the car.

The fiend-hound tore through the roof, flinging crumpled blue Subaru into the street. It ripped down to the chassis and shoved the halves of my car aside, each one smashing into a luxury sedan on either side.

"And there go my insurance premiums," I muttered.

CHAPTER
SEVENTEEN

The fiend-hound ripping my car apart had the effect you'd expect.

People screamed and ran.

On the one hand, that was great. It meant they weren't in my way when the monster lunged for me, its tentacles snapping up fist-sized chunks of the sidewalk. On the other, it was distracting.

On the other-other hand, nobody was looking at my face.

Gunshots exploded over my left shoulder, near enough I knew I'd have my ear ringing for the next few hours at least. Loredana fired three bullets without flinching, and I don't think she would have moved out of the fiend-hound's path if I hadn't pushed the two of us behind a planter full of gardenias. We hit the concrete hard. Pulpy bits rained on us.

"Clear as many people as you can out of here." I spat a petal from between my teeth. "The quicker I kill this thing, the better, before the cops show up."

"The police, or our unidentified friend."

Right. Forgot about our special forces ninjas.

My phone started buzzing. Seriously?

The fiend-hound grabbed the planter and threw it into the middle of the street. It bashed the front end of a cab, stopped the vehicle in its tracks, and bounced against a bus. More cars collided with each other.

I dove under a pair of tentacles that were intent on stabbing me, and swept the pulsar stave up through the tangle. One of the appendages flopped onto the pavement, wriggling and sizzling where the stave's energies had severed it.

The fiend-hound shrieked at me. A clawed stump whipped around. I blocked it with the stave, and for a split second, we were locked in position. The creature snarled at me, its creepy, glistening eyes reflecting an irritated Mercury Hale.

I looked pretty good in my suit.

A second swipe came from the right, and it was only Loredana's gunshot that saved me. Blue goo sprayed from the paw.

The wound gave me time to spin free and fall back to a better defensive position. I realized then that the clawed stump was on the same leg that Skipper had cut. Which meant the fiend-hound could regrow limbs.

Wonderful.

The phone kept buzzing. I finally put it into speaker mode. "What?"

"Hey, Mercury! Did you see the tracker's results? I couldn't believe it, but the tachyon pulses were off the scale!" Liz squeaked. Like she was a mouse. Or saw one. "It's just sooo cool!"

"It'd be a lot cooler if the fiend-hound weren't right in front of me!" I snapped.

The beast lunged for me, but I pulled power from the

stave so I could vault over its head. I landed in the street, as a car horn blared. It had missed running me over by a few inches.

I slashed at the fiend-hound's haunches. Too slow. It spun around so fast I thought it had pulled that inversion trick the astral fiends could do. I ducked a swipe that ripped a sleeve from my jacket.

Well, great. That was one of my best pre-Procyon sets of clothing. Which was an odd thing to worry about, fighting for my life in the middle of the dinner rush hour in downtown San Camillo.

"Wow! Is it staying there?" Liz yelled. "Okay, I'm charting everything that comes in through the tracker. Don't turn it off!"

"Don't worry, I won't!" I slit another tentacle, but the fiend-hound was growing them back. At least with the old monsters I could trim them down to size and then deliver a killing blow. This beast was a whirlwind of claws and spikes, its fangs gnashing at air and spraying saliva.

"Draw it in!" Loredana reloaded her pistol. "I can't get a clean shot!"

Easy for her to say. I tried to slide by, as I'd done in countless battles before, but the fiend kicked with a huge hind leg. He could have made Manchester United a great striker. That's football. Well, soccer, for us Yankees. Either way, that kick nearly took off my head, if I hadn't put the stave between me and one gnarled, slimy claw.

It gave me the chance to split the stave in half and stab it as deep as I could into the fiend-hound's side.

I was expecting the death knell of an astral fiend, the swift and smelly sublimation that followed, and a feeling of triumph. That would have been the best end to the evening.

Instead the critter bellowed in my general direction. Two more tentacles burst from its hide and wrapped around my arms. Cold snapped through my body, faster than and with greater intensity than I'd ever experienced from an astral fiend. I was sure I'd be dead in seconds without the pulsar stave's energy protecting me.

As it turned out, this beast wasn't hungry, because instead of draining my life, it flung me at the building.

A quick somersault in mid-air saved me from impacting headfirst, and I used the pulsar stave's energy to prevent my bones from breaking. But my body slapping against the wall still knocked the air from my lungs. I landed shoulder-first.

Half the stave rolled toward the front door.

The beast made an immediate beeline for it. Since when did the monsters go *toward* my weapon? They're not generally fans of its power, which spelled their death.

Loredana slid out from hiding and kicked the stave half toward me. She fired all six shots from her revolver, point blank at the fiend-hound.

I didn't see where they all went, but two of them blew part of its collection of eyes into purple and blue gunk.

I staggered upright, but it wasn't without a fair amount of shaking. Here I was, sweating out a San Camillo summer night, the stink of ozone and garbage cutting through the air, and I could have used a parka.

The fiend-hound did some staggering of its own, shuddering, thick blue slime streaming down its face. It bellowed at Loredana, and my guess was it was sizing her up for another attack. Sure was taking its time, though.

Meanwhile the area had cleared out of vehicles. I mean, there wasn't a car left on the street. A quick glance confirmed that the traffic lights at either intersection at the ends of the block were both red. Without any cars caught between.

Since when did that ever happen?

Loredana edged toward me, gun trained on the fiend-hound. I wondered if the beast could count shots fired, because if it could, it would recognize Loredana was out of ammunition. "Are you hurt?"

"No more than usual." I put a hand on her shoulder so I could steady myself. The pulsar stave was doing its thing—that is, healing my body at an accelerated rate. It also helped that my biology was slightly different from the average Earth-bound person's. "How about we kill this thing while it's sitting here confused?"

"After you."

I reconnected the stave and let its power build, yellow-white light streaming from one end, the sparks cascading up and down its length. It backed away, shrieking at me, tentacles whipping up a storm, but it didn't attack.

"Good riddance." I struck with the full might of the stave.

The thing disappeared.

The *snap-crack* sounded like a huge firecracker. Wind whipped around me. I spun, broke the stave apart again, and wasn't disappointed when the fiend-hound rematerialized behind Loredana.

"Run!" I threw one of the staves.

She dodged from its attack, but not quick enough to avoid a slashing tentacle that tore across her bare shoulder. Loredana's cry was enough to push me over the edge from dull anger to white-hot fury.

This abomination had killed innocents in my city, caused enough mayhem to bring the police barreling back down on us—which is what I assumed the car engines racing up to the intersection represented—and now hurt the woman I cared about. To top it off, its granddaddies probably murdered my parents.

Enough.

The fiend-hound writhed, with one of the stave halves embedded in its back. Must have felt like the world's worst wasp sting. I built the stave's power again and flung myself at it, using a trick I'd done in the past—covering a couple dozen feet in the blink of an eye.

That time, he wasn't fast enough to teleport.

But a stunning flash of light knocked me to the ground.

Everything was intense ringing. Spots swam across my vision. Took me a minute to realize the men I saw surrounding us weren't upside down. I was.

A hand yanked me upright. The world righted itself. I stared into a mask. Night vision goggles.

Not those guys again.

Eight of them, clad in the by now familiar gray special forces gear. Four of them prodded the fiend-hound against the restaurant's exterior wall, using long sticks that sparked with—electricity? It was a purplish light. Whatever it was, each poke elicited a howl from the fiend-hound.

Two more of the men had Loredana at gunpoint. Since she had an unloaded revolver, and their MP5s had what I assumed were full magazines, she stayed seated, seething. If the scrape along her shoulder blade hurt, she didn't let the pain show through, other than for the tears that smudged her mascara.

I saw two gray vans parked in the street. More men were wheeling out a big glass container braced with metal. Tubes and pipes protruded from one end. What looked like a couple computers blinked on the other.

The guy holding me put more pressure on my arm until I was sure he was gonna wrench it off. "I told you the pulsar stave would be ours."

That same strange voice. "I'll give you guys ten seconds to leave. If you do, I promise I won't kill you right after I carve up the critter you're playing with."

He chuckled. "You're brave. That can't be denied. I think you've earned a peek behind the wall."

He slid the goggles and mask up. Have to admit, the guy was good-looking—square jaw, brown hair trimmed short and curly but messed with sweat from being under his mask, with a thick beard.

But his eyes were that eerie purple on black.

"Just because you're brave, doesn't mean we'll submit to your proposal. We've come all this way to bring back what is ours. Thanks to you, we've succeeded." He gestured.

The men with the Taser-poles jabbed them deep into the fiend-hound's hide. A sharp *crack* rent the air. I could feel the shockwave crinkle my skin.

The creature collapsed. It heaved a tremendous sigh, like a high school kid who'd taken his last exam, except this was filled with more phlegm. That was the soldiers' cue to push and pull it into the box, which they quickly sealed. Good plan, because no sooner did they have it shut than the fiend-hound twitched, snarled, and sprang back to life. It bashed at the transparent sides of the box.

No broken glass there. Whatever material they used was reinforced.

"Quiet our guest," the leader ordered.

One soldier input commands through the computers. More purple pulses bombarded the fiend-hound until it lay docile, whimpering under the onslaught.

Another soldier picked up the half of the pulsar stave that had been embedded in the beast and handed it to the leader. I still had the second half.

He turned it over in his hand. Inert metal. Meanwhile, mine shimmered with its effervescent energies. "It's remarkable when you realize a weapon like this is only accessible by a tiny fraction of humanity. And yet, how many have converged on this city in recent years? Yourself and at least two others."

"And one of yours," I snarled. "Until we killed her."

He slammed the pulsar stave into my gut. The blow drove me to my knees. I tried to swing back with my powered half, but this guy was as strong as if the stave really was powering him. He stopped my strike in mid-swing and hit me across the jaw.

"Let him go." That would be Loredana. She was on her feet, fixing her hair as if a squad of soldier ninjas hadn't just apprehended the monster I was trying to kill. She could have been ordering dessert upstairs in Saito on Sky, except for the messed-up makeup and the blood smeared on her arm. "That weapon and its owner are our assets."

"By 'our,' you mean Procyon's." The leader nodded. "We know who you people are. Deceivers. Ruiners of destiny. Despoilers of humanity's true fate."

"Nice monologue," I coughed. "Get to the part where you reveal your devious plan and I'll only break your face."

"There's isn't time for that. What's Procyon's will be ours." The leader aimed the defunct stave at Loredana. "Everything."

He glanced at his men. One gave a thumbs up. Those purple-black eyes targeted me again. I felt like they were sucking me into the Interstice, miniature rips in space-time that wouldn't let go. "You're the key to giving us this weapon's power. We'll find a way to use you."

Sirens. Oh, no. "You guys better clear out before the cops arrive."

"Don't worry for our sakes. They won't cause us any trouble. And we'll leave them something with which to delay their interference."

The second van's back doors opened. A throaty set of shrieks issued forth, but they were too low-pitched to be an astral fiend, or even another fiend-hound. Feet shuffled against a ramp that banged against the pavement. One by one, people loped out of the back.

Not people. Bodies.

Great.

The first one was the shriveled corpse Ramos had first shown me, down by Court Street. There was no way I could have forgotten the sight. Yet, here it was, limping into the street, missing its right arm. Because two tentacles had sprouted in its place. And its mouth was mangled to three times the size of something a person should have. It featured the same fangs as the fiend-hounds.

Four more followed, and I instantly recognized the stragglers as the young homeless couple from Rosa Roja. I guess Ramos had decided not to call me about more bodies gone missing from the morgue. Or maybe he didn't know yet.

"They were left wandering the city, when the fiend-hound came for them. It had them corralled at one of the sites it transported to. Like they were cosseted in a nest." The leader grabbed my neck and made me watch. "Before we go, we'll watch them tear Ms. Lark limb from limb. And once they've drained her, she'll join our ranks."

Our?

Despite the lack of oxygen, I was able to grab ahold of the stave half the leader had taken. It pulsed to life.

He realized his mistake a second before I tossed him at the van.

The other soldier holding me raised his gun, but I'd already melted it with the stave. I smashed both halves into his mask, making him snap over backwards at an angle that broke some bones. I heard them.

Loredana hurried toward me. Wait, how'd she escape from her captors?

They were already at the vans, dragging their leader aboard.

Several things happened all at once:

Six squad cars sped through the intersection, reds and blues dancing off the glass on all the surrounding buildings.

Two silver SUVs braked from the opposite direction.

Skipper hurtled from the open door of the first SUV, hatchet in one hand, stolen ninja sword in the other.

The first man who tried to shoot him expended bullets on a lot of air. Skipper whirled through them like he was avoiding raindrops, not looking the least bit concerned. His hatchet struck the gun, sending it clanking across the street.

That soldier brought his sword out, and their blades flashed in the police lights as they dueled. Whoever the soldier was under the mask, he had no chance, because even though he had some martial skills that matched mine, Skipper made sword fighting look like something he did in his sleep.

It ended with the soldier on his knees, weaponless. Skipper held the blade to his chest. "Surrender."

The guy fast-drew a pistol from his waistband. He got

off two shots.

One grazed Skipper's ribcage.

It didn't prevent him from stabbing the guy through the heart.

"San Camillo Police!" That was Ramos shouting through a bullhorn. I was never happier to hear the grump right then than I was to hear anyone's voice. "Drop your weapons! You're under arrest!"

The staccato of automatic weapons fire and the howl of the corpse-fiends drowned him out.

CHAPTER EIGHTEEN

Everyone was shooting at everything. It was up to me to find the spaces between the bullets and put a stop to the fiasco.

Easier said than done.

The police had taken shelter behind their squad cars and were trading shots with the soldiers. It was turning into a lopsided battle, because while the SCPD had an assortment of semi-auto pistols and rifles, with a smattering of shotguns, the enemy all carried automatic weapons. Pretty soon every cruiser was punched full of holes and missing most of their windows.

It didn't help that the corpse-fiends didn't keep slouching but ran.

Truth is, I couldn't tell whether they were running or using a version of the fiend-hound's teleportation ability. One second, they were approaching the line of cruisers, then next they were among the police.

So, that's where I went.

A leap powered by the stave landed me behind one of the former homeless couple—the guy, I guessed by his build. I don't know. Maybe I just thought he was uglier and figured the other one was the woman, okay? Either way, I slashed across his back with the stave.

It left a deep cut that filled with a nasty tar but didn't put it down.

Tentacles burst from its shoulder blades, slapping into me. The slimy appendages slathered goo across my suit, trying to envelope me, but I rolled backward over a patrol cruiser's hood, severing one as I went.

"Mercury!" Ramos was there. He pulled me aside, which wasn't really helpful because I wound up firmly seated on the pavement. He emptied half his pistol's magazine at the corpse-fiend.

Decomposing flesh splattered, and decomposing bone sprayed. Wherever it landed, which included the hood of the next car over, it sizzled before evaporating in a spray of particles that hitched a ride on the dank breeze.

"Hey, Ramos." I wiped blood from my nose. Blood? Yeah, there was a cut on my forehead. Worry about it later. "What brings you out on such a nice evening?"

He glared at me. "I was at home, having a nice but tense dinner with my family. Would you like to care why it was tense?"

How would I know why his family was having problems ... Oh, no. Sunday night? "Man. I'm sorry, I uh ..."

"For once, please, shut up." The corpse-fiend dragged itself over the hood. Ramos fired more bursts, as did officers around us. "I'll manage. Olivia's on the warpath, though, so I suggest you think of a creative and expensive way to apologize."

"I would have been there, I swear but, I had something come up and it, ah, overruled most of my rational thoughts."

I caught a glimpse of Loredana, resplendent in her dress, firing her pistol. Ramos snorted. "I won't argue. Why don't you tell me why these things can't be killed?"

"Because they're already dead. Don't you recognize one of your morgue guests?" I ramped up the stave's power and brought the tip down on the creature's face. Yellow-white light coursed through its body like electricity through a live wire. It shuddered and slumped, then melted into nothing.

There. That was better.

"How did they get out? What did this?" Ramos reloaded. "Bradley! Where's S.W.A.T.?"

"Stuck in traffic!" Bradley was tucked behind a cruiser, shoving fresh shells into a shotgun. "Which means we've got five minutes without them!"

Speaking of fresh, a new round of automatic gunfire swept across our hiding place, plinking holes in the cruisers. Ramos and I ducked. "Then get on the horn and tell those idiots we're going to need body bags if they take any longer!"

Bradley shouted orders into a radio, every third word an expletive. His command of their usage was impressive. But not as impressive as Skipper's hand to hand.

Yeah, he was still cutting his way through the soldiers, taking out any who opposed him. The good part about them trading shots with SCPD was that no one had paid attention to his arrival, allowing him to duel his opponents one by one.

"Don't even try to rationalize what I'm seeing with your new friend," Ramos said.

"Can't. He's not from around here."

"Like you?"

"Close." I waved a hand at the chaos. "Cliff's notes version: these guys are somehow linked with Marigold and Winston. They've got the fiend-hound in a stasis box, I guess you could call it. Tasered its brains out. Then they dropped off their zombie pals. Oh, also, their leader's holed up in the same vehicle."

"I gathered that, because they've blocked all our approaches." Ramos hazarded a couple shots over the top on the cruiser behind which we were hunkered. His bullets caromed off the van like it was a concrete bunker. "Where are they getting this kind of hardware from?"

"It's got something to do with Syndax." My heart rate spiked. Where was Loredana?

"Provable?"

"Not yet."

"That's not going to cut it. We can barely hold these things off. If they let the fiend-hound loose—"

A woman screamed. In that second, I thought I was going to die. A horrible, helpless sensation of sickly cold enveloped me. Worse than an astral-fiend's attempt to drain me lifeless.

Loredana?

No. A female SCPD officer held her hands in front of her. Her face was contorted in pain, because as everyone around her watched, they disintegrated into withered, gangrenous versions of their healthy selves, charred and black but riven with purple pulses. The infection smothered her head to toe, until she looked like a burnt version of the corpse-fiends.

Then the same thing started up in two more officers.

"No!" Ramos hurried from shelter, ignoring the gunfire around him. He dragged other officers away. "Get back! My god, what happened?"

A nearby cop, a young guy with his head shaved gleaming bald, had tears in his eyes. "Gomez, sir—we shot one of those zombies to bits—but some of it got on her. It ... it's doing this ..."

The connection formed in my mind, way too late. "Ramos! pull your people back. Concentrate on the soldiers and leave the corpses to me."

"What?"

"Do it! I can kill them without leaving a mess, and if that mess is what's transforming your people, we can't risk anyone else falling prey!"

Ramos gave me maybe two seconds in which I thought he was gonna argue, then nodded. "Everyone stay clear of the creatures! Hold your line until help arrives! I want those vans disabled!"

He backed off, issuing commands, while I engaged the next corpse-fiend.

This one was shorter, and grosser. More gross? Its tentacles whipped at me even though it was walking the opposite direction. I dodged them, but not with as great a margin as I'd have liked. The protracted battle, back to back with the first one against the fiend-hound, was taking its toll. Even the pulsar stave seemed to dim. It was impossible to tell, yet I started to feel sluggish, nonetheless.

One thing was for sure. I wasn't about to let those monstrosities touch me.

As I lopped spiked tentacles loose, I wondered why the slime on my shirt hadn't infected me like those three cops. Did it have to do with the destruction of the corpse? Spreading through explosion?

Didn't matter right then. I slipped past an incoming flurry of tentacles and struck the corpse dead-center in its back. It howled its dismay, because I guess even a reanimated dead body can lament its end. Again. Golden sparks shot through its torso and it sublimated in the old familiar astral fiend fashion.

Two of the newly transformed creepers grabbed onto my arms. Intense cold stabbed through my skin, deadening muscles, slowing circulation. I dropped to a knee but willed enough power into the stave to melt one of them right off my back.

The second one lost its gnarled arms to a sweeping silver blade.

Skipper raised the hatchet for the newly disarmed corpse.

"No! Hold on!" I pushed him aside and swept the pulsar stave into the creeper. It shrieked and melted into a steaming blue puddle that quickly evaporated.

"Don't put yourself between my blade and the body in which I intend to sheathe it." Skipper radiated anger. I was glad he was on my side. At the moment. "Ever."

"Yeah, well, these things tend to spread their infection when dispatched in the standard mode." I glanced around. "What about the soldiers?"

"Formidable, but they have retreated inside their armored wagons."

He was right. The reason we could hear each other to talk was the gunfire had slackened. The last of the soldiers were pulling their wounded inside one of the vans. The dead? The remaining corpse-fiends were happily infecting them.

That's when I spotted Loredana. Garvey was with her, shielding her from attack behind a toppled car. He aimed his favorite Mossberg over the tire, letting the van have a couple slugs that didn't do much but leave dents.

"You should get someone to look at that wound." I crouched beside Loredana.

"I'll manage." She touched my face. "You look positively dreadful. Haggard."

"Not my best, I'll admit." I tapped Garvey on the

shoulder. "Get her back to Procyon. Skipper and I can manage with SCPD."

Garvey nodded. He nudged Loredana, like a child trying to be respectful of his mother yet get her to safety.

"I'll remain until we see this through."

"Listen, I don't want ..." Something was wrong. The soldiers had stopped shooting all together. SCPD swarmed toward the van, even as the corpse-fiends staggered toward my new hiding place. Why weren't the soldiers protecting the second van?

"Ramos!" I sprinted from behind the car. "Ramos! Pull your people back! The van! Like at Syndax!"

He knew what I meant. The fear on his face was plain, even at that distance. "Take shelter! Move move move!"

Give SCPD credit: their men and women were trained to respond and obey. Everyone hit asphalt, and that's when the second van exploded.

Shrapnel cut apart two of the corpse-fiends, spraying their particles around and up into the air. The others ignored the blast, increasing their pace as they closed on our spot.

I braced myself, pulsar stave in hand, with Skipper by my side. "Come on, Garvey! I told you to get her—!"

A yelp interrupted my latest irritable order. Garvey dragged Loredana into the waiting SUV, as she kicked, smacked, and squirmed in his steel grasp. The poor guy took a nasty hit to the nose, which finally had the added effect of bringing Loredana out of her frenzied state. Last I saw of her was the SUV door slamming shut and the vehicle screeching away in reverse before spinning in the right direction.

"That was chivalrous of you." Skipper slashed at a corpse-fiend, sending it spinning in range of the pulsar stave.

"Don't you start." I melted the critter.

What I really wanted to do was disable the van carrying the surviving soldiers and the fiend-hound, but it was already barreling away. Ramos rallied his officers to their vehicles. Good lucking finding more than two that were still able to drive.

Speaking of drive, I realized then that Skipper and I were slaying the rest of the corpse-fiends in between the severed chunks of my Subaru.

It was satisfying. Not as satisfying as owning a new car that was in one piece, but I'd take what I could get.

The van was gone. So was the Procyon truck in which Garvey had stashed Loredana. Skipper and I stood among disintegrating puddles of corpse-fiends.

The stave powered down. A wave of nausea struck me.

Skipper caught me by the arm. "Are you hurt? We should seek Arne the healer."

"Yeah. Not a bad idea." The police were swarming throughout the street. S.W.A.T. trucks came barreling around the corner. A couple squad cars raced by, lights blazing, sirens blaring, intent wherever the soldiers' van went. "I have a feeling we don't want to answer any questions these guys have."

I let Skipper guide me to the other Procyon SUV. Ramos saw me. He took a step, like he was going to run and intercept me, but stopped. Whether he knew I didn't want to be dragged into this mess or not, I couldn't tell, but I wasn't about to get him in trouble. Not with everyone watching us. Watching this disaster.

Watching?

The whole time, people were near. Evacuated to the ends of the block, sure, but still around, cowering in buildings, hiding behind cars.

The phones were coming out. They were everywhere. And I didn't have a scrap of clothing on my face.

Dr. Arne was even more upset about my physical condition than I was. "This is insane. You shouldn't be out in the streets fighting monsters. No one has any idea what repeated tachyon exposure does to a person's cells. I'd strap you to this bed for weeks if I could get away with it."

"I don't think you can. I wouldn't let you." I let my feet dangle off the edge. The room wasn't spinning, and I didn't feel sick, so that was a plus.

"Fatigue. Exhaustion. Call it whatever you want. Your vitals are shot. I haven't run blood tests yet because I'm afraid no one's going to like the answers I uncover."

"Relax, Doc. I'm tired. You just said so."

"'Tired' doesn't begin to cover it. You're a young man who's spent years tackling those monsters. I want a full battery of tests—"

"Enough, okay?" I stood. Shakes hit, but they didn't last more than a couple seconds. Skipper stood by, bandages adhered to his face and his arms and a big one along his side. The guy was seriously muscled, tanned. He had some nasty scars on his chest, his ribcage—besides where the bullet had grazed him. Like he'd lived a rough life at sea, or on the streets, of wherever he'd come from. "C'mon, Skipper. I've got to find Loredana so we can get this sorted out."

"There's nothing to sort out, Mercury!" Arne followed us to the door. "You're hurt, your weapon is on the fritz, I've got no idea who *he* is—" He pointed at Skipper. "—and the only thing I can tell you is the fiend-hound that's out there is capable of rapid healing. Then you bring me news of infections spreading in dead bodies."

"Look!" I pushed into his space, nose to nose. "Syndax had bits of astral fiend. They lost track of them, somehow, either because they're evil or incredibly stupid, so we've got a new monster that's infected dead bodies and they're, in turn, infecting other people. Syndax just took that monster, tonight, and the bits could be spreading. We don't know. What I do know? I've got a temporary measure to keep the pulsar stave from draining entirely, and I'm gonna use it to stop Syndax and their crazy soldier boy band. That's why we brought one back."

Yeah. The recovery room next door to the infirmary was home to one drugged and so far, very quiet, soldier. Soon enough, I'd get him awake and get some answers.

Arne backed away. "This is a bad idea. I'll go on record with Ms. Lark and Manager Alvarez."

"You do that, right after we make our plan."

I hustled for Tracking, because I knew Loredana would be there with Liz. Where else would she be when everything was spiraling out of control?

She was, too, standing in front of that kaleidoscope of computer monitors, a silhouette against brilliant light. That comforting sight. The one I wanted to see every time I showed up at Procyon.

What I didn't want to see was Alvarez there, with her.

"Before you say anything, let me interject, I don't want to deal with your stupidity," I snapped. "You might not like me, Alvarez, but I get results. I'm the one to whom the pulsar stave was given."

Alvarez scowled. "I understand that. The board's already taken me to task for that. Your security clearance has been restored. Ms. Stojan has a badge for you."

Ms. Stojan—Liz—she didn't look happy about it. In fact, she was crying. She blew her nose into a clutch of tissues.

"Okay. That's good." I nodded. "Come on, Loredana, we have work to do."

"No, Mercury, 'we' do not." Loredana turned around. I'd never seen her so ... despondent? Since when was Loredana despondent?

"You'll work with Ms. Stojan to fix this," Alvarez said. "Ms. Lark is to be removed from the premises. Mr. Garvey will accompany her to her apartment and, with a contingent from security, will make sure she remains there."

"What? You're ..." I worked my mouth but couldn't come up with anything rational. "She's under house arrest?"

"She's disobeyed my direct orders. For that she has to be taken off this matter." Alvarez left the room without another word.

Garvey and three security guys took his place. Garvey winced when he saw me. "Sorry."

I stood there, staring. What was I going to do? Fight all these guys? They were on my side. I was all set to do it, though. The pulsar stave started to glow.

Loredana touched it. Our gazes met. She shook her head. "Find another way, Mercury. Find Mr. DeBarthe and the fiend-hound."

Then she was gone, leaving me halfway out the door after her.

"Mercury?" Liz sniffled. "What are we going to do now?"

I couldn't answer. All I could do was look down. My phone was in my hand. Didn't remember taking it out. And didn't remember messages.

One from Ramos.

<Department's in an uproar. Manhunt's expanding for the soldiers. Your fight is all over the web. But no one was watching for this. Tech traced the email Gary DeBarthe sent.>

It was an address. In Rampart.

The other message was Loredana. The timestamp told me it came to my phone while I was arguing with Dr. Arne.

<My home is 13311 East Sheridan. We must get to Syndax. I have a mode of transportation ready for such an emergency. I'll entertain myself with Dr. Who reruns until you and your friend can free me. Don't tarry.>

"Now that's more like it," I murmured.

CHAPTER NINETEEN

I thought about calling Ramos first. He had enough on his plate without having to wade into Procyon's personnel mess. Besides, Alvarez could always deny Loredana was being held at her apartment against her will—and she did accompany Garvey's security boys without resistance.

Upside? I finally got paid. Mark Hale's checking account received a sizeable boost. The next morning, I converted a good chunk into cash, just in case Alvarez changed his mind. I mean, I didn't think he'd really take back my pay, but at that point, I wasn't willing to risk it.

What I was willing to risk was a conversation that should have taken place a long time ago.

Skipper and I took the bus forty miles up the coast to Bulwark State Prison. It was a good chance to put San Camillo behind us, especially since social media feeds were blowing up with images and videos from last night's fight at Saito. My luck was holding. No one had been near enough to get a good image of my face. It helped that the ensuing fracas had broken streetlamps and exterior lights on Saito Tower.

My passenger was silent the entire ride. He spent most

of it with his eyes shut. Sleeping, or meditating, or lost in prayer, didn't matter much to me. My brain was churning with how I was going to track down Gary DeBarthe in Colorado and get Loredana out of her illegal house arrest.

The morning air was cool and sharp, without a hint of humidity. It was the perfect day for relaxing on a beach, like the dozens of people with the same idea that our bus had passed or hiking through the forest trails on the other side of the highway.

It even softened the supermax prison.

Bulwark State was tucked back in the trees, away from the residential neighborhoods and the suburbs. Chain link fences and razor wire kept hundreds of the worst and most violent offenders permanently locked up. Had a real Stalag Luft feel to it—concrete, massive, forbidding.

Getting in to see people was next to impossible. Especially for someone like Winston, who was being held indefinitely on pending charges of domestic terrorism. What else were they going to charge him with? He was cut off from all contact with the outside world—no visitors, no phone calls, no email or social media or even messenger pigeon.

However, having a Procyon badge was like finding the magic key in a video game. Of course, there was another reason I didn't have any trouble as a visitor.

He'd listed me as a "Next of Kin."

The guard let me into a small room. Like the rest of the place, the walls were bare concrete and the floor, shiny white tile. I sat in front of a window. There was a silver speaker box below the window, like you might see at a bank teller's drive-up.

Two guards brought Winston Yen in the other side.

He was thinner than I remembered. Still stocky, yeah, but the orange jumpsuit hung off him, as if they hadn't been able to find the guy's size. The normally clean-shaven Winston was well on his way to achieving full beard, and the dark roots were showing through bleach blond hair dye.

Winston smiled, thin-lipped, when he saw me. I froze up. Except I wasn't cold. Anger took over. My heart thudded. Memories of the North Beach Battle flashed through my head. Wrenching sounds. Booming gunfire. Unrelenting shrieks of astral fiends. Strange smells, too, like the stink of smoke and the sickly stench of slain monsters.

We sat without speaking until the guards left. "Mercury." His voice was scratchy, though the English accent was clear as ever. "Charmed to have you here."

"Wish I could say the same."

"To what do I owe the pleasure of a visit? It's rare for me to see a friendly face. Or any other face, for that matter. Have you ever seen the inside of a supermax cell?"

I glared at him. Really hadn't anticipated this reaction. I guess a part of me had wished I could have talked to him like we were still buddies, Winston in charge of Tracking, me the one sent out to destroy astral fiends. We'd been a good team.

Until he and his wife had tried to import monsters here permanently.

"It's a cement box." Winston continued as if he didn't notice me trying to melt through the glass wall between us with my angry stare. "The walls. The bed. The shelf. The stool. None of which move, of course. Well, the walls *shouldn't* move. That would make for a poor prison, don't you think? They lock me behind a metal door that could fend off the most determined band of soldiers, with bars behind that, and all the solace I receive is a four-inch slit for a window."

"Let's assume I don't care, and you answer my question," I snapped. "Why did Gary DeBarthe come to see you?"

"Ah, yes. Gary. A rather cynical fellow, yet one on whom I could always rely when it came to Tracking operations. His skills with Procyon's tachyon detection technology were unparalleled. It seems he couldn't simply stand down from his role after I was … detained. The poor git took it upon himself to continue the work I'd overseen. Admirable, really, even though the way to the Interstice was sealed. Thanks to you."

"Thanks to me."

He must have expected some kind of rebuttal, like I was gonna argue with him about having saved the world, because Winston blinked, his smile static. "Ah. Yes."

"Gary."

"Oh, as I was saying, poor Gary noticed anomalies. Not new rips, mind, but—"

"Breaches in space, linking two points. Yeah, I know. Our new people cracked that one, thanks to the goons at Syndax."

Winston had been decent at poker. The emotionless mask he slapped on now reminded me. "I'm sure I don't understand."

"We know Syndax took Gary."

"It's fascinating to me that you're wound so tightly, Mercury, when you're outside these walls enjoying freedom and I'm incarcerated." Winston rested his elbows on the counter. "Perhaps you misunderstand your role in what's to come. Gary knew. The astral fiends will return. It is only a matter of time. This reprieve from their incursions is temporary. And that is why he came to me. You see, he'd tracked the new creation's progress to San Camillo. He realized the danger it held—as well as the promise."

I remembered what Moira had said about her ex-husband's worries, and the text of his e-mail warning to her. "Seriously doubt he was looking forward to it. Gary came to you because he thought you'd have a solution. But you already knew about it, didn't you? Because you're in league with these soldiers from Syndax."

"Whatever would give you that idea?"

I held up my phone, with a zoomed-in image of a tattoo front and center. "The guys who took him had these stamped on their arms."

Winston's eyes widened. "Ah. So they do. How lovely to see the blade again, this side of the Interstice."

"Why did they take Gary? Was it to keep him quiet, so he couldn't alert us to the fiend-hound?"

"Fiend-hound? You know, I quite like that name." Winston shook his head. "Gary is far more important than simply as a man who will sound the alarm. He'll serve their purposes nicely."

"I need specifics, Winston."

"I'm not inclined to share, Mercury."

I slapped my hand against the counter. "You listen to me! I've had enough of people's secrets, all the stuff they've decided isn't important for me to know."

"No, you've never been comfortable handling classified information, have you? Especially when it's been kept from you for important reasons." Winston tapped the glass. "Take your land of origin. Had you not found out that fact, things might have turned out differently. This wretched world would be much cleaner, had we succeeded in letting the astral fiends loose. I don't think we knew what to expect upon further examination of the samples—the 'bits,' as you call them. But events often follow the call of destiny."

"Your crazy plan to mutate an animal isn't destiny. It's a really bad idea."

"It would be, yes, if that had been the goal. Quarantine failed. How could it ever be fully successful, when dealing with entities that can move across dimensions and bridge space-time? The mere fact that it became something more fearsome, more wondrous than even an astral fiend is further proof we were meant to succeed."

"Don't count on it," I said. "Your boys have crossed one line too many. San Camillo PD is onto them, and so's Procyon. I'll find Gary and clean up your mess."

"And then what?" Winston sneered. "You've lost your way, Mercury. You don't have a purpose. Without the astral fiends, what good are you? Oh, I've read the blogs and seen the videos. Skulking about the streets, hitting the same lowlifes I wanted to obliterate forever. It's pathetic."

"What's pathetic is me believing I needed to bother talking to you. But you've been pretty helpful."

"Why shouldn't I? You must know where to find Gary, because you've never asked me where he's being held. And I would never hide the fact from you. You're meant to find him, Mercury, because you're meant to go to Syndax. They need you. They need the pulsar stave. And they need your friend."

Whatever I thought Winston was going to say, that wasn't it. "What friend?"

Winston closed his eyes. "The older man waiting for you in the coffee shop. He seems so lost, and yet so at peace. This isn't his home. He doesn't know it, yet, but he's vital to the return of all we've hoped for. He's such a brave soul. That bravery will cost you all dearly."

He opened his eyes and leaned back in his chair. As much as I hated his guts, my heart twisted to see him so pallid. Run down. This wasn't the boisterous, cheery Winston I'd worked with for years. This was a ruined man, haunted by his wife and the conspiracy they'd shared.

And somehow, he knew about Skipper.

I pushed away from the desk and headed for the door.

"Mercury?" Winston called. "Don't be upset. You'll find all the answers you need at Syndax. Unless you're happy in your ignorance. Remember that."

"You know what I'm gonna remember? The failure of your dead wife's grand plan to destroy everyone on Earth. What'd she say? Seven generations of effort, and I flushed it."

"Mari is not dead. She's merely suffered a setback." Winston closed his eyes again. "And by the by, she says 'Hello.'"

It was a long walk from the prison to the strip malls where the bus let us off. My legs were aching by the time I got back. I gave every shiny Subaru that passed by a dirty look.

Procyon owed me a new car.

Skipper wasn't at the bus stop. He wasn't in any of the restaurants I walked by, either—Thai, Mexican, Italian. He wasn't in the massage parlor, either. And that was a guy who could use one.

There was a coffee shop, though.

I stood outside the window for a good twenty seconds. There was a crowd inside, lined up and seated in comfy chairs. Skipper was by himself, ensconced in a corner. He was moving pieces around on a chess board. He saw me and nodded.

I waited for him to exit. "Mercury," he said. "How was your conversation?"

"I found out more than I thought I would, but not enough. Winston's not all there."

Skipper cocked an eyebrow.

"He wants us to go to Syndax, which either means that's right where we need to be, or else it's a very bad idea. Probably both."

"We do, however, have someone else we can question."

I socked him playfully in the shoulder. "Now you're thinking."

The soldier in Procyon's recovery room was awake. Badly bruised, his face puffy and purple, but awake. His bed was angled so he could be upright. security hadn't taken any shortcuts when it came to that aspect—there was a strap across his chest, and both his wrists and ankles were restrained. He was a young, thickset black man with a thin layer of curly hair.

His eyes were deep brown, instead of the purple and black I'd expected.

"I'm against this." Dr. Arne waited at the door. "We're not supposed to keep people as prisoners. This isn't the jail, and we're not police."

"Duly noted, Doctor." Alvarez was with him. Keeping him, I hoped, from interfering. "We have to find out all we can about the Syndax property. Ms. Stojan can ascertain details of a floor plan from city records in Rampart, but we know nothing else—and our enemies have already shown they can strip a building down to the drywall if they need to leave quickly."

"Don't worry," I said. "I'm not a fan of this part either. In fact, I'm new to it." And, I thought, it was ironic, given the last time I was anywhere near this room was when Procyon had my brother locked in it.

"You should know, then, that this man is experiencing withdrawal symptoms. He's a mess. I don't like the way his vitals are elevated." Arne folded his arms. "And if you're going to press him too hard—"

"A monster is in our enemies' possession," Alvarez snapped. "We need to know what Syndax has in mind for it. And despite my personal dislike for Mr. Hale, the board has decided he's the one to stop them."

Skipper stood behind the soldier, where the kid couldn't see him. "What would you have me do?"

"Hold him, so he doesn't get out of control." I willed the pulsar stave to life and separated the halves. I ran both ends over the soldier's chest, the energies sputtering across his shirt. "Listen, pal. You got caught. I have to imagine your bosses are disappointed with that. So, we'll make a deal: tell us everything we need to know about Syndax, about where Gary DeBarthe is being held in their facility, what this purple-eye thing is you guys have going on, and what the plan is with the fiend-hound. Do that, and we'll keep you in protective custody. Sound good?"

He glared at the ceiling.

I sighed. My stomach churned. "Not looking forward to this, but you're not giving me any choice."

I pressed the end of one half of the stave to his shoulder and sent a surge.

The soldier shouted, more out of surprise than pain,

I guessed, but then again, I'd never been shocked by my weapon. He hissed through his teeth.

"What were they doing to you that made you stronger?" I asked. "How were you able to stay in sync? And why'd your boss keep talking about 'we'?"

"We're stronger together," he said. "That's why we'll win."

"Doubt that. Twice now we've stopped you."

"We have the fiend-hound. Arkwright won't ..." He clenched his teeth.

"Arkwright." The name from Gary's email. "That's the boss? Is he the one you helped grab the pulsar stave for at the Saito fight?"

The kid pinched his eyes shut and clamped his mouth.

"That's not gonna work." I zapped him again.

He flinched, grimaced, but didn't talk.

I tried not to think about Teget and my grandfather, about Wilhelmina, and especially not about Ramos. About the spirit of heroism they'd instilled in me. I was supposed to be fighting for a greater good, whether I was slaying astral fiends or saving the people of San Camillo from their criminally inclined neighbors. This, though, was pure vigilantism. It didn't matter what the soldier had done. We were illegally detaining him, and I was using the pulsar stave as an implement of torture.

But you'd better believe I was desperate.

Beeps sounded from the other room. Arne was there, snarling something subdued at Alvarez. To which Alvarez just raised a hand, as if to silence Arne, and continued watching me.

It was one thing to have the boss approving of your job well done. It was another to have him sternly giving that approval while you were doing—this.

I pressed the business end of the stave under the kid's chin. The room stank of his sweat. "People have died because Arkwright—because *you*—messed with something that should have stayed destroyed, something that never should have been allowed refuge on Earth. Now, you're gonna tell me every last detail you know about the Syndax building and the people there, or you get to find out first-hand how the astral fiends felt when I cut their limbs off and stabbed them straight to hell."

Before he got a chance to answer, I slashed with the other half of the stave. A blackened chunk of the bed's corner hit the floor.

CHAPTER TWENTY

The kid blabbed everything he knew.

Which, unfortunately, wasn't much.

All that gut-wrenching, Dr. Arne's yelling, and Skipper's silent admonition, for so little. Sure, we had an estimate of how many people were on-site at Syndax, and we knew where the labs inside the building were, but the kid wasn't high enough in their organization to know the master plan.

He did know some of why he was acting like he'd come down off the biggest drug high every.

"We inject before every mission." He choked back tears. His nose ran. "I ... I didn't know who I was after the first time, but each one got easier, except for when it wore off. Then I wasn't strong anymore and ...I couldn't hear them. The others. We could hear each other, knew what we were doing and saying and thinking."

Arne had one of the used syringes analyzed, after the soldier's gear had been thoroughly searched. The guy got quiet, like he was going to take a knee and touch up with holy water before entering a church's sanctuary. "There's traces of the same biological material that makes up an astral fiend. It shares aspects of the genetic code from the fiend-hound, though it's not as corrupted. There's way too little of it to manifest as a creature, though, and it's kept in a suspension that dissolves upon contact with the human bloodstream."

"Unbelievable," Alvarez said. "They've made themselves, what, a steroid? Using the DNA of astral fiends?"

"That's a crude way to describe something elegant, but, yeah, it's not a bad way to put it." Arne shook his head. "I'll need to run more tests to be sure."

Alvarez turned to me. "You'll depart immediately and infiltrate the Syndax building in Rampart. There's a benefit gala at our new office—"

"The new Procyon office, yeah, I know." I crossed my arms. "Loredana told me. I think she was planning to go before, you know, you locked her up."

"We've done no such thing. She's a highly valued member of our team, however, her repeated disobedience necessitated her temporary sabbatical. Since she is so highly placed, we can't afford her leaking information."

"Loredana would never spill Procyon's secrets."

"I believe you, especially since we have cut off all her communications. She needs time to clear her head. You, therefore, are in charge of this operation. I'm authorized to give you whatever support you need."

I glanced at Skipper. "He comes with me."

"Absolutely not." Alvarez pointed. "That man has no business in our dealings. He's not even of this world!"

"Careful how you talk about people who aren't from around here, Alvarez. Skipper comes with me—"

"I said you get support, not whatever you want." Alvarez

straightened his tie. "Mr. ... Skipper's weapons have been confiscated. Escort him to the police and tell Lieutenant Ramos this man needs to be remanded to a shelter until such time as his identity can be confirmed."

"Don't be an idiot!" I snapped. "If you want to get rid of him you could ..."

Hang on. Alvarez hadn't said anything about the portal we'd found in Cavill Cemetery. Maybe Loredana and Liz had kept that from him.

Skipper touched my shoulder. "Let's not quarrel. I will submit to your commander's wisdom."

"Finally. Someone who does." Alvarez's phone buzzed. He checked the incoming call, then aimed the device at me, like one of those obnoxious business people who wielded tech the way Skipper held a hatchet. "Keep me updated and put summaries in my inbox every few hours."

I glared at him as he left. "I'll put the stave in his inbox if he doesn't watch it. Come on. Let's go."

All I wanted to do was sleep. That luxury, unfortunately, would have to wait.

Isaiah ducked his head out of his apartment. "Hey, Mark."

"Hey, Isaiah."

"Boy, you look all sorts of beat up. What'd you do, get into a fight with the old lady?"

"Nah, she's fine. How'd your talk with the super go?"

He waved his hand through the space in front of him. "Got the AC fixed. Cooler than my icebox in this joint. You had a visitor, though. Cop."

I winced. Yeah, there was a sticky note on my door. The

annoyingly perfect penmanship made its intent clear: *Stay here. -Ramos*

Great.

"See you 'round, kid. Stay out of trouble." Isaiah shut his door.

Sure, Isaiah. I think I was getting better at getting into it than staying clear.

The couch was an island of comfort in the midst of the storm of trouble. I kicked back, and at that moment, didn't care if the entire city blew up. I'd stay put, butt glued to the cushions, shoes off.

Except Loredana needed my help. And Syndax wasn't gonna stop itself from playing with extradimensional forces.

"Am I to be turned over to your police?" Skipper frowned. "I'm not familiar with the laws here but I can see none I've broken."

"It's more the fact that you don't exist, and don't have an identification." I rubbed my brow. Headache. "That bothers people. I'm not about to hand you to them, so don't sweat it."

"I apologize if I've become a liability. Other than the presence of that creature, calling to me in the night, I cannot find a purpose for my actions—or my sojourn here."

His mention of purpose led me back to Winston's eerie comments. "Hey, don't apologize. You saved my life plenty and prevented more bloodshed. Granted, it was with bloodshed on your part, but things would have gotten out of hand without a partner at my side. Last time I had that kind of help was from my brother."

"He's not here?"

"He's not from our world. Or, this world. He's—a long way away, and I don't know how to get back to him. Doing so could put San Camillo in danger again."

Skipper sat on the couch's arm. "You're concerned he may forget you. Don't be. No matter how long the journey, or great the distance, a family's bond remains."

"Thanks for that, Doctor Phil." I didn't want to admit how badly my throat had tightened up with that assurance. Man, what a sap I was becoming.

He looked to the window. Sun caught his features, and for a moment, I could believe he'd been on a boat somewhere—on an alien sea, a churning ocean that no one in San Camillo or on this Earth had seen. His steadfastness must have calmed his crew in the worst tempest, as solid as he was right now. Just having him to talk to got me focused, helped me climb up out of the muck of self-pity I kept sliding into.

My door opened. Ramos stormed in.

"Um, sure, come on in. Make yourself at home." If that was bitterly sarcastic, good. I was tired of people shoving their way around my life. Last person I needed it from was Ramos.

"What do you think you're doing?" Ramos stood in front of me, hands on his hips. The posture made me more aware than ever of the badge gleaming on his belt and the gun holstered opposite. "Where is he?"

I pointed at Skipper.

"Not him. Though he'd better be prepared to come downtown and answer questions. I'm talking about the soldier, Mercury."

"Thought you had a few of them in custody."

Ramos fumbled with his phone and pushed it under my nose. The face on it belonged to a dead man—pale, eyes rolled back, white foam squeezed between clenched teeth.

Judging by the gray fatigues and the tattoo on one shoulder, visible where a sleeve was ripped away, he was one of the soldiers from last night's fight.

"We had this man for questioning. He killed himself. Suicide pill." Ramos shoved his phone into a pocket. "Where have you been? I've been messaging you all day."

"Had my phone off. Skipper and I went on a road trip up the coast. I had to talk with Winston and figure out what was driving these guys to steal a fiend-hound."

"You're unfocused and getting sloppy. While you've been off playing interrogator, we've seen an uptick in reports of walking dead. This is escalating, Mercury. I have panic rising in my streets. The captain wants me to bring you and Skipper in, because the commissioner is leaning hard."

"How hard?"

"This isn't a joke!" Ramos snapped. "This isn't something you can make fun of, swing the pulsar stave a couple times, and go back to slinging sarcasm! The consequences of your actions are rippling across San Camillo. Have you seen the videos? It's getting harder to conceal the truth from people."

I pushed up off the couch. "So don't! Tell everyone the truth. They're not idiots, Ramos. People know what they saw, and all the official talk of hallucinations doesn't cover that up. It doesn't convince people they're crazy. I can't spend my time worrying about who sees my weapon or my face! If you're not gonna be my partner on this, no problem. I've got a new one."

Ramos flicked a glance at Skipper. The latter had turned from the window, and was sizing both of us up—estimating, I guess, which one was gonna win this argument. "I'm not blaming you for what's happening," Ramos said, his tone softer. "But who else is going to challenge the darkness?

This isn't in SCPD's purview. You've tackled worse—*we've* tackled worse. I'm worried that you're losing your way."

"You shouldn't. I knew exactly what I was doing."

Apparently, my lie convinced exactly no one in the room. Ramos rolled his eyes. "Keep telling yourself that and you'll get killed. I'd rather that didn't happen. Listen. Contact your superiors and get them to turn the soldier over to me. That way I don't have to explain why a supposedly civilian nonprofit foundation is taking prisoners. We can run the questioning from here."

I pulled out my phone and gave him Alvarez's direct number. That ought to enrage Alvarez. See, Mercury? Day was getting better already. "Thanks for stopping by, Ramos. I mean it. Even if you are a pain."

Ramos smirked. "It's difficult to be anything but when paired with the likes of you, Mercury. Whatever you have coming next, I hope it's effective."

"Tell you what—I'll leave you out of my plans, and you won't have to worry about whether I'm in danger or, perhaps, planning to break a bunch of laws."

"Let's do that." He shook my hand. "We'll be praying for you."

I didn't ask who was doing the praying, but I was happy with it, nonetheless. Ramos had spoken of *la paz*. I could use peace with me right about now, wherever it came from—and I guessed that Ramos had access to the most reliable kind there was.

"If we are to take the next steps," Skipper said, "I have a suggestion."

"Go for it."

"Your commanders confiscated my weaponry. I'll need something fast and flexible, yet strong." He smiled. "I don't

213

suppose I can borrow one from a similar shop from which I liberated the hatchet that proved so useful?"

"Not without drawing a whole lot of attention we don't want." Then I grinned. "But I got a better idea."

I dialed Liz.

Confession time: I didn't have much of a plan.

Loredana's home was in the northeast section of San Camillo, dubbed Tabb Terrace. Don't know why, because there wasn't a single terrace or anything terrace-like about the landscape, but Ramos once told me the developers picked the name because it sounded fancy and, thus, could attract big spenders. Plenty of condos were packed into four blocks by ten, with Sheridan bounding the north edge and Campos, the south. The rows of identical white and cream-colored buildings were broken up only by the infrequent two- and three-story houses that probably were sixty years old.

Skipper and I hopped off the bus at the stop a couple blocks over. That made it easier to spot the silver SUV and Taurus sedan parked on the opposite side of East Sheridan, across from 13311. There was a silhouette in each one—tinted windows, so I couldn't make out who. Best bet? More guys were probably upstairs, inside the condo.

"Second floor, Unit C." I kept a leisurely pace, trying to fly casual, as Han Solo would recommend. I was grateful for the pulsar stave's holster, which let me beat the heat without a jacket and hide the weapon until it was needed.

Skipper didn't have the same advantage. I'd loaned him a windbreaker, which lost all its bagginess when applied to his robust frame, but it offered decent concealment. The hilt of his new toy protruded just enough he had to flip the collar up. And he still had on that flannel shirt, so he looked like a lumberjack trying to play tourist.

"How are you not sweating to death?" I asked.

"I feel quite cool most of the time." Skipper frowned. "Freezing, at others, as if I've fallen into icy waters."

I nodded. Poor circulation, maybe. I stopped a couple doors down from 13311 East Sheridan.

"What is it?" Skipper scanned the street. "Has the beast returned?"

"No. I'm ... having second thoughts. And third through fifth after those."

"Doubts assail you."

"Yeah, I figure everyone who's about to break a friend out of solitary confinement has those." I blew out a breath. "This used to be a lot simpler. As chaotic as my life was when I faced off against monsters, there was a routine. I hang around, I get the call, I kill the beast, I start all over again. Now nothing's stable. Nothing's reliable."

"Except for the people in whom you put your greatest trust, like the constable, Ramos. And Lady Lark."

"They're as constant as I can hope for." I look up at him. "You don't have to do this, you know. There's no monsters around."

"You've shown me greater kindness than anyone I've encountered in this strange world. I know not why I've traveled here, but if you are the one fated with destroying the evil things, then I will do my best to lend my blade. The Most High would not task me with anything less."

"You sound like you should talk with Ramos more often." I nodded. "Thanks for that. Finding a helping hand in this part of the work—out on the streets, I mean—isn't something I could request on Upcycle."

He gave me that quizzical expression he seemed fond of, by which I mean, he probably had no clue what I was talking about. But that was okay. He had my back. I was convinced.

Which was good, because we were going to need that kind of support.

I waited until a mother with twin toddlers in a stroller approached the door to 13311. Bingo. She was petite, and her kids' ride was bigger than her. She still managed to get both kids out and wrestle it partway up the steps.

"Ma'am, can I give you a hand with that?" I grabbed the stroller bar and tugged.

"Oh! Thanks, that'd be great." She smiled at me, but the smile froze up when Skipper approached. "Both of you."

"We'd be delighted to lend you our assistance." Skipper half-bowed.

Right then, the boys attempted to escape, heading for the curb. The mom hollered at them, that simple, sharp, "*Boys!*" that cracked like gunfire. They paused, momentarily weighing the consequences of free exploration versus inevitable punishment, until Skipper scooped them up, one in either arm. They squirmed, but Skipper spun them a couple times, until they were giggling hysterically.

If the Procyon guys were paying attention, they didn't care, and sure didn't leave their cars.

"I appreciate the help." Mom and I pulled the stroller into the hall. She retrieved the boys from Skipper. "They're not usually so comfortable with strangers! Do you have children?"

"I have." Skipper's expression brightened. "Yes, I believe I do."

The mom looked to me, like she was about to ask another question, but I was already herding Skipper down the hall.

"You're welcome. Glad to be of service. No charge!"

Let her puzzle that one.

Up the flight of stairs at the end of the hall, and we faced two Procyon guys standing about, drinking coffee. Man. Wherever they found their brew, it was just the right combo to give me pause—as in, I'd rather ask for a sip than spill it. Part of me wanted to warn them, so they could set it down and not lose a drop. "Hey, guys."

They looked up. Garvey the first one to frown. "Mr. Hale? I wasn't notified Ms. Lark was getting visitors."

"Not visitors, Garvey. She's getting *out*." I drew the pulsar stave and ignited it. Its energies crackled in the silent hall. "Don't touch your phones. Let's make this easy. Open the door."

Garvey's partner let one hand dip to his belt, where a phone was protruding from his pocket—not a gun, thankfully.

There was a flurry of movement to my right, and a *swish* through the air. Metal shone in the midday light coming through the window behind them. I could see Garvey's reflection in the blade, gaping.

Skipper brandished a sword. I'd begged Liz to loan us the full-steel falchion from her living room. How he'd drawn the weapon without gouging the hallway walls, I have no idea, but there it was, the angled tip hovering inches from the guy's throat.

"Stand aside, and let her go," he murmured. "I have no desire to harm either of you."

Garvey's hand was on his belt, near his gun, but I really hoped he wouldn't do anything stupid. He stared at me.

I shrugged. "Hey, he's the one with the sword."

CHAPTER
TWENTY-ONE

Nobody shot at us. That was a win. Whether Garvey and his pal considered it a bonus, too, I didn't really care. I thought they were more worried about whether Skipper was going to stab them.

"So, look, he's not going to stab you," I said. "Is anyone else in there?"

Garvey's nostrils flared. I mean, that sounds stereotypical, but they really went quadruple wide, so big I could have poked the pulsar stave up either one. Which I doubt he would have liked. "One man. Seated in the vestibule."

"Okay. Give him the secret knock or whatever you do to let him know things are copacetic out here."

"They're what?"

"Copacetic. Hunky-dory. Alright. Groovy. Whatever!" I gestured with the stave.

Garvey glowered at me, but his eyes kept training on Skipper's sword—and I had to admit, he was intimidating, as ridiculous as his outfit seemed. Garvey walked around his security partner and knocked on the door. "Travers. It's me."

I made sure I was behind Garvey, standing to the right

of the door, where Travers wouldn't see me. Locks clicked, and it opened. "What's the deal, sir? Sounded like you had a debate club going—"

He broke off in a hiss of indrawn breath. Oh, right. I forgot he could see Skipper's sword as a straight silver line behind Garvey's back. So much for the element of surprise.

See? I should have stuck to fighting monsters.

Whatever. I pushed by Garvey and jumped at the door, kicking off at a sharp angle that ricocheted me into the vestibule of Loredana's condo.

Travers was a tall, athletic young guy, probably my age. If he'd still been in high school or even college, I wouldn't have been surprised to see him in a varsity football jacket. With his Procyon security employment, he had the black polo shirt and pants uniform.

He also had a gun and a Taser—and apparently, the wherewithal to assume I wasn't a lethal threat. His hand went from the pistol to the Taser in the couple seconds it took me to slam into his chest, his shoes squeaking on the tile floor.

The Taser came up, sparks crackling from the prongs on the business end. Funny. I had a Taser of my own. I wrenched his grip aside, just in time for the wires to shoot out left of my shoulder. There was a dull *thunk* where they hit the wall and the angry crackle of a couple thousand volts coursing into what Travers had hoped was my chest, I assume.

He dropped the Taser and punched, but I was already underneath, delivering a blow to his solar plexus that was bad enough on its own. Mine was augmented by the pulsar stave's energy, so it threw him out of the vestibule, into the living room, and onto a couch.

I stalked after him, flipping half the stave over in my

hand. "Hands off the gun."

"Mercury." It wasn't an astonished question, or an incredulous exclamation. Loredana said my name with that curious combination of relief and "What took you so long?" that I'd come to adore.

"Hey. How's it going?" I grabbed Travers by the shoulder and rolled him over, so he was face down in the red upholstery. "Sorry about this, man. No hard feelings."

A tap to the base of his skull rendered Travers insensate.

Loredana was seated at the bar counter separating the kitchen from the living room. She was wearing a black T-shirt that featured a collage of nearly every actor who'd played Doctor Who—don't ask me the names—and jeans. How many of those fan shirts did she own? Anyway, with red hair and blue eyes, those colors clashed against an apartment that was six shades of white and cream, the furniture the only accents. Gorgeous watercolor paintings hung at intervals between tall windows. Each one depicted a lush forest. Men on horseback, wearing long coats, pursued a fox in the largest.

She caught me staring and folded the print issue of the *Bayside Breeze* she'd been reading. "My great-grandfather, on the hunt, as painted by my uncle. I find it reminds me of the happier aspects of home and serves as a reminder of the work we do for Procyon. As hunters."

"If you say so." I grinned. "Got a place I can stash our guests?"

"Of course. Bring them in, don't be rude." She smiled back.

Skipper guided Garvey and his disgruntled sidekick at the point of his sword. He bowed and offered up a smile of his own that, while not as cocky as I figured mine looked, was bold and confident and made me ready to launch myself at an astral fiend with his guy guarding my side. "Lady Lark. I trust you're well."

"Quite." Loredana rummaged through a drawer under the counter. "Ah. Here we go."

A silver roll flew toward me. I speared it, ring-toss style, on the stave. Duct tape. "Garvey, you carry zip ties, right?"

Garvey muttered something.

"Sorry, all those astral fiend shrieks and gunshots messed up my hearing." I tore off a strip of duct tape. "Try again."

"Left rear pocket," he said. "And it's probably the Aerosmith, Mr. Hale."

"Won't argue that." I gave the duct tape to Skipper. "Batten down the hatches."

He taped their mouths shut while I bound their wrists with Garvey's handy-dandy zip ties. I made sure to pocket Garvey's phone, which had a bunch of recent calls made to and received from various numbers, all within the last half hour. Travers, who was drooling peacefully onto Loredana's couch, required some trussing, and we got his ankles strapped, too.

"I have a guest room, back there." Loredana pointed to a hall that branched out of the living room. "It locks."

"I won't ask why, but great. Window?"

"Yes, but if you tie their ankles like you did Mr. Travers' ..."

"Good point."

The three of us got our security entourage stashed in what must have been Loredana's office. Very old school—wooden rolltop desk, lots of stationery, a printer, corkboard. No file cabinet. A divider that held folders was empty, and it looked like cards had been torn from push pins in the cork board. And there was a rectangular blank space on the desk.

Loredana locked the door and shoved the keys in her pocket. "Well. That should suffice." She turned to me, and started to say something, but closed her mouth. She brushed hair from across her eyes. "I'm sorry for all this. I wanted to thank you—"

I kissed her.

She returned the gesture, and the sentiment. I backed against the wall, perfectly content to stay there, embracing her, until the world fixed itself and we could, as she'd be the first to put it, go on our merry way.

Only Skipper's oh-so-subtle clearing of his throat from living room brought me back to the massive pain that was reality. He had a sly smile, as if he was trying his best to be a disapproving parent but failing. "As joyful a reunion as this is, Mercury, it's best we consider how to deal with the security men waiting in the vehicles outside."

"Yeah. I'd been thinking about that." I winked at Loredana. "Not, you know, the whole time."

She elbowed me. "I don't suppose you've procured a new car since yours was destroyed last night?"

"Way to bring up a sore subject. Nope, no new car for me. But yours is parked around here, somewhere, isn't it?"

"It is, but as you imagined, one of the first things they did was confiscate the keys."

"Ah. That's a problem." I glanced at Skipper. "How do you feel about theft."

He frowned.

"Yeah, that's what I thought." I shrugged. "Okay, I don't suppose you know how to hotwire a starter."

Loredana shook her head.

"Okay. So, we need a car with keys. Sorry, Skipper, we're

gonna have to put your principles to the test. Come on."

"One moment." Loredana disappeared into the hall. I heard something bang against furniture, then she emerged with a bulging messenger bag and a suitcase.

"You're—planning a road trip?"

"To Rampart, as we discussed." She cocked an eyebrow. "Surely that's our destination."

"Well, yeah, Skipper and I were gonna bust in there and—"

"Absolutely not. We're doing this together. That's the way we've always worked. I'm not about to upset the status quo. If you are heading into harm's way, without proper support, you'll die, and ... I can't allow that, either."

Always nice to hear. "Do we have a way to keep in touch with Liz?"

"Of course. I took the liberty of establishing clandestine communications through my personal phone. Elizabeth is ... quite proficient in such methods."

"Good deal. Okay, we'd better swing by my apartment so I can get some stuff. Like the tracker. And a change of clothes."

"We'll need to get you new formal attire, as well, since your last was ruined when our date suffered an interruption." Loredana removed her revolver from her purse, loaded it, then slung the purse over her shoulder. She took her luggage to the door, sunglasses perched atop fiery hair, like she was headed to a beach.

I checked the hall and beckoned for Skipper to join us. I had Garvey's phone in hand. "Hey, look, if we're gonna grab this ride, I need a way to sneak up on them."

"I'll draw their attention, since I'm unfamiliar with how to helm one of those vehicles."

"A distraction would be great. What do you have in mind?"

Skipper patted the hilt tucked in his collar. "Something memorable, Mercury, don't despair."

My man. "Whatever car we grab is gonna need to be gassed up, and we'd better hope we miss traffic between here and Rampart."

Loredana shook her head. "It only needs to get us to the airport. Once we take off, you can brief me on everything you found out from our captive soldier."

"And Winston." I blinked. "Hang on sec. Airport?"

"Oh, yes," she said. "I have an airplane."

Skipper's distraction, it turned out, was rudimentary, but more than effective. He waded out the front door, sauntered into the middle of traffic, and drew his sword.

The two security men scrambled from their vehicles, guns drawn, shouting commands. They were young, too, like Travers. Made me wonder how many new people Procyon had brought in during the reorganization. They sure didn't look familiar—a short Latino and a tall, spindly white kid with blond hair and goatee.

"Drop the weapon, sir!" I thought his voice was gonna crack. "Put the sword down and your hands up!"

"Relinquish your firearms and I'll not remove them myself." He swung the sword as he walked, like he was spinning an umbrella, except this was a couple feet of tempered steel. Yeah, Liz had bought the real deal, not some flimsy knock-off.

The stopped cars created the perfect barrier between the showdown and me as I skulked across the street, Loredana crouching behind me. Sure, we didn't look like crack spies, what with Loredana dragging a suitcase that grumbled and clattered across the asphalt. But since everyone was busy gawking at Skipper and taking pictures with their phones, I didn't care, because they weren't watching us.

I chose the SUV, because it was nearest and because it had more power under the hood. Downside? It had their logo etched on the side. Can't be picky when you're on the run, I guess.

And the newbie left his keys in the ignition, because really, when a guy with a sword challenges you to a fight, the last thing on your mind is whether or not someone's going to drive off with the company truck.

"We have only five minutes before Procyon realizes something is amiss." Loredana slid into the passenger seat and shut the door. "I suggest we move quickly."

"I suggest you're right." I started the engine. "Hang on."

I steered into traffic, scraping the left bumper against a compact car. Driving a giant SUV that fast out of the gate was crazier than I was used to, especially with the V8 growling under the hood.

Skipper's reactions were up to the job. He swung his sword at the Latino, who dodged what looked to me like a sluggish swipe. Skipper ran at our approaching truck, planted his foot on the bumper and stepped up onto the hood.

"Go!" he shouted.

I popped the truck into reverse and jammed the accelerator. We hurtled to the curb, mashing a bike rack and its two occupants. So much for rideshare.

The newbie security officer spun around and aimed at us. We locked gazes for a moment, as I shifted back into

Drive. I pictured him pulling the trigger, shooting the truck full of holes—killing me and Loredana and Skipper—and I wondered whether Procyon paid extra for reinforced glass.

He hesitated.

I stomped on the pedal.

The truck roared ahead, and I swerved at the last moment, not wanting a dead Procyon guy's blood on my hands—not when other innocent people were already dead because I wasn't good enough. The officer dove for cover.

Skipper slammed onto the roof.

I drove like a maniac.

Loredana lowered the rear right passenger window. "For heaven's sake, slow down so he can get inside!"

I skidded us around an intersection. Came three feet from wiping out an ice cream truck, which, even if it had been unoccupied, would have been a tragedy. "You said we needed to hurry! This is me hurrying!"

"Haste will do us no good if you kill our allies!"

Boots poked through the windows, blocking the rushing air. The rest of Skipper followed soon after, with a grunt.

"Happy now?" I found a rare empty lane and let the SUV tear down the street.

"I trusted you weren't going to let me fall over the edge." Skipper was gasping for air, his face pale. "Still, the prospect was terrifying."

"What, you're afraid of heights? Bad time to let me know."

"Eyes on the road, please." Loredana turned in her seat. "Are you having flashes of memory?"

"Only confusing ones. Images that don't make sense—and yet, provide comfort." Skipper rested his sword on his knees. "I saw myself on an island, but I was up so high ..."

"A little less reminiscing and a little more navigation for your pilot," I muttered.

"Turn left at the next intersection and take Hanover in three blocks."

"Got it." I checked the rearview mirror. No one following. Not yet. But there was no way the police weren't going to get wind of this.

I just hoped we could stay off their radar for a while. "Call Ramos, while you're busy dialing. See if he can clear our way."

Loredana put her hand over the phone's receiver. "Are you certain you want his involvement?"

Did I want Ramos risking his job along with everything else he'd done for me? For the people he cared about? I thought about his family, and those police officers who'd been killed and absorbed by the corpse-fiends.

I also thought about how many risks everyone else was taking. Loredana, with the only career she'd ever known. Skipper, with his very existence, lost in a strange land.

Me. With everything.

"Call him," I said. "I'll apologize later."

We detoured only for a couple minutes, so I could jam clothing into a bag. Then it was off to McAllen Field. Loredana's plane was stored in a hangar at that small landing strip to the southeast, instead of at the sprawling international airport. Could we have taken a regional jet, to expedite the trip to Rampart? Sure. But what were the odds Procyon had tipped off local PD to watch for us when we tried to get through the ticket lines?

McAllen had twenty-one hangars arranged in neat rows,

at the head of twin tarmacs that crisscrossed in a gaping V. We pulled up behind one. I spotted a sporty dual-engine prop plane waiting as I handed Loredana one of her bags. "That looks cozy. Kinda slow."

"Charming, yes, but not mine." She led the way to the front of the hangar.

I should have known a woman like Loredana traveled in style.

Her aircraft was one I'd seen featured in an aviation history magazine. What? I read things. Anyway, it was a Cirrus Vision Jet, a sleek, hot rod of a passenger plane with a V-shaped tail and a turbofan jet on its back. The thing looked ready to jump off the ground, and sounded equally prepared, I realized, because the engine was running.

A young woman in coveralls stained with grease tipped her cap and helped Loredana load baggage into a small compartment. "She's all set, Ms. Lark! Anything else I can do for you?"

"Simply provide your customary discretion." Loredana shook the woman's hand. There were folded bills pressed between their palms.

Then she shouted over the howling engine, "Well, gentlemen? Shall we?"

CHAPTER
TWENTY-TWO

I thought I'd be climbing into a coffin, but Loredana's jet was roomier than any car I'd ever owned. Smelled new, too. I felt like I was sliding into the black leather seats of a Jaguar, or a Mercedes. Not that either had ever graced my parking spot, but I'd test driven a few.

It wasn't an X-wing or the Millennium Falcon, but I'd take it. Come to think of it, the plane was more like something Lando the gambler would own.

"I'm guessing you didn't buy this on Procyon's salary." I spoke the words into a microphone. We all wore headsets. Otherwise, we'd be hollering to be heard over the jet's constant roar.

"My family's influence, I suppose," Loredana said. "And some of their finances. But we have more pressing concerns."

"Right." I told her about my visit with Winston, and the subsequent interrogation of the soldier who—I hoped—was on his way to the police station instead of being illegally detained by Procyon. "It's all stored in my phone. Liz had the particulars compiled into a little light reading for me. But, yeah, the Syndax lab is crawling with their own security and technicians."

"Then it seems evening will be the prime opportunity for an incursion."

"Few people, quieter, darker. Sounds good to me."

"I trust the suit is operating within its parameters?"

"As far as I know." I jerked a thumb toward the rear of the cabin. "The pulsar stave's been behaving itself, so there's plenty of its power to siphon off. I'll need it, to stay off Syndax's figurative radar. Unless they have literal radar. Can you do that on an office building?"

Loredana smirked. "I'm certain that masking your body heat and the pulsar stave's tachyon emissions, in addition to camouflaging your physical appearance, should suffice."

"My new favorite word of the day, 'suffice.'"

"What of the method in which the stave was restored? The portal?"

"Well ..." I glanced at Skipper. He was staring out the window, and for a moment I thought he was super excited about flying in a lavish private jet, but then I realized he simply seemed ... content. Could've sworn he was getting teary-eyed on me. "I can't really tell you how it worked. Only that it did. When I used the stave at the portal, though, it changed. Expanded, I guess. Don't know what it was about to do because we were in a hurry and I didn't stick around to run more tests."

"The data Liz collected was quite instructive."

"You said last night it leads to another dimension, through a direct connection."

"Possibly."

"Maybe I should try to return Skipper that way."

"I'm hesitant to experiment with such a theory, Mercury, because of the risks involved. Even if it is his point of origin, we cannot be certain malevolent forces do not lie beyond."

"Fair enough. But we ought to get his take. He isn't a lab subject. This is a guy who may have a whole life wherever he came from. When this mess is cleaned up, I want to make it our priority to get him back there."

"Let's endeavor to do that."

I craned my neck. "Enjoying the view back there?"

I wasn't imagining it. Skipper *was* crying. "It's beautiful. It's as if I'm home again."

"So, you're a pilot?"

"Nothing about this craft seems familiar, but the sights out this window—the sensation of the deck beneath my feet—there's nothing as reassuring. I feel ... completely at ease, for the first time since I arrived in this place."

"Look, you probably heard us. We'll try to get you back there. Wherever there is."

"I'm thankful for that. This, though, is near perfect."

He wasn't kidding. Despite the engine noise, the view out the wide cockpit canopy was breathtaking. Lush valleys split dusty mountain ranges. Thick gray clouds swaddled forest fires. Lakes were shiny patches of blue, dotted with tiny splashes of color trailing white wakes. If I squinted, it could be me flying, sans aircraft. Made me daydream about the vigilante Drake City was dealing with on the other side of the country, the guy who could reportedly give Superman a run for his money. Jury was still out on whether or not it was an elaborate Internet hoax.

But seriously, with the horrors I'd faced and the journey I'd taken, who was I to question something remarkable that broke all the rules?

That was *me*, for crying out loud.

⌘ ⌘ ⌘

231

Three hours later, we touched down at Rampart Regional Airport, a big L of runways with single-story terminal of matching shape. It was on the northeast side of the city, across the Van River from the grid of streets. The city itself clung to the river on a pallid tan plain between a cluster of buttes and hills. Green circles of irrigated farmland were the only colorful relief.

Loredana got her plane stashed away while Skipper and I rented a car. It wasn't until we were settled in at a hotel downtown—which Loredana paid for in cash—that we dug into the plans.

She emptied the messenger bag's contents across one of the two queen-sized beds in the room I was sharing with Skipper. If there was something on a city planning record about Syndax's Rampart facility, Loredana had it printed out. We spread the documents out as far as we could, interspersing photos that were grainy but gave us an idea of the surrounding area as recently as a week ago.

"Syndax's facility is a four-story structure spread across four city blocks, off Federal Street. Entrance is permitted through a guard post at a gap in their fence. The fence itself bristles with motion detectors, infrared-equipped cameras, and—" She circled four spots, at the points of the compass, with red marker. "Tachyon detectors."

My turn to raise an eyebrow. "Seriously? Tachyon detectors? Since when does anyone need to worry about astral fiends robbing a place?"

"I don't think the fiends have changed their modus operandi that drastically. These are recent additions. Photos taken within the past month show them in place, whereas the original schematics from their archives indicate only the other security measures were in place."

"Awfully handy to get your hands on their schematics."

"They're not all public record, if that's what you're implying."

"Nice." I grinned. "Remind me not to let Liz anywhere near any electronic device I own."

"I hardly think that will prove an inconvenience." Loredana shuffled through the stack, until she produced a photo of a yawning garage port. "This is the entry for all supplies delivered to Syndax. It is behind the security checkpoints but is kept open at all hours of the day."

Skipper leaned over the images. "If your pictures are true, this is the destination of the van carrying the beast."

"I believe so."

I traced my finger across the building schematics. "Looks like it connects to an elevator shaft. Leads up to the fourth floor. What's the deal with this bunch of unmarked rooms on the fourth floor? There's only one way in or out, and it's set up like an airlock."

"That is what I surmised—a room between the lab and a quarantined space."

I ran a hand through my hair. Actually, there were a lot of those unmarked rooms. So many that what should be a targeted strike and retrieval was rapidly resembling a scavenger hunt. I hated scavenger hunts. "Our soldier-slash-prisoner wasn't clear on where Gary was being kept. What would be really nice is if we could pinpoint his location before I sneak in. Less chance of me getting shot or arrested."

"I agree. That's why I have Elizabeth attempting a breach of their building network this evening. If successful, we should have results while at the gala." Loredana smiled. "I trust you've not forgotten."

A second chance at our date? And the first chance to dance with Loredana in one of those gorgeous dresses I'd seen her in? I'd have to be brain dead and dismembered.

"I trust I have a role to play in this quest," Skipper said.

"Well, I don't have an extra superhero suit, so I can't get you inside invisibly." I shrugged. "You could pass for one of their soldiers, though, but the problem is, they can hear each other in their heads once they've taken the injection our captive talked about. No faking that."

"No, indeed." Skipper folded his hands. "There is another alternative."

He was watching Loredana. She didn't look up from the papers but nodded. "He is correct."

"Okay, that's great, but how about spelling it out for me."

"He can offer himself up to Syndax." Loredana grimaced. "He is, after all, the man who rescued you from the fiend-hound and killed several of their soldiers."

"I ... no. That's a stupid idea."

"It is not," Skipper said. "It is the only way I can gain entrance to their fortress. Captaining one of your vehicles is out of the question—I have no time to learn the mechanics. Nor can I employ stealth and subterfuge to get past their detection systems. But I can do what I am best at."

"Which is walk right up to them." I shook my head. "I don't like this."

"I don't either," Loredana said. "But the gala is in two hours. Slipping out from there, under cover of darkness, is the prime opportunity to infiltrate the facility."

"We have time to steal one of their vehicles, or get ahold of some soldier's clothes, or ..." I spun my hands, as if I could manufacture the best plan out of the dry, cold hotel air. "Something else."

"Don't be afraid." Skipper clapped me on the shoulder. "I'm not."

"I'm more concerned about you getting captured and dissected."

"Then you should do your best to prevent that from happening and make certain I don't fall into the hands of the enemy."

"Sure. With you walking right up to their front door." I rolled my eyes. "No pressure."

Procyon's newest offices were a block away from the Van River, and when I say newest, I mean you could still smell the paint. Three towers of white concrete were connected by a dome that housed a garden. The parking garage was in the middle of the towers, with spaces on every floor except the seventh. The windows were strips of gleaming glass that ran down the sides, top to bottom, reflecting the oranges and reds of sunset.

The dome served a purpose beyond looking awesome. It was a ballroom.

Okay, so I'm sure it had some other purpose, like for meetings or planning sessions or even for training. But given how much effort Procyon put into its actual charitable efforts—which simultaneously helped the community and formed the perfect cover for their extra-worldly activities— it made sense for it to be a posh gathering space. Panels retracted in the roof, like an observatory's, and there was a string quartet playing classical music at the far end. No Aerosmith for me, alas.

The only thing more surprising than the fancy ballroom

atop what should be an office building was the fact that we even made it through the door.

The security men took our IDs and scanned them at a computer. Red lights flashed.

Loredana's hand tightened on my arm.

"This could be a problem," I muttered. "Somebody might have put out an inter-office APB on your escape from your condo."

She kept a smile firmly in place, dazzling as ever, even with her nails digging into my sleeve. "Mr. Alvarez's reach is not universal throughout the foundation."

One of the guards touched an earpiece, as if he were listening to instructions. Five seconds later, he got them, and nodded. "You're cleared; however, the manager has asked that you not access any sensitive areas of the building."

"Understood. Thank you." She glanced at me as we entered with the other party-goers. "You see? Managers are granted considerable oversight when it comes to the individual offices. And if it so happens that an operative and his handler have support on the board, well, that helps all the more."

"So, you're saying, Alvarez doesn't have pals here."

"Alas, he does not."

"Yay for us."

Loredana had managed to find a charcoal gray suit for me in the short span since we arrived in Rampart. I'd look even more slick if not for the bruise on my jaw and the leftover scrape on my forehead.

Didn't really matter what I was wearing, though. My job was to be the box for the jewel. Loredana had on a strapless red dress, and enough diamonds around her neck to use as a blunt instrument against muggers. Her hair was pinned up.

I'd seen her in the same outfit a few times before, usually after she'd returned from one fancy soiree or another. She had on the same sapphire earrings she wore to our first date at Saito on Sky, too.

I couldn't help grinning at the sight of every guy's head turning as we walked by.

"The gala is supposed to last well beyond ten o'clock." Loredana sounded as if she were reading off a family restaurant's menu, not walking through the crowds of Rampart's upper crust. She fit right in among beautiful young women and elegant older ladies, escorted by guys ranging in age from, well, me to some who probably shouldn't be out of reach of a walker. "Once the speeches begin at 8, you'll have plenty of time to slip out and make your incursion."

"I got it." A waiter wove between the mingling, chattering guests, keeping a silver tray of twelve full champagne glasses expertly balanced. I twisted and snatched two from him as he executed the slightest pause, smiled, then sped along. "Here. Drinks on me."

"How generous." Loredana clinked her glass with mine. "To our evening together, once again."

"As long as there's no monster attacks planned, it's got a few hours of potential." I indicated the couples already swaying in the middle of the dome, those few brave ones who didn't mind showing off their dancing skills—or lack thereof. "While we're here, care to join me?"

"I didn't know you danced." She took my hand anyway.

I slugged back the champagne. Not classy, I know, but there was barely a thimbleful in the glass. "Sure. It's how I stay in shape to backflip over monsters. Come on, you never saw my amazing moves while I was sparring with the practice arms in the gym?"

"I certainly never observed you waltzing with them."

"It was more of a tango." I winked.

She set her champagne aside, equally drained, and I led her onto the dance floor. All cards on the table: I did dance, yeah, but it was more infrequent than the change of seasons and more of the minimum movement required in a nightclub. Spilled a drink all over someone else last time I went—and it was a guy on his own date.

But I was a quick enough study to pick up the motions of the couples around us. Fred Astaire, I was not. Neither was anyone else, though, and as we circled the small space I'd carved out among the other guests, even that didn't seem to matter. There was only the music, and us. Cheesy, I know, but it was true.

"I wanted to thank you," I said. "For sticking by me. No matter what."

"It's hardly a bother." She smiled.

"No, I'm serious, Loredana. Ramos is a good man, doing his duty, and he's got this gruff fatherly vibe that I appreciate, but I don't count on him like I do you. Are you much of an Arthur Conan Doyle reader?"

"I've read all the Sherlock Holmes collections."

I searched through the text in my head, grasping for one of my favorites, because even though it perfectly described the rapport between two buddies, it summarized how I felt: "It makes a considerable difference to me, *having someone* with me on whom I *can thoroughly rely.*"

"*The Boscombe Valley Mystery.* I'm impressed, Mercury. Something you've committed to memory besides the contents of your latest binge-watching session."

"Can't all be spaceships and cop shows."

We both laughed, and it was goofy, just fun. I don't think

I'd felt that relaxed in months, let alone years. We were inches apart, hands clasped, with my left on her hip and her right at the back of my neck.

"You've always been a great mystery to me," she said. "I can't say I've met anyone quite like you. And ... there were nights when you went out to face the astral fiends, that I found myself fearing the worst."

"The worst being what?"

Her voice dropped to a whisper as she said, "That you'd never come back to me."

I touched her chin. Perfect time for another kiss. And this time, with Skipper waiting for us elsewhere, there was no one to—

Loredana's eyes snapped open from sapphire slits. "Mercury ..."

Really didn't want to look behind me. But I did.

A man had just entered the ballroom, with a lithe blonde woman—girl, really—dangling from his arm. The guy could have been Bruce Wayne. Everything about him, from his navy-blue suit to his gold-plated watch to his smartly cut brown hair and well-groomed beard, screamed Rich Boy. He ignored the sycophants surrounding him, the men clamoring for his attention and the women trying to squeeze between him and his date and grinned at *me*.

It was the leader of the Syndax soldiers.

Minus the evil purple and black eyes, of course.

CHAPTER
TWENTY-THREE

I turned back to Loredana and kept dancing.

"This complicates matters." She'd gone all stiff, but hey, who could blame her? One minute, we were trading our feelings and moving far out of our professional territory. The next, we had to deal with the sudden appearance of the guy who'd captured the fiend-hound and tried to take the pulsar stave from me.

Twice.

"I have to say." The guy's voice cut across the murmur of conversation as he approached us, guiding his lovely date around the dance with such ease that I wondered about *his* exercise regimen. Apparently, it included shooting up with astral fiend leftovers, or so his captured flunky said. "Procyon throws the best parties in this town. Or any other, for that matter."

"I shall pass your compliments on to the manager," Loredana said.

"You can indeed, Ms. Lark." He let a balding, gray-haired man cut in on his dance, and the girl's face went from enraptured to bewildered in three seconds flat. It felt awkward in the extreme to try and dance with him standing there, smirking, so I stopped and folded my arms. Nope, nothing adversarial about that. "We haven't been properly introduced."

"Yeah, I don't think it was proper at all," I muttered.

"You obviously have us at a disadvantage." Loredana could have been pitching a budget solution to her board, as pleasant as she spoke. "Loredana Lark, Operations."

"I've heard your name about Rampart and San Camillo, and, frankly, anywhere Procyon pops up." The guy took Loredana's hand and kissed her knuckles. "Charmed."

I rolled my eyes. My turn. "Mer—ah, Mark Hale. Also, Operations."

We shook hands. Nice and manly. Pressure contest? Oh, sure. But we both came away smiling grimly. My fingers ached. His had better, too. "You're more an enigma, Mr. Hale. I pride myself on having the latest information on anyone who crosses Syndax's radar."

"Don't worry about it, pal. You can't always get what you want." I grinned. "Or even *half* of what you want. Sometimes you choke."

The smile tightened, like he'd stopped pretending to be human and gone for full-on Terminator robot. "Sense of humor. I like that."

"And I didn't get your name."

"Alexander Arkwright, Chief of Logistics for Syndax Multinational."

Logistics, huh? That was a nice bland name for the guy who ran a covert squad of private soldiers hopped up on astral fiend energy. "Bet you travel a lot. Meet interesting people. See some unique … stuff."

Loredana's shoe stabbed my foot.

"I prefer it that way," Arkwright said. "I'd be no good to Syndax all cooped up in a lab. More gets done on the streets, wouldn't you say?"

"Definitely." I clenched my hands into fists. "Maybe next time you're in my city, I'll show you around."

"Why not? We could all use a different perspective." He grinned. "If you'll excuse me ..."

Then he was off, mingling and glad-handing, acting like he hadn't tried to kill me or kidnap me, and make off with the pulsar stave. Just another rich benefactor at this soiree.

Speaking of the stave, it pressed against my side, a freezing metal icicle, taunting me with its presence. And by taunt, I mean I could imagine it saying, "Let me loose so we can beat this chump."

Except there'd be no beatings handed out in the middle of the city's fund-raising gala of the year. "Slipping out to Syndax isn't gonna be easy with him here," I murmured. "I'm guessing he didn't come alone."

"Hardly." Loredana leaned in, her breath tickling my neck. She was acting all coy again, but her words were out of sync with someone whose body language said she was ready for a make-out session. "Two standing by the door, on the left, talking. Tan and gray suits. Similar build. Paying more attention to the party than to each other."

They were easy to spot, now that she'd pointed them out. Both men were Garvey's size. Putting suits on them was as good a disguise as sticking a rhinoceros in a kindergarten classroom, giving it glasses, and telling everyone it was the day's substitute teacher. "I see them. Maybe we should split up and ask both if they want to dance. You'd have better luck than I would."

"Hardly a practical alternative." But she smiled as she

said it.

"Or I could take Arkwright over to the window and smash him out of it. Seven floor drop might help."

Loredana cocked an eyebrow.

"Kidding! I'm kidding." Mostly. Something nagged my memories, though. Something I'd heard or read recently ... "Arkwright," she murmured.

"Right. Gary's email. 'Arkwright wants to conjoin.' Which sounds bad, if it's in the context of the astral fiends."

"Most especially if he and his men have been using the fiends' biological material as a catalyst for human enhancement."

"Also bad. And I'm guessing Procyon's gonna revoke our get out of jail free card if we start a brawl with Syndax's chief of logistics in the middle of their party."

"An astute assumption."

My phone buzzed. Incoming call. Now? Ah. It was Liz. "Yello."

"Mercury! Oh, good, I was hoping it was you."

"It's my phone, Liz."

"Right. Oh, right! Anyway, I cracked into Syndax's network but I can't stay in very long because whoever they have running their security is reeeeeally good at his job or maybe her job so they can find out any—"

"Liz!"

"Sorry. Gary DeBarthe is on the fourth floor, in the laboratory area. There's a single entry and egress. All other details are classified."

"Isn't that why you're breaking into their network? To declassify it?" I smiled at Loredana, hoping she'd get the hint that this was a call nobody else needed to know about. She did, thankfully, and put herself in between me and the view of the bodyguards. She even grabbed the arm of an old bald guy who'd been in the middle of a conversation with other old bald guys, and they were suddenly laser-focused on every word she said.

"Declassify."

"Whatever, Liz."

"I'm sending you updated guard locations. The schedule was easy to grab. But I can't touch their systems. If I take a single camera offline, they'll know."

"Back out, then. We don't want them knowing what you've been up to."

"Be careful." Liz coughed. "Um, about my sword—"

"It's been very helpful."

"It was kind of expensive."

I sighed. Gonna have to pull some late nights to make up for that loan. How many crimefighting hours were needed to pay her for it if Skipper broke the thing? "Tell Alvarez to give me a raise and I'll get back to you."

"'Kay. Good luck!"

Right. I tucked my phone away and touched Loredana's arm. "I've got an idea, but I don't think you'll like it."

"Why not?"

"Well, *I* don't like it."

Loredana pursed her lips. "I dance with him, giving you the opportunity to leave the gala."

"Bingo. See? Told you it was no good."

"It's actually quite clever."

Rats. So much for getting out of that one. Way to use your brain too much, Mercury. "His guys are still going see me head out of here, unless you've got my supersuit tucked in that dress."

"The only thing I've concealed is a pistol." Loredana

smiled. "Let me worry about gaining the attention of Arkwright's men. You get into Syndax and retrieve Mr. DeBarthe."

"And whatever else I happen to get my hands on." An unpleasant thought occurred to me. Not that I was going to mince words about it because, hey, it was me we were talking about. "We're not taking the fiend-hound back to Procyon, are we?"

"No. Kill it." Loredana's expression hardened. "Preserving such a creature goes against everything for which our organization stands. Our goal is the elimination of threats to this world, not weaponization of the creatures that desire our destruction."

The string quartet finished off their sound, and the round of applause would have lifted my spirits even if Loredana hadn't just confirmed what I'd always known about her. I kissed her and, eyeballing Arkwright in my periphery, said loudly to be heard by the immediate neighbors, "Sounds like we need another drink."

"Let me have one more dance, first." Loredana approached Arkwright, who swiveled away from his blonde date. "Would you care to join me?"

"A man would be a fool to say no." Arkwright took Loredana by the hand and together they swayed into the crowd as more couples filled the floor along with the rising strains of the band's next song.

Watching another guy dancing with her would have irked me more than a little bit if I wasn't on the lookout for Arkwright's goons. They might be tough and fiend-doped in the field. Here? The advantage was on my side, because if push came to shove, I had the pulsar stave freezing my ribcage, waiting for a chance to join a fray.

But Loredana's plan became obvious as she subtly steered Arkwright deeper into the morass of tipsy, well-dressed bodies. Soon enough, the goons were straining for a glimpse of their boss. One was even on tiptoes. Their frustration couldn't have been louder if they'd broadcast it on a monster-sized TV screen for the entire crowd.

Me? I wound a path through the dancing couples, even accepting the offer of a dance from a giggly brunette—long enough for me to get obscured from the goon's view.

Finally, those guys lost their cool and pressed two paths into the mix, one of them staying near to the edge of the dome, the other trying for the direct approach but getting bogged down in worse traffic than I'd seen on DeLeon at rush hour.

Which left me a clear path to the door.

I glanced back for Loredana as I hurried out of the gala. I couldn't see her, couldn't hear her, but I had to trust she knew what she was doing. There was too much at stake for me to doubt in her abilities. After all, I'd just given her a great—and heartfelt—speech about her having my back.

No way I could forgive myself if I didn't do the same.

Skipper and I left the rental car a block away from Syndax and made our way the last couple hundred yards on foot.

The building sprawled across its property like an ancient citadel, albeit one built with the most modern and elegant materials. It was pale gray, with charcoal panels and long, amber-frosted windows. Few lights shined from inside. The roof seemed exceptionally tall, until I remember that the papers Loredana had gotten her hands on showed the fourth floor lacked windows. Those papers weren't wrong about the extent of its security. Four guys wandering the fence, two in the booth. The cameras were obvious, and so were the brilliant halogen lights turning the perimeter into a sickly, glaring version of daytime.

"My spectacle should provide time for you to gain access," Skipper said. "We should move quickly."

"Then don't wait up." I engaged the suit and watched my hands as they faded to a mimicry of the asphalt.

"Shark's blood," Skipper muttered. "I know not whether there are things such as magic in this world, but that surely approaches it."

"Not gonna argue." I moved across the street as stealthily as I dared, grateful for the soft footfalls of the suit's padded boots. A cat had nothing on me. And getting up to the fence surrounding Syndax would be virtually impossible without the suit, because there was no way to approach the building without crossing a wide city street. Federal's traffic was light, but I was actually glad for the periodic cars. They gave the guards something else to watch.

I huddled behind a bus stop bench and offered up thanks to whatever civil servant decided Rampart's transit system needed shelter right in front of Syndax's fence. It was bathed in the glare from the halogen floodlights, but the Plexiglass was streaked with enough grime and peeling stickers from a bazillion businesses that I was pretty sure I could have waited all night.

Then Skipper did his thing.

To his credit, he waited until traffic was clear, unlike when he'd waded into the middle of East Sheridan outside Loredana's condo. He made it across the striped travel lanes and onto the sidewalk, his hands brushing the tops of the emerald shrubbery lining the driveway. He paused at the dark granite sign carved with "SYNDAX" in bold white letters. Their logo was stylized "S" laid atop a blocky, futuristic "Y," inside a hexagon of triple lines.

"Sir, this is a restricted facility." One of the men left the guard house. Not as burly as the soldiers or Arkwright's goons back at the Procyon party, but athletic, trim, dark-skinned. He could have been an accountant or a realtor, except for the navy-blue polo shirt, khakis, ballcap, and, most importantly, pistol in the holster on his hip. "If you'd not registered to do business, I'll have to ask you to leave."

"I don't think you're going to do that, lad." Skipper kept walking. "Surely your commanders know why I've come. For what other purpose would I approach this place? I seek the beast in your possession, for I alone know its secrets."

Any other private security firm would have Tased a wacko spouting nonsense like that, or at least called the cops. This young guy muttered something into the radio clipped to his shoulder. "Sir, I'm going to ask you again, leave the premises."

"No." Skipper passed him.

"Hey! Sir!" The kid drew his gun. "I'm authorized—"

"If you shoot me, the people to whom you answer will have lost what they need to know, and who do you think they'll blame for that? Do you need proof?" Skipper drew his sword. "Does this not prove who I am? Ask the leader of the forces you sent to San Camillo."

I wasn't sitting still for all this. As Skipper gave his monologue, I crept behind the shrubbery, sidled through a gap in the bushes, and entered the gate. The garage was dead ahead. None of the guards walking the fence had responded—check that, two of them were walking towards Skipper and the man holding a gun on him.

Taking these fools out and storming the place would be my preferred method. I had the itch to will the pulsar stave to life and wipe the pavement with them, literally. But if I did that, the tachyon detectors would light up like the Fourth of July fireworks over San Camillo bay. Which would be stupid, because we'd both get caught, and have to scrub the mission. We'd lose our one window.

So, I descended into the garage, resolutely ignoring Skipper's taunts. More guards were yelling. The noise stayed the same volume; a quick glance confirmed they were herding him in my direction. Good. Getting him inside would only help me. He wasn't any good as a getaway driver.

But if it came to a fight later ...

Skipper's diatribe ended with his sword getting confiscated and his wrists getting zip-tied. Two guards wearing the same cap and polo combo corralled Skipper into an elevator, one a young Latino with a thick moustache and the other a burly, freckled fella with close-cropped orange hair who could have passed for an overly protective older sibling of Loredana's. They were barely ten feet away.

I backtracked, holding my breath and really, really hoping I didn't have to sneeze. Slow steps, but not too slow, because the elevator doors weren't going to stay open forever and if I lost track ...

The doors trundled closed. I ducked in, turned sideways. A sole squeaked.

One of the guards looked my way, but as he did, Skipper stomped his boot. "I demand to see your superior. I have unfinished business—"

Redhead guard punched Skipper in the gut. I pressed against the back wall, hoping beyond hope they didn't bump into me. Skipper doubled over, groaning, and steadied himself against the elevator door. I could tell he was hamming it up. Seriously, he'd taken way worse hits in the couple of fights I'd seen.

"You killed a friend of mine," Redhead snapped. "If it was up to me, I'd put a bullet in your head and find room for you in the incinerator. But that's not our orders. You're lucky."

Lucky was right. Skipper straightened, sweat beading on his forehead. He folded his arms, stoic, unbothered about ending up in the mouth of the lion, or the lion's den, or whatever dangerous-place-with-lions was worth mentioning.

Which was good, because I was headed there with him.

CHAPTER
TWENTY-FOUR

As soon as the elevator opened onto the fourth floor, the guards shoved Skipper out. Which was nice, because then it gave me a chance to duck into the corridor behind them and find a place to hide.

The suit was stealthy, but not totally invisible. If someone looked closely enough, it would seem like the background over which I passed had undergone a bad Photoshop adjustment—poor lighting, or distorted patterns. Blink, and you might miss it.

These guys were either too tired or still irked by Skipper's deranged appearance at Syndax's gate to notice.

I followed them down a windowless corridor, boots treading lightly on obsidian tile flecked with silver. Potted cacti protruded from alcoves set at random intervals. Note to self: Don't lean on them if it came to pressing myself against the wall to avoid guards again.

My brain was crammed full of conflicting worries, outright fears, and other random thoughts—including how hungry I was, because me being of genius intellect I'd skipped out of the party before hitting the hors d'oeuvres—

but somewhere in there I had the fourth-floor layout from Loredana's pilfered plans. There was only one corridor that wrapped around the entire perimeter of this level. The wall to my right was an exterior surface. No rooms. Doors were spaced every twenty feet along the left, leading to an assortment of offices, supply storage closets, and a greater number of unnamed spaces.

Skipper's guards passed these by. I stayed back far enough to keep them in sight, while I moved slowly enough to not tax the suit's camouflaging abilities. The surveillance cameras weren't exactly subtle. Glossy black domes, each as big as a snack cracker topped with pepperoni and cheese, clung to the corners of the ceiling every three doors. Man, I really was hungry.

The trio ahead of me turned the corner. Skipper's sword slapped the leg of the redhead guard, who had the blade tucked into his belt. I sidled up to the same bend in the hall and peered around. Nothing but another long, straight corridor lacking windows. That matched the plans, so far. All the rooms were squashed in the middle of the fourth floor, with a single point of access. Which Skipper and his new buddies stopped in front of. One of the guards pulled an ID card from his belt and whisked it over a white panel affixed to the wall. The card snapped back on a retractable cord. A door whooshed open with a subtle hiss that would have made the most diehard *Trek* fan giggle.

Skipper didn't move. "Am I to be held prisoner? I demand to know where your commander is, so I may face him like a man, unless he lacks a spine like his comrades."

Well, that earned him a kidney punch. Had to admire his stamina—and his planning. Only reason I could figure for him to deliberately antagonize the guards was to stall their entry into the central core of rooms until I could get near the door, because if it slid shut, I was locked out. I moved as fast as I dared along the wall, keeping the mental image of the plans fresh in my head. The compartment beyond the door was an airlock, with little spare room. If I timed this wrong ...

"Shut up and keep moving," Redhead grumbled.

Skipper shuffled through the door, head hung like a puppy who's been kicked one too many times for peeing on the carpet. Wow. He was not going to act in Hollywood anytime soon, but if the guards cared about him hamming it up, they still didn't show it.

I was ten feet from the door when the Latino guard's heel disappeared through the frame.

Move it!

My jump landed me inside the airlock, crouched in the nearest corner, as the door slid shut behind me. I jerked a stray foot out of the way, resisting the urge to let out a big old "Whew!" because when you were wearing what was effectively an invisibility suit, it's best not to talk, because I was pretty sure bad guys would shoot at ghosts as readily as they did at real intruders.

The door stuttered six inches from closing, made a whining noise like gears were stuck on tracks, and opened partway.

One of the guards glanced back.

I froze, hand resting on my leg, where the pulsar stave was secured in a covered pouch. Its energy pulsed under my touch. The thing was spoiling for a fight. *Easy. Bad time for it.*

The door got over its funk and slid shut without further complaint.

Redhead guard, the one who'd done all the punching, rolled his eyes so badly I was waiting for his mother to show up and tell him they'd get stuck that way. He sighed. "What now?"

"The door hiccupped."

"Doors don't hiccup, you idiot."

"That's not what I meant." The Latino guard squinted at me. "It stopped closing like something was in its way."

"That's because those tech trolls can't figure out how to adjust the sensors. Remember last week, when Hank held up the lab coats for five minutes because his shoelace was hanging over the threshold?"

"Yeah, but—"

"Just get up here and swipe your card."

The Latino guard muttered something that I'm sure Ramos could have translated for me into a searing insult, but I was busy with my own internal muttering. *Listen to the Redhead. Nothing to see here.*

"I need to get my contacts checked." The Latino had an ID card, too, leashed to his belt with a retractable cord like Redhead's.

"You need to shut up." Redhead pointed to the dual panels, one on either side of the metal door, and they swiped their cards in unison.

There was a gust of air throughout the small room, like the entire room had sighed, which I guessed meant either we all got decontaminated before entering a clean room or the air pressure equalized. My ears popped, for whatever that was worth. The doors slid open.

The room ahead was a huge, cavernous space, spreading out into vast, dark corners that hid their secrets well. Pale purple lights glowed in the floor, and the ceiling, but you couldn't get much illumination until you were right over or under them. Computer terminals and lab stations were scattered throughout, most of which were in the open, but some of which were cordoned in glass enclosures with their own airlocks.

I followed Skipper and the guards deep into the lab, taking care not to step on any loose panels, because the floor here was metal grating that rattled. I hazarded a look down. Yeah, the grating was wide enough for stuff to pass through, and there was another floor, this one shiny metal, underneath. Ten feet in, I spotted a drain. Really didn't want to know what that was for.

"Put him into the cell next to the geek," Redhead ordered. "We'll let the boss decide his fate when he gets back."

"'Kay." The Latino guard stopped by a wall that appeared to be glass, given the dim reflection that mirrored his moves. There was a panel on this wall that was chock full of buttons and switches. He punched one.

The room brightened into a nightmare.

The fiend-hound was there, slumped inside the containment box the soldiers had shoved it into back in San Camillo. The computers' lights flickered in a slow, steady rhythm, like a heartbeat.

I sank back and braced myself on what felt like another glass wall, calculating how fast I could get across the room, take out the guards, and stab the fully-powered pulsar stave through the creature's hide. Of course, then I had to get us both out of there.

The wall the Latino guard faced was an empty room, a small cell, really, complete with bed, desk, and a semi-transparent partition that had a toilet and shower stall behind it. There were two more cells to its right.

One held Gary DeBarthe.

I could have thrown my hands up and whooped right there, except for being in stealth mode. Gary looked even more pale than he had from his photos, and had shed a couple pounds, which, considering he'd barely been gone two weeks, meant Syndax wasn't exactly the Radisson when it came to meals. That didn't do him any favors, physically, because he was already rail thin. But the blond hair, the left blue eye and right brown eye, the retro '50s glasses he fumbled for from the side of his bed—my brain checked off the list. It was him, in blue jeans and a grungy brown T-shirt that featured Captain Malcolm Reynolds from the canceled—and best TV show ever—*Firefly*.

"Um, you guys are back early." Gary sat up in bed and rubbed his eyes so hard I wanted to warn him he should have washed his hands first. "I told Arkwright, there's nothing more I can do today with the injections. They can't be—"

"Nobody's talking to you." Redhead shoved Skipper toward the empty cell. "You get a roommate, at least until we turn him into a zombie."

Gary squinted. "Okaaay ..."

Something moved, out of the corner of my eye.

A corpse-fiend, its teeth ravenous, its jaw unhinged and oozing, lunged for me.

I leapt away, boots rattling on the grating. No way I was gonna become an Interstice-fueled zombie for ...

Hang on. The corpse-fiend was stuck. So were the others around it. There had to be twenty, shoulder to shoulder, packed into a room walled off by reinforced glass. They scraped and pounded at their prison, but no sound escaped, which frankly made them more terrifying because I couldn't hear a thing from them.

Of course, after my brain cleared away the sheer, screaming panic and relapsed into tactical mode, I realized I'd made enough racket—and put on a spectacular light show—to give away my position.

Talk about an idiot.

"What is that? What is it?" The Latino guard approached me, his pistol trained to the right of where I stood.

"Don't shoot it! It could be part of the experiments."

Don't shoot it? Well, that meant they could see me. I glanced down. Yeah, my arms were rippling like someone had thrown a pebble into a pond. Must have been taxed by my suddenly leap out of harm's way.

"What if it's that guy?"

"What guy?"

"The one at Procyon! The monster slayer!"

Ah. Reputation precedes me. Behind the guards, Skipper was rearranging his hands. I stayed as still as I could, hoping the suit would adjust and I'd disappear.

Didn't work.

"Boss is going to want him alive. Especially if he's got his weapon on him." Redhead reached into his belt and came up with a Taser. He moved past the Latino guard, heading straight for me.

Skipper kicked his sword. The sudden blow wrenched Redhead sideways, because the sword was still hanging out in his belt. Skipper spun him the rest of the way and punched him in the nose. Blood spurted onto his knuckles.

The other guard aimed for Skipper instead of me, which gave me the chance to body slam him against the glass wall. The corpse-fiends launched into a silence frenzy, their desiccated fingers leaving trails of ooze.

"Aaah!" The guard's scream surprised me more than the

initial appearance of our zombie roommates, and he took a wild swing at me.

I ducked, feeling the breeze from the end of the gun inches away from my nose, then grabbed his wrist from the reverse side. I brought the arm down and my knee up until they met with a *crunch* of bone against bone.

The guard screamed again and dropped the gun. I caught it. Sig Sauer. It was a nice, new gun with a pleasant heft that I appreciated even more when I clocked him in the face with its grip.

He went down, unconscious, but his buddy was still fighting, even with the world's worst bloody nose. Redhead fired his Taser. All but one of the prongs missed Skipper, who just grunted and ripped the offending projectile free of his shirt. Redhead must have been too startled to remember the next step, because Skipper jabbed the prong into his arm and pressed the trigger. Redhead collapsed, twitching and moaning, as his own Taser did the dirty work.

Skipper grabbed him by the hair and *clonked* his head against the metal grating, for good measure. All while zip-tied. I was impressed.

I pulled up the bottom of my mask and grinned. "When we get back, I'm gonna get Alvarez to put you on the Procyon payroll so we can give you an immediate raise. Like right now."

Skipper nodded. "I'm glad you approve. We shouldn't, as you say, hang around."

"Right." I approached the cell. "Hey, Gary."

He was on his feet, hands pressed to the glass, eyes wide, mouth open enough to admit Loredana's jet. "Mercury? Mercury Hale? I knew it! I knew you guys would come for me! It's been …I don't know how long. They don't let me have a clock but … oh! The phone. You got my email? The one I sent to Moira?"

"We did. She did. She got it to the police and then to me. Why'd they let you have access to email, anyway?"

"They didn't. A couple of the scientists got careless when they made breakthroughs with their experiments. I found a cell phone on the counter and dashed off a message. I thought for sure they'd catch on, but it must have slipped by." Gary blinked. "So, someone figured out the code."

I tried not to puff out my chest like the world's most egotistical gorilla, but hey, let's face it, I finally found the guy I'd been searching for and was poised to rescue him from the bad guys. Yep, I was bragging. "I got it decoded, yeah. It helped that Syndax blackmailed you or whatever it was they did with the money."

"The money? That was me." Gary pumped his fist. "Great! I thought it would help. Like breadcrumbs, you know? I offered it to them, pleading for them to take it if they'd promise to let me go, but I figured they wouldn't. I just wanted to someone to notice the huge withdrawal."

"Well, it worked. Cops sure got wind. What was the deal with the rat-trap apartment? You could have afforded the gulag."

"Oh, that. I had to change where I lived and didn't want to tip off Syndax. Didn't work, though. Winston still found me. Plus, I figured if I drastically reduced my standard of living, it would get someone's attention. Right?" Gary looked way too pleased with himself, until he peeked over my shoulder. "Who's that? Someone from security?"

"Sort of." I scratched the back of my neck. "Okay, back up. We've got to get you out of here. Part One of my mission."

"What's Part Two?"

"Eliminating the fiend-hound."

Gary glowered at the containment box, where the fiend slumbered. It shuddered and moaned, then scratched at its hide with a huge back claw. Did the creature dream, like dogs did? Marigold would have been a great one to ask about the metaphysics of that, if she hadn't turned evil and been absorbed by the Interstice's keeper. "That thing. I was watching for a way to kill it since they brought it in. Bad enough they've been messing around with astral fiend genetic codes and blood. They've engaged in human experimentation! I can't tell you how many body bags they've hauled out, and how many of those ... abominations they've herded back in."

He pointed past us to the corpse-fiends. "Yeah, don't worry, I'll deal with them, too," I muttered. "Hey, Skipper? We'd better figure out how to open Door Number Two."

"I don't see a lock or chains." Skipper yanked his sword from the redhead guard's belt and used it to cut loose the ID badge. "But I'll endeavor to open it nonetheless—if you're sure you want to engage an entire cage full of those demons."

"Easier than asking them to come out one by one." I took the card from the Latino guard's belt. One of the two badges had to trigger the cell door, right? I swiped it in front of panel. No luck. I took the other badge from Skipper and tried that. Still nothing. But there were plenty of buttons. And, thankfully, Syndax was organized and not counting on people breaking into their top-secret lab. I picked the green button for Cell 2.

The glass door slid open.

Gary shook my hand like he was running for re-election. "Thank you. Thank you so much! I can't wait to see my little girl again."

"Hey, no problem." I jerked a thumb at the fiend-hound's cage. "Open her up."

Gary froze, in the middle of shaking my hand. "I-I don't have access. Only the techs have the code."

I sighed. Fine. Hard way, it was. I drew the pulsar stave. "Let's start this party."

I willed it to life. Yellow-white energy pulsed.

"No, wait!" Gary reached for my arm.

The room was bathed in red light. Klaxons pounded at my ears.

Good news was, the fiend-hound's box popped open, and it didn't jump out, but raised its head, as dazed as pot farmer.

Bad news was, the wall of the corpse-fiend enclosure also opened.

The entire horde tripped over each other, clawing their way to us from the end of the huge room.

CHAPTER
TWENTY-FIVE

G reat. More zombies.

I ripped the first two apart with the pulsar stave, their bodies withering and then disintegrating under the weapon's onslaught. That gave me room to pull power from the stave, hurtling myself backward twenty feet in a split second. "How're we looking?"

"I would rather be affecting our escape than wading into this muck again." Skipper beheaded a corpse-fiend that got too close. Particles sprayed free. "Although it's better we contain this here than endanger innocents outside."

"Amen to that!" I had to shout over the klaxon just to hear myself speak. I swept the bits he'd left on the floor into oblivion with the stave's energy. No point taking chances with us or Gary getting infected. Speaking of whom ... "Hey! What else do you know about this room?"

Gary had edged away from the center of the room. He kept eyeing the fiend-hound, which was wobbling onto its feet. "Um, nothing about weapons, if that's what you mean. There is a stun protocol the researchers have in the containment box, to keep the hound subdued."

"Figure that out! I don't need it gnawing on me while I'm trying to clean these up." A zombie grabbed the pulsar stave, and its raspy groan morphed into a shriek way too similar to an astral fiend's. Its hand vaporized, leaving behind a molten stump. Since he wanted the stave so badly, I let him have it right in his cadaverous chest.

"Okay. Yeah, I can do that." Gary pounded commands into one of the computers attached to the far end of the containment box. The screen cast his face in glowing blue stone, haggard but determined. Nice to have the object of your rescue not panic when things got out of control.

"Mind your enemy!"

I jerked away from a pair of corpse-fiends whose bony, clawed hands raked against the suit. Fortunately, the thing was tough enough to withstand their sharp scratches. I impaled one, then broke apart the pulsar stave and slashed through his neighbor with the free half.

Skipper kicked an incoming corpse into its buddies. He smashed the pommel of his sword unto its face and followed up with a flurry of strikes than left the monsters in a heap, missing various and sundry parts of their anatomy. I made sure to crisp the entire pile.

"They're persistent!" Skipper hadn't even worked up a sweat.

Inside the suit, I felt like I was Santa Claus in the Sahara. "I'm more concerned with why we're locked inside with these guys!"

The klaxon shut off halfway through my inquiry, leaving the room dipped in red but mercifully quieter. Gary grinned, and pumped his fist in the air, but otherwise kept his focus on the computer monitor. Whatever he was doing made something rush through the pipes on the containment box, which was good, because the fiend-hound hissed through the glass at him. "The pulsar stave's tachyon pulses. I was too slow to warn you. There's very few objects that can produce the kind of intense tachyon emission that the stave and the other two weapons do, so Syndax has the lab rigged with detectors to warn of intruders."

No wonder those guys assumed I was—well, me. I ground my teeth. Great. Winston was right. This is where I was meant to be.

Because Syndax *wanted* me in the belly of the beast.

Arkwright had said as much. He'd called it the breaking of the wall. And he'd deliberately shown me his face. That coy greeting at the gala was his way of him letting me know he knew exactly who I was ...

The fiend-hound slammed against the inside of the box. It staggered in a circle, then peered out—right at me. It shrieked, the sound echoing into the lab. The corpse-fiends writhed, their onslaught slowing, until they stood in place. They swayed with each burst of sound from the creature.

"Heavens above," Skipper said. "They heed its command?"

"I really, really hope they don't." I glared at the fiend hound. Fine. It wanted a piece of me? I'd oblige. "Hey! Dinner time, ugly!"

I pointed the pulsar stave and, boy, did it get the message. It rumbled down the length of the box, tentacles smashing the sides, as Gary frantically pounded on the keyboard. "Don't get it outside! The stun protocol won't work!"

"You've got about three seconds to make it so!" I charged toward the opening. No way was I gonna get myself stuck *inside* the box. Fighting the fiend-hound in a super-enclosed space would have been the height of stupidity. I could catch him at the entrance, though before he could get loose in the lab. Or worse—teleport himself into Rampart's streets.

I was happily surprised when the Gary whooped and pointed into the box.

Purple bolts of energy whipsawed from one side to the other, wrapping around the fiend-hound. It clawed at the air, screeching, but managed to make it to the mouth of the box. Tentacles snapped out into the room, battering my shoulder, knocking some of the walking corpses over. Skipper shouted a warning.

Good thing, too. The hound had released its zombie buddies from their trance.

I took the head off the one clawing at my backside. Didn't have to worry much about the rest, because Skipper strode among them like he was handing out presidential pardons, except for pardons all he had in his hands was the sword. It sounded like an angry storm, a great rush of air accompanying each swipe. Within seconds he'd cut down three more and let out a thunderous cry as he engaged more.

Which left me free to get at the main event. The pulsar staves hummed in my hand so loudly the sound could have filled a cathedral. I waded into the fiend-hound's embrace and stabbed them deep, ignoring the cold searing my arms, the despair flooding my mind, the pain wracking my body. The critter was doing its best to drain the life from me, urgently feeding even with the suit blunting the bulk of its efforts.

Yellow-white energies flared around me. Blue slime spattered onto the glass. The tentacles released me. Sensation started to flood back into my limbs.

Then the stave sputtered and died.

No! Not now!

The fiend-hound barreled into me. I flew into the lab, careening off a computer terminal and sliding into a cabinet. My head left a nice dent in the metal door. I scrambled for the stave's halves, but they were dead metal sticks again.

This must be what it's like when Ramos is desperate for a prayer to get through.

Skipper ignored the continued splash of whatever energies the containment box used to stun the fiend-hound and launched his own attack. He parried the spiny tentacles with his sword. One, two, three of them got cut off. He plunged the sword into the beast's hide, and let me tell you, hearing it caterwaul at somebody else was nice for a change.

I willed the pulsar stave to come back to life, give me something, *anything*, and it finally sent a tremor through my fingers.

But when I struck, all it did was give the fiend-hound a nasty sunburn. Slimy skin sizzled. That was one smell I'd never get out of my nose.

Suddenly a great hum shook the box. It felt like someone had the bass on their speakers cranked up to eleven, and my eardrum was pressed to the surface.

"Get out!" Gary cried. "Get out now!"

Skipper's sword was stuck in the monster's hide.

I joined him, and we did our very own joint version of King Arthur, until we wrenched it free.

We made it out of the box one full second before those purple arcs lit up the interior. The fiend-hound howled in abject misery as it absorbed the brunt of the stun pulse. It writhed for what seemed like forever until it slumped to the floor.

Skipper and I leaned against the bent frame of the containment box, panting. I wiped ooze from the suit.

Skipper pawed at his beard, as if he could get every molecule of blue slime free of the matted hairs.

"Blue's not our color," I said.

"I would disagree. I'm partial to the shade." Skipper grimaced. "Only, not in this form."

Gary shut the door to the box. He made sure the latches were in place. The guy must have run his hand through his hair, because it was sticking up at crazy angles. "That was amazing! I mean, I can't count how many times I'd heard you fight astral fiends while I was at my station in Tracking, but to see it …! And your partner is great!"

"We aim to please." I slapped Skipper on the shoulder. "We're not done yet. Zombies, remember?"

The corpse-fiends were standing as if at attention. The fiend-hound getting zapped must have put them into standby mode. Heck, I even waved my hand in front of one of them.

"Bewitched?" Skipper asked.

I shrugged. "Whatever. Makes this part of the job way easier." I jabbed a half of the pulsar stave into the nearest corpse-fiend and got it to sizzle in the most satisfying sizzle. Granted, the stench was awful, but the sound reminded me of pizza left in the oven for too long Which made me think of pizza, which, in turn, made me ravenous all over again.

"We may have another problem." Gary stepped over one of the unconscious guards and headed for the airlock door. I kinda forgot they were here. Must have whacked them pretty hard, because they were only now squirming.

"Let me guess. More alarms?"

"No. The door's locked."

"That's easy." I had both cards in my pocket. I tossed one to Gary. We swiped them over the panels simultaneously. The doors slid apart.

Arkwright stood there, hands clasped behind his back. "Good evening, again."

I brought the pulsar staves between him and Gary, but I don't know what I was expecting to achieve because he had six soldiers crammed into the airlock. Four of them trained automatic weapons on us.

And Loredana was right behind him.

At least she didn't look hurt. More than likely he'd taken her from the party at gunpoint. She was seeing red, though. Probably not literally. I was glad I wasn't Arkwright and that glare was directed nowhere near me.

"Your resourcefulness and determination impress me. I'd offer you a job, if I thought you'd be open to the possibility." Arkwright gestured with two fingers. "Secure the scene."

His soldiers stepped into the room. They took Skipper's sword—again—but didn't touch the pulsar staves. I guess surrounding us all with machine guns was good enough.

"So, you restrained the hound." Arkwright knelt over the mushy puddle that was all that remained of it. "I'm glad you didn't kill him, as vital as he is to the keys."

"Keys."

"Yes. Them." Arkwright got up, brushed off his slacks, and headed for the corpse-fiends. "Well, they're more than that: they're the perfect marriage of humanity and Interstice life."

"Probably why I've never been married," I said.

Arkwright chuckled. "Me neither."

I glanced at Loredana. She was the only one of us—well, besides Arkwright—who looked out of place. "Are you okay?"

"I've done her no harm," Arkwright said.

"I'm capable of answering for myself," Loredana

snapped. "Though he is correct. I've not been harmed; however, I cannot say the same for his men."

"You did give Roland a decent hit to the groin." Arkwright shook his head. "Never underestimate anyone in a fight, even if she looks harmless."

"Look, Arkwright, if you're going to kill us, how's about you get it done with. Otherwise we'd gonna hop the next flight back to San Camillo."

"I'm not going to kill you. Yet. Or possibly at all." Arkwright shrugs. "I haven't decided. First, though, I want you to witness the breaking of the wall."

I gestured at the containment box. "Pretty sure we did that."

"The wall separates us from the Interstice. You should know. How many times over the past few years did you halt astral fiends at their rips in the space-time continuum? And despite the best efforts of our sentinels, you succeeded in closing what should have been a permanent gateway to that realm."

"If by sentinels, you mean Marigold and Winston Yen, then it was Mercury's duty to stop them," Loredana said. "As it was mine to stand by his side. Procyon would never allow the Interstice to be opened onto Earth."

"And yet you did." Arkwright walked among the corpse-fiends, as nonchalant as if he were strolling through Rosa Roja on a warm evening. "You allowed the rips to continue, year after year, decade after decade."

"We had no way to manipulate their appearances. The night's blade was lost, or so we thought."

"True, you didn't know the sentinels—Marigold's ancestors—had searched for and then located it. But the rips themselves were naturally occurring. Sealing them for good created an imbalance. The wall must have breaches, periodically. The astral fiends must be allowed to pass through. If they don't, then other portals start to misbehave. Such as the one that brought your friend to us."

He was staring at Skipper.

"Don't know what you're talking about." I shrugged. "Bad case of memory loss but other than—"

"No lies, please. We know who he is. Don't you think we can analyze DNA and blood here?" Arkwright spread his arms. "He's not from our Earth! And more importantly, he's not from your home, Mercury, the place of your parents. It's a natural disruption of the links that traverse the Interstice which brought him here. Which is, of course, why I'm so happy you two came as a package deal."

The chill I felt had nothing to do with the fiend-hound's attempts to drain my life away. The soldiers had Skipper hemmed in, and with six of them—and the pulsar stave halves flickering—I was uneasy about attempting to break free. Especially with Loredana and Gary held at gunpoint, too. Way too much potential for collateral damage.

"I've been trying to tell you," Gary said. "Procyon's not going to help you reactivate the rips or send anyone through a portal."

"I don't need Procyon's help." Arkwright shook his head. "I need the pulsar staves, and I need this brave warrior who shows no qualms about facing my strongest men. They'll suffice. The rest of you are insurance to make sure Mercury here goes along with my wishes."

"You're not gonna use us to open the gate to the Interstice again," I said. "I'll kill every single one of your men before I let that happen."

"We're not interested in getting back to the Interstice."

Arkwright clapped me on the shoulder. "We want to control the paths to everywhere else. For example, to the place you come from. The place where the weapons have gone to. Meda."

I stared at him. So much for maintaining a poker face. "I ... don't ..."

"Yes, I know, you don't know of any such place, you disavow the name, et cetera. Please. You think you're the only source of information about the Interstice and the land where relics of great power are kept? Marigold knew. Or rather, she *knows*."

Not possible. She may have merged with the—being or whatever he was that stalked the wastes of the Interstice, but she was locked in that dimension as surely as my brother Teget was locked inside Meda with the night's blade and the ax.

"Gentlemen?" Arkwright withdrew a tiny glass and ceramic syringe from his jacket. Violet and sapphire granules swirled in a viscous black suspension. "I need a word."

He injected it into his wrist. The soldiers, in near unison pressed something on their wrists. Shudders traveled around the room.

The corpse-fiends moaned. They stretched out their arms.

When Arkwright opened his eyes, they were the same haunting, stormy purple as his men, the same color of the rotting orbs in the heads of the corpse-fiends. But when he opened his mouth, it wasn't his smooth bass voice that emerged. It was a twisted version of a woman's, discordant, like several speakers had overlapped.

It stretched the syllables of my name in a way I'd never, ever wanted to hear again.

"*Mercury* ..."

CHAPTER TWENTY-SIX

I f I could have snapped my fingers or clicked my heels together or do whatever that teleporting thing was the fiend-hound could pull, I would have.

Arkwright walked toward me, but the bold saunter, the kind of Tony Stark or Elon Musk strut, was gone. This was a graceful stroll, yet there was something majestic at the same time. Like a ballet dancer and a king mashed into one body that didn't belong to either of them.

Skipper murmured something that sounded like, "Preserve us."

"Mercury." Marigold in Arkwright's body smiled. "I've missed you."

"I ..." Had to clear my throat. It had dried up beyond all usefulness. "That's hard to believe."

"Whatever our conflict, you must know that, prior to our last meeting, my feelings for you as a colleague and a friend were genuine." She touched my cheek.

Scratch that. *Arkwright* touched my cheek.

I recoiled. "Easy, there. Your husband's in prison, not dead, and you're—you're not here. This can't be real."

"It's very real. The boundaries between this world and the Interstice are flimsy. The rips through which I sent the astral fiends in times past were calculated, crude assaults. This is more a ... comingling." She—he smiled. "Yes, I am still here, with Marigold Yen."

The voice took on a rumble, a more masculine hiss, that had nothing to do with Arkwright's voice or Marigold's dreamy tones. I tried to say something, either commanding or quippy, but hadn't a word to spare.

"You may have trapped me in the Interstice for the time being, Mercury Hale, but there are always other paths that can be taken. Marigold Yen's family tree has many branches. Did you not think others would be willing to give their lives to the same cause? Her matriarchs are not the only ones among your quaint species who yearn for the day when the light of my Realm can break forth and wash away the darkness that festers among humanity. When you and your kin cut the path to the Interstice, when they ended the rips by sending the blade back to Meda where it gathers dust in their pathetic warehouse, they upset all my careful manipulation. Something had to be done."

Arkwright's body shuddered. His eyes stayed discolored, but the smirk that graced his lips was his, no question. It was the self-assured sneer of a man who had power and knew it. "So, here we are. Thanks to the work of Syndax—which owes its funding to the generosity of the Yen family's quiet connections—we have everything we need. Willing soldiers who have become one with the Interstice. But for the wall to be taken apart brick by brick, they must give all."

He turned around. "Are you willing?"

"I'm willing," one man said.

"Sir, I'm willing."

273

One by one, they answered in the affirmative. Even the guys on the floor had gotten to their feet, albeit shakily, and affirmed their allegiance.

"Good." Arkwright patted them on the shoulders as he walked into their midst. He could have been a football coach encouraging his boys before the playoffs. "I'm proud of you all."

He glanced at the two guards Skipper and I had knocked out. "Except for you. Your failures are inexcusable. I wanted Hale and his traveler inside, but your incompetence meant the fiend-hound lost some of its power before it transferred to me. That's poor performance, gentlemen. You'll serve the cause another way."

Before those poor souls could ask what he meant, a quartet of corpse-fiends lunged for them.

"No! Don't do this!" Gary tried to intercede, but what did he think he was going to do? He had no weapons, no abilities. He was just a guy. Still, he strained under the grip of the soldiers guarding him.

The security guards screamed as the corpse-fiends' hands disintegrated, the particles burrowing into every inch of exposed flesh. In half a minute, Redhead and his Latino counterpart had been shriveled and twisted into corpse-fiends.

Loredana's eyes were brimming with tears. Her voice shook with an anger I'd never heard before. "I'd slaughter you here if you'd give me the chance."

"Not very ladylike, Ms. Lark."

"Return me my revolver and I'll demonstrate gentility."

"I'll pass, thank you." Arkwright wagged a finger at her. "You don't get it, do you? Their bodies are serving a greater purpose now that they're unburdened of their souls. Those husks are capacitors."

I knew the word. "Storing what?"

"Tachyons." It was Gary who spat the answer. And then he spat for real, the glob landing on Arkwright's expensive Italian leather shoes. "Those—those things he's made. They can store and focus tachyons in their cells. That was part of their experiments. They were forcing me to find a way to combine their efforts, to pull the tachyons out once they were—"

"Turns out you were more helpful than you realized." Arkwright shrugged. "For all your obfuscating, you eliminated options we could have spent months chasing. And every false answer you gave, well, I knew when you were misleading. Or rather, Marigold and the Whisperer knew."

There it was. The Whisperer. The nebulous being who inhabited the Interstice and, as far as I knew, marshalled the astral fiends. He'd merged with Marigold when she was obliterated—or when we thought she was obliterated. Nagging doubts filtered through my head. He could listen in on me? On us?

Stop it. Don't second guess yourself.

Why shouldn't you? How many mistakes have you made? Look at how rash decisions have compounded over and over into this moment, this reckoning that will lead to your destruction?

I gritted my teeth. Stay out of this.

"It doesn't matter," Arkwright said. "We know what needs to be done. You see, I'm prepared. And so are my followers. We're all bound together. Even those who no longer serve us in life."

He opened the containment box.

"Whoa, hey, wait a minute." I started for Arkwright

but got a gun's muzzle aimed at my skull, so I opted to stay put. "We just put Fido there to sleep. I don't think he's done with his nap."

Arkwright stepped into the box. "That won't be a problem. He's gone through enough. Time for him to know the only peace in his miserable existence."

He felt across the fiend-hound's hide for something. His hands kept searching until they found the wound Skipper's sword had made. Then he jabbed his fingers deep into the congealing ooze. Nasty.

Bolts of energy arced through the box's interior, bold and bloody in the crimson light of the room's alarm system. The fiend-hound was suddenly bolt awake. Its screams bludgeoned us as it thrashed at its confinement, its tentacles cutting into Arkwright. Particles swarmed around him. The pulses rippled, making my bones rattle in sympathetic vibration. With any luck, the monster would suck the life out of that idiot and Skipper and I could jump the guards.

But it was the fiend-hound who withered, its skin cracking, its form shriveling until crumpled in on itself. The tentacles stuck to Arkwright and then, with an awful tearing sound, pulled free of the monster's hide.

Arkwright stood over the ashes. I could have sworn he was six inches taller. His muscles bulged against his clothes. The jacket sleeves ripped.

"It's even better than I hoped." His voice had that overlapping, rhythmic cadence. He walked free of the box, his expression euphoric. "I can ... see it. The wall. The shadows of the Interstice beyond. But it's not enough."

He plunged his hands into the sternums of two corpse-fiends, the ones who'd been the unlucky Syndax security guards.

I struck then, putting the end of one pulsar stave into the gut of the nearest guard, while planting the other onto a second soldier's face. The stave sputtered and sparked, enough for my will to draw a surge of power out.

I shot aside, slamming shoulder-first into one of the men guarding Skipper. Together we bounced off the far wall of the lab, spilling the contents of three cabinets. Medicine bottles and other supplies rolled across the floor.

Skipper used the distraction to pound on his guard, managing to yank the gun free from his grip. The gunshots were loud enough to drown out the shouts from Arkwright and Gary. The soldier crumpled. Blood sprayed across the cell walls.

He turned toward Loredana.

She ducked as Skipper's fusillade peppered the soldiers who had her cornered. Skipper wasn't an expert shooter with a fully-automatic weapon, because half his shots went wide. The soldiers took cover behind a work station. One yelped as a bullet cut through his leg.

I punched the soldier with whom I was entangled until I was sure he wasn't getting back up. Then I hurtled for Arkwright. I couldn't let him absorb any more of the corpse-fiends. No idea what he was becoming, but it was guaranteed bad news.

"Mercury!" Gary shouted. "Don't touch him with the stave!"

It was already raised over my head, combined and powered up, ready to strike before it glitched out on me again. What was he talking about? Arkwright had to be killed, right now.

But this was the guy who knew everything there was to know about Tracking astral fiends and rips. That included tachyons.

To which the pulsar stave was irrevocably linked.

I adjusted my aim in mid-strike, missing Arkwright by a hand's breadth.

A tentacle struck out from his back, sprouting from out of nowhere. It wrapped around the stave. Part of me was glad, ready for the weapon's energies to reduce the offending appendage to a melty blue mess.

Instead, the stave flared even brighter.

Its yellow-white energies struck *me*, a lightning bolt to the chest, if a lightning bolt could be freezing. I thought my heart was going to stop—and that was just from the shock of the weapon's reverse actions, nothing to do with the pain.

The pain was worse.

Every cell of my body ... It was like the stave was trying to reclaim the power it had loaned me for years, compounded with a ton of interest I didn't have. It was greedy, hungry, scraping the life from my insides.

And my hands refused to let go.

A body collided with mine, breaking me free. The impact on the metal grates was a blessed relief from the agony. I squirmed, blood dripping from my mouth. I'd bit my tongue. Of all the inane things to notice.

Loredana had knocked me loose. She held my face in her hands. "Stay with me, please. Focus on my eyes. Can you hear me?"

"I ...Yeah. I can." I pushed onto an elbow. The pain lancing through my limbs made me want to vomit. My vision swam.

Arkwright's tentacles passed him the pulsar stave. He turned it over in his hands, its power arcing around him, gouging holes in his clothing and leaving burns on his skin.

Yet, the purple energies he'd just siphoned off a grand total of four corpse-fiends intercepted those strikes, warring for supremacy.

"It's a strange thing, trying to hold this weapon, and feeling it was nothing more than a cold hunk of metal." Arkwright shrugged. "That obstacle's been overcome. Thanks to Marigold."

Of course. No wonder Gary had tried to warn me. Arkwright was merged, in some weird, extradimensional way, with not only the Whisperer but Marigold Yen. Marigold, who was descended from a line of individuals who—like me—carried a hidden genetic marker that let them use the three weapons. The pulsar stave. The night's blade. The ax.

Arkwright had absorbed the same genetic marker. My guts clenched, and I wanted to punch him in the face. Or anywhere, really. How dare he. My parents came to Earth and died in its defense, giving up their lives—giving up *me*—to destroy astral fiends, just like the warriors who'd traveled between the dimensions had done millennia ago. His perversion of the gift passed down through those bloodlines from the few who'd stayed behind to protect this world was worse than even Marigold's. At least the ability to wield the three weapons was her birthright, no matter how badly she'd abused it.

This guy stole what should never have been his.

"I've wanted this for a long time," he said. "The strength to reach between the worlds, to bring what's been banished from Earth and return it to its rightful place. Think of it, Mercury: you won't have to spend your nights in fruitless pursuit of common criminals. You're snuffing lit matches in the middle of a raging forest fire. When the wall is down, and the doorways are opened—"

"Just shut up." I let Loredana help me to my feet. Gary took my other arm, providing leverage until I was upright. Skipper joined us, brandishing the automatic rifle he'd taken from the soldiers.

"I understand. I'd be upset, too, if I learned I had no special role to play, no purpose anymore." Arkwright lifted the stave. "But I want to thank you for fulfilling your role up to this point. You've made this transition possible."

The pulsar stave sent a burst of light flashing across the room. I thought, for an insane second, I was going to die at the business end of the very tool that I'd used to save the world.

Instead, the blast knocked Skipper out cold.

"Take him," Arkwright ordered.

His remaining soldiers, including the injured ones who'd gotten their second wind, dragged Skipper's stunned form into the midst of the corpse-fiends. The whole entourage filed out the airlock, the doors of which they left open at both ends of the small chamber. Guess they weren't worried about containment.

Gary eyeballed the sword, and then looked at me, eyebrows raised. I shook my head, hoping that was enough to dissuade him from trying something heroic and/or suicidal.

"I wish you could join us, but I'd rather you not interfere with what's to come." Arkwright was the last one, blocking the open hatch. "It'd be simple enough to kill you, but, if I have to be honest, I don't want you dead. Far from it. I'd like to you witness the moment of our triumph, when the light floods this dimension. What happens to you after that is a matter I leave up to the Whisperer."

He turned around.

I'd never seen Loredana sprint so fast, her heels discarded in a lopsided pile on the floor. It made me wonder where she found the time to exercise, because she covered the distance between us and the airlock in no time flat. She stuck her hands in the gap, clinging to the edge as the airlock doors whined in protest at whatever was preventing them from closing the last six inches.

"Watch it!" Gary lent all his inconsiderable weight to the other door, but they weren't stopping the inevitable. By the time I limped over, their fingers were almost touching each other's.

The door mechanism grumbled and jerked inward.

Loredana cried out. She yanked her hands back, as Gary did the same. The doors slammed shut. Heavy metallic *clanks* sounded down the frame. Air hissed.

Sealed in.

"How could you let them take it?" Gary turned toward me, his expression crazed. "I thought I was going to die in here, and then you gave me hope by showing up to rescue me, but you've gone and screwed it all up!"

He grabbed my shoulders and shook me like he wanted to rattle sense into my brain. All it did was compound my headache, so I did the only logical thing—slammed him against the wall. "Look, Gary," I snapped. "This may come as a surprise to you, but I hadn't planned on Arkwright being able to activate the weapon."

"Steady." Loredana touched my arm. "Contact Liz."

"Right." I dialed her up. "Liz?"

"I wish I had good news." She sniffled, whether from sadness or allergies, I couldn't tell. "Whoever just left the building locked down the entire network. Data, backups, operating systems—scrubbed clean. The building itself is physically sealed, too. It's airtight. Independent power supply. Let me see what I can do. Oh! Maybe there's—"

The phone went dead. So did all the electronics in the room. Even the blood red emergency beacons extinguished. All that was left were pale, white LEDs set into the floor. I swore I heard the HVAC system grind to a halt.

We were stuck.

CHAPTER TWENTY-SEVEN

I tried rebooting my phone. Nothing. I might as well have been holding a brick, or a shoe.

"EMP." Gary rubbed his face. "Electromagnetic pulse. It must have disabled the electronics throughout Syndax."

"That won't do Liz any good," I muttered. "Or us, unless you know if those guys kept a pry bar in this lab."

Gary shook his head. He started pacing. "We're never gonna get out of here. Whatever Syndax is planning with the pulsar stave and your friend there—"

I looked at Loredana, who had her hands pressed to the door as if she could will it to yield. "The portal."

"The one through which Skipper arrived."

"Yeah. Could it access Meda?"

"I ... don't know. If it is similar to the portal of which I have prior knowledge, its construction is more that of a tunnel than an instantaneous link between our world and the Interstice."

"This is insane," Gary said. "You have to get us out of here. My daughter! If Arkwright is heading back to San Camillo ... I won't let anything happen to her. We have to get word out!"

"I know that, Gary, and also, shut. Up." I refocused my attention on Loredana. "How would Skipper access the portal? He doesn't have any means that I know of. Otherwise he would have headed back home first thing, right?"

"It is possible Arkwright could use the pulsar stave to activate it," she said. "I have no idea of whether or not it would remain stable."

"What about the other portal you said Procyon had experience with?"

Loredana wouldn't meet my eyes. "It's a classified file, you see."

"And we all know how I feel about those."

"I'm not at liberty to divulge—"

"Look, Loredana, I think you're great, and there's no one I'd rather be spending a lot of time with alone, but frankly, having Gary as a third wheel was not what I'd had in mind, and your habit of keeping Procyon's secrets secret when we're all very likely gonna die is annoying. To say the least. So how about you cut the mental red tape and pretend like I'm capable of keeping the same secrets as a tech dork like this guy."

"Hey," Gary said.

I raised a finger. "One more word, Gary, I swear ..."

"The portal has been accessed." Loredana crossed her arms. She paced, her lips pursed. If I could have looked inside her head, I bet I would have seen her rational, by-the-book personality arguing with the we-need-to-escape-or-the-world's-doomed passionate self. That would have been fun. "On a regular basis."

"That's ... bad. Why couldn't you have sent Skipper home?"

"I'm speaking, of course, of the other portal which Procyon has recorded."

"Does the pulsar stave—?"

"I don't know," Loredana snapped. "We haven't conducted as much research on it, simply because it did not come to our attention prior to the last decade. The technology which activates it is similarly mysterious, though ... when we traveled to Meda and the temple from which the pulsar stave hails, I suspected we learned part of the answer."

"Okay. Good to know."

"Mercury, the portal of which I speak does not instantaneously transport one to the Interstice. It bypasses it, in a manner of speaking, connecting our world with another dimension."

"Another. Like, other than Meda and the Interstice."

She nodded.

"Maybe the one where Skipper came from?"

"I sincerely doubt it. Its similarities to our own are too numerous."

Gary slapped a work desk. "This is all fascinating stuff. If I was back in Tracking, I'd really like to dig through the archives and run some tests on the properties of these dimensional breaches. But if we don't get out of here, the world's going to be overrun with monsters and my family won't stand a chance against them!"

I sighed. "Loud and clear, Gary. You have anything to contribute, besides freaking out every five seconds? Because we could take turns."

"There's nothing we have left in here to use for communication." He picked up a cell phone from the floor. "They're all dead."

Not a comforting phrase. "What about a manual release

for the door?"

We checked every wall panel surrounding the airlock hatch. Gary used a scalpel from one of the experimentation rooms to pry open a panel. Lots of wires, sure, but they all linked to controls that were zapped. At least, no matter how Gary fiddled with them, they didn't work.

"Scour the room," Loredana said.

She didn't elaborate but we got the message. There had to be something in there we could use, either to break out, or to communicate with Procyon. I kept thinking of Skipper. The guy had done nothing but his best to help me, going so far as to risk his life, with nothing in return but my lame promises that I could maybe help him get home. And what did that get him? Trapped by Arkwright, as easily as a mouse who'd hung around for the cheese.

I thought the pulsar stave made me invincible. All it took was one happenstance recharge of its power for me to set aside all worries about its potential failure. I worried so much about what it was doing for me and how I would benefit from its continued use that I never once stopped to consider that someone else could twist its purpose. To be fair, I didn't think that was possible. But come on. I should have been a little *wary*. What were the odds of Marigold having no family left? And hadn't I already run into Wilhelmina, my mentor and Procyon's former operative, who shared the same genetic marker that filtered down through the generations from those very first Meda warriors who protected our world from the astral fiends?

Talk about a grade-A idiot.

"Nothing." Gary shut what must have been the fiftieth cabinet. "A lot of computers, but with the fried electronics and the network down, they're useless hunks of plastic."

"Keep looking. There might be—"

My pocket buzzed.

Everyone froze. The sound was like jackhammer in the silence. I unsealed the pocket's flap.

The tracking device. The one I'd taken from the soldiers back in San Camillo.

I thumbed the power button, slowly, hoping it wasn't going to, I don't know, blow up or something.

What I'd come to recognize as the standard, Main Menu graphics lit up.

Gary shook my shoulders. "It works! Syndax must have shielded them! Made them ruggedized for work in the field."

"Yeah, it's great." Best part? Message from Liz. <Are you guys OK? I can't get through. Whole building dead. Hello?>

Downside: it was a one-way stream of communications. I told Gary as much.

"I can work with that." Within a couple minutes he had the thing's guts spilled across a table, poking and prodding at it. There was a lot of muttering, too, so I steered clear.

"Mercury, we must come to the realization that without your family's aid and the other weapons locked inside Meda, our chances at success are slim." Loredana leaned against the door.

"This would be a great time for you to tell me you've got a metaphorical ace up your sleeve." I nudged her bare arm. "Even if you don't have literal sleeves."

She smirked. "If we can get a message out, I should be able to expedite our return to San Camillo, though my asset won't be of much use to us in a battle."

"Asset?"

"Hey! Got it." Gary held up the tracker, grinning as if he'd just delivered his second child solo. Of course, this second child was a half-dismantled electronic device that was either incredibly sophisticated or on its way to the garbage, depending on which way you looked at it.

"So, you broke it?" I asked.

"No! I reversed the process Liz used to send messages." He gestured to Loredana. "We can tell her whatever you want."

"It's not her we need to contact." She approached the table and frowned down at the near-unrecognizable device. "May I?"

Gary nodded.

Loredana typed a long string of numbers into the tracker, then added instructions: <Gemini. Retrieval.>

"Gemini?" I made a face. "You're into the zodiac?"

Loredana checked her watch. Too small to be affected by the EMP, I guessed. "Hardly. Give it a few minutes, Mercury, and we shall be delivered from our captivity. Mr. DeBarthe, how is your constitution?"

For a weird, injury-addled moment I thought she was asking him about the governing document of America. "I'm, ah, prone to motion sickness in aircraft."

"Might want to warn him about the leather seats," I murmured.

"That won't be a problem. We're not bothering with the plane. Mr. DeBarthe, gather whatever technology was left unscathed by the EMP. We'll need access to Syndax's data if we're to determine Arkwright's next step."

"On it." He pulled the side panel off a computer hard drive. "If you guys want, you can round up anything with a computer in it for us to carry back."

I dug up a duffel bag from the other side of the room. Loredana helped me shove laptops and cell phones into its depths. "I don't know if we've got enough time for Liz to rebuild this stuff. The internal components are fried."

"We have to gamble on her being able to reconstruct whatever data was not lost. Depending upon what she's able to ascertain from her connection to Syndax's network prior to the attack, we may have an advantage."

"Don't forget your files."

Loredana make a face, but she sent a couple additional messages through the tracker—one telling Liz to do exactly what she'd told me was the plan, and another to have Procyon's Rampart staff pick up everything from our hotel rooms in town.

It was about then I noticed the breeze.

It was easy to pick up the sensation of cool air blowing across my face, since the HVAC system had died with everything else. This breeze, though, got colder, and harder, like it was suddenly the dead of winter inside the lab.

"Over here!" Loredana had to shout over the roar.

She was standing by a bizarre ripple, a bulge in—nothing. Like a part of the room was distorted by the presence of something invisible.

Hey. Just like the portal in Cavill Cemetery, only inverted.

I shouldered the duffel bag. Hang on a sec. The sword. If we found Skipper, he'd need it, and in the meantime, it would make a decent substitute weapon for me. Besides, I wanted to make sure Liz got it back.

I dragged Gary over to Loredana, leaning into the bizarre hurricane that blew papers into a spiral and toppled computer stations. "Hang on!"

"I've—I've never done this!" he blurted. "Traveled by a rip!"

"This doesn't look like a rip, so don't bet on a vacation

cruise!"

White light exploded from the center. It coalesced into a ball no bigger than a marble, but insanely bright. Even a glimpse left a violet afterimage in my sight. The dot widened, pulling itself into an oval that a hazy image filled in.

It looked like ... an apartment?

There was a silhouette of a man in the middle. For a moment, I wanted to cheer, because it reminded me of when I first saw Teget on Earth—my brother, the Icon, who'd traveled through the rip from the Interstice to help me defeat evil. Pretty exciting stuff.

Except, this figure's wrists were glowing like pieces of the sun.

The oval expanded, and the three of us fell in.

My body reacted poorly. As in, I felt like I was standing in two places at once.

That was me, in Syndax's abandoned lab, the air stale and stinking of fiend goop.

That was also me, in a comfortable loft apartment, with wood floors and bare brick walls. The tiny part of my mind that wasn't screaming at the madness of having body split between two points in space wondered if there was beer in the fridge. Or pepperoni pizza.

The light died, and we collapsed. I let go of Gary and caught Loredana, who passed out. Her head lolled against my chest, eyes, half shut.

Gary landed on his face.

"Is she hurt?"

The silhouette was a guy, sure, but he was fuzzy, indistinct. Or maybe that was me. He knelt in front of us. His face was solemn, with very regal Arabic features. He was dressed professionally, in a teal Oxford with the sleeves rolled up and top button undone, plus pinstriped black pants and shoes of the same color. "Loredana? What's going on?"

"Please ... deliver us to Procyon in San Camillo. It's urgent." She wasn't even talking in the right direction. Could she see him? Or had the trip affected her vision? It sure hadn't done me any favors.

Gary held the sides of his head and groaned.

"I can do that. Hold tight." The guy stood. Silvery bracelets encircling each wrist started—moving. No joke. They spun around, pieces levitating from his arm. "If you need help, I can be there."

"No. Please." Loredana was on her knees now. I helped steady her. "They can't find out about you. Doing so would further jeopardize our operations. Your service to us—your true abilities—are of the utmost secrecy."

He glanced at me. "Then I trust these men know how to keep things under their collective lids."

"If you'd hung out with me this week," I muttered, "You'd know better than to ask."

"All right. Don't hesitate to call me if you need anything."

"Godspeed, Dominic."

Dominic ...She'd written him an email, at least once, back in the spring.

I didn't have time to ponder further because the portal reopened. The three of us floated a foot off the floor, and I got one last look around the rustic but retro apartment. It made me wish I was at home, on the couch, doing something—anything—other than risking my neck and assorted body parts to save the world.

But if I didn't, well, we were toast.

This second transportation was worse than the first. I felt like I was back at the Syndax lab and in the loft *and* in

Tracking at Procyon's San Camillo building. My brain argued with itself, turning any semblance of coherent thought into rambling nonsense.

It stopped, thankfully. But only when we hit the floor of Tracking. That place is *not* covered in comfy carpet like its companion office in Forecasting.

"Oh! What are …? How did you …?" Liz's face spun before me, upside down.

I closed my eyes and counted, slowly, until I didn't feel like I was going to come apart at the seams. When I hit thirteen, and didn't have the desire to vomit, I opened them again. "Hey, Liz. We're back."

"You're okay!" She hugged me. And Loredana. Which would have been funnier, had Loredana not been deathly pale and short of breath. "I thought you guys were stuck in Syndax's building and I was working on a way to reboot their systems but when the power went off—"

"Great to see you too, Liz." I patted her back, then disentangled myself from her embrace. "Where's Doctor Arne? We need to get Loredana checked out. She looks awful."

"I'll be fine. We haven't the time to tarry with a medical exam." Loredana's arms trembled.

"I think you'd better get her looked at, Mercury."

Ramos? He was standing guard by Liz's desk, frowning, glaring, arms crossed and every inch of him the grumpy cop. I could have kissed him, I was so happy to see the living embodiment of my normal life. "Ramos! Man, am I glad you—"

"Explain to me why I shouldn't haul you to a cell right now," he snapped, "And maybe you'll begin to pay for the damage you've done."

CHAPTER
TWENTY-EIGHT

The travel between portals messed with my brain in a bad way. As in, I'd completely lost track of the time. It took a good ten seconds of staring at Ramos before it kicked me in the face: this was less than half a day after Skipper and I had broken Loredana out of her house arrest, flown to Rampart, danced at a gala—Loredana and I, not Skipper—and gone through our ordeal at Syndax.

Having Gary sprawled on the floor, his eyes wide and his mouth even wider, solidified the notion. "Wow. I can't believe we just did that! How is it possible to link two points in space—three points! And we didn't breach the Interstice, did we? I don't recall any of the data on the rips looking like that."

"Let's geek out later." I nodded at Ramos. "Want to run that by me again?"

"I see you found your missing man."

"No small thanks to him and his email. Things didn't go the way we planned."

"They rarely do."

The sight of the young Syndax soldier being wheeled on a gurney past the door to Tracking distracted both of us from the conversation. The men wheeling the gurney were Procyon, not SCPD. I guess Alvarez wasn't willing to let other cops onto the seventh floor, filled as it was with all Procyon's secrets. "I guess you called Alvarez."

"That's all you have? Of course, I called your manager." Ramos gestured at the door "We discussed it, remember? The part where your organization isn't supposed to take prisoners off my streets?"

"Yeah, I remember." I braced myself on a computer desk. The room didn't wobble, and neither did I. A bottle of water would have hit the spot. Plus, a couple beers. And pizza. But I doubted Ramos would react well if I paused our conversation for an emergency call to Carlito's. "What I don't remember is you being triggered when we parted ways."

"Those consequences of which we spoke? They're coming to bear, Mercury." Ramos tapped a panel on Liz's computer.

I knew Loredana must have been feeling bad because she didn't freak out or call security back when Ramos touched Procyon property.

Nothing happened.

"It's, um, the second panel over." Liz handed Loredana a water bottle and helped her drink most of it in one sitting, like she was born to be a nursemaid. "I configured Cyril so his controls linked to the main monitors would cycle through different panels depending upon which programs I was running because I don't like having them in the same old place every ..."

She trailed off when she saw everyone was staring at her. "Um, never mind."

Ramos punched the correct panel. The monitor's maps blinked out, replaced by various images of new reports and downtown San Camillo. They were from different angles, with commentators and station logos blotting out much of the scenes. The videos streamed off YouTube lacked the officialness, but made up for it with colorful commentary, most of which was better left unrepeated. But I got the gist.

"Three square blocks downtown are blacked out," Ramos said.

I sighed. "If you're telling me, I'm guessing it's not a utility issue."

"We have no communication with anyone still there. No cell phones, no landlines, no emails, not even a radio. Two officers on patrol drove their unit across the boundary half an hour ago. They've been MIA since. And it's getting worse."

"Worse, how?"

This time Liz took over the controls. "The anomaly appeared two hours ago. It's slowly expanded to encompass the nine blocks."

A map appeared inset in the videos. My stomach twisted, and it wasn't because I was low on fuel. I knew the location. Thirteenth and DeLeon. "Cavill Cemetery."

"That's the locus, yeah, as far as Cyril can pinpoint and since we're dealing with tachyons that's pretty easy. But it's not a single spot, you know, it's a bunch of indistinct emission points that when taken as a whole, signify a bigger anomaly than I've ever seen. Like this." She typed, and the red blotches crept away from the cemetery, as individual spots and in clusters.

"Huh. How about that." Gary had his nose practically pressed to the monitor. "It's very disorganized. You'd expect uniform expansion in a phenomenon like this."

"That's what I said! I mean, to Cyril, and he can't answer, duh, but—"

"It's the corpses," Ramos snapped. "Those reanimated bodies that were supposed to be gone. And the biggest surge happened within the last half hour."

"Surge ..." I rubbed my forehead. The headache was a constant companion, now. Thanks, Arkwright. "I've got a bad feeling about that. Syndax is behind the corpse-fiends. Their boss—he's, ah, merged with the fiend-hound. And he's using the corpses like batteries full of tachyon particles."

Doctor Arne burst into the room. He halted, face twisted into a scowl, probably trying to decide what to do with the three sickly looking individuals and their bag of stolen equipment. Also, the sword, which was tucked through the straps of the bag. "What is this? I've got a patient, and you're letting her sit there unaided? Move. Now!"

Ramos slid out of his way, unperturbed by the doctor's brusque orders. He was way too intent on me to care, apparently. "Arkwright. This is the leader of the soldiers, I take it."

"One and the same. He had Gary working on a method to harness tachyons. He's after the weapons stored in Meda, the blade and the ax."

"But he can't get to the Interstice, can he? You couldn't ..."

"He has ascertained a way to bypass the normal access." Loredana put her hand to Arne's chest, keeping him at arm's length. She finished off the water bottle clutched in the other. "I'm recovered, Doctor. The mode of transportation we used can drain certain individuals."

"I don't care if you walked on the ceiling," Arne

muttered. "I need to check your vitals."

"Not. Necessary." The customary impatient bite reasserted itself. "Lieutenant, I advise you to evacuate the area before any—"

"None of you are listening, is that it?" Ramos waved at the monitors. "We can't send anyone in, because no one comes back out. The corpse-fiends are overrunning the area."

He wasn't kidding. A shaky camera image showed three corpses staggering down a street. The police at the edge of the frame must have thought them far enough away to avoid infection, because they shouted commands and then opened fire. Commands? At what, the corpse-fiends? Like a zombie was worried about its Miranda rights and the threat of arrest. Their bullets did a much better job of tearing the corpse-fiends into tiny bits. And while I kept hoping a well-placed headshot would drop each one, there was no such luck. They kept on keeping-on until they couldn't stagger, and then they fell apart, before disintegrating into swirling clouds of the infectious particles. I watched as the remnants withdrew deeper into the three-block area.

"We've cordoned off the neighborhood as best we can." Ramos paced among the computers. I don't think I'd ever seen him do that. "There's officers at every intersection. The captain's hollering for airborne units but the commissioner's vetoed her so far. He doesn't want us getting a clear view of what's down there, for fear it would incite public panic."

I gestured at the screen. "Like that's not?"

"You have to get down there. Stop this." Ramos looked around at all of us. "There is a plan to handle the situation, isn't there?"

I glanced at Loredana. "There's a complication."

"What sort?"

"Arkwright has the pulsar stave. And he can use it, just like I can."

"*Dios mio.*" Ramos fingered the crucifix tucked into his shirt. "Is this true? How can it be possible?"

"Long and complicated story. Short version? He's possessed by Marigold."

"Marigold Yen."

"Yeah."

"She's … dead."

"Sort of." I scratched the back of my neck.

"There is no 'sort of,' Mercury. She's either dead or she is not. Her soul—"

"Not gonna debate heaven and hell with you, Ramos. I saw her before the Interstice closed up. She'd combined with the being who bosses the astral fiends around, and through Syndax's experiments, Arkwright gained the ability to merge himself with them, across the barrier between the dimension. He calls it the breaking of the wall."

"This is exactly what I was talking about." Ramos poked me in the chest. "This situation has gone completely out of hand. I trusted you to handle it. To do your job."

"What do you think I've been doing?" I snapped. "I'm lacking guidance these days, in case you haven't noticed. All you've been good for is having me chase down leads like a second-rate detective, which, last I checked, is what I'm not! Point me at the monsters, sure, and I'll take them apart. But they come out of the portals, one or two or a bunch at a time. This isn't what I trained for, so instead of standing here sniping at each other, how about we get business done?"

Ramos murmured, whether in thought or in prayer, I couldn't tell. At that point I'd take either. Nice part? He wasn't barking at me anymore. "How do you stop them?"

"I don't know. That's why we brought this stuff back."
I knelt and unzipped the duffel bag.

"Oooh." Liz clapped her hands. "Is that all Syndax
property? Like from their secret lab?"

"Merry Christmas." I handed Liz her sword.

"Perhaps you should retain that for the time being."
Loredana seemed much better. She tucked stray red hair
behind her ear. Doctor Arne frowned over the readings on
the blood pressure cuff wrapped around her upper arm, but
removed it, apparently understanding that Loredana wasn't
going to sit still like a good patient. "We're at a decided lack
for weaponry."

"No kidding."

Liz gazed at the blade, which showed flecks of blue and
stains of red. Skipper had cut down both men and monsters
with that thing. I wondered if she was calculating how much
she could get for a genuine battle sword on eBay. "She's
right. Mercury, um, you'd better keep it. For now, I mean."

"Sounds good to me." I took it from her. The thing had
serious heft. I swung it a few times—mindful of the bodies
around me, of course. It wasn't the same as having the pulsar
staves, linked to my body via their otherworldly energies,
but it'd do.

"I'm taking you downtown to handle this disaster."
Ramos was at my side.

"I suggest we formulate a plan first." Loredana helped
Liz and Gary transfer the electronic equipment from the
bag onto a table in the corner of Tracking. She brushed file
folders, each one perfectly stacked atop the other, onto the
floor, where they spilled their contents in a mix of paper.
Times must be desperate, indeed. "Rushing into the situation
will only result in more death."

"Don't talk to me about more death!" Ramos stepped toward her, but I slapped the flat of the sword's blade across his chest like the barrier on a toll booth. "There have to be hundreds of people in those nine blocks! If they're not dying, they're dead already, transformed into those abominations. I would like nothing more than to roll S.W.A.T., but until we can figure out how to destroy those things without endangering my people and even more residents outside the cordoned area, there's nothing I can do about it. You people are my only hope to avoid the destruction that's coming."

That sounded more apocalyptic than it should have. Then I remembered the steps Ramos had taken last time monsters had tried to invade San Camillo. "National Guard."

He nodded. The breath he sucked in was a mere shudder, like it was going to be his last. "It's out of my hands. The commissioner has contacted the commanding general. They can have soldiers here in a few hours, but the ANG can have units even faster."

"ANG. Air National Guard." I felt even queasier.

"Helicopters? Are they going to evacuate people?" Gary looked puzzled. "I don't think there's enough room in that part of town to land that many aircraft quickly."

"No, lint for brains," I snapped. "He means if we don't get this under control, they're going to bomb the neighborhood into the Stone Age."

"Contain the infection." Ramos scowled. "His words."

"Then you're right. We have to go." I plunked the tip of the sword on the floor. "Ramos, can you get me downtown ASAP?"

"That's why my car's been left running. Stan Bradley's already at the cordon, keeping the media and gawkers away while keeping the corpses in." Ramos cleared his throat.

"Ms. Lark, I could use whatever help your organization can provide."

Loredana stopped in the middle of plugging in two laptop computers. "I can have twenty people there in five minutes—provided your department is willing to overlook the firepower we may have available. Gary?"

"Hmm?" Gary was staring at a dizzying array of files that opened one by one on a nearby monitor. He'd rigged it to a battered hard drive emblazoned with Syndax's logo and was downloading who knew what from the brains. I just hoped it was worth something.

"If there are any projects in the laboratory or armory to which I was not privy—projects your former supervisor arranged, as he did with Mercury's suit—I suggest you bring them to our attention."

"Sure. Yeah, I can do that." He tapped his lips. "Now this is fascinating. Liz? You see where they had figured a way to absorb tachyons directly into the DNA of a host? The first results were messy but when they got here ..."

"Oh! Wow, that's impressive. Let me crack this encryption on the biological results. Shouldn't take me a minute ..."

And so, the nerd herd was off, combining their equally brainy brains to the problem. "We can't wait around for them to figure it out," I told Loredana. "Give me an earbud and you can quarterback from here while Ramos and I rally the troops, before the real troops show up."

"I'll get us both earbuds, thank you very much, because I'm coming with you."

Pretty obvious neither one of us wanted to relent. I didn't want her anywhere near the fight—but seriously, last time around, she'd been in the thick of it with everyone else. Who was I kidding? If I had to wade into battle against evil forces, there's no one else I'd rather have on my team. Well, her and Ramos. "Okay. So much for arguing you out of it."

She smiled. "We both know that's not a possibility."

"Tell me about it." I took her hand and kissed it in the most gentlemanly fashion possible. "But you'd better get changed into something more comfortable."

"Indeed. I thought perhaps slacks, and Kevlar." She headed out the door.

Ramos watched her leave. "Things have progressed, have they?"

"We're getting there." My chest was probably puffed out so far, I was surprised I could still see the sword.

Ramos clapped my shoulder. "You're maddening and infuriating, Mercury Hale, but I'm happy for you in that regard."

"Aw, shucks." I grinned. At least the budding relationship had distracted him from wanting to murder me. "Not kissing your hand, Ramos."

"*Cállate.*"

"Mercury?" Loredana leaned back around the corner of the door. "I cannot believe I'd forgotten—there's something that could be of use already available in the lab. Your brother left it here during the North Beach Battle."

Ramos shook his head, scowling. I chuckled at Loredana's adoption of my name for the fight. Well, my name and all the Internet's. But I blanked on what she meant. "No way. He took the ax and the blade back to Meda. Hence us being worried about Arkwright getting his hands on them."

"Not those. Your temporary substitutes."

My face must have looked as empty as my brain, because Loredana raised her eyebrow in that less-than-patient way she did. Then the memory clicked.

I grinned. "Oh. Those."

The daggers were locked in a cabinet at the back of the lab, labeled with red and white emergency stripes and the warning, "Classified."

Loredana's badge opened it.

They were exotic, slender versions of machetes. The lab's sickly lighting glittered along the hair-fine carvings up the center of each blade as I twisted them around, the sword strapped to my back with an equipment belt I'd found in the armory. "Don't I just get all the best toys."

"I'm glad this makes you happy," Ramos said. "Feeling better about our chances?"

I swung the daggers left, then right, then brought them across a faucet. They sliced it off without the slightest tug on my grip. Water sprayed on my face. Loredana yelped, shaking it from her hands.

"Oh, yeah." I flicked a drop off my nose. "Much better."

CHAPTER TWENTY-NINE

The drive downtown happened in total silence, among the passengers, I mean.

Ramos's Dodge Charger roared the whole way, the engine vibrating its chassis. Sirens howled from every angle. Voices scratched over the radio.

Never been in the front seat of a police car. The roof? Sure. I glanced up. Yeah, the metal had been patched and the ceiling recovered. You never would have known I held onto the car for dear life by stabbing the pulsar stave into the top.

Ramos seemed as calm as a guy who had plenty of time to get himself to church—hands loose on the wheel, body slouched in the seat. Otherwise, he drove like the Indianapolis 500 track was part of his morning commute. Reminded me of Loredana's jet taking off.

We bypassed the normal evening traffic and wound up cruising a street that was empty. Not a vehicle in sight, not even parked ones. What had SCPD done, towed the ones whose owners were gone?

We found a huge crowd of people a block away. They were shouting and raising fists and generally being obnoxious, but if it were me with my family trapped in a zombie-infested part of the city, I couldn't say I'd blame them. Our convoy of five vehicles—Ramos's Charger and four Procyon SUVs—pulled over well to the side of the street, clear of the crowd.

Detective Stan Bradley was at the head of the police cordon, his usual sour-faced self, except he'd accessorized his wardrobe with Kevlar and his shotgun. I would have guessed seeing Ramos would have improved his mood, but Loredana and I accompanying him had the opposite effect. "Lieutenant? What are they doing here?"

"They're our chance to clean this up before the ANG makes this neighborhood look like Syria." Ramos slung an M4 rifle over his shoulder. "Spahr! Jimenez! Get those barriers separated so we can get our vehicles through."

"Are you crazy?" Bradley blocked his path. "Have you seen what's comin' down that road? I've got S.W.A.T. snipers on the rooftops to take out any more before they can get closer. But I don't have enough people to clear out these wackos who're trying to get through, and now you want to go sightseeing?"

"Stan, not now. Mercury—"

"Is a dangerous vigilante who couldn't stop those, those things from killing our people." Bradley had the muzzle of the shotgun prodding my suit. "I oughta put a hole the size of a dinner plate between his legs."

I left the bottom half of the mask pulled back so he could see my sneer, which went along nicely with the daggers and the sword.

"Is that him? That's Mercury?" The shouted question came from a reporter stabbing a microphone through the air like her own melee weapon. "Sir! What can you tell us about the situation? Are there really reanimated corpses? Is the city co-opting the services of a vigilante? How will this impact taxpayers?"

"My parents!" A girl was sobbing into her hands, making the statement semi-coherent. "They live across from the cemetery! Has anyone seen them?"

I grimaced at the memory of the video Ramos had shown us, with SCPD gunning down a handful of corpse-fiends. There was no doubt in my mind the creatures were not only originating from the cemetery but killing and infecting anyone in that neighborhood who hadn't managed to hide.

"Listen, Bradley," I growled, "You could shoot me, but then there's no one left to kill the enemy soldier who's become his own version of a fiend-hound, complete with tentacles sprouting out of his back, and playing general for the corpses. So, who's gonna turn back the monsters? You?"

Bradley stared at me, stunned into rare silence, while Ramos radioed instructions and shooed his officers out of the way. They opened a big enough gap in the barricade that the Procyon SUVs could slip through.

"Come on." I led Loredana and Ramos on foot. The cemetery was a block and a half away. Procyon security, led by Garvey got out of the trucks a few buildings from us, in the shadows where the crowd couldn't see them well.

"Lieutenant!" Bradley helped officers replace the barriers, as reporters shouted questions around him. "What do I tell the captain?"

"Tell her I'm working the problem!"

I nodded. "Good answer."

"I thought so."

Ramos's radio crackled. "Lieutenant? Rooftop Unit here, at your eight o'clock. Got ten targets inbound."

"Roger that. Hold your fire. I've got people down here to handle it."

I saw the corpse-fiends spotted by the sniper just ten seconds later. They shambled out of the gloom, ahead of the Procyon SUVs. The security people had spread out, seeking cover behind steps and a bus stop, in addition to their vehicles. Garvey saw us coming and waved. They were all armed with shotguns. There were also MP5 machine guns in the mix.

"You were serious about your foundation's access to firepower." Ramos unlimbered his rifle.

"I was." Loredana wore a T-shirt, Kevlar, and fatigue pants. She had her hair secured in a ponytail, and little of it was visible from underneath the unmarked gray ballcap pulled down low over her eyes. There was no way you could match her up with the best-dressed woman at Rampart's gala just a few hours ago. "With the threats we face, we find it is best to be prepared."

I got to the security personnel first. "Hey, Garvey."

"Mr. Hale." He blinked when he saw the long sword hanging from my belt, and the slender daggers clutched in my hands. "You're, uh, prepared."

"Not my usual arsenal, but a man's gotta make do."

"Sure thing." He gestured with the shotgun. "Ten in front, six more coming along the sidewalks."

He was right. I bet the snipers hadn't seen the extras, what with the trees blocking their lines of sight. "Okay, then. Ramos, give the word."

He shook his head. "This is your show, Procyon."

"Don't call me that."

"I was talking to your handler, Mercury."

Loredana smiled primly. "Thank you, Lieutenant." To

Garvey, she added, "You may fire when ready."

Garvey barked a command, and weapons erupted around us, the booming of shotguns intermixed with the harsh chatter of automatic fire. The first five corpse-fiends went down, their bodies shredded, emitting the noxious cloud which seemed to be their signature side effect.

The rest of the gang, though, sped up. I mean, they flat out, *ran*. And as if that wasn't bad enough, fifty feet away, two of them flickered, their bodies outlined in purple sparks, and I had double vision for a second. Then they disappeared.

And reappeared in our midst.

One of them speared a Procyon security guard with its tentacles. The guy screamed, his MP5 shooting wildly into the air and the adjacent vehicles. Garvey dove, taking Loredana to the ground with him. She put several shots into the corpse-fiend as she fell.

I stepped in and delivered the disintegrating blow with one of the daggers.

I had no idea whether the weapon, which Teget said was forged in Meda, would affect the monster in the same way as the pulsar stave, but my prayer was answered. It fell apart without spreading its particles across the street, leaving the spot where it stood clean.

Our security guard wasn't so lucky. I stabbed him next, because he'd become a shriveled, snarling corpse himself.

"Snipers!" Ramos shouted.

The heads of two corpses exploded, but they weren't nearby anyone, so the particles whipped around in the air before swirling along the street toward the cemetery. Ramos put them onto the pavement with well-placed shots of his own. He fired from a kneeling position, taking his time with each target.

Our security boys weren't nearly as disciplined, as busy as they were scrambling in the midst of the corpse-fiends that kept appearing around us. Gunfire became more sporadic and, well, poorly aimed.

A bullet creased my suit. "Hey! Watch it!" I lopped the arm off a corpse and melted it down with the daggers.

We had the first wave struck down, at the cost of just one of our people. It was one too many. Garvey leaned against the truck, tears welling up. He stared at the smudge on the pavement where his young protégé had been. Don't ask me the name. I had no idea. Just another face I'd seen around the Procyon complex.

This was Arkwright's fault. And Marigold's. Their obsession with emptying the contents of the Interstice into our world like the bottom of a trash bag spilling onto the kitchen floor was the cause of all this death, this destruction, this terror.

Not after tonight.

"Come on!" I hurried up the street and was happy to hear the rumble of boots and shoes on the asphalt behind me. It wasn't much of an army, but it was better than nothing.

Especially when we found our target.

The street was thick with corpse-fiends just before Cavill Cemetery. They were packed in dozens, hundreds of them, milling about. Milling, that is, until they saw us. Shrieks rippled outward from the front ranks, spreading to the wings.

Then the gunfire started up. But it came from *inside* the horde.

"Get to cover!" Which was easy for Ramos to say, because he was already tucked behind a bench, the M4 propped on top.

Me? I was running down the middle of the street, like an idiot, the sword strapped to my back. But it felt right. Better than skulking around, searching for answers, or dropping off fire escapes to punch a mugger in the face. This was the battle I needed.

Four of the corpse-fiends did their teleport, materializing around me at the points of the compass. I let myself get lost in the fight, blades flashing in the pale glow of San Camillo's lights. I sliced a head off, kicked one corpse into another, impaled them both, chopped tentacles off the fourth one, parried his counterattack, got knocked to the ground, brought the daggers up into its chest. It was a blur of images and sounds, each more disorienting than the last.

Next thing I knew the horde was pressing around me. The Procyon guards were there, shooting—from above me? Since when could they levitate?

Ah. Since Garvey put aside his mourning and got the SUVs rolled up behind me. He stood on the hood, blasting corpses apart with his shotgun. More Procyon men lent their fire with MP5s from the roofs, lying prone or crouching. It was a good way to keep them out of the monsters' grasps and was doing a heck of job clearing the field for me.

Loredana, of course, snuck up to my right, MP5 held in a two-handed grip. It bucked burst after burst, punching holes in the corpse-fiends. But the bullets weren't holding back as many creatures as she would have liked. A couple swiped at her with their spiked tentacles. She drew back, her balance lost.

"Look out!" I hurtled into the space between her and the attackers. A tentacle slashed across my side, snaking around my arm. Ice spiked through my chest. I chopped the critter's appendage off with a dagger, let it melt off as I slaughtered the first corpse fiend and then its buddy.

This wasn't like the way I fought astral fiends. That had an element of grace, almost a dance, in a twisted way. It took skill and foresight to stay a step ahead of their eight tentacles and the constant shift in their positions, with a gymnast's skill. But the corpse-fiends? They were a mob. It was a matter of destroying them faster than they could kill us.

Simple. Except they had mutated human soldiers with them.

One of the Procyon guys toppled off the truck, blood spraying across his partner. More shots riddled the front of an SUV, making Garvey roll onto the pavement.

Syndax soldiers came out of the horde, using the corpse-fiends for cover as they blasted at us with what had to be the biggest guns I'd ever seen on San Camillo's streets. They were military-grade, probably SCAR model battle rifles. Made the MP5s look like water pistols. And being linked together via fiend DNA meant they moved in unison and with incredible reflexes. I saw a guy dodge a flurry of bullets. Another took a direct hit from Garvey's shotgun without slowing his stride.

He did stop, however, when Ramos put a bullet between glowing, stormy violet eyes.

"Hold your ground!" Loredana waved to the Procyon guards. "Use the trucks for cover!"

It was like those stories you hear about the settlers circling wagons against understandably aggravated Natives, except the trucks bumped against each other, some nose to nose, others bumper to bumper. The bullet-resistant glass was holding, sort of, because while it must have been designed for added protection, it was not meant to fend off a full-blown assault.

Numbers weren't in our favor, either. We were down to fifteen, including Garvey, plus Loredana, Ramos, and me. Facing a hundred or more corpse-fiends, with probably two dozen soldiers in their ranks. Whenever one of ours put down a corpse-fiend, the soldiers used the body as a barricade from behind which they could shoot.

I kinda wished the ANG would bomb this place, just to wipe them all out, but I knew it wouldn't do us any good. I cut down a corpse-fiend, then obliterated a second, before I found shelter at one corner of our SUV barrier. "So much for conventional tactics."

"Can you see Arkwright?"

"Not from here. Hang on." I pressed my hand against the earbud riding underneath to suit's hood. "Gary! I need some good news."

"Good news? We've got a lot of data decrypted off the Syndax computers. And also, if you can get the pulsar stave, I'm pretty sure we can use it in conjunction with the portal, this tachyon nexus if you will, to stop whatever Arkwright has in mind."

"Yeah. About that …"

"You're probably not near it." Gary muttered something and I heard Liz clap her hands together. "Got a drone flying over right now."

"Give me a peek."

The drone buzzed overhead, red and green lights blinking as it hugged the buildings on the right side of the street. The soldiers shifted aim, blasting skyward. Had to hand it to Liz—she was an ace pilot, because that tiny thing juked like the best Mustang in a World War II dogfight. That is, until one shot clipped a rotor and it spun out of control. Another couple of blasts spewed plastic and wires across the road.

"Transmitting video now!" Gary yelped. "Oh, and tell Ms. Lark—"

"The THEL has green lights!" Liz's exhilaration made the earbud's audio crackle and sent a jolt of pain into my head. "She's ready to go whenever you are! Cyril has the controls routed through the server so we can monitor the fuel levels and make sure it doesn't, you know, blow up if it runs too hot, which is a distinct possibility because I think we've only tested it twice and never in a city street because that's just crazy—"

"Loredana!" I gave her a thumbs up.

She sprinted to the back of a nearby SUV and flung the rear hatch, which was actually two doors, open. "Position and fire!"

Whoever was driving the rig had some skills. Not quite Steve McQueen, but definitely some *Fast & Furious*, because the tires screeched, and the truck spun around until the backside was pointed squarely at the oncoming horde.

The soldiers must have figured something bad was gonna happen, because they tried to withdraw. Which didn't work out well, because their hesitation gave the SCPD snipers and Ramos time to drop another four of them.

I caught a glimpse of the SUV's cargo—a tan sphere perched on gimbals, braced against the interior of the truck. It was surrounded by all kind of wires and tubes. Metal cylinders were clustered behind it. The front of the sphere was a set of three lenses, the smallest the size of my fist, the largest with the same diameter as a beach ball.

A deep, heavy hum filled the air. Then came a series of clicks.

The particles released by destroyed corpse-fiends highlighted sections of an otherwise invisible beam as it pulsed across the horde. The creatures turned white-hot everywhere the beam touched and then vaporized, looking like a bunch of coals that got way too hot before exploding. The laser roasted a half dozen corpse-fiends in the first strike, then five or six, until the THEL had cut fifteen, twenty, twenty-five ...

Oh, yeah. THEL. Tactical High-Energy Laser. One of Procyon's toys. Nice and mobile, too. The military was playing with them, but as far as I know, they frowned upon you stuffing one in the back of an SUV.

I grinned. After about the fortieth zombie melted, I figured they wouldn't complain.

By then, the soldiers had all taken shelter in and around abandoned storefronts and alleys. The zombies rushed us, flinging themselves across the gap between our trucks and their front ranks. THEL caught several in mid-lunge, moths caught in the good old bug zapper. With the laser targeting the largest concentration to our right, I headed left, to where Ramos was hunkered down. He was still patiently putting down zombies with two-shot bursts and had just paused to swap out magazines when the tip of their incursion reached him.

I kicked a corpse-fiend backward and stabbed the daggers through his chest. He was only halfway disintegrated when the next one ripped through his poor pal, clawing for me. I swiped through his face with one dagger and slashed diagonally with the other, leaving two lumps of blackened blue goop sublimating on the sidewalk. "Can't let you have all the fun."

Ramos wiped his forehead. "I think Loredana is the one having fun—she and whoever is controlling your ...is that a laser?"

"Oh, yeah."

"Mercury!" Gary shouted so loudly in my earbud I jumped. Swore he was standing right next to me. "There's a massive buildup of tachyons and ... energy readings I don't recognize. It's as if the Interstice itself is bleeding into our world, a rip but more focused, a tiny but powerful space."

Okay. Give me a target and I'd hit it. "What's that mean?"

Half the corpse-fiends had been obliterated when a sickly purple light shot through with undulating black waves flashed from the cemetery. It rolled over the reanimated bodies. Each one it touched became enmeshed in a pulsing, glowing web. Then the wave reversed. It dragged the corpse-fiends into each other, their arms and legs jostling, at an astonishing speed. Wind tugged at my clothes. It blew leaves off the trees.

The monsters howled, one ghastly sound that cut off in the snap of fingers. And then they were gone.

With them vanished, I had a clear view of the cemetery, albeit at an angle. The soldiers were standing on guard, weapons ready, their eyes like flashlights, purple lighting crawling along their bodies.

Arkwright stood in the center, the pulsar stave raised. He was two feet taller, with bulging muscles, tentacles that protruded from his chest, arms, and legs. Thick obsidian scales ripped through his clothing. His eyes—there were nine of them now, hideous and glistening purple orbs.

"The wall is in ruins!" His voice could have been filtered through a hundred megaphones.

Blinding white light tinged with purple shot from the pulsar stave, right into our group. I dove across Ramos, shielding him.

The SUV that was home to THEL took the brunt of the blast, exploding into a huge fireball. Two more vehicles went up in smoke with it. The rest were toppled on their sides, windows shattered.

My ears were ringing. I couldn't see anything. My head spun. Was I out? Concussion 2.0?

Soldiers swarmed us. Blows to my stomach and my head put me on the ground. I heard Ramos cry out.

Nothing I could do.

Finally, I managed to look up. Soldiers dragged Ramos and I and the remaining Procyon guards away. Loredana, too, thankfully. She was singed. Bruised. But kicking.

And captured.

CHAPTER
THIRTY

O nce the ringing in my ears tapered off, it was peaceful in the cemetery.

I was on my knees about thirty feet from the clearing, with Loredana at my right and Ramos on the left. Twelve Procyon guys were lined up behind us, including Garvey, who was visible off my right shoulder. That meant eight of our people were dead.

I glanced at Loredana. Her chin was at her chest, her eyes red from tears or exhaustion. Did she have to contact families? Write letters or send emails to parents and wives and children, making up some story about how all those men were killed? It had to tear her apart, being unable to tell their loved ones the truth.

Those guys were the heroes.

"I should be stronger, you know." Arkwright walked toward us. My brain screamed at his appearance. No one should look like that. The sheer otherness triggered an automatic response that everything was *wrong*. "The more the risen bodies I absorb, the greater my link to the Interstice becomes. You've proven more a thorn than I anticipated."

I wanted to be defiant, to slam him with a gallant speech, but I was aching and tired and just fed up. "Not my fault you couldn't figure that out. I did save the world a few months ago."

Arkwright chuckled, which was worse than ominous silence. Multiple voices—including Marigold's distinctive musical tones—overlapped. "Good point, Mercury. If I'd wanted you dead, well, I should have pulled the trigger myself. But I really did want you alive for this. All the better that you made your way here, through some minor miracle no doubt, and can see in person the glory of what I'm going to achieve, of what we're all going to be a part."

"Glory has nothing to do with this." Ramos wiped blood from the corner of his mouth. Dark red stains speckled his shirt. The first couple buttons were undone. His crucifix poked through, its fine silver chain tangled in the gap. "Desecrating the dead. It's vile."

Arkwright knelt before us. He reeked of astral fiend, that peculiar, wrenching smell that emanated from their slimy bodies. But, oddly, I also got a whiff of cologne. Arkwright's eyes shimmered. They lost some of their alien hue and, for a moment, I could see normal brown human eyeballs. "I don't think that's possible. What do the dead care? The beings I created with their discarded flesh were empty shells. Surely you agree. Whether or not I'm a religious man, like you, I know the soul is gone when death overtakes us. Where does it go? I'll leave that for you and the theologians. But the body's left behind. They were batteries for tachyon particles. Nothing more."

"It doesn't make it right." Loredana's voice shook.

"Ms. Lark. I didn't figure you'd be the one to lecture me about what's right. After all, those men out there are dead because of your foundation's existence. And how long did Marigold and Winston lurk in Procyon's shadows? How long did you unwittingly support their goals without realizing who they truly were?" Arkwright touched her cheek. The hands had deformed into three gnarled digits, each with a black claw that would have made a velociraptor proud. "But go ahead. Make your righteous protest. I'd rather you feel good when the light takes you."

I grabbed his wrist. "Nobody's taking anyone anywhere."

Maybe he'd throw a punch. Maybe I could dodge the blow and retrieve my daggers. They were jabbed in the ground, twenty feet to our left, where a bunch of the Syndax soldiers stood. The rest were split into two groups, one behind our guys and the other arrayed across the cemetery's entrance.

Neither plan worked, because Arkwright reversed his hand in a direction that wasn't humanly possible, latched onto my wrist, and threw me.

I hit an obelisk forty feet across the clearing, upside down.

That's where I found Skipper.

Half his face was a maroon bruise that had gone black and blue around the edges. He was tied to a tree, sitting cross-legged. Four Syndax soldiers surrounded him. He squinted. "Mercury? Thank the Most High. I thought they'd put all of you to the sword."

"Nice to see you too." I coughed. Blood trickled from my mouth. Fortunately, it felt like a damaged tooth or maybe a cut inside my mouth. I was really hoping it wasn't internal bleeding. "Be ready."

"I stand at your side." The corner of his mouth crooked. "If, that is, I could stand at all."

I chuckled. Poor timing, I know, and, ow, but in the face of what was probably going to be something terrible, humor's about all that makes me human.

"I have no desire to kill your friend." Arkwright loomed over me. He was good at looming, with those extra two feet of height. He cut Skipper's bindings with a single swipe of his newly clawed hand. He used the other to pull Skipper off the ground and hold him at arm's length, boots dangling. "He's my way home."

He carried Skipper into the clearing. The portal's distortion intensified. For a moment, it looked like there were three of them. Then the forms coalesced, though there was a silvery tinge to them. "I don't know where this portal goes. But I know it passes through the Interstice. And as you've no doubt discovered—though I'm sure Procyon would rather you did not—there's more to the interdimensional barriers than merely poking a hole through a rip so astral fiends can have free rein here on Earth. The Interstice operates as the transit station, the terminal, if you will, between dimensions. There's an old saying: You can't get there from here. Well, from the Interstice, you can get *everywhere.*"

Arkwright slammed Skipper into the ground. Skipper tried to get back to his feet, but Arkwright slammed a monstrous, clawed paw onto his chest. Skipper's hands pulled at the grass as he gasped for breath.

"Hold still." Arkwright willed the pulsar stave to life. *My* pulsar stave. Its yellow-white energies were tinted a sickly violet and writhed with an imbalance I'd never seen before. "It'll be over soon enough."

He thrust the pulsar stave into the core of the portal. It strikes nothing I can see, but the effect is immediate. The outside of the bubble swirls, reflecting me, the Procyon and

Syndax people, the headstones and trees, even warm glow of San Camillo's night sky. But it stays transparent, somehow, so I can still see Arkwright and Skipper. A shadow forms, tall and narrow, its edges crackling with purple energies. If didn't know better, I'd say he used the pulsar stave to create or capture a rip. Maybe I don't know better.

Arkwright drew the halves of the stave apart, and as he spread his arms, the shadow widened. It expanded and inflated, forming a second sphere, even as the outer shell extends its boundaries. This new circle flashed with smeared shapes. I couldn't make them out. But when I struggled upright, it looked like a tunnel. I walked the edge, and the illusion—or reality—stayed the same. No matter from which angle I looked in, I'm was looking down a swirling tube.

The Syndax soldiers stayed near me, at a distance. They didn't strike me or try to restrain me. No doubt they'd shoot if I tried something.

"It's working! I wasn't sure if it would. You plan and hope and yet, when it comes to the moment—" Arkwright smiled. He's still got a nice smile, if not for half his head being mutated into a monster's visage.

"No matter what you let loose into this world, I'm gonna stop it." I stood beyond the outer sphere. No way I was stepping inside. Not yet. I glanced at Loredana. She watched the whole thing with wide eyes. But when our gazes met, I was hoping for—and got—that mutual reassurance. That look that says, I'm here for you. I hoped she could sense it in me, too.

Of course, her gaze flicked left. Toward the daggers, which the Syndax goons were ignoring, because they were just as enamored with the portal's gyrations as their boss.

I knew Loredana wouldn't let me down.

She nudged Ramos, a subtle touch of her fingers to his shirt sleeve. He frowned at her, then looked at me. I kept my finger at my waist and pointed.

He got the hint, too.

Arkwright finally let off Skipper. "This is it. This is the broken wall, and you're privileged to see beyond it. I've waited a long time for this—for the light to come through, yes, and cleanse this world, but more importantly, for me to leave it."

Good. He was in a talking mood. "That's got to be disappointing. You're going to revamp Earth, and you're not even sticking around to see the results?"

"Oh, I am. I'll make sure everything here is put to the purifying fire. But then, I'll go home, and bring the same cleansing with me." Arkwright's fingers brushed against the rip-shadow or whatever it was with surprising gentleness, like he was reaching for—a flower? A lost pet? A loved one?

"Give it a rest, Arkwright. You're gonna blow everything up. You don't have to justify it. I assumed you were crazy, just like Marigold and her wacky family." I shrugged. A hiss of static bled through my earbud. What? The thing was still working? Maybe the microphone in my suit, the one through which I could talk with Liz and Gary back at Procyon, was up and running, too. "For all her grandiose yapping about a new world, I get what she was saying: Letting astral fiends kill people."

"Sounds crude when you put it that way. But accurate. It's for a better purpose, though. Once we're all linked together, even this improvement—" He rapped a stave half off his armor. "Won't count for much. We'll see each other as we truly are."

"If you say luminous beings, I'm gonna have to beat you

for misquoting Yoda."

Arkwright gave me a quizzical smile but wagged the stave in my direction. "You don't get it. I'm surprised Ms. Lark hasn't told you. Then again, maybe she's used to keeping secrets."

"Procyon guards the public from secrets that have to be kept." Couldn't believe I was saying it. "People are freaking out because of what you've done! Nobody wants panic."

"Of course not, but the truth—the truth is always paramount. And the truth is why I'm here. Truth is, Mercury, I'm leaving here to go home."

"Home. What, Colorado?"

"Oh, yes. Just not your Colorado."

I must have taken one too many blows to the head. "Now you're talking like a crazy supervillain, which I guess is to be expected since ..." I waved my hands at him.

"Let me clear it up. I'm Alexander Arkwright, but not *your* Alexander Arkwright. Not *this* place's Alexander Arkwright. I was part of a classified experiment to breach the boundaries between dimensions. Nobody was more surprised to find out this place existed—so close to my world, yet different enough for me to risk the mission."

He scowled. "And, of course, when I went through, when I found myself here, I learned the truth. I was abandoned. Left with no support, not hope of return. Alone. For twenty years. Twenty years!"

Arkwright lashed out. The pulsar stave's insane power-up produced a blinding flare when it struck the nearest headstone. The marble exploded into orange embers that brightened to yellow, then faded to gray. Ash settled on Skipper, who just stared, mouth agape.

Blinking lights caught my attention. I thought they were

overhead, but when I tried to pinpoint them, they were gone.

"Now, that's not to say I blamed them." Arkwright walked around Skipper, glaring at him. "Why should I? I volunteered for the mission. I understood the risks involved. What right did I have to complain when they left me here to rot? So, I did what I was supposed to."

"You killed him," Loredana said. "You murdered Alexander Arkwright."

That made even less sense than the wild images I was seeing through the bizarre lens of the modified portal. Then I spotted those blinking lights again. This time I saw the drone they went with. The tiny machine disappeared above the cemetery's trees.

"Mercury!"

For a second, I thought Marigold was speaking to me through Arkwright's body again, but I realized this voice had a hiss of static as an undercurrent. It was Liz, whispering through my earbud.

"I know you're surrounded. We can see you through the drone's cameras and have an audio feed, too. What did they do to the portal? The tachyon readings are through the roof! Anyway, we've got an idea. Scratch your cheek if you hear me."

I scratched, still staring at Arkwright and trying to make sense of his monologue.

"Of course I did." He chuckled and waved the pulsar stave at Loredana. "It gave me twenty years to fit into place, to put myself in a position where this could come to fruition. It helped considerably that Alexander Arkwright was an aimless 21-year-old partying his way through college. Mom and Dad were delighted when he finally and suddenly sobered up, boosting his grades, graduating with honors, putting a theretofore undisclosed technical and scientific aptitude to work."

"Okay, Mercury, I know this sounds weird, but you have to let Arkwright breach the barrier between dimensions even further," Liz murmured. "Get ahold of the pulsar staves and use them to redirect the energies he's released. It's not as simple as linking the weapons like you did before. This requires you to follow our instructions. Gary's monitoring the portal from there."

From there? Where was he, under a tombstone? And more importantly, why was Arkwright bragging about killing himself? The only feasible answer hit me so hard I was out of breath. "You're—Alexander Arkwright. A different one."

"Only different in two places." He tapped his head, and then his chest. "DNA, blood type, both identical. I'm sure if Procyon ran some tests, though, you'd find subtle genetic differences. That's to be expected, considering I'm from a parallel Earth."

"I should have known," Loredana snapped. "Did Zein send you?"

Arkwright frowned. "I don't know any such person. Probably he was after my time—twenty years, as I said. So, you've had experience with my world. Doesn't matter. I have my means. The only thing I lack is the proper access."

"Mercury!" Liz's interruption startled me. I moved around the portal, edging closer, but must have hit the point of no return, because when I was at arm's length from the outer sphere, Arkwright's soldiers blocked my path.

"Easy, fellas." I held up my hands and smiled. "Just want a closer look. I mean, come on, who wouldn't?"

"It's all right. I don't need him." Arkwright extended a hand to Skipper. "I need you."

"What possible use could a monster have for me?" Skipper stood braced for a fight. "I'll die before I come to your aid, and I shall remove you from this world when I do."

"No, you won't. Let me ask you this: how did you find the fiend-hound? When you were hunting it throughout San Camillo. You don't have anything like the technology Syndax or Procyon possess. Certainly, you lack the financial resources. What was it?"

"Its presence called to me, like a distant bell. Whenever it appeared, I could be there, drawn to it. And my desire was only ever its extinction. It does not belong anywhere but the deepest pits of the underworld."

"I can see how you'd make that mistake. The fiends, they're not an infection. They're harbingers of the light. They bind the dimensions, and yet, they lack awareness of their purpose. Drive. Will." Arkwright reached for Skipper. "We have that. Mankind, yes, but aren't we more than the common species? Better. Gifted."

"The only gift I'm aware of is your death, should it be granted to me." Skipper's hands clenched into fists.

"Come on, don't give me that. You want the same thing I do."

"Your destruction?"

"To go home," Arkwright murmured. "To be in the presence of the ones you love. To make your lands pure."

Skipper's face twisted in evident confusion, like he was trying to decide something but couldn't recall what his choices were.

"Don't deny it. You miss home."

"I don't ... remember it."

"Not even pieces? Smells? Sensations?"

Skipper touched the side of his head, as he gazed

somewhere beyond Arkwright. "Shards."

"It's in there. I can help. I want to go back, too, but this—" Arkwright indicated the swirling tunnels around him. "This is too much for one mind to comprehend. But two minds—minds that have already experienced the passage from other worlds through the Interstice—can. They will. I had a partner here, a man with whom I traveled from the other side. Let me extend that partnership to you, so we can restore your memory and bring us both to rest."

"Are you insane?" I blurted. "Skipper's worked with me the whole time to stop your fiend fest! He's one of us!"

"He isn't. For crying out loud, Mercury, *you're* not even one of us!" Arkwright scowled at me. "You belong in Meda. I belong on my Earth. And this Skipper, he belongs on his world. The only thing that unites those places, that should ever and will always link them, are the fiends. They're the living extension of the Interstice!"

"Skipper, listen. Help me defeat him." I pushed against the soldiers. "You've done what's right, without any reward, and yeah, I know what it's like to want to go home."

He looked at me, but Arkwright blocked the way. "I'll be glad to pass a message to your family, Mercury, when I get to Meda. A side trip on my way back. You didn't think I'd forgotten, did you?"

Arkwright's face distorted and smoothed into a delicate smile. When he continued, it was Marigold's melodious voice, the one that made my skin crawl. "My mother and my mother's mother and my grandmother's mother would be pleased to know you had a hand in returning the blade to our family. More than that, our lineage will finally possess all three weapons. Things will be as they should."

I shoved a soldier. He tried to bring his weapon into

my gut, but I caught it, reversed its trajectory and cracked him across his mask. The second guard had his gun pointed inches from my nose, but I pushed it skyward and hit him in the throat. The muzzle flashed. Bullets sprayed overhead.

Two jokers down.

I had the gun ready to mow the entire rank of soldiers behind Loredana and Ramos when intense cold wrapped around my midsection. Arkwright's tentacles, stretched out a good eight feet, coiled over my shoulders. He whipped me into the portal. A swift swipe with his claws smashed the gun to pieces, and a second blow put me on the ground. Again. I was gonna have to pay the cemetery rent at this rate.

"I wish you had been on our side." He shook his head. "There's still time."

"Go to hell." I spit on his shoes. Probably didn't have the same effect, since their fine Italian curves were mangled by his protruding claws.

"It's not on my way, sorry." He kicked me.

Skipper reached, like he was gonna help me up, but stopped.

"Give me a break." I coughed. Blood again. If I'd had the pulsar stave in my grasp, it could have accelerated my healing, but fat chance Arkwright was going to lend it to me for some first aid. "Please. You've got to help us."

Skipper turned away.

"Don't do it!" I shuddered. My insides were full of needles where Arkwright had touched me. It was like the life was still being drained from me, or the worst hangover in the history of the world.

Skipper didn't look at me. Nor did he look at the men with their guns behind our people, poised and ready to shoot them. I tried not to think of the empty graves around us.

Arkwright held out half the pulsar stave. "Will you help us both find the way?"

Skipper took it. Since Arkwright maintained his grip, the energies continued to pulse from the carvings. Then Skipper went and blew our last chance out of the water.

"Yes."

CHAPTER THIRTY-ONE

Two things happened simultaneously.

Arkwright's and Skipper's outlines exploded with the same pulsating multi-colored hue of energies as the portal's interior.

And Ramos attacked his guard.

He wasn't alone. Loredana headbutted the nearest soldier in the groin and came up onto her feet swinging. The soldier blocked her furious blows as best he could, but still stumbled backwards into his buddies.

The confusion gave Garvey and his people the perfect opportunity to go on the offensive. The brawl expanded, pitting our guys against Syndax, until it was a whirling melee of fists, arms, and legs.

Gunshots rang in the crowd. I couldn't tell whether Procyon or Syndax forces had fired, but it didn't matter. I wasn't gonna let anyone get killed.

I grabbed one of the pulsar stave's halves.

There was no way I was getting it away from Arkwright, unarmed. Skipper didn't make a move to stop me, but his new pal did, bashing me out of the portal with a thunder strike to the chest.

Even as I slid into the trunk of a tree, sharp pains shooting up my spine, I grinned. The grin was still there as I wiped dirt from my teeth.

That single touch? It was enough for me to use as a siphon.

A smidgen of the stave's energy coursed through me. Time to see how long a smidgen would last in a fight.

I threw myself toward the fracas and was happily rewarded by a burst of acceleration that was way outside the speed of a normal person. Eat that, Usain Bolt.

The Syndax soldier facing me stared, wide-eyed, over his face mask. Guy looked perplexed, even with his pupils glowing eerie purple.

A single punch put him on the ground.

Now that was more like it.

"Mercury!" Ramos planted the back end of a shotgun into a fallen soldier's midsection, then kicked him in the helmet. There was a joke to be made there about police brutality, but I'm not that guy. "Catch!"

He tossed one of the daggers.

I caught it in mid-slide, because I was busy ducking an explosion of bullets from a soldier's SCAR. Took one swipe to cut the gun in half, but that didn't stop the soldier from reaching for a second gun, the pistol in its holster.

I stabbed him in the chest.

It wasn't like going after an astral fiend. No simple snicker snack, as the poem goes, but a subdued crunch. The blade came out bloody. This guy wasn't going to melt away, like the monsters I'd faced. He was dead, and he was real.

One more image to add to the nightmares.

More shots buzzed around us. The soldiers on the other

side of the cemetery were shooting, disregarding the safety of their comrades. A Procyon guard fell, as did the Syndax man with whom he was grappling. Well, that was one way to solve the problem of enemies amongst your buddies.

I pulled Loredana behind a crypt. Shards of chipped stone flew overhead. "I'd like to say things will get better, but, you know, I'm still working on that."

"What word from Procyon?" Loredana propped a SCAR rifle—who she'd taken it from, I had no idea—and fired. Someone screamed. A thud followed.

"Liz and Gary have a plan, and Gary's nearby. Got a drone watching the proceedings. They went silent when I got knocked into the portal zone."

"Our success hinges on retrieving the pulsar staves."

Ramos joined us. He had a radio pressed to his mouth. "I don't care what the commissioner says! Get those S.W.A.T. units down here *now!* We've got people dying!"

A rumble grew overhead. It sounded like aircraft, except I'd never heard one over downtown San Camillo that loud, or with that pitch to the engines.

"Air National Guard," Ramos muttered. "If you have a plan—"

"Like I said, working on it!" The remaining Procyon guards had killed or incapacitated their Syndax captors. They were hidden behind tombstones and trees, trading shots with the last of the Syndax soldiers across from us.

That left Arkwright and Skipper unattended. Whatever their joint presence was doing for the portal, it wasn't good—and by not good, I mean it was working to Arkwright's advantage. The wildly swirling patterns were slowing. Images coalesced. I thought I saw an ocean, then futuristic metallic corridors, then an ancient stone structure. They were there and gone in a blink.

As if that weren't enough of a pain, wind picked up all around us. Leaves shuddered on branches that bent in all directions, like we were at the edges of storm. Purple lightning skittered across the grass, and on the walls of the neighboring buildings, and even midair out in the street. The shapes opening among the sudden surge of otherworldly electricity were way too familiar.

Rips.

And with rips, came astral fiends.

Lashing tentacles, some studded with spikes, and dark slimy hides—they squirmed, trying to get through the rips, but something was keeping them tethered. They shrieked clamoring for our attention and, I'd bet, a taste of the life they wanted to leech from our bodies.

"What on Earth?" Loredana muttered. "That isn't possible."

"Mercury!" There was Liz, yelping in my ear again. "Gary's almost on scene. As soon as he gives you the high sign, get your hands on the pulsar staves."

"And do *what*?" I snapped. "Arkwright's in the portal's nexus! He's bracing it open! We're getting rips tearing things apart here!"

"I've got them on my tracker, Mercury." That was Gary. Whatever he was doing, he was short on breath. I thought I heard someone shout at him, but the sound faded quickly. "Liz and I were able to modify existing equipment from Winston's lab to sync with the tracker and—okay, just be ready. I think we can destabilize the portal to the extent it should implode."

"That's good, right?"

"Yeah, definitely. Except there's a possibility of

catastrophic collapse. Should be localized."

"How localized?"

"City-wide."

I rubbed my forehead. "Of course."

"I surmise the plan is not without risks." Loredana ducked as bullets clattered off our makeshift hideout.

"Pretty much as bad as usual. Listen, can you guys cover me? I've got to get inside the portal."

Loredana removed the magazine from her rifle. "Sadly, I'm out."

"Here." Ramos pulled a new one from the body of the soldier I killed. "Give us the high sign, Mercury. We'll be ready."

"Good deal. Now all I need is—"

"Mr. Hale?" Garvey slumped behind us. Blood soaked the side of his shirt. But he was alive, and he had the second dagger in his possession. It, too, was coated crimson. "You'll need this, sir."

I took it and smacked him on the shoulder. "Hang in there, Garvey. We'll get through this."

"If you say so, sir." Garvey leaned against a tombstone as another security man applied a bandage to his wound. Looked like a gunshot that had stayed clear of his vital organs. "But I'll need you to verify to Manager Alvarez that I'm taking a sick day."

I grinned. "Count me in." I crouched, ready to spring across the crypt.

Loredana grabbed the front of my shirt and pulled me in close. "As your handler, I forbid you to die."

"Wouldn't dream of it." I kissed her, which was fantastic but also a terrible mistake, because that rush, that pounding in my heart that had nothing to do with the battle around us, made me disinclined to throw myself into the fray. In fact, I wanted to find her jet and fly as far away from any other frays.

But that wasn't gonna happen. I had a job to do. A duty to fulfill. I'd already turned my back on my true home for this one. I wasn't about to let Arkwright destroy San Camillo so he could unleash devastation on a whole bunch of other worlds.

I jumped into the hailstorm of bullets.

First thing: when you tell people to cover you, it translates as, "Shoot a bunch toward the bad guys from nearby me." It sounded like a couple of lightning bolts had landed on my heels. I landed in a run, weaving between tombstones, on a straight line for Skipper and Arkwright and the center of the portal.

They were still linked together. The portal's various corridors had stopped, and more than that, had smeared their edges until they formed a continuous band encircling the duo. A dizzying array of landscapes and structures flashed by, more than a dozen at a time, and I couldn't watch the display, or I'd throw up.

Arkwright saw me coming and snarled. I'm not talking the sneering expression of an angry man, either. I'm talking full-on bestial growl, with visible fangs and the whole nine yards.

I lunged at them, daggers drawn.

Arkwright disengaged from Skipper, blocking my attack with both halves of the pulsar stave. Purple-white sparks exploded around us. Bonus points: the daggers didn't melt under the onslaught. Which was great, because I'd only ever used them against a weapon from Meda was helping Teget fight Marigold. This time, I didn't have a partner.

And Arkwright made Marigold seem as dangerous as a toddler mimicking swordplay with a stick.

No matter how hard I struck, no matter how fast I moved, it wasn't good enough. He intercepted every blow, parried every thrust, until I was sweating and aching from sheer exhaustion. If Arkwright was tired, he didn't show it. I swore he was enjoying himself.

Skipper staggered out of the portal area, grasping the sides of his head. Now there was a guy who was about to vomit. "I don't ... understand. What's happening? Where has the voice gone?"

Voice? If he meant Arkwright, my adversary had apparently given up speeches in favor of cold, hard silence as we fought. Arkwright struck at me with a pair of tentacles, spiked appendages that lashed over his shoulders, but I severed one and sidestepped the second, even as I used the other dagger to intercept the combined might of the pulsar stave. He'd snapped it together and was hammering at me with blows that I would have used to kill an astral fiend.

I refused to back away. Refused to run. Even when the voices hit *me*.

Let me send you home. Across the void, to Meda. You will not have to brave the wastes of the Interstice. I can give you back your family, and the weapons which you obsessively covet. When the light floods this dark world, Earth will be reborn, and you can be as far away as you like. Give up. Put down your weapons. Let me help you.

As tired as I was, as bitter as the constant threat of death and the sight of the dead had made me, that sounded good. Really good. Arkwright and I slowed our attacks. Maybe he was getting tired, too. Whatever. The guy just wanted to get out of here. Could I blame him? It'd be nice to rest, for once, and let someone else do the fighting—or better yet, let the fighting end. Maybe the light coming to Earth wouldn't be so bad ...

A cry shattered my calming thoughts. Outside the portal spheres, Loredana helped Ramos regain his footing. He'd been nicked by a bullet. Blood covered an arm. He kept shooting, though, muzzle flashes illuminating his face. I'd never seen him so brutally determined.

And Loredana? There was a wide-eyed frenzy to her expression. Then she saw me.

That's when I realized the only things that had slowed were Arkwright and I. Everything outside the portal's realms was moving at normal speed.

Rest. It would be nice, would it not? To let someone else do the fighting. You have been a warrior for so long you have forgotten what it is like to live.

Wait a second. My words? Or his?

The Whisperer.

I gritted my teeth. Couldn't separate the two. And worse, I didn't care. But I had to save everyone. It was up to me. Most of all, Loredana—she relied on me. I couldn't let her down. I had to be there for her. I'd give up everything so she could survive.

I loved her.

Seriously?

You can be safe. You won't have to give anything up, Mercury. If you truly cared for her, you'd leave this vile place, this foul pit. I can help you. We can bring her away from the darkness. She can live with you in Meda, a life of peace and tranquility, and you and your family can grow old together until you pass in your sleep.

Hot tears stung me. That's all I ever wanted. My grip on

the daggers wavered.

Mercury ... Marigold. Her song lulled me.

I could just ... let go. Drop the weapons. Take the pulsar stave offered by Arkwright. He stood there, holding the glowing end of the stave toward my chest. Not attacking. Not trying to kill me.

"Mercury!"

Ramos?

"Don't fall for it! He's telling you lies. You know what has to be done!"

I cringed. "Can't. Sorry, Ramos. I ... failed."

"You've never failed. Never once." He was at the barrier. He reached for me, but a flash of light singed his hand. "Never once. I'm proud of you. Son."

For a moment I thought Arkwright had stabbed me. My heart should have broken free of my chest. I gasped, clutching the daggers against my suit, feeling the tattered fabric where it had been slashed by the pulsar stave. *My* pulsar stave.

What had I been thinking?

Ramos smashed his hand against the barrier again, and this time, even though he cried out in pain, his hand penetrated the sizzling energies. *"¡El Señor te reprenda!"*

Something screamed in the back of my mind. I clutched the sides of my head. The fog lifted. All those crazy thoughts evaporated like mist off the bay in the morning sun.

I couldn't leave.

I couldn't let them down.

Ramos was inside the barrier, all of a sudden, and fired at Arkwright. The bullets ripped through him, but Arkwright roared a challenge in return. He brought the pulsar stave down on Ramos's head, the twisted light shrieking through the air—

And I blocked it with the daggers.

Arkwright swung again and again. I battered aside his attacks, until the daggers were inches from his face. He changed up his next strike, faked me out, and a searing pain lanced through my left forearm. One of the daggers hurtled into the portal wall, disappearing.

"You could have had *everything*!" he thundered. "I could have taken you home! You and your loved ones! But you're opposing me!"

"I'm already home," I snapped, "And shut up, already."

Metal flash. Arkwright shrieked.

His left hand was on the ground, clutching the pulsar stave. Blue ichor oozed from the wrist.

Skipper stepped up to my side, the falchion blade gleaming. "I've had quite enough of this foul beast and his tampering with my mind. What say we banish him and be done with it?"

I grinned. "After you."

Arkwright's rage exploded.

Tentacles burst from his entire body, slamming into us like cyclone's front. The injury to my hand was nothing compared to what happened to my right leg. I writhed on the ground, clutching the knee, hollering. I didn't want to look. I bet it wasn't even there.

But it was. Twisted, broken. And the suit was barely flickering with energy, which meant there was precious little with which to heal my body.

Meanwhile, the portal was flickering. The stability of those corridors was failing, I'm assuming without Skipper to help Arkwright stabilize.

Ramos wrenched the pulsar stave from Arkwright's

severed hand and threw it.

The moment it touched my palm, I could have cried. The surge of power rolled over me. Not enough to return my leg to battle-ready, but enough to energize the rest of me. Screw this sitting around.

"Hold still." Loredana put my arm over her shoulder. "We have to get you out of here."

"No." I ground my teeth. "Gotta get back in there."

"You're in no shape to fight!"

"I'm in no shape to sit around, either!"

Sirens were approaching. And the jet engine noise wasn't getting any closer, but it wasn't abating. I imagined fighters circling the city like vultures waiting for a meal to die.

But the first vehicle to arrive outside the cemetery wasn't the cops, or the national guard. It was a bicycle. A mountain bike, with a brilliant red frame.

Gary DeBarthe hopped off, his shirt soaked with sweat. He had a bulky—contraption on his back. The Syndax tracker was lashed to one side. It looked like a police officer's radar gun, only three times as big.

The last few Syndax soldiers took aim.

"Gary!" I shouted.

He froze, fifty feet from the portal and a long, long way from doing us any good. Then he lifted the device and slid a switch on its left side.

The entire apparatus glowed a sickly purple. Bolts of energy, wild as a summer's thunderstorm, lanced out. They struck the portal, wrapping around it. It looked like it was simultaneously trying to suck the portal in, while the portal was retaliating by pulling away.

Gunfire lit up the night again. Bullets ripped up grass near Loredana and me.

Gary stood his ground.

"Stop!" Arkwright fought off Skipper, holding him at bay with an endless swarm of tentacles. He stomped to the edge of the barrier.

"Mercury! He can't leave the perimeter!" A bullet creased Gary's side, spraying blood. He yelped, and faltered, but before he could fall, he braced himself on a headstone. "I can't close it without him as the focus! He's absorbed too many tachyons!"

Right. I could stop him.

Loredana held a hand to my chest. "If the rips reopen, you'll be needed here."

All around us, astral fiends were still struggling to enter our world. I shook my head. "Arkwright's the threat! Let me finish him!"

"You're not doing this alone, Mercury." She touched my cheek.

Then she shoved me away.

I collapsed, my broken leg not willing to support me. "Wait!"

Way too late. She had already breached the perimeter of the portal, where Ramos stood. Loredana looked back at me and smiled.

Ramos made the sign of the cross.

"No!" I dragged myself upright, limping as fast as I could. Just twenty feet ...

Together they grabbed Arkwright, one on each arm. Loredana drew her revolver and emptied the cylinder into his chest.

Arkwright's keening wail synced with that of the astral fiends. The lightning storm intensified, until bolts careened wildly throughout the cemetery.

Ten feet from the edge ...

A burst of light rippled along the beam between Gary's device and the portal. It shattered the perimeter.

Skipper cut himself free of Arkwright's tentacles, half of which had gone limp. He stabbed Arkwright deep through the back. The blade's tip protruded from his chest.

Still, he wouldn't die.

Five feet ...

I held out the stave for Loredana to grab.

Her fingers brushed the end, an inch away.

"He's destroying it!" Arkwright's voice was his own, without Marigold or the Whisperer to augment his speech. I thought he meant Gary, but Arkwright shied away from Ramos, who held onto his arm with both hands, pulling him deeper into the portal. "I can't find the way!"

Suddenly three overlapping circles stopped spinning, their images as clear as if they were in the building next door—the temple of Meda, the stormy nightmare of the Interstice, and a bombed-out city block.

A wave of energy dragged Arkwright into all three.

Ramos tumbled away, still clinging to him.

I threw myself at Loredana.

My hand caught hers. But it was slick with slime from Arkwright's wound.

She slipped out of my reach.

The last I saw of her was blue eyes on a startled face, red hair whipped wildly, as she vanished into the mass of portals.

A thunderclap echoed off the walls. It knocked bricks loose and shattered tree limbs. Tombstones crumbled.

Every person standing fell.

The cemetery went dark. It was like the battle had never

happened. The rips were gone. No sign of astral fiends, though their screams echoed in my head. The bodies of Syndax soldiers and Procyon guards were strewn about.

"Sir." Garvey crawled to me. He was pale. His face was smudged with dirt and blood. "Sir, what happened? Where are they?"

I could only stare at the shimmering, diaphanous shell where Loredana and Ramos had disappeared. They were gone. I half-expected them to emerge from behind a crypt, shaky, but alive.

Nothing.

Gary whimpered. His hand reached up, trembling. He tried and failed to pull himself onto a tombstone.

I staggered to him, with Garvey helping me—not that he was in much better shape, with his ribcage still bleeding. But Gary ...

He'd been shot at least three times. None of the wounds were in places I could expect him to survive.

"We did it?" His voice was reedy. Every breath was a struggle. "We're okay?"

"Yeah." I fought away tears. Barely knew the guy, but they were an accumulation. For him. His daughter. His ex-wife. The dead Procyon men. Even the soldier I killed.

Ramos.

Loredana.

"It's okay. You did it. We stopped them." I tried a smile.

Gary closed his eyes. "Okay. Good. You tell Liz ... I mean, Isabel. Daddy misses her and loves her. Okay? And Moira. I miss her, too. I'm sorry ...I'm ..."

His breaths faltered, became wheezes, then ceased.

Garvey swore. He rubbed at his face.

The world was safe, yeah, but the price was too high.

My God, what did I do?

I pressed my forehead against Gary's. "We won."

CHAPTER THIRTY-TWO

I drew Loredana's smile first.

It was a rare thing, so it stuck foremost in my memory. From there, the rest was easy. The sweep of her neck, the lines of her hair, the eyes. No matter how I sketched the latter, I couldn't get the glint right. That sly look she gave me.

Oh, well. There was plenty of time to practice.

I was in a secure room on Procyon's seventh floor. That level was off the guided tour, for good reasons. The secure room, which didn't have a name and wasn't labeled on the blueprints, had only one purpose.

It was for keeping operatives out of danger when things went off the rails.

Didn't matter whether if it was to protect me or everyone else. I was put in the room for three days. There was a bunk with a mattress that felt like cardboard, a sheet that should have been washed a year ago, and a bathroom in the corner. Mini-fridge was well-stocked.

I ate some macaroni and cheese, I think. Mostly I drank when I got really thirsty. Water and soda, alternating.

It was a good thing I'd spaced the sketchpad. It must gave

stayed neglected in Tracking after I'd brought it to Procyon and showed to Loredana after I'd sketched the night's blade.

My leg ached. Shocking, really. It was in a splint. The breaks were healing faster than any person could manage, but hey, that was me. Dr. Arne grumbled and cursed, but said things were looking good. I wasn't up to full speed, though. It was more an accelerated gimp.

I stared up at the wall. No view for entertainment. There were no windows. Just a couple of naked fluorescent bulbs. They say the bare furnishings aren't punishment, but I didn't care if they were.

The people I cared about were gone.

The images wouldn't stop. Loredana's hand slipping from mine. Ramos falling into the dimensional rifts. Gary dying.

Nobody asked me any questions. SCPD had me locked up for less than an hour before Alvarez himself was on scene, with a handful of Procyon flunkies I assumed were lawyers. They sure weren't security.

Next thing I know, I'm ushered in here and the door's locked. Seventy-two hours ago.

The room was soundproof, too. If anyone out there was yelling, I can't hear it. Fine. I wasn't in the mood for any of Alvarez's complaining. Hey, at least I was in the building. Not bad considering the man wanted to bar me from there permanently.

There was a knock on the door.

Finally. Had to be the cops. Alvarez had reached his limit, and without Loredana around as my advocate, the board had stepped back. I was gonna be locked up.

After all, a cop was lost on my watch. More than one, if you count the officers killed by Arkwright's corpse-fiends.

I heard the electronic beep of buttons being punched.

Then the heavy click of locks being disabled. The door opened.

It was Alvarez. The man was dressed in a black suit, white shirt, black tie. Like he'd been to a funeral. In his case, I'd guess it was several.

"Ten men." His voice lacked his signature snark and arrogance. If anything, he sounded as tired as I feel. "Ten sets of families, friends, colleagues, neighbors. All people know is that they died protecting the city, as volunteers who stepped in. A kind of community policing effort, if you will. The police have been kind enough to downplay our involvement in the events at the cemetery. They confiscated our weapons, to be sure, but there's no word of our true capabilities in the media. That's helpful."

I set the drawing aside. "What are you doing here. Telling me I served my sentence?"

"I'm telling you it's not up to us anymore. The police have your friend Skipper in custody. Homeland Security is on its way for you, and then to question him."

My adrenaline spiked, for the first time in days. I shot up from the bunk, which was a terrible idea, because pain stabbed through my leg. "What am I supposed to do? The board—Loredana always said Procyon had friends in the federal government."

"It's not like I know who those people are, Mr. Hale. All I understand is that we're being offered a modicum of grace." Alvarez straightened his tie. His hands trembled. "The board has kept them away from our most intimate secrets, but Homeland wants a word with you. I have no idea what steps they'll take."

I nodded. The pulsar stave leaned against my bunk, same place it had remained since I got here. I picked it up and limped over to Alvarez at the door. I willed it to life. Yeah, it was fully charged again. Back to normal. Part of me wished it were still a dead stick. "Here. Hide it. Do whatever you need to keep it safe. Hey, I understand there's an old lady visiting Drake City who did a great job with it back in the day. Maybe she'd been interested in—"

"Will you please kindly shut up for three seconds?" Alvarez touched the stave, but instead of putting it in a plastic bag or whatever you do with interdimensional weapons when the operative entrusted with them is gonna get arrested, he pushed it back to me. "I said I have no idea what steps they'll take. I know exactly what my plans are."

"You should turn me over. My actions resulted in a lot of people getting killed."

"They also resulted in you preventing the end of days, again." A young man entered the room. Tall, well-dressed, like a business professional, except for the hints of bulky jewelry protruding from under his cuffs ...

Hang on. I pointed. "You're the guy who pulled us out of Syndax."

"Dominic." He offered a hand to shake.

I declined, because I was still trying to figure out what was going on. "Alvarez, you better talk."

"He's going to get you past the federal agents our people are stalling downstairs. Do me a favor, Mr. Hale, and don't argue this executive decision." Alvarez straightened his tie, again. It didn't need straightening. He looked like he might be sick to his stomach. "There is a lot for which you must answer, yes, but there's no denying you halted another disaster from endangering our world. That's why the board is taking a hands-off approach. As of an hour ago, when inquiries reach them, they will state under penalty of law that they have no idea where you went after you escaped Procyon's facility."

"Escaped."

"Yes." He smirked. "There's not a single image of you leaving this building. That's curious, given that your suit is in tatters, undergoing repairs with Liz Stojan's input."

I glanced at Dominic. "So, you're my ticket out of here."

He nodded.

"To where?"

"Home." Dominic unbuttoned his cuffs. "We've got a few stops to make along the way, though, so I hope you haven't eaten too much. Don't worry. You'll adjust to the transits. Eventually."

"Ralphing up your lunch didn't seem to be a problem for you."

"That's because these operate in sync with me. My body's attuned to the travel." He wore silvery ... bracelets, for lack of a better word. They looked old, semi-tarnished, yet they didn't match any design I've ever seen.

Of course, same thing could be said about the pulsar stave.

"Why'd you call this guy in?" I asked Alvarez.

Before the manager could answer, Dominic cut in. "He didn't. Procyon keeps me apprised of dangerous situations. I step in where I can, when I'm not ... busy with other pursuits."

"Gemini."

He smiled. "Loredana liked her code names."

My muscles tensed. "Likes. Not liked."

"Sorry."

Alvarez cleared his throat. "Get Skipper out of the SCPD's hands, keep the stave safe, and keep your head down until such a time as we can bring you back. It's the best we can do. Procyon's secrets have to stay that way."

"Sounds good to me." I scratched the back of my neck. "Thanks, by the way."

"Just don't screw this up. Consider it your last chance." Alvarez dug into his suit pocket. "Here."

He dropped something tiny and sapphire into my hand. Never mind. *That* was when my heart broke. It was one of Loredana's earrings, with the backing attached.

"It was found in your suit's pocket. Liz thinks it was deliberately placed there. I was hoping you could tell me its significance."

I was too busy watching our dinner at Saito on Sky, seeing flashes of her face, interrupted by our dance at the Procyon-Rampart gala. She'd worn the earrings at both places. A memento? She must have slipped them into my pocket before I'd made my final attack on Arkwright.

I clenched my fist around it until the stone dug into my palm. Forming words was difficult. My lungs didn't want to cooperate. "Nope."

Alvarez glanced at Dominic, who seemed to be observing us with an expression of regal dispassion. This new guy could do aloof really well. "Good luck."

His departure left me standing with Dominic in the awkwardest silence ever. "So," I finally said. "Skipper?"

"In police custody, unfortunately." Dominic rolled up his sleeves.

"Ah." I grabbed my sketchbook and my phone. The last couple messages on it were from Ramos. I couldn't stand to look at his name, because I knew there'd be one more terrible thing to do before we skipped town. "Better buckle up, then."

Someone ran up to the door. For a moment I thought the feds had made it upstairs, and Alvarez had turned into a complete idiot who would let them into Procyon's most secure floor. But it was Liz, panting and teary-eyed, with a plastic shopping bag clutched in one hand. Her hair was a blast of pink in the otherwise drab room. She hugged me about the waist and rested her chin on my shoulder. The bag crinkled. I thought I smelled—food? "Oh, Mercury. I'm so sorry."

I patted her back. Didn't really know her, still, but I wasn't the only person who suffered loss. "Gary was a hero, Liz. Don't forget it."

She sniffed and dabbed at her eyes with her sleeve. "I'm going to see Moira today. She was at the funeral. So was … so was Isabel."

If this kept up, I was going to be too beaten down to accomplish anything. "Sorry about the mess with your sword."

"I'm not ever going to wash it. It's been in real battles, and I need something to remind me of what was sacrificed so it's going by my desk because I've found a really nice place to hang it and even Mr. Alvarez thinks it's a cool idea, but he didn't say 'cool' because—"

I smiled and pantomimed zippering my mouth shut.

She smirked. "Did he give you the earring? He made me run, like, eighty tests before we could clear it for release."

"He did. Thanks for that."

"Oh, I got you something for the road, too."

She presented the bag like a peasant giving royalty treasure. I unwrapped it.

A package of pepperoni slices. And a cell phone.

"Encrypted by Cyril. It's got its own copy of the Big Bad

Wolf to break into other systems, too. You can stay in touch with us." She took my phone from my hand and touched the two together. "As soon as we transfer your old data to the new one."

"You're the best, Liz."

Her smile faltered. "Thanks, but ... I don't know what we're supposed to do. The pulsar stave should be losing power again, but all the tests I ran show it operating just like it did before the North Beach Battle. I can't figure out why, unless—"

"Unless they're coming back. The rips. Like they had for a century and a half."

"There's been no tachyon spikes. I have drones surveilling the city, ever since we recorded those emergent rips at the cemetery. If something shows up, we'll see it." Liz bit her lip. "I'm scared."

"Me too. No sense lying about it. We'll figure it out."

She looked at Dominic. "Take care of him, okay? Please."

"That's my purpose." Dominic gestured to the center of the room. "Are you ready?"

I sighed. "Not in the slightest, so, let's do this."

He was right. The portal trip this time wasn't nearly as bad as the first two. I did ding my shoulder against a cinderblock wall.

Skipper smiled. "Ah. I was wondering how long I was to languish in this dungeon."

I glanced at Dominic, and the swirling remnants of our portal's energy. "You don't seem surprised by us appearing out of nowhere in your cell."

"After the wonders I've experienced in this land, nothing

more can surprise me." He stood and clapped both my shoulders. His expression turned grave. "I am truly sorry for your losses, Mercury. Have faith in the outcome."

"I can't. Not now." The bitterness surprised even me. Me, Mr. Cocky.

"So say all who find themselves at the bottom of a dark well. The difficulty is knowing when to stop trying to clamber out. Thy right hand shall save me."

"We'd better continue this conversation elsewhere." Dominic kept his face turned from the cell's bars. Voices echoed nearby, even though we couldn't see anyone else. "Preferably, at Cavill Cemetery."

I clenched my fists. "I'm not going back there. Why would you even suggest it?"

Dominic activated his wristbands. Their pieces separated and spun, floating of their own accord, until the portal reignited. "Because it's time for your friend to leave."

Gotta hand it to SCPD. They made things easier for Skipper's departure.

They'd erected a barricade in front of the cemetery's fence, blocking all view for ten feet up. I heard papers fluttering in the breeze.

"Memorials." Dominic paced the edge of the distortion, the area in which the portal resided. His image split and then recombined as he circumnavigated it. "People have been taping photographs, love letters, mementos, anything you can imagine. I have a picture on my phone ..."

"I don't want to see it." I rubbed my face. When would this end? When would the night stop haunting me? I felt sick. It had nothing to do with lack of food or portal travel.

"How's this work?"

"Like the other one." Dominic activated his wristbands. The portal opened with a rush of wind, except instead of a clear view, all we got was a black shadow.

The pulsar stave sure hadn't gotten those results.

"The disorientation isn't too bad," Dominic told Skipper. "Just don't touch the walls of the corridor. You could fall through, into the Interstice."

"Seeing as I am currently unarmed, that seems unwise." Dominic gestured for Skipper to step forward.

Instead, he took both my hands. "I must thank you."

"For what?" I snorted. "You saved my life time and again."

"True, but if not for you, I could not return home. I pray you'll encounter the same joy soon, Mercury. Keep the memory of your loved ones near. Should you ever find your way to my realm, know that I would gladly serve in battle at your side once again."

Heat flushed my face. "Yeah, okay. I'm gonna miss you, too."

He crossed the threshold. The portal swept him up, until he was floating in the middle of the shadow, drifting in a slow circle. Ever see a guy do one of those skydiving booths? Think perpetual fall.

"Hey, Skipper!" I had to shout over the rush of wind coming at me. "You seem like you're doing a lot better!"

"I am indeed!" He laughed. "You see, Arkwright, though a vile creature, unlocked my memories when he tried to use me to get home! I recall everything! And I must say, it feels fantastic to soar again!"

A white light flashed. I had to block the view, unless I wanted crispy retinas, but I heard Skipper cry out. Couldn't make out the words. They were happy though, like a guy who'd ridden a roller coaster for the very first time.

When the portal cleared, and the winds calmed, ice coated the trees and nearby tombstones.

Dominic insisted we get out of town as soon as we had Skipper safely on his way. He zapped us back to his apartment because, apparently, that's how his portal-deal-thing worked—he had to return to the point of origination after each trip. I had one more place to stop, and since I was the operative and he was just my teleporting version of Uber, I overruled him.

So, he stood at the far corner of a bungalow porch, his back to the white post, arms folded. He glanced into the street every five seconds, like that would make a difference if SCPD dropped the hammer on us without warning.

I was kind of surprised there weren't cops already at the house.

Olivia answered the door on the first knock. The feisty grin I knew from Ramos's family photos was a soft frown. Her eyes were red from crying, but there were no tears I could detect. Not now, three days later. When she saw me, she put a hand to her mouth.

"I can't say here long, Mrs. Ramos. I wanted to see you before I leave." This was stupid. What was I gonna say? Sorry I missed dinner, and then lost your husband in an interdimensional rift? She had her arms wrapped around her midsection, as if she were preventing herself from flying apart. "Ramos—I mean, Gabriel—he was never one to back down from a fight. I could always count on him to do the right thing."

It would have been a lot easier if my throat didn't tighten up like I was in the throes of an allergic reaction. "He, um, he was the one to keep me pointed in the right direction. Or at least, he tried. He told me so many times the right way to go and I didn't always listen, but he never gave up. Never turned his back on me."

I lost the rest of my speech because she hugged me.

There I was, trying to comfort her, and before I knew what else to say, tears streamed down my face onto her shoulder. I embraced Olivia like she was family, instead of just the wife of a cop who was a hero.

Maybe that's who she really was.

"Wherever he's gone," she whispered, "I have faith you'll bring him home."

At that moment, she was probably the only person on this or any world who believed it.

CHAPTER THIRTY-THREE

Our last trip was to Rampart.

Dominic and I were back in the loft, which, it turns out, belonged to him.

"Home away from home." He opened the refrigerator. "Can I get you a drink?"

"Yes, please." I sank onto a couch and turned on the TV. No catastrophic news from San Camillo. Okay, so the datelines were full of rumors from "unnamed sources" whispering about federal investigations into the monster outbreak downtown. That's what they called it. No more hiding the reality. How could they? Even the city acknowledged that something terrible had happened, stopping short of calling it "zombie" attack while also admitting it wasn't mass hallucination. A hundred and twelve people were dead.

A hundred and twelve.

"I'm short of food, but that's nothing a quick trip to the store wouldn't fix." He held up a white cardboard container. "There's leftover chicken fried steak from Caerphilly."

"Good?"

"Better than McDonald's, if that's what you mean." He handed me a bottle of Alaskan Amber. I could have used about ten of them right then.

He reheated leftovers and I dug out the pepperoni Liz had given me. I ate half of it. No sense in scarfing it all at once.

We dined in silence. Night fell. Dominic cracked some windows. A cool, dry breeze filtered in. The evening sounds of Rampart's busy streets accompanied it.

This guy wasn't so bad. I figured I should attempt to be sociable. "We never got formally introduced. Mercury Hale, operative for Procyon." I tipped my bottle in salute before sucking down half of it.

"Dominic Zein, likewise."

"Zein. Huh. I've heard the name before. From Loredana. She asked Alexander Arkwright if Zein sent him here, but she meant from another world ..." I frowned. "Don't tell me you're from another dimension, because I'm about sick of that."

"No, I'm not. Of course, I'm not the only Dominic Zein." He grimaced. "Let's worry about that later. What's your plan?"

"My plan?" I gestured at the TV. "What do I have left to do? SCPD and the feds are hunting for me. My guess is, I need to change my identity—again—and find a new life. Monster hunting's out of the question."

"Everyone has a purpose. The trick now, is discovering yours. Or perhaps rediscovering."

"Yeah, okay. Don't talk to me about destiny."

"Maybe that isn't a bad idea." He tossed something gold onto the coffee table between us.

A crucifix. Bits of grass clung to it.

"I found that in the portal. Yours?"

I dangled it from my fingers. "No. But I'll hang onto it."

"Listen, Mercury. I'll be frank: I think you're too reckless and arrogant for this kind of work."

"Gee, thanks."

"But it's my job to protect you, so that's what I'll do." He pointed his bottle my way. "You've got to be willing to cooperate. Can I have your word?"

"My turn to be frank, Dominic. I have no clue—"

My phone went nuts. Not my phone, I mean, the new one Liz gave me. I hit speaker and answered, "Hello?"

"Mercury! Oh, good, I thought maybe you'd been arrested!"

"Pretty sure Alvarez would have heard about it, Liz."

"Okay, so, never mind, but the earring! You have it, don't you?"

"Liz, that'd be the last thing I'd forget."

"I know, right? Put it next to the phone!"

I rolled my eyes but did so. Those Tracking geeks and their projects. "Okay."

"Activate the scanner. It's one of your apps."

Helpfully labeled, "Tachyon Scanner." Talk about bells and whistles. I tapped it.

A readout bar appeared. It spiked from green, through yellow and orange into red. I frowned. She had to be kidding. I moved the earring away.

The bar plunged.

"There's a transmitter embedded inside!" Liz squealed. Honest to goodness, little kid squealed. "I missed it before, because it wasn't activated."

"Did you turn it on?"

"No, Mercury. And it gets better! I have Cyril linking results from your scanner app back to Tracking. The earring points—well, somewhere! Somewhere not here! The transmitter's been quantum entangled. I did more digging through the projects confiscated from Winston Yen. He was working on a transmitter that could do more than reach anywhere in the world. He wanted it to breach dimensions! Guess who the last person to access the project was?"

I grinned.

"My God." Dominic stood. His beer bottle spilled its dregs on the wood floor. "She's alive?"

"Someone is! Someone activated the transmitter's partner!"

The second half of the earring pair. I turned it over and over in my hand. "That's—awesome."

"Yeah it is! Okay, but the problem is, the transmission itself appears to be triggering an instability in Gemini's apartment."

Gemini? Took me a second to realize she meant Dominic. "Is that bad?"

"It's only bad if you don't want a rip to open."

"Old school, classic rip?" My turn to leap up.

Yeah, there came purple lightning.

Dominic had already lit up his wristbands, only this time he aimed them at the burgeoning rip. "Should I be worried?"

"Only if you've got a big security deposit on this place." I willed the pulsar stave to life. Its power surged into my core, wiping away ever ache and twinge, even the pain of my broken leg. I could have really used a tussle with an astral fiend to take my mind off everything awful. "Because you're probably gonna lose it."

The rip opened, and I vowed to kill every last astral fiend in my way between the apartment and Loredana. I prayed—yeah, prayed—that Ramos was with her.

Except we didn't get a single tentacle. Instead, a man pounced through the breach. He was young, with hazel eyes, a black beard and matching goatee, shaved head ...

Teget.

The Icon, defender of the relics of Meda—which included not just the night's blade, but the gleaming ax with a brass handle that he gripped in both hands.

Dominic glanced from Teget to me and back again. "Mercury, do I need to shoot?"

I shook my head. "Um, no. This is my brother."

Teget took four strides to stand face to face with me. He was stone serious, right up until and through the bear hug he crushed me in.

"Hey!" I wheezed. "Missed you, too."

Teget released me, but he didn't look any happier. "I wish our reunion could be under more joyous circumstances, my brother."

"You and me both. I've got friends to find and an enemy to destroy. Interested?"

"That is why I am here. Our world is in peril."

Our world. Not Earth. "What happened?"

"The Whisperer has taken physical form, and invaded Meda."

"Physical form. Let me guess: handsome guy, lots of tentacles, claws, scaly armor, bug eyes for part of his face?"

"Then you know."

"Man, do I ever."

"If we do not return, all worlds will suffer death when the temple's relics are added to his arsenal."

He stepped into the rip. Light exploded from the ax.

The rip expanded. Dominic disappeared in the glare.

I gripped the pulsar stave, ready to fight whatever we

were up against.
Before I lost any place I could call home.

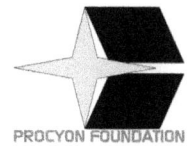

PROCYON FOUNDATION

Mercury's adventures continue in

Mercury At Risk